Chasing Uncle Charley

SOUTHWEST LIFE AND LETTERS

A series designed to publish outstanding new fiction and nonfiction about Texas and the American Southwest and to present classic works of the region in handsome new editions.

Chasing Uncle Charley

Cruce Stark

Southern Methodist University Press
Dallas

Printed in the United States of America

First edition, 1992

Requests for permission to reproduce material
from this work should be sent to:
Permissions
Southern Methodist University Press
Box 415
Dallas, Texas 75275

Library of Congress Cataloging-in-Publication Data
Stark, Cruce, 1942–
Chasing Uncle Charley / Cruce Stark.
p. cm. — (Southwest life and letters)
ISBN 0-87074-333-3
I. Title. II. Series.
PS3569.T33573C48 1992
813′.54—dc20 91-52777

Cover / jacket illustration by Barbara Whitehead
Design by Whitehead & Whitehead

For Nancy,
and yet again,
for Nancy

Folks

The Town

The Border

The Plains

The Thicket

Indian Territory

Folks

here we could start is when Old Uncle Biles was walking across a log that kind of lifted up its head and looked at him.

Because there hadn't been any gators around for a time, not since we started being a town. We figured what got them back was Simon McCallister. Not that he had any fondness for creatures, whatever their kind. But Simon ran the butcher shop, and he was the sort when he got through with anything, there wasn't a whole lot left to do something else with. But back then, what *was* left, he'd put in his wagon, haul it halfway over the bayou bridge, and just dump it in.

The first gator, maybe it was Uncle Biles's, could have gotten lost going someplace else. Or maybe it'd been there all along, sleeping on the bottom for years, only we hadn't noticed. But when it finally got awake and was passing under the bayou bridge just at the right time, he probably thought he'd discovered alligator heaven. And with so much left over even after he'd finished, he must have spread the word.

Pretty soon, every day at dumping time, they would be thrashing around, like they had just found what they'd spent a long time looking for. But then the gators got lazy. So we managed to get most of them. It had been a long time since we'd had any reason for real shooting. Living in town, there simply wasn't the need. But then they got fat, slow, so we got most of them. Not all, and there were new ones always arriving. But one we got to recognize. He was different, not just big, although he was certainly that. But mean. As though he took pleasure in it.

He had a way about being up and then under, none of us could keep him in gunsights long enough to matter. Afterwards, we might not see him for days. Then there'd be a carcass, maybe of some kid's pet dog, lying on the bank half-eaten, only enough left to let us know how it had gotten that way.

None of us knew how to get rid of that one. And while it stayed around, new ones kept showing up. Because Simon wouldn't stop feeding them off the middle of the bayou bridge. His argument made sense. Kind of. He said we wanted his meat. We didn't want to go out and kill our own, and we didn't want to buy what was left over and bury it ourselves, and Simon said he sure as hell wasn't going to spend any time with a shovel. Or pay anybody else to, for that matter.

So we told him to go up around Cypress Point, dump it there. Anybody who wound up on the bank half-eaten at Cypress Point shouldn't have been there in the first place. Or the fellow that found him either. Simon said all we had to do was pay for a cart and a driver and it'd be all right with him. Every day, of course, only so long as we wanted to eat meat.

He had us. He knew the town wasn't going to get itself fenced in with that kind of expense, not knowing when if ever it'd be over. But we had to do something. Kids played around that bayou. Sooner or later one of them was bound to fall in. Then it wouldn't be only the kid's dog lying on the bank. Besides, a town just couldn't have things like alligators running around loose. That might have been allowable a few years back. We'd gotten farther along than that by now.

So what we did was hire a professional, a Mr. Chester Thibodeaux from over the border in Louisiana. Once we got rid of this bunch, then we could do something permanent, string wire across the bayou or something. But nobody was about to get into the water, not with that big one floating around down there somewhere. So Mr. Thibodeaux came into town, a big fellow running to fat, which was about as close to moving as he seemed inclined to, as though we ought to be honored if he managed to get up from his chair to say howdy. But he had a rifle. It looked heavy, with a long barrel. He said he'd used it once to hunt buffalo, but we suspected he was talking about somebody else.

About the only thing that seemed to stir him was the idea of getting it done so he could go back and find his chair at the hotel bar. So we showed him where the bridge was and he rested the barrel of his buffalo gun on the railing and told Simon to go bring the alligators their dinners. As soon as the scraps hit the water, they started arriving from wherever they'd been. And about as soon as their snouts broke the surface, Mr. Thibodeaux blew their heads out of the water.

So all of a sudden, it was raining alligator. Those of us watching had to stand back to stay clear of the splatter, shoving what seemed like all the kids in town away from the bridge, since we had an idea how their mothers might feel about working out alligator stains. Even if they knew how, which nowdays wasn't likely. But Mr. Thibodeaux was as cool as could be. He didn't even much move. Except for his trigger finger, he seemed able to manage that. And he got most of them. Maybe even all. That is, except one. Which was too mean. And smart. As though he knew this was a good time to stay hungry. And us, it was almost like we'd expected it.

So Mr. Thibodeaux sighed and belched, the first sounds he'd made for awhile, outside, of course, the shooting, and started back to the hotel.

"Those wasn't the one we wanted," we said.

"Of course they wasn't," was all he answered.

He wouldn't let Simon feed them the next day. But Mr. Thibodeaux did fine himself. We'd agreed to pay room and board, which was a mistake. Only we couldn't have known, it could have been a more moderate man. But the day after that, we were all back at the bridge. When Simon dumped the scraps this time, nothing happened, not at first. Then we could see kind of a ripple coming toward the scraps, real slow, and then stopping, right underneath the floating food. Then the ripple moved away somewhere, to get another breath maybe. Before long we saw it again, heading back toward the bridge. Only this time, Mr. Thibodeaux was concentrating, glaring through the sights of his gun. But when he fired, all that rained down was water. Mr. Thibodeaux sighed and belched and leaned his gun against the railing.

"Why're you stopping?" we asked.

"Cause I done killed myself an alligator," was all he said.

And sure enough, farther down the bayou, in a shallow part on the other side, we could see a blur of white, then the gator, floating belly-up.

"That's a big 'un, sure enough," Mr. Thibodeaux said, leaning against the railing, waiting, making sure the gator stayed dead.

"Yep," he said after awhile, "that oughter do 'er. They ain't built to do that while they're alive. Whatever else their ugly carcasses're built for, that one ain't on the list. Here, sonny."

Billy Wattle, the livery stable owner's kid, was standing beside him, staring.

"Here, sonny," he said and gave Billy Wattle a coin, "go get that dead limb over there and poke him over here to this side so we can take a look. He's a big 'un."

And before any of us could stop him, Billy was off the bridge and wading in the water, holding the stick. When

Billy nudged the dead gator with it, the gator started floating slowly toward the other bank, closer to us. When the gator stopped moving, Billy followed it, nudged it again, this time a little harder. Only this time there was a mighty thrashing in the water, and I swear the gator grinned up at us while he was turning over. Billy didn't even have time to scream before we lost sight of him, and when his body came up, it didn't do it all at the same time.

None of us could get a handle on what had just happened, we couldn't even take it in. Except for Charley.

In the quietest, politest voice imaginable, we heard him saying, "Excuse me for a moment, Mr. Thibodeaux?" And when Mr. Thibodeaux turned around, he was looking down the barrel of his buffalo gun that he had thought was still leaning against the railing. But he only looked for a second, because then Charley blew Mr. Thibodeaux's head off, down into the bayou. And when the gator came back to get it, Charley blew the gator's head off as well.

Then Charley kind of lost his head, too. Up to then, he'd been a little rash, it'd be hard arguing the other side of that, but nobody was going to hold much of anything against him. Mr. Thibodeaux for Billy wasn't by any means a fair trade, but it was probably the best anybody could do at the time. Truth be known, I suspect most of us wished we'd done the same thing, or at least something similar. So unless Mr. Thibodeaux had friends and relatives who missed him, which seemed unlikely, we could live with his sudden departure. But Charley didn't stop there. He turned around and shot Simon McCallister.

That was going too far, and Charley knew it. While we were running toward Simon, Charley finally came to his senses and was getting on his horse.

Word drifted back he was seen riding toward Indian Territory, which didn't surprise us. It's not unusual for people to head there when for one reason or another they feel crowded. Or have a suspicion they're getting ready to be. And when they leave, they tend not to get back, even those that do the chasing. So none of us had much stomach for following.

And some of us figured that Charley had been feeling crowded, one way or another, maybe for a long time. Probably not by the town, although it was growing pretty fast. But somehow inside his head. As though there was more going on in there, in his head, than any of us was ready to know. I'm not suggesting that anybody else saw it this way, but it was as though there was something inside Charley waiting for this to happen. As though something was waiting to be set loose, wanting to chase Charley, or at least the Charley we knew, across a line he couldn't get back across. As though the shooting was a way of showing on the outside, maybe even to Charley, what was happening down below. As though he needed a reason for getting out of town.

I'm not saying Charley intended on it ahead of time, just that he was ready once it came. At any rate he wasn't your ordinary fellow. But he also wasn't the kind you'd expect to blow a man's head off. Whatever the reason.

The Charley we'd gotten to know had been a quiet sort. He read a lot of books, about the only thing he ever got in the mail. People in a town notice that sort of thing, even when they don't talk about it. Maybe he had time to read because he'd never gotten married, at least not while we knew him, we heard different stories later. But there weren't the usual responsibilities, maybe he had more time at night than most of us to do what he wanted. Or could be he was just lonely, reading was about all that was left. The only company he seemed to have was his mother, and she was about as talkative as he was. She may have read the books, too, for what we knew.

Or maybe he read so much because he felt it was part of his job, being the town's schoolteacher. That could be the reason he took Billy Wattle's killing so much to heart, knowing Billy the way he did, day in, day out, watching him growing, seeing it stop.

So Charley was a little strange, nothing serious, just not like most other folks in town. But not the kind of strange you'd expect to start shooting people. And not the kind you'd think would manage too well outside of town, especially so far outside as the Territory. But after awhile, five years, maybe ten, we more or less stopped thinking about Charley. Not that we forgot, he just wasn't much on our mind.

That is, until his mother died. It was a shame Charley couldn't be there to see her off properly, they'd been so close. Or we guessed they had, they hadn't said much on the subject one way or the other. But we did the best we could, with the service and the burying. She'd put some money aside, only not enough for a tombstone. But then lots of people have rested pretty comfortable, lying under wooden crosses.

Then a month or so later, out of nowhere one morning there was a tombstone, all white and smooth, shiny and engraved with her name and dates and some words out of Shakespeare. It wasn't fancy, but it wasn't made out of wood.

That same day, Jason Miller, who runs the hotel, discovered that somebody had taken his bay mare, the one with the white spot like a quarter moon on its flank, and in its place was a big fine sorrel and a small cart. The sorrel was looking pretty worn out and likely to stay that way for awhile, but it was more than a fair trade. It just wasn't the normal way of transacting business.

At first we couldn't figure it out. Then we could.

"Somebody's got to tell him," we said.

"Tell him what?" a new fellow in town asked.

"That I ain't dead," Simon McCallister answered.

Both things were true. Simon had just been grazed and somebody had to go chase down Charley and tell him he could come on back and finish his reading. He'd been gone from home too long as it was.

But then the question was, who? It might likely be a long trip, and most of us had responsibilities.

Somebody said, "What about me?"

It was young Mirabeau Lamar Johnson standing there, his shirttail hanging out.

We kind of laughed. At least at first.

"Why Bo," we said, "you've just barely finished being a boy. What we need here is somebody a bit farther along."

"I'm old enough," he said. "And besides, I've got a right. He's kin."

That was true. Bo had always called him Uncle Charley. Only lord knows how many times removed. I couldn't recall Charley's having any brothers or sisters who'd gotten lost somewhere along the way.

So we said yes. Bo was bright and resourceful enough. He and his family lived on a farm not too far from town, but far enough that except for going to school, Bo wasn't around as much as boys living closer by. Besides, he was usually needed at home. We knew his father worked him pretty hard. Not because his father wanted to. We knew Mr. Johnson, he tried to be a fair man. But farming wasn't like selling groceries or tending school. There wasn't a whole lot of time off. So none of us knew Bo as well as we probably should have.

But Bo had been around animals, we knew he could ride better than most, probably even shoot some. He appeared quieter than others his age, as though he spent a good bit of time inside his thoughts, there seemed to be an independent streak running somewhere pretty deep. But he was the responsible sort, his folks had raised him that way, the sort of a boy a man would be proud to call his son.

So if he was a little young, the trip was probably going to be a long one. If he did start off just on the other side of being a boy, he more than likely would come back the far side of becoming a man. A person could do worse than do his growing up trying to chase down his Uncle Charley.

His mother cried a little, his father frowned and didn't say much. He seldom did, sometimes it was hard to know Mr. Johnson's feelings. But they were good people. And fair. They both knew Bo was of an age. If he made up his mind about something and that something was worth doing, then it was best for him to be doing it. His younger brother was old enough now to help with the crops.

So we got together and gave him a good horse, we collected some traveling money and wished him godspeed. We couldn't offer him much more, there weren't a whole lot of clues about where to look. But we figured Bo and Charley'd be traveling the same road, at least for awhile. There wasn't but one going through town. Since one end of it pointed back toward Louisiana and more towns, more people, Charley wouldn't likely be interested. The other way headed west, toward the insides of Texas.

So Bo did, too, and it was a good life, or so the story goes. Up till now, I've been pretty certain about things. It stands to reason. I was there looking and hearing and some of the time getting out of the way. And if I wasn't, if work kept me away, there were other folks, neighbors who could fill me in. Even if all of us got confused, we could talk it over till we'd arrived at something we'd at least call the truth. That's one of the things about being in a town. So if somebody still felt different, that was his business, but he most likely was being crotchety.

From here on out, though, I just can't be that sure. At best, the telling has got to be secondhand. There've been gaps, there had to be. I've tried to fill them in. I hope I've been fair. But it's hard sometimes, knowing what a boy might be thinking, even if you know what he's doing. So if Bo, or for that matter Charley, ever sees this, I want them to know, I did my best filling in the gaps, trying to understand.

Because nobody I know has seen anything at all of what follows. We may have once or twice felt that way, maybe even acted similar, though somehow I doubt it. But none of us has ever gotten to chase an Uncle Charley, at least not like Bo did. Like I said, it wasn't that we didn't want to. We simply had responsibilities.

At any rate, Bo started out, we know that for certain. He missed his folks, but not too much, they'd be there to come back to. For someone Bo's age, family doesn't seem so much like separate people as parts of a place called home. So although his mind might have been full of thoughts, there couldn't have been many that were bothersome, the land he was passing through was full of game, lots of water, plenty to eat, and nothing to worry about. As though both the world inside and the one outside were somehow full and empty at the same time, mainly happy in just being.

So it seemed the best of all worlds. To be free, living off the land and still having most of the comforts of home. And none of the work or even the worry. All Bo had to do was ride and look for places where he could ask about his Uncle Charley.

So that's what he did. Anywhere somebody might've had a chance to notice, he'd ask about a man riding a bay mare with a quarter moon on her side. Most hadn't, still more than enough had. Strangers were common along the road, but they were noticed. Folks who'd worked hard at keeping things peaceful didn't want something foreign unexpectedly causing trouble. So there were sightings enough for Bo to be comfortable. He figured his uncle didn't have any reason to worry about being followed. There wasn't any need for either him or Bo to be especially careful.

So the road turned into a trail, and the trail turned into directions, sometimes across country to the next town, most often to the next ranch or farm. But being in open country was no problem. The ranches and farms were small and close together, roads were mainly a matter of convenience. Folks knew how to get from one to the other without them. Or give good enough directions to someone else who might. And more often than not, when Bo stopped to ask about the horse with the quarter moon, he'd be invited in to rest, have something to eat, even spend the night. It was a good life for a boy getting ready to be a man, traveling with no strings attached, except the one, the looking for Uncle Charley.

So one day about sundown, he rode up to a little ranch, not a lot more than a farm. But well kept, Bo could tell in a glance. What Bo was noticing, although he probably didn't know it, were things other people might think didn't matter—flowers, clean curtains blowing in the windows, everything looking swept. A woman, short and a little bit plump, was standing on the porch like she was waiting for him, smiling, wiping her hands on her apron. Even that looked clean.

"Afternoon, ma'am," he said, taking off his hat. "Could I get maybe a little water. For my horse?" There'd been plenty in the creeks and ponds along the way, but he had learned this was a good way to begin. It wouldn't do to start by asking for supper.

"You're a bit of a young one, aren't you?" she said. "Well, take your horse on around to the stable. Then get yourself back here. You could use a little water on yourself before supper."

"Why thank you ma'am. That's certainly . . ."

"Now hush up and get going. I got things that need doing." So Bo knew it was going to be fine, at least for the night. He just didn't know how fine until Miranda.

When he sat down, there were four at the table, not counting himself. There was Mrs. Potter, the mother, but she was hardly ever sitting, she was so busy getting up for this, taking away that, filling things up that weren't even empty. There was Mr. Potter, who didn't say much, but when he did everybody stopped what they were doing and listened. There was Rafe, the hired hand, who looked five or six years older than Bo and talked a lot, mostly with his mouth filled with Mrs. Potter's supper. There was a nice family feeling. Bo almost felt a longing for home. Except there was Miranda.

She was about Bo's age, maybe a year or so younger, and she was the prettiest thing, not just person, the prettiest anything Bo had ever seen.

Not in a citified way, not delicate looking or putting on airs. But blonde hair hanging down to her shoulders, and skin that hadn't been afraid of the sun. Yet it looked so soft you wanted to reach out and touch it, just to see if it was true, if it could possibly feel the way it looked. You knew it couldn't, but you wanted like everything for it to be true. And she looked strong, fit, as though she'd be the match of anybody riding after cattle or milking. And, well, Bo couldn't really get it into words, she was just, well, she was pretty.

He could tell Rafe thought so, too. Rafe kept talking to her, saying things intended to please. But Bo could see she was used to it, she wasn't paying much attention. Still, Rafe was doing better than he was. Bo was so taken aback by sitting across from Miranda, he couldn't say anything. It didn't seem to matter. She didn't say much to Bo, but she smiled a lot in his direction.

"I said, boy, are you asleep with your eyes open, or are you merely deaf?"

Bo jerked his eyes away and refocused toward the head of the table.

"Oh, no sir, Mr. Potter, my ears are fine. I was just so wrapped up in Mrs. Potter's supper, I guess I wasn't paying much attention to anything else."

"That's very well and good. Satisfied eating can be a pleasure. But around this table, when I ask a question, I expect it to be answered."

"Yessir, I can understand that sir, it sounds like a good policy."

"What I asked, boy, I see you can ride, and I expect by that rifle I saw on your saddle, you think you can shoot. But what I asked, boy, can you read?"

"Why, yessir, I've read whole books, lots of them, cover to cover."

"Oh, that's wonderful!" Mrs. Potter broke in. "It's so difficult to find people Miranda's age around here who have culture. Back in Kentucky, before we moved, it was different. But there's hardly anybody around here who's like that."

"Don't see why reading's so important," Rafe said. "Don't see what good it does you on a ranch. Just a fool way to waste time."

"You may have a point there, Rafe, my boy, you may have a point," Mr. Potter said, getting up from the table. "But these days, with what's happening here and about, a man's got to read to keep up with other folk that do. Things are changing, son, right at this table, you see a fellow younger than you are . . ." Bo felt edgy, like he was somewhere in the middle of an argument that wasn't his. "Not smarter, mind you," Mr. Potter kept on, "we don't know anything about that. But unquestionably younger, who already can read, least says he can. So let it be a lesson, son, you keep busy with what Mrs. Potter's trying to teach you."

Mr. Potter was headed toward the porch when he turned around. "But you may have a point, boy, you may have a point. Myself, I fail to put as much stock as Mrs. Potter does, making sense of squiggly lines on a sheet of paper. Except of course for the Bible. And bills, you've got to make certain you get what you asked for, you've got to be careful about that, you plan to run a ranch someday."

Mrs. Potter didn't say anything, just beamed in Bo's direction.

It was like back home, after supper was always a nice time of day. The chores were done, except for cleaning up the kitchen, and Miranda and Mrs. Potter made quick work of that. Bo offered to help. Since he didn't have sisters, he was used to it. But Mrs. Potter shooed him out on the front porch with Mr. Potter and Rafe, who were leaning back in their chairs and looking out at the sky while they smoked their pipes. They didn't say much, Bo was used to that, but it felt a little strange, sitting there on the edge of the porch, staring back in the direction he'd just been coming from. He thought about asking his questions, but it didn't seem quite like the time. It would have been nicer back in the kitchen, drying dishes with Miranda.

Mrs. Potter came out with her sewing. Miranda followed a little later, holding a book. There was still enough light, but she didn't open it, just sat down, catty-cornered from Bo, where she could look in his direction without seeming to make any effort. Mrs. Potter didn't feel the need to be cagey.

"Young man?" she said.

Neither Mr. Potter or Rafe moved or apparently took notice.

"Ma'am?"

She hesitated, but not long. "You heading out or coming back? Or do you mind my asking?"

Mr. Potter gave her a quick look. It wasn't always the thing to do, asking a stranger his plans or his reasons. But then Mrs. Potter probably figured Bo was only just past being a boy.

"I'm on my way, ma'am, I've been at it awhile. I'm trying to catch up with my Uncle Charley."

Mr. Potter took his pipe from his mouth and banged out the leftover ashes. "Your Uncle Charley?"

"Yessir. I suspect he was riding this way. On a bay. Quarter moon on her flank. It'd be awhile back."

"Couldn't say. Don't spend much time keeping track of strangers." He put his pipe back in his mouth and went on studying whatever it was that had been holding his attention.

"Me neither," Rafe said. "Maybe you'd best go ask someplace else."

"Or maybe you could wait for the Preacher," Mrs. Potter said. "He'll be here before long, soon as he finishes his circuit. If your Uncle Charley's about, most likely he'd know. Besides," she said, going back to her knitting as though it was settled, "the Preacher told us last time he was here, we ought to be watchful, especially watchful he said, over the needs of strangers."

Bo glanced at Miranda. She had her finger inside her book, marking her place. She didn't say anything, nothing called for it, but she smiled.

"Would that be all right, Mr. Potter? For me to wait? I'm used to working, I can earn my keep."

All Mr. Potter did was grunt, then he kept on looking.

In the bunkhouse Bo took a bed as far away as he could, but Rafe was good at snoring. So Bo carried his blanket outside where the sound of cattle, complaining for some reason in the corral, was almost as bad. But he was more used to that, it was steadier and sounded more natural. Besides, it was nicer thinking about Miranda without company. Particularly who snored.

Breakfast in the big house was businesslike, mainly a matter of refueling. When they were through, Bo followed Rafe to the corral. The cattle inside were all cows, and by the size of their bags, pretty recently calved. Their udders were swollen, like badly made balloons about ready to burst, near to dragging the ground, in danger of being stepped on by neighbors. Most of their eyes were bloodshot and rolling, looking confused, as though they weren't able to understand which would hurt more, standing still or moving, trying to leave the hurt back where they'd been. So whichever they found themselves doing, they tried the other, only it never seemed to make things better.

"Dad blast it, Rafe, who in hell takes care of milking?" Bo was halfway over the fence before he glanced back.

Rafe just laughed and started rolling a cigarette. "Let me remember myself, boy, you grow up on a ranch or maybe it was a chicken farm? I seem to forgit. But you do seem to know a hell of a lot more about milking than running cattle." He licked the edge of his rolled-up cigarette and lit it.

"Rafe," Bo said without raising his voice, "I don't have any idea and I don't care what you're talking about. But what I do know is, there's animals out there hurting for no good reason, so it makes sense for somebody to do something, and there ain't anybody around much closer than us."

He was ready to drop to the other side when Rafe said, "Hey, boy, you best wait up."

Bo did, one foot still on the fence, the other hanging in air.

"Don't go getting bothered about something you don't know nothing about," Rafe said comfortably. "Just cause you don't know a good reason, no sign there ain't none."

Rafe sucked in some smoke, making a point of taking time. Bo just hung on, ready to finish jumping as soon as he was through waiting.

"Take for instance," Rafe said, "back on your chicken farm, you ever need to move a herd someplace, away from where they've gotten themselves good and settled? And somehow the mamma cows get wind of it, they start hiding their babies, putting them where they think they won't be bothered?"

"Sure, that's what cows do, it's their nature."

"Well then, sonny, what's your nature? What you find yourself doing about it? Hope they miss their mammas and come wandering home for supper, so next week maybe you can get them headed where you want them?"

"Whatever you're aiming at, Rafe, hurry up and say it. These cows aren't likely to get much pleasure out of lengthy speeches."

"Well, I reckon they just ought to consider that next time they get a notion to start hiding their young'uns."

He smoked a bit more. "You ain't answered me, back where you're at home, what you do about it?"

It wasn't his business, they weren't his cows. He just didn't see the need.

"What anybody would do. I go find them."

"Must be a pretty small piece of ground you got, back wherever you come from."

"It's big enough. I know where to look."

"Sure you do. Bet you even learned it from reading a book. But what you got to understand, sonny, out here, it ain't so simple. There's about a couple million places, and that's just the ones we know about. So we got a better way."

Bo knew about cattle, Rafe didn't need to explain. What some people did was bring in cows who clearly had milk but didn't seem to have anybody to give it to, and they penned them up overnight. By morning, the cows were so full and hurting, when the gate opened they made a beeline for their hidden places. Then you followed them to their calves and drove them to where you needed them to be.

Rafe could tell he understood. "Pretty smart," Rafe said. "Lot quicker than just looking."

"Does Mr. Potter know this is the way you do it?"

"His idea in the first place. The Mrs. ain't too excited about it. 'Why Hiram, I don't see why you have to do it that way!'" Rafe's voice took on a high mincing whine, nothing at all the way Mrs. Potter really sounded. "'Don't you recall,'" Rafe kept on, "'when Miranda was just a little thing . . . '" Something inside Bo jerked around when Rafe mentioned Miranda's name. It somehow wasn't right, but Rafe didn't seem to notice.

"'When she was just a little thing,'" Rafe kept going, "'how bad it hurt when it was time and for some reason or another, maybe the little darling was asleep, she wasn't able to suck on my titty, don't you remember how that hurt?'"

Here it wasn't just inside, here it felt like something outside jerked Bo around, and he saw himself moving, getting ready to climb back down on the other side of the fence. This time Rafe did notice, but he just grinned.

"'Don't you all just remember how bad that all hurt?' And Mr. Potter," Rafe said, "he takes his pipe out of his mouth and says, 'Now Lucinda.'" Rafe pitched his voice low, and although it sounded more like Mr. Potter than it had like Mrs. Potter, it still wasn't very close. "'Now Lucinda, you must also remember, my dear, that this is a business. And you must also remember, my dear, you are my wife. These are merely cows. If we are going to survive, we can't worry about giving them a little pain in their tits.'"

Rafe laughed and ground out his cigarette under his heel. "Come on, farm boy, let's saddle up. The sooner we get going, the sooner they're going to cut out that bellowing."

Mr. Potter and Miranda were waiting at the gate when Bo and Rafe got back from the stable. Bo noticed that Miranda was wearing pants, he couldn't remember ever seeing a girl doing that before. But what he noticed more, she sat her horse like a man, as though her bottom, without any effort, was permanently attached to the saddle, like her body from the waist on down knew what the horse was going to do, then moved with it. But Bo felt awkward, thinking too much about Miranda's body from the waist on down, there was some sort of line he'd be better off staying one side of. So he stared hard toward Mr. Potter.

"Okay, Rafe," Mr. Potter was saying, "you and the boy tail them on up north. They'll probably stop somewhere around the crevasses, so you be careful, it's just about time for the rains. The girl and I'll follow toward the brambles, down around the creek. Once you find any, head 'em on back here."

"I know what to do," Rafe said. "I've done it before."

"I know, son, I know you have. There's others riding that ain't."

As soon as Rafe opened the gate, the cattle started out at a trot, separating into clear streams, one heading to the right, uphill, the other toward the left, back from where Bo had ridden the day before, downhill toward where there were creeks and thickets, a lot of green, where although he hadn't thought much about it at the time, he remembered the land as being friendly. Uphill, where he and Rafe were going, it quickly got drier, barer, there were large patches of sandy clay, and then there weren't just patches, there wasn't anything else. The cattle kept moving at a slow trot, still moaning, their bags every now and then catching on a rock or a ridge, and then their sounds became deeper, somehow thicker, but they never slowed down or showed any doubt about direction.

Rafe seemed in a hurry, too. Bo didn't see any reason why. He didn't like the sounds himself, there was too much hurt in them, but at least now things were heading toward an ending. Apart from that, it was a nice morning, the air was clear and clean. Both he and his horse were rested, and it wasn't like on the trail, he knew where he was going back to once the day had ended.

But Rafe was in a hurry. He kept urging the cattle on, even though they seemed to be going about as fast as they could under the circumstances. Besides, pushing them faster, you not only caused more hurting, you stood to run off weight, which didn't do anybody any good. But Bo didn't say anything. Not until they got to a gully that was steep on the far side. The lead cow took one look and said forget it, and turned to find another direction.

"Shee-yut," Rafe said. "These dumb titty-bags think we got all day."

Rafe rode up alongside the lead cow and turned her back, driving her down into the gully, forcing her to scramble up the other side, scraping her bag against the top of the ridge, turning her moaning into a bellow.

That was enough. Bo didn't say anything. He rode to the front and turned the rest of the cattle back, toward where the lead cow had been going before Rafe had interfered. Bo led them, not all that far, to where the land flattened, where they could keep on going without increasing their pain.

Rafe, of course, hadn't waited, but he didn't take long to find, Bo's cattle had been hurrying to catch up with their leader. When they were back together, nobody said anything, Rafe just looked at Bo hard and spit off to the side, making a bit of dry clay splatter. Then they just rode.

The cattle slowed as they came to a plateau, wide, empty, with suddenly shallow arroyos, twisting, ending sometimes in miniature box canyons, sometimes wandering like they weren't going to stop but still not sure where they were going, winding back on themselves, separating, coming together.

There could be multitudes of things hidden down there, herds of wild buffalo, no one could tell.

At the edges the cattle stopped, letting out the first wholesome mooing Bo had heard all day, all night for that matter. Calves started appearing, some of them spindly-legged, others ready to romp, all of them seeming hungry, all of them scrabbling one way or another up the slopes.

A few of the mothers risked going down themselves, but they seemed to know easy places, and even then they did it gingerly. With those, Rafe and Bo followed. When they found a mother with her calf, they interrupted the reunion long enough to get them to the high ground, where all the cows and calves could be kept together. Then Bo and Rafe waited until everybody finished breakfast.

Except for one cow and her calf who got through early and wanted to ramble. Bo, not even thinking, rode off leisurely in a sweeping circle to cut them off, but Rafe was moving quickly. Almost immediately he was beside Bo, riding strangely hard, forcing him back.

Bo was confused, more than that, he was irritated. But he was the stranger, he let Rafe turn him. After both of them had slowed, Rafe just looked at him and said, "Shee-yut, farm boy, let me show you a little something."

They rode easily in the direction Bo had recently been heading. Without warning they were on the edge of a giant crevasse, a wedge of open space, dark at the bottom, fifteen, maybe twenty feet below. Rafe spat down into it.

"You fall down there, sonny, you're in trouble."

"Why?" Bo asked. "What makes it different from the others?"

"Them others ain't so steep for one thing. But you notice how none of them mothers left their little darlings down here, you did notice that?"

"Not to think about," Bo said. "Why's there a difference?"

"Main difference, those holes back there, they been here awhile. These here, last year they weren't."

Bo looked down again. The crevasses beneath him still looked more or less like the rest.

"It's been a dry year," Rafe said. "Don't let the creeks in the bottom fool you, most times they're twice as high. Up here it gets bad even when down there it's flooding. And when it goes dry, real dry, the land up here just sort of opens up, there's big cracks all of a sudden. One day there ain't nothing, next we got these. And they go away just as quick, you got to be careful. One of those real fast rainstorms, before you know what happens, they snap shut, it's like they never was. And whatever's down there, it's a lost calf or a curious coyote or just some dumb farm boy, it don't make much difference, what's down there, it stays. So you'd best remember, this ain't back home, there's things here that ain't in your books. You best be careful. I can't be around all the time looking after you." He spat again and turned his horse and rode off after strays.

They drove the cattle back to the ranch where Mr. Potter and Miranda were waiting. Then Rafe and Bo moved what now was a small herd to another range, where the grass hadn't been recently grazed. When they got back to the ranchhouse, Mrs. Potter had lunch waiting, and after that everybody split up for separate chores. Rafe gave Bo an ax and pointed him toward a woodpile.

Bo was still at it when Miranda came out to do the evening milking. He managed to finish quicker than he might have, and when he'd carried the last load into the woodshed, Mrs. Potter happened to be standing outside the kitchen on the back steps.

"My, you work fast," she said, wiping her hands on her apron. It was still clean when she'd finished. "I hate to put you onto something else so quick, but maybe you noticed Miranda heading down to the barn?"

"Yes ma'am," Bo said.

"Would it be a whole lot of trouble seeing if she might need a little help?"

"No ma'am," Bo answered, "I don't see how it could."

He wasn't so sure once he got to the barn. There wasn't any question, being there felt good down inside. It was just getting the inside to the outside that made him nervous. The problem was, he didn't have any sisters. He wasn't sure how he should act. At least not with girls that made him feel like he was starting to now.

"You milk real good," he said.

She looked up from kneeling beside the cow and smiled. But she didn't say anything.

Which didn't help. He had to think of something else. "Except maybe your trousers, don't you think you might be getting them dirty, being on the ground like that?"

She glanced toward her pants, clearly cut down from her daddy's, looking more like two towsacks than trouserlegs.

So at first she blushed, but of course Bo didn't notice, then she flicked her head back, tossing hair, and she stared up higher, like she was interested in the shape of cow ribs.

"It doesn't much matter," she said. "They're just old stuff, I only wear them for things like this. Besides," she said, seeming to return to her milking, but not really doing much. "Besides," she said, "why aren't you back doing whatever it is you're supposed to be doing? Instead of standing here, telling me about my clothes? If I wanted company, I'd have asked."

"I just finished," Bo said. "I thought maybe I could help." He hadn't considered before how talking could be so hard. "Mrs. Potter, too. She thought it might be a good idea."

Now she looked like she was going to stare right through the ribs and out the other side. "Oh," she said, in a tone as though she couldn't in the least be concerned. "So the two of you, you got together and decided, just because I'm a girl and you just happen to be a boy, the two of you decided you know more about milking cows than I do? And how come you're so worried about my pants and not about yours? I suspect I got more changes in my closet than you got in those little saddlebags of yours."

It still wasn't happening the way Bo had planned. He was beginning to understand that maybe with Miranda most things didn't.

She turned around toward him, waiting, her nose still higher than she normally kept it.

"What I meant to say was, well, you seem to be awfully," Bo thought for a good word—Miranda seemed to be awfully particular about such things—"you seem to be awfully . . . *interesting*. And since I was through and I was by myself, Rafe's someplace else, and besides we don't have a lot to talk about anyway, so I came here to see if I could find you because . . . well, because . . ." He gave up. "Because I wanted to."

He didn't have any idea how he was doing. And she wasn't helping, she was just kneeling there. He gave up. He'd try again later. You could hear it in his voice. "And Mrs. Potter, she really didn't have a whole lot to do with it. And my worrying about your trousers, that was kind of an excuse so I could help you, because dirty trousers don't seem to me to be any problem, and I think you milk real good."

So of course it was now that she straightened up and dusted off her pants, and Bo wondered if she knew how pretty she looked.

"But now that you mention it," she said, "my knees *are* getting a little tired."

So Bo sat on his heels and started to milk. The rhythm of the milk hitting the pail was all the sound necessary, as though now they didn't have to fill up the silence. So now when they talked it would be because of wanting to, not because of any need. Especially since now there was a reason for both of them to be there.

A week later, maybe, they wouldn't know what they talked about, but they'd remember what was important. That this was the first time they'd been together by themselves, and it didn't just happen by accident. They were together because that's where they'd wanted to be. And they'd both probably remember the sound the milk made when it hit the pail, since it's that sort of thing people somehow manage to keep ahold of. But I suspect they wouldn't remember much about what they actually said. It was probably what most folks their age might have talked about. How their lives were alike, how they were different. Not yet getting around to mentioning what they hoped for, or dreamed about when they shut out the present so they could live hundreds of futures inside their heads. They probably didn't talk about those things. But they probably hinted, just to test the waters.

So everything was going fine as long as Bo kept his eyes on his work. He didn't need to worry about his mind. He'd milked enough cows, milking one more didn't need any thinking. But after awhile, it wasn't enough just to hear Miranda in between the squirts, he wanted to see her, too. And that shouldn't have been a problem, either. His hands knew what to do.

So he turned around to see her, how she was leaning back against the side of the stall, looking better than anything he could ever even imagine. It was just then he started feeling strange, not just red in the face but that way all inside, and he didn't know why, not right at first. He only knew that he felt funny and wanted to be someplace else. Although he knew that couldn't be true. There wasn't anyplace in the world he'd rather be than right where he was.

He looked back around at his work, and then something inside made connections. He'd done milkings hundreds, probably thousands of times and hadn't thought about it, just went out to the barn, put a bucket under the back end of a cow and got started. He hadn't thought about it, he just did it. But there hadn't been anybody around like Miranda before, looking at him, talking to him all the while. Then all of a sudden he knew, what he was doing wasn't just milking a cow, what he was doing was milking a . . . *female* cow. And the parts he was doing it on . . . He didn't want to be even thinking about it. But he couldn't help it, he turned his head and looked at her again, without even deciding to, and she was still there, leaning back, looking at him. And Bo felt the redness inside him starting to creep out, up through his scalp, into his hair. And he felt so awkward he missed a beat.

By this time, the cow had gotten used to Bo's hands, she'd understandably come to take his talent for granted, and so when he messed up the timing, she was annoyed. She looked around and stomped a hoof, then she swatted Bo with her tail. And since he didn't have his mind on what he was doing in the first place, Bo lost his balance. But he had enough presence to reach out and steady the pail while he watched himself falling. It was bad enough to lose self-respect without losing the milk as well. But Miranda had seen the swat coming, knew that Bo was starting to tumble, and since she was a rancher's daughter, she sprung over, reaching for the pail, too.

So there they were, Bo lying on the ground holding on to one side of the pail, Miranda bending over, holding the other, their faces so close they could hear breathing. And then they started laughing, neither could have told anybody why. But they didn't need to, at least not to each other. They both knew it was really the same laugh, only split in two.

And it was hard to stop doing it, even while they stood up, brushing themselves off. And all the while, the cow was just staring, chewing her cud, waiting, in the course of things, for life to go on.

That night, after supper and the porch sitting, Bo took a walk. He didn't really have anywhere he wanted to go, and if you'd asked, he probably couldn't have told what he was thinking. But there was an unaccustomed feeling he didn't want to get rid of. And he was afraid if he stayed in one place too long, somehow he might stop feeling it. The last thing he wanted was sleep. There wasn't any way to be sure the feeling would still be there in the morning. He wasn't used to this sort of thing. He needed to be careful. But tomorrow was a work day, and sooner or later he would have to risk it. So he went back to the bunkhouse for his bedroll.

Bo planned on sleeping outside again. He didn't want to share his feelings right now with anybody, except just one, and Rafe most certainly wasn't it. When he walked into the bunkhouse, Rafe was already in bed, only he wasn't asleep. Which isn't to say he wasn't busy. Bo had walked in so quietly Rafe hadn't noticed, at least not at first, and he didn't have time to get his blanket pulled up. It took Bo a moment to register, and when it did, he got mad. He almost felt mean.

He walked over to Rafe's bunk and stared down. "I don't care what you do," he said. "That's your business. But while you're doing it, I want you to be real sure, I want you to be especially sure even inside your head, there's at least one person you're not doing it to."

Rafe at first seemed flustered, then only confused, but at last back to being his old self. He sat up, still keeping the sheet over his bottom half, but pulling his arms outside and folding them across his chest.

"Listen, farm boy, I'm gonna think about anybody I want. And what's more, I can think about doing things you ain't even considered yet. I can think about doing things you can't tell me not to, cause you don't even know what to call them."

Well, of course, this could only make Bo even madder, but he wasn't sure what to do about it. What he wanted to do was pull Rafe out of bed and slam him up against the wall. Then part of Bo got a look at himself and started feeling the whole conversation was getting foolish, probably had even started out that way. But another part was still getting madder, knowing all he could do to stop Rafe's imaginings was maybe cut off his head. Which seemed extreme. So he gathered his blankets and just left.

Outside, lying under the stars, Bo felt urges, too. While he was doing it, he told himself, he could think of somebody else. One of the girls back home, one from school, maybe. Or somebody he could even make up.

He couldn't take the chance. The person he made up at the last minute might start looking like somebody else, somebody he hadn't made up, somebody he couldn't have imagined, no matter how hard he tried. And that wouldn't be fair. And it might also get in the way of how he was feeling. Then it wouldn't be a good trade, was what he thought, turning over, settling into sleep.

He woke up happy. Even Rafe, bustling around getting ready, didn't change things a lot. The only problem was to keep remembering why he was here in the first place. Because now there was some confusion. Bo was discovering more parts of himself than he found useful. One part knew he was waiting for the Preacher so he could find out about Uncle Charley. But another part, one he wasn't quite used to, and the one that right now had his attention, didn't care at all about that. What it cared about was a lot closer at hand.

But not that near, at least not during the day. Because he found out at breakfast that after work everybody was going to a party at a neighboring ranch, one with more hands, more cattle, and a lot bigger living room. It also had a daughter, older enough than Miranda for them not to be best friends, but closer than anybody else in both age and distance so they could pretend to be. And Miranda was going to spend the day there, getting ready for the evening. As she got up from the breakfast table, ready for her ride over, she looked at Bo as though she wasn't too happy about leaving, as though she was waiting for him to say something. But for reasons Bo didn't understand, he acted like he didn't notice, looking down at his plate, paying attention to chewing.

Bo and Rafe rode range all day. They didn't say much, they didn't have the opportunity. They weren't all that busy, but they were seldom close enough to talk even if they'd had something to say. Or wanted to say it. But after work and a quick supper, they seemed overly conscious of each other getting ready for the party.

Rafe acted as though it was nothing special, or if it was, that was mainly because *he* was going to be there. He whistled and talked about his dancing and how everybody kept asking him how he did it, and about his special party bandanna and the shirt he kept just for dances. To hear him tell it, he didn't make any real effort, he just couldn't help being the center of things once he got there, so he owed it to people to get himself ready.

All of which couldn't help but make Bo nervous. It wasn't that Bo wasn't used to socials, they had them back home all the time. Only now those seemed kid stuff, like doing party games. And he'd been as good at it as anybody, but not any better, at least not enough to talk about. So he couldn't believe Miranda would pay him much attention once she was around other people. He didn't have anything close to a party bandanna, and his shirt was going to be a clean one, but it wasn't going to be anything special. So he had reason to be afraid that in spite of herself, she might overly notice Rafe.

Of course, she'd probably been going to these sorts of things all her life and Rafe must have been at some of them and she hadn't been taken in. At least not yet. But Bo wasn't clear about how these things happened. If Rafe was so sure of himself, maybe she'd pay too much attention without being able to help herself. Then all of a sudden, Bo wasn't certain when, he'd stopped worrying about himself and started considering that Miranda herself might need some taking care of. If she was too nice a person for himself, and he was pretty sure about that, she was way too good for someone like Rafe. Bo couldn't have explained how he knew that, and he wasn't too proud about thinking it. But he knew it just the same.

Still, as Bo glanced over while he and Rafe were back of the bunkhouse bathing, splashing water out of two large basins, Rafe didn't look all that bad, if you didn't know any better. He was kind of tall and lean and hard looking, maybe even a little bit handsome, although Bo never could figure out how girls decided things like that. In fact, it occurred to Bo, someone might think Rafe was something of a catch. That is, if Rafe kept his mouth shut. And Rafe, Bo thought with relief, wasn't likely to be caught doing that.

They left for the social a little earlier than necessary, at least according to Mr. Potter's figuring, although he didn't complain too much. Of course, Mr. Potter never did complain too much, he just changed people's minds for them. But this time he only let everybody know what his figuring was and left it at that.

"That girl's going to be the death of me yet," Mrs. Potter said, like she was explaining something Bo needed to know, "running around all the time in those pants. It's not civilized, I keep telling her, but she says cattle don't seem much to mind. So I need to get there early, make sure she doesn't put her dress on backwards or something."

But Bo could tell she couldn't wait to get there herself. In fact, she'd seemed kind of lonely all day. While the men were out working, Miranda was about all the company she had, and when Miranda was gone riding or visiting, something seemed missing from everything Mrs. Potter did. It was kind of strange for Bo, thinking that way about Mrs. Potter. He couldn't remember wondering about what his mother felt when she was home by herself, while he was working in the fields with his father. And for his mother, there wasn't even a Miranda.

He simply didn't remember thinking too much about either one of his parents. Maybe he had, but if so, he'd somehow forgot. They just seemed to always be there. Like that was what they were for. But now that he was traveling, looking at other people's families, at other people's lives, he seemed to be noticing things in different ways.

Mr. and Mrs. Potter and Bo rode in the buckboard, Bo in the back, leaning against the side, but Rafe insisted on riding his horse. Bo was a little surprised Rafe didn't have a different horse hiding someplace, maybe next to his bandanna and his shirt, stored away special for parties. Bo figured Rafe thought he'd make a better entrance coming in that way, up high and riding, but Bo decided his own horse needed the rest and besides, the only reason he was going to be there, he was the Potters' guest. It was only fitting he should keep them company.

He also suspected they'd be coming home late. Miranda might tie her horse to the wagon and ride inside, and about the only place where there'd be room would be in the back beside him. It was at least something to think about. He'd let Rafe worry about entrances. He'd be thinking about the ride home.

When they got to the neighbors', it turned out that Mrs. Potter had known what she was up to. There was a gaggle of buckboards already outside, so at least a handful of women had beaten her there, probably for the same reason.

Mrs. Potter lifted up her skirts so they wouldn't drag in the dust and climbed down. Without waiting for anybody else, she headed for the door. "I bet that girl is still upstairs talking and not even thinking about time," she said with a smile that suggested she'd spent some time upstairs herself, back in Kentucky when she was a girl.

The men stayed outside talking and smoking. Bo could hear the kids off somewhere doing whatever kids do until they figure the refreshments are ready. The younger men gathered to another side, Rafe and one or two others not quite ready to get off their horses, in case there might be a few girls who hadn't yet arrived. But the rest of the younger men were standing around trying to look comfortable, maybe a dozen in all. Some of them had probably ridden half the day to get here, and would probably ride half the night, or what there was left of it, getting back to start work the next morning.

Bo stayed with Mr. Potter. He wasn't likely to add much to the conversation, but he still liked it better beginning the evening as Mr. Potter's guest instead of seeming like Rafe's. And if Mr. Potter didn't pay him much attention, he also didn't seem to mind.

So Bo stood and listened while the older men talked about weather and screwworms and horses. But mainly what they stood around doing was filling up time. It wasn't that they were waiting for something different. They'd be happy to keep on doing what they were doing all night if the womenfolk would let them. Which of course the womenfolk wouldn't and the men knew it. But now they were simply feeling good with the company, not really needing even to talk, since most of what one might be saying was pretty much what the next one was thinking anyway.

But that wasn't what Rafe and the younger folk had in mind. As soon as there were scurryings inside the house, Bo could see them getting edgy, wondering who was going to be first to make the move, to do what everybody couldn't wait to start doing himself.

Inside the house, there was a long narrow room that seemed made just for dancing. All the furniture that must have usually been there was now someplace else. Instead, there were benches back against the wall leaving the middle space clear, like it was begging for folks to fill it. Off in a side room there was a table fixed up for a punch bowl, and standing around it were an awful lot of women, some of them girls, the younger ones doing more giggling than talking. The older ones, the wives, a few of them young themselves, but most of them more like Mrs. Potter, were just kind of smiling, glad to see themselves as women at a social, not only wives and mothers back in the kitchen. All of them were dressed up special, some even had on storebought. Some of the others, you could tell, had spent more hours than they could spare staying up late with a needle. A few were even wearing their wedding dresses, and not just those looking the youngest.

Bo did some quick calculating. Even counting the older women, there were a lot more men hanging back with him than there were women around the punchbowl, but nobody seemed bothered.

"Well, lookey all who's here!" a big smiling woman said, looking like she had on an acre's worth of petticoats and all of it storebought. As near as Bo could tell, she belonged to the house. "I reckon since so many folks decided to drop by we ought to see if anybody here can make music. 'Less, of course, you want me to sing and Joshua over there to whistle." Everybody looked toward a skinny dry-seeming man whose lips were pressed so hard against each other they'd probably break if he tried to pucker. But he managed a bit of a smile. Almost. At any rate his mouth moved a little.

By the time Bo looked around, somebody had a fiddle and a couple of fellows pulled out guitars and they were starting to get in tune. Bo looked around again. He still didn't see Miranda, or for that matter her mother, except she wasn't a major concern.

The fat woman, who probably had to smile a lot to make up for Joshua, was clapping her hands, getting everybody quiet, and then she held up a handful of handkerchiefs.

"Okay, you menfolks, it's almost choosing-up time."

A few of the younger fellows started edging out the door, until the fat woman pointed over to them. "That's right, you Jim and Buck there, you go on outside and see if anybody's skulking around and you tell them, anybody that ain't here by time the music starts, they get to wear the last bandannas. And that means the two of you, too." Pretty soon the two of them came back, along with three or four more. Rafe included.

"Don't you think you scalawags can fool me," the woman said. "I been keeping my eye on menfolk before you young'uns been born. And I've told you before, but I reckon it needs doing again," she was still smiling, but talking in a tone that meant business, "if we gonna keep having these parties, you young fire-eaters got to act civilized. We may not be in some fancy opry house, but then this ain't the middle of the wilderness either. So you young folk better get used to cooperating, else nobody's gonna have any fun, including yourselves. There's times you got to be what you ain't, you want to keep the party going. So just cinch up and fit with the crowd. Everybody's gonna get a chance to dance with the ladies, and sooner or later all you rascals is gonna get a chance to wear one of these pretty bandannas."

So all the men started lining up, the older ones included, except maybe three or four who looked like they didn't intend to have much fun anyway. And three or four others who looked at first like they didn't either, but whose wives went over and decided for them differently.

Bo started to join in, but just then there was a stirring and Mrs. Potter and Miranda were coming down the stairs and Miranda was wearing a blue dress so soft Bo thought she would start floating down the rest of the way, like on a cloud, and it wasn't just soft, it showed a lot of her neck that looked even softer, and Bo had to swallow at least twice before he noticed Mrs. Potter was motioning him to come over by her.

"We got us a first-time guest with us," she said, "and it only seems fitting we make sure he has some fun and doesn't get stuck with any bandanna." She stopped and smiled so everyone could take a look at Bo. But of course since he was the only stranger around, everybody already had. "At least not this first time," she said and took Bo by the arm and led him out of the line, over next to where Miranda was standing. Miranda smiled up out of her blue dress, and all Bo could do was stare down at his feet, it was like she was too pretty to look at.

When he did look up, the fat lady was holding a handful of hay straws, and when each man passed by, he took one. Those that got the longer ones were relieved, those who got middle-sized didn't seem to mind, and those with the short ones got bandannas tied to their arms. Including Rafe.

"It ain't fair," he was saying, as the fat lady tied it onto his party shirt. "I had to wear one of these the last time."

"I guess you just got lucky," she beamed, "and you do make such a lovely partner."

"But Rafe's right," Mrs. Potter said, sounding considerate. "He did have to dance with a handkerchief the last time. So for his turn, why don't we let him stay in the back room."

"Oh, no ma'am, that's all right," Rafe said, talking faster than was probably necessary. "I don't want no advantage, I'll take my chance on the back room straw like the rest of the boys."

"Nonsense," said Mrs. Potter. "Nobody'll mind, if it's only this once."

"That's right, Mrs. Potter," said one of the rest of the boys. "We won't mind. Besides, that'll just be Rafe's kind of thing. There's probably some females back there already dying for his assistance."

"Leastwhiles crying for it," another one said, and they all laughed. Except Rafe.

"That's right," said another of the boys, "and there might be one who'll even listen to such stuff you always want to be saying."

"That's right," said another one. "Cause over there in the back room they ain't got much choice."

"That's right, and you might just find one that'll believe you."

"Nah, that's too much for Rafe to wish for, there ain't any, not even back there, who's all that little."

What Rafe did was glower and stalk off to a back room where Bo could hear babies crying. Women were already scarce enough, you didn't want to waste any on babysitting.

In fact, they were sufficiently scarce, there had to be bandannas, and those that were wearing them had to dance the parts of women. Or at least they were supposed to, some did better than others. Bo had to dance with them occasionally himself, when there was a reel or a square dance and he had to swing someone else's partner. But when the fiddles and guitars started playing, he happened to be standing next to Mrs. Potter, and of course Miranda, too, so the pairing off came natural. Although he couldn't help but notice some of the younger fellows didn't take it kindly. For that matter, some of the older ones either. Women were scarce, young ones scarcer. So being with one of the mothers, especially young ones whose husbands weren't much for dancing, that wasn't bad, nowhere near so bad as pairing with a bandanna. But when you looked at Miranda . . .

Most of the dances Bo already knew, and the rest he didn't mind learning from Miranda. After awhile the men with the bandannas took them off and gave them to those who had drawn the middle-sized straws, and all in all everything seemed good-natured. Except maybe for Rafe, who was more anxious than most for the changing.

But wasn't real happy when it happened, because he came out of the back room just in time to see a slow dance starting. There weren't many of that kind, most of the dances were like the parlor games Bo was used to, "Old Dan Tucker," that sort of thing. Only there were others where you got to hold your partner for more than just a swing or two. Which was fine for everybody who wasn't partnering or wearing a bandanna.

It wasn't like you got to be real close. Still it was close enough to feel like it was. Especially if you were Rafe, standing in a corner by the punchbowl, thinking about just how close it was, and how it wasn't with him.

So even though his time in the back room was done, he walked outside like he wasn't happy. Bo, of course, didn't give Rafe much attention. He naturally had different things on his mind, some of which were happy, but other developments were getting bothersome. The dance was about to end, and Bo was acting nervous. Miranda could tell, and at first she was worried it was something she had done. Then she noticed.

"It's okay," she said after they had just done a swinging twirl and now were back together, closer than usual. "When the music gets over, we'll just stay together and go out like we're taking a walk. Nobody'll pay any mind."

So that's what they did.

They both were a little self-conscious once they got out the door, but Miranda said, "Don't worry, Bo, I live on a ranch, I know about things like that." She smiled. "And it's not the first time it's happened at a dance, though it's nicer happening with you."

Bo didn't know what to say. Being this close to Miranda, having her talk like this wasn't helping things any. It just made the front of his pants feel even tighter.

"Though what I worry about," she said with a serious look, almost a frown, "when it happens, when it gets like this, does it hurt any? I mean, is it like with the cows yesterday, does it just keep hurting," and for the first time she seemed embarrassed, "until it . . . goes away?"

Bo was getting ready to tell her it hurt a lot, only not in the way she seemed to mean, but he didn't have time because out of nowhere Rafe was appearing, looking like he knew where he was heading.

"I've had enough of this, clodbuster," he said, lunging toward Bo but doing it kind of slowly. And as soon as Bo smelled his breath, he knew what Rafe had been doing outside. So did Miranda. "Rafe, you cut it out. And if Daddy finds out you've been drinking, you know what that's going to mean!"

Rafe, at the time, wasn't too interested in conversation. But Bo had figured as much and was ready. As Rafe came at him, Bo moved out of the way, tripping him, letting Rafe's own lunging carry him past, sending him sprawling into a watering trough.

"Oh, Rafe," Miranda said, "now you've gotten yourself all wet. And with your party shirt on, too. Climb on out of there and get dried off before someone starts paying attention."

But Rafe had found a piece of firewood on the bottom of the water trough and came up flinging water and rushing toward Bo again, waving the wood ferociously.

"Oh, Rafe," Miranda said, and matter-of-factly kicked him in the crotch, "once your manners get better, come on back inside."

She took Bo by the arm and nudged him toward the house. "You've got to ignore Rafe sometimes," she said. "Sometimes he gets carried away."

Things inside were winding down. Only some older women, who were probably thinking about how long it would be before they'd be dancing again, seemed reluctant to leave the floor. And some younger ones who couldn't bear even to think that far, who couldn't believe there wasn't music still coming, not sometime else, now, just as soon as this song got finished. But for most, the night's dancing was about ready for remembering.

Then there was a bustling, and a little man came from somewhere, Bo couldn't be sure where, but it was in the direction of a side door right next to where Mrs. Potter was still standing. He moved through the folks laughing, his belly more or less made for the activity, bouncing comfortably as he made his way to the front, up next to the band. He was wearing a black coat and his pants were likely the same color once, but that had been a long time ago, before a lot of traveling.

The room became unusually still, so quiet that Bo turned to Miranda for an explanation. But she only looked at the floor, like she was ready for more dancing and was just waiting.

"No preaching tonight," the little man said. "Got more of that maybe for tomorrow. Tonight, what we got is dancing."

He said a few words to the musicians, and Bo thought the man may have even stared for a moment at him. But Bo was long past wondering why folks might look hard at someone standing close to Miranda.

Then the band started playing and folks started dancing, and Miranda pulled him out onto the floor. The little man in black started clapping his hands to the music. "What the lord wants is folks that are dancing. That is," and he laughed devilishly, "so long as those folks keep doing it proper." Then he clapped louder. And everybody started doing the right moves.

Bo did, too. The tune was familiar, so the words the stranger was calling out didn't matter. At least not while he was dancing with Miranda.

Take her by the lily-white hand
And lead her like a pigeon,
Make her dance the weevily wheat
Till she loses her religion.

And almost without knowing it, Bo was remembering, even while he was dancing, he was waking up in the middle of the night, noticing a lantern still burning in the parlor. And it felt strange. Things were still going on around him, the music was playing and folks were moving and he knew for sure Miranda was there in his arms. But things were happening inside his mind as well, and they were just as real. They were already over, they had to be, he wasn't making them up, he was remembering. But they were happening again, not so much side by side with the outside, but somehow right in the middle, happening and at the same time already over.

And yet they were different, because they weren't just happening anywhere, they were happening here, in the middle of the floor while he was dancing with Miranda. So while he was promenading to the music, he was also getting out of bed, checking on the light, and at first he couldn't understand. His mother and father were standing together close in the middle of the room, moving back and forth, looking at each other but not talking. And then he realized they were dancing. The only music was inside their heads, and they were dancing. He was too sleepy to think about it then, so he went back to bed and until now, he hadn't thought about it since.

And he couldn't think about it much now, because something was changed with Miranda. All night, dancing with Miranda had been like floating, particularly once he got through his uneasiness. But now she seemed nervous herself, glancing every now and then over Bo's shoulder at the caller.

A little more of your weevily wheat,
  A little more of your barley,
A little more of your weevily wheat
  To bake a cake for Charley.

No matter, she was still smiling. It just seemed she'd been happier before the new caller had showed up.

Charley, he was a nice young man,
  Charley, he was dandy,
Charley was a nice young man,
  Until he got too handy.

Bo all of a sudden was listening. When he looked over, the little man was looking right back, but he kept on calling.

Charley here and Charley there
  And Charley over the ocean,
Charley he'll come back some day,
  If he doesn't change his notion.

Then the fiddle took over and Miranda smiled up at him and they danced around the room, and by the time Bo thought to look again, the little man in the black coat was gone.

The next morning at milking time, Miranda had already started by the time Bo got there. She didn't turn around, just kept on milking.

Bo decided not to notice. He still felt too good about last night, dancing with Miranda. On his way to the barn, everything seemed to know it, all the world seemed to give off the same feeling. The air smelled fresh, waiting, as though the day couldn't start soon enough, and even if it didn't, even if nothing else happened, ever, right now was almost enough. The way the sun seemed to shine exactly right on the grass, the dew making everything look polished, the light shining on the wagon bed, unhitched, waiting, even the few places where the paint was flecking, even that was just right, the sun shining there, too, making designs as though they had been intended, and up over everything a bird singing, like it was a message about nothing else but the song. Bo felt as though his insides were spilling out over everything, like a blessing.

Except Miranda, the cause of it all, seemed to have slipped outside Bo's new world.

"You want me to milk some?" was all Bo said.

"You think I don't know how to do it? You think I won't know how to do it again after you're gone?"

"Of course you know how to do it, I didn't say anything like that, or at least I didn't mean to. But as long as I'm here, I'd like to do something, not because you can't do it, only because I'd like to be doing something for you. And that's the only thing you happen to be doing just now."

She turned around and looked at him, like she was mad.

Bo wished he'd had some sisters.

"And I don't need any more talking like that. You just go on, get ready to do whatever you plan on doing and leave me alone. So I can get used to doing what I got to do."

Bo decided it would be better to leave. He didn't know what he'd done to upset Miranda, but he didn't want to stay around if that was going to make things worse. Then something made him stop. Something made it cross his mind that maybe, just maybe, Miranda was saying one thing and meaning different. It was taking a chance, Bo was accustomed to taking words for what they said on the surface. But this time he decided it might be up to him to do some explaining, to try as best he could to put what he was feeling into words, even if the words weren't there and he ended up sounding silly.

"Look, Miranda, last night when we were dancing, I got this feeling the two of us, we were kind of together, like you wanted to be with me as much as I wanted to be with you, and I almost couldn't believe it, only it was true. It felt so good I could hardly sleep last night. Except I wanted to, I wanted to sleep as fast as I could, because I knew the sooner I did, the quicker I'd be seeing you again. And now, it's like you were trying to fool me last night, you were trying to make me feel that way so you could make fun of me in the morning. I don't know a whole lot about girls, but that doesn't seem a real good way to treat a friend."

Miranda looked up from her stool, her eyes brimming over, looking like the grass did covered with dew. "Oh, Bo," she said, "why are you gonna have to go? And so soon? Just when . . ." Then she stood up and didn't even look at him, only moved around him and started running toward the house.

Bo squatted down and finished the milking. He really should have had some sisters.

Nobody said much during breakfast. Nobody usually did. But now they didn't even more than usual. Except Mrs. Potter. She was still feeling the aftereffects of the night before. She was talking to everybody in general and nobody in particular while she was putting plates down and picking them up and seeming never to be standing still. She made as though she was talking to Mr. Potter, but his mind was already somewhere else, it was hard to be sure just where. Only it wasn't here at the table, and knowing Mr. Potter, it certainly was a long way from last night. Rafe was sitting next to Mr. Potter, but not saying much either, like he was announcing how he wasn't listening, as though he'd cleared a space around himself so everybody could tell he had reason to complain. But nobody except himself was paying attention, certainly not who was supposed to. She was helping her mother with the serving, though not with the talking. Still, she probably knew, even when she was quiet, somebody was trying to listen.

As soon as everybody was finished, without saying a word, Miranda headed out the door. Bo felt confused, not knowing what his chores were going to be for the day, but except for knowing he had to earn his keep, he didn't really care what they were. His concerns were directed right now over to the barn. He looked at Mr. Potter. But Mr. Potter was still wherever he'd been all during breakfast. Bo glanced over at Mrs. Potter, who was already looking at him. She smiled and nodded, motioning with her head toward the door.

Outside it was getting cloudy. The air felt heavy, like something was waiting to happen. But Bo couldn't bother with that, right now there were more bothersome clouds waiting over at the barn. And by the time Bo caught up with her, Miranda was already saddling her horse. She still didn't give any sign of talking, but she didn't seem in a hurry to leave before Bo had finished saddling his. It was only when she was getting into the saddle that Bo noticed she wasn't wearing pants today. She was still sitting like a man, except she had on a calico dress. It was nothing like the dress she was wearing the night before, except it did seem awfully pretty for only a ride around the ranch.

But Bo didn't say anything. She didn't either, just rode off toward high country, first at a lope, then she slowed to a walk. Bo stayed right beside her.

They kept riding until they were where Rafe and Bo had found the calves that first morning, up on a plateau, right near the crevasses. Miranda got off and started walking, leading her horse. Bo got down, too.

She stopped and pointed toward a crevasse. "That's what I feel like, Bo, that's what you're doing to me. Right over there."

Bo looked, but didn't notice anything out of the ordinary. He decided it'd be best to wait for whatever was coming next.

Miranda turned toward him, a look of tears and anger mixed with an appreciation of good drama flickering across her face. "That's just the way I feel inside, Bo, just like that." She was still pointing toward the crevasse. "Why did you even bother to show up if you're going to just go off and leave like this, like nothing even ever happened?"

Bo wasn't sure what he needed to say.

"Who said anything about leaving, Miranda?"

She glared at him, like he was being stupid on purpose.

Bo was still trying to decide what to say next, when suddenly there was a bleat from somewhere below.

"That sounded like a calf," Miranda said, immediately up to business, back to being the rancher's daughter. She moved quickly to the edge of the crevasse, too quickly, too close, looking down for a moment, then starting to fall. Bo reached out for her, like he'd been wanting to, but not like this, and she kept slipping. He could hear the dirt crumbling under her feet. He lunged, and this time he reached her, and they both were falling. Bo could smell the hot clay and feel its edges on his back as they fell, and he tried to hold her away, on top, so that only he would feel it as they bounced toward the bottom.

They got there. And when they did, the calf was over them, looking down with a puzzled look in his eyes. It bleated again.

Miranda didn't say anything, just got up and brushed herself off and looked up at the top of the ridge. It was a long way away.

Bo glanced, too.

"Looks like rain," was all he could think of to say.

Miranda stared at him, at first like he was making a bad joke. Then she looked up again, and back toward him like she was waiting for an answer.

"First thing," Bo said, "we're going to get ourselves out of here."

Miranda didn't look convinced.

"Look," he said, "what we've done is fall down into a hole. So the next thing we're going to do is climb out of it."

"But if it rains . . ."

"The next thing we're gonna do is not think about rain. It didn't rain yesterday or the day before that or the day before that. It's not gonna start doing it today just because we fell in a hole."

"But if it does . . ."

"But it's not." All the time he was staring at the sides.

"Our horses are still up there," she said. "Yours doesn't do stuff like in the books, does it? Drop down a rope, do things like that?"

Bo looked at her like she'd lost her mind.

Climb out of the hole, he'd said. The sides were practically sheer. There was something, maybe ten, twelve feet up, an outcropping, almost a ledge, then there was the top. But no footholds to get to the ledge. He wasn't sure he could stay if he got there, it was so narrow if you weren't looking for a way out, you wouldn't notice. And he didn't know exactly what he'd do next even if he got there. But right now, none of those problems was important. They would come later if at all.

The bottom, where they were, wasn't wide, not enough to take a running jump. Not straight across anyway. Bo picked his way sideways, far enough to see that the end of the crevasse, at least down that way, was as sheer as the sides. When he came back, he could tell that Miranda had been looking in the other direction. She shook her head.

Bo nodded toward where he'd just been. "Not down that way either," he said.

She was doing fine, Bo thought. At first he added, at least for a girl. But once he heard himself thinking it, he knew that wasn't right. She was doing fine, pure and simple. He thought about Rafe, he couldn't imagine what Rafe would be like if he was down here. He not only couldn't imagine, he didn't intend on trying. Rafe wouldn't be down here in the first place. He wasn't the sort to risk falling into crevasses for a person, let alone for a calf.

Who was still standing where he'd all this time been. Still staring with the same confused look, moving his mouth up and down, as though at least it was something to be doing.

So Bo went back in the direction he'd just been exploring and took a running jump. He grabbed the ledge all right, but it totally gave way, crumbled, and he came tumbling down, trying to keep himself upright, for self-respect if nothing else, but he couldn't, or at any rate didn't, and wound up sprawling spread-eagled across the calf, who gave out not only a confused bleat this time, but something akin to terror, and scrambled as far away as he could from whatever this was that not only was trying to squash him a little deeper down in the ground than he already was, but was taking a running start to do it.

Miranda came over to see if Bo was all right. He knew from the beginning he was, but it felt good to have her there, bending over him. But he told himself now was no time for thinking those kind of things. He had work to do. Miranda was depending on it.

So the next thing to do was try it together.

"Maybe if you stood on my shoulders," he said, "you think you could make it to that ledge?"

"Then what?"

"Don't be in a hurry. Do one thing at a time."

He felt a drop of water.

Sweat, he told himself.

He kneeled down so Miranda could climb up, her feet on his shoulders, her hands bracing against the side of the crevasse.

"Climb down, try again," Bo said. "Only this time, take your boots off."

She did, and Bo stood up. He was surprised how light she seemed. Looking at her, you'd think she was sturdier, strong, like she could hold her own with just about anybody, and in a way she could. But that must have come from someplace inside, because now that he was holding her, she felt almost fragile. He stopped himself, he didn't have time to think about things like that. Particularly now that she was kind of jumping up and down on his shoulders, trying, Bo could only guess, for a grip on the ledge.

Then, right at the top of a jump, her calico skirt flapped up and then over his head, and everything became dark. Bo jumped a bit himself when it happened, he wasn't expecting anything like that. But he managed to keep holding her ankles, then he reached up to steady her legs. And when he did, he had to tell himself again, whenever the time might be, even considering it might ever be, which was hard to believe, right now wasn't it, right now just wasn't the time. But he couldn't help it.

He looked up.

The sun was shining through the calico. He could see the outlines of her legs going up. Miranda's legs. He could see the loveliness as their shapes moved toward coming together, merging in the darkness. He couldn't see any more than that. It was too dark. Inside the dress. Inside the calico dress. Inside Miranda's calico dress. He could only see the shapes as they moved toward the joining. He could only imagine. So that's what he did. He stood there, caring about nothing else, not even the climbing out, caring about nothing else but imagining.

And all the time, Miranda was still struggling to reach the ledge. Finally she said, "Hold on tighter," and Bo did, he didn't mind at all. Then she was trying to step up on top of his head, so he held his neck steady. But there must have been mud maybe on the bottom of her socks, because she started slipping and Bo couldn't stop her. And she was sliding down him, and then he was slipping, too, falling backwards, and the calf bleated again and got even farther away.

So the two of them lay there. And Bo could feel her body on his, and that was a wonder just in itself, but he could also feel rain, there was no way now to pretend it might only be sweat. And it was like both of them were thinking.

"Bo?" she said.

He didn't answer. He didn't know what to say. So he just waited.

"You know, don't you, what's gonna happen, once it starts raining?"

"I know what Rafe told me."

"Bo?"

"Should I start calling out? To see if somebody might be around, maybe even looking?" He didn't want to, but he started getting up.

She shook her head and held on. "We both know there's not anybody even close. So if it really does start, what Rafe said, what Daddy told him, it's going to happen."

Bo wanted to say that it wouldn't. First off, he had a job to do. Nobody back home would know he hadn't done it yet. And besides that, well, besides that, it just wasn't going to happen.

"But if it does," Miranda said, and then she was quiet.

This time, Bo tried to answer.

"If it does?" He wanted to say more, to be a comfort, but the words weren't quite there.

"Bo? I don't want to die not knowing what it feels like."

Bo still didn't know what to say. But he knew what she meant. And knowing, it was strange, but it made him feel more alive than he could ever remember feeling.

"Do you know?" she said.

"No," he answered. "Not really."

"If it does rain," she said, "and it's already starting, I think I want to know."

"Do you reckon we have time?"

"I don't know," she said. "How long does it take?"

Bo shook his head. He felt helpless. "I'm not real sure," he said. "I've seen horses. And cattle. But I suspect it's somehow different with people."

He felt helpless, still he knew what she was saying. He wanted to find a way out, but if they tried and failed, and then it was too late . . . except a part of him couldn't stop believing. If you felt like this now, you couldn't help being alive forever.

All of a sudden the calf was bleating.

"Well, you young folks can lie down there all day, if that's what you want," a voice came down. "But I sure ain't staying. It's working up to being wet."

Miranda jumped up. "Hurry, Bo," she said. "Get up and start moving. It's the Preacher!"

Bo got up, too, and if he had thought about it, his feelings might have momentarily been mixed. Only there wasn't time, because the Preacher was lowering a rope, and the rain was falling harder. Bo tied the rope around Miranda's waist and then he helped her, just supporting at first, then pushing while she started to climb, the Preacher pulling hard from his end. So after slipping back a couple of times, she finally made it to the top. Then the Preacher untied her, and threw that end of the rope down to Bo.

"Okay, sonny," the Preacher said in a raspy, twangy voice, as though he had a deathbed cold, or at least had lost most of a vocal cord. "Okay, sonny," he said, "you'd better get in a hurry, that rain's gonna make this crack start snapping, maybe real soon."

Bo understood what he was saying, he believed it. But he'd grown up on a farm. He'd spent too many nights in the barn trying to get animals born. So first he headed for the calf. There wasn't any sentiment attached, at least not at the moment, and he wasn't particularly trying to do Mr. Potter a favor. But he had grown up on a farm. A calf was something you tried not to lose.

Having just fallen down a hole in the world, this particular calf was understandably confused. And having folks not just falling down on top of him, but running and jumping and then falling, the calf couldn't be sure of Bo's intentions.

So when Bo started toward him carrying a rope, the calf started moving in the other direction.

By this time, the bottom of the crevasse was getting muddy, clay was beginning to muck up everything even close. So when Bo, more out of desperation than hope, made a diving lunge, he got more than calf, he got several pounds of gummy clay. Except now he had the calf in his arms, bawling, kicking, squirming, helping distribute Bo's muck more evenly. But Bo had been born on a farm. He held on and dragged the calf back underneath where the Preacher and Miranda were standing. When Bo had finished tying the rope around the calf, when he looked up to tell them to start pulling, he could see through the rain that they were looking worried.

And just about when the calf was halfway up, still bawling, one time even kicking Bo on the side of his face, just about when the calf was halfway there, Bo heard it for the first time, at the beginning only a creaking, like it was coming from somewhere down inside, it was low enough, Bo couldn't tell whether it was coming from in front or behind or from under, it was soft enough he wouldn't have had to notice, if that was all it was going to be.

But of course that wasn't all it was going to be, and so Bo didn't pay any attention to the way the side of his face hurt, he just kept stretching up, pushing harder. And then over the calf's squealing he started hearing the sounds louder, and more of them, now not just creaking, it was more like a grating and then not even that but a rumbling, and he didn't even ask himself where it was coming from, it was coming from all around him everywhere, and he pushed harder, and he could tell that the Preacher, and Miranda, too, she was at the end of the rope helping, they both were pulling harder. And as soon as the calf was at the top and untied, scrambling away, the rope came back down to Bo.

And now it wasn't only the sound, Bo could feel it, the earth itself was vibrating, right beneath him at first, then not just vibrating, but starting to quiver and then shake, and while Bo was grabbing the rope, he could see the ground actually moving, closing up the hole that had opened in the first place only by mistake. He could see it, feel the gummy clay coming together beneath him, and he started to climb, holding on to the rope while the Preacher and Miranda pulled, the rain coming harder, they didn't even have time to use a horse for help, they pulled and Bo started to climb, holding on to the rope, trying to walk up the side.

But the side wasn't only muddy and slippery and hard to get a foothold on, now not just the bottom, but the side itself was quivering and shaking, and he kept trying to go faster, but it was as though the earth could tell, and was trying to close quicker, trying to claim him, trying to show that if he'd had the audacity, the temerity to invade the earth's territory, then the earth had every right, maybe even responsibility, to keep him there. And so the sides were moving faster, like a jackknife getting ready to shut.

But Bo kept on scrambling, the rain slamming into him now, the mud plastering his face, closing shut his eyes, but he was scrambling and they were pulling and he was close to the edge. They were reaching for him, only just then, just when they were reaching, the foothold he had found, that he was using to hold himself while they were reaching, it gave way, and he fell, not so far they couldn't reach for him, but far enough they had to lean even farther, he had to stretch even harder. And so he pulled himself up again. But the earth was closing. He got himself over the edge, the top part of his body was over, and they were pulling the rest, and they almost made it, all of him was almost over, all but one leg, when with a wrenching and a booming, the earth was snapping shut, and he was almost out, but the earth was shutting, and it still had his leg and it wouldn't let go, and Bo was reaching out, he was clawing, but it wouldn't let go. They pulled and he clawed and he could feel the ground pressing, coming around, enclosing his leg, but they refused to give up, they kept pulling, now all but his ankle was out. So he tried to let it keep his boot, if it would only let go of his ankle, but the foot wouldn't come out of the leather, but with a final mighty jerk he was free and they were all on the ground in a jumble and the earth was shut. There wasn't any opening at all, only a slight fissure where something, nobody would be able to tell what, where something might have once been.

At first they just sat there, the rain streaming down on their faces, they just sat there and waited. Then the Preacher blew out a breath, a long one, through his teeth.

"Well, sonny," he said. "I reckon a leg for a healthy calf's a fair trade most days. Let's see if what you've got left is gonna be any good to you."

Bo tried to get up. Then he tried again. Then he decided to stay sitting down.

"That's more or less what I figured," the Preacher said. "Okay, little missy, you get on your horse and head home. I've got the boy's gear on the back of my horse and we've got to be going. At least if he still wants to find his Uncle Charley."

So Mrs. Potter had been right. The Preacher knew.

"Now?" Miranda said.

The Preacher didn't answer, just started helping Bo to his feet.

"But what about his leg?"

"It ought to stay latched on till we get to Junction City."

"But can't you stay till you get him fed and cleaned up?"

"I'll clean him up first creek we come to once it stops raining. But I got to be moving. Stay around here, folks'll start thinking I'm still on my circuit. First thing I know, people'll start dying and marrying and birthing again just so they can get me to do preachings over it. You head on home. We got to be going."

Miranda looked at Bo, who was by now leaning on the Preacher's shoulder. "See, Bo," she said, "that's what I knew. Soon as I saw the Preacher at the dancing, that's what I knew. He'd be packing you off, taking you someplace else. I don't think I care much for your Uncle Charley."

"Well, you got to remember, missy," the Preacher said, this time more gently, like he understood maybe even more than she did, "you got to remember, it was looking for Charley that got him here in the first place. Course, if he wants to stop chasing, settle in and act like it's home, that's for him to decide."

It seemed that the Preacher knew more about Bo's business than he had any right to. Bo could see that Miranda was looking at him, waiting, and he could feel the Preacher's eyes, too. And for a moment it was tempting.

But that wasn't what he'd set out to do.

And that's what he said, the best he could.

So the Preacher helped Bo over to his horse. Still, when he got there Bo turned back again toward Miranda. She was looking at them like she was trying to smile but not quite managing it, like she was getting ready to ask.

But when Bo saw that look, there wasn't any doubt about his answer. And when Miranda saw him looking that way, it was all the answer she needed.

So she gave Bo a smile, not just a trying, a real one this time, although it was a smile he didn't quite understand. Then she got back on her horse and rode away.

The Town

Once Miranda was fully gone, the Preacher puffed a little and propped Bo in his saddle. Except Bo had an inkling, even in the middle of his hurting, that the Preacher wasn't straining quite so much as he seemed. But an inkling was as far as he bothered to get. His leg was aching, the side of his face was on fire, he felt wet and muddy and clammy, and besides that, he still wasn't all that sure about leaving.

The Preacher stood down beneath him, looking up, one eye squinting.

"Troubles you, don't it boy? Even if you ain't quite figured out the words, I suspect the time'll come when you will. It's one of them things that's easy to learn and terribly discomforting to live with, how hard it is, getting back to places you one time decided to leave. What's important though, boy, and you hear me out, don't you let nobody lead you wrong. No matter how much it seems to the contrary, it's possible. Maybe not likely, I didn't say that, I said it's possible. Not that it's gonna be the same place, not just exactly, things don't work that way, they need to change, it's in their nature. But don't let nobody say you can't ever get back. The biggest problem most times is the still wanting to."

Bo had already stopped listening. His leg was hurting awful.

The Preacher started toward his own horse, but before he got there, he turned around again. He seemed more willing to talk than Bo was wanting to listen.

"But what you got to consider, boy, what you want to think about, you've already got yourself one direction. Which is about all any man can handle at a given time. You think how you'd have to feel, giving up, letting it go. You've got a right to do it, stay back, let here be where it ends.

"Right now, what you're worrying about is how you're gonna feel tomorrow, leaving, seeing the girl going. But what you need to be thinking, boy, how'd you feel tomorrow, you decide to stay? How you gonna feel once you start wondering if you stopped too soon, only right after you got started? Thinking about how you'll never know if you didn't lose something you never even knew was out there, since you hadn't ever tried to catch up with it? You ready for that kind of wondering?"

Bo didn't say, just slapped his reins and started moving. Which felt strange, since he didn't have any idea where he was going. But at least he was moving. And his leg was hurting and the Preacher seemed in the mood for long-range talking.

The Preacher looked at him leaving. "Makes sense," he said. "Sure beats listening." Then sprang into the saddle more sprightly than you might have expected. He kind of pointed in a direction, but he let Bo do the leading.

Bo had never ridden with only one leg before, it kept him out of balance, it made his whole body hurt even more. Things simply didn't fit together in the customary ways. The Preacher didn't seem to notice. As a matter of fact he seemed happy, even considering the rain.

So Bo was out front, feeling wet and hurting, not really knowing what he was doing or why, only knowing what he was losing by doing it. Except Mrs. Potter had said the Preacher might know about Uncle Charley, and Bo tended to trust Mrs. Potter. About the Preacher, he was withholding opinions. Which might have been harder to do if he'd been hurting a little less.

Of course, it wasn't just the leg.

At first, it was only the humming.

Then it got worse.

Like most people who ride a long time alone, the Preacher had discovered his ways of staying amused.

It wasn't that Bo had anything against singing. In fact, that was usually the best part of church service back home. But the Preacher had been at his job too long. He not only knew all the verses, he intended to sing them. And he started from page one and he seemed set on not skipping any till he caught the tail end. Or if he didn't know them all, at least he covered a lot of different words. Bo never was too sure about the tunes. Considering the Preacher's scratchy voice, they all may have been the same one, or might as well have been for all Bo could figure.

After awhile the rain stopped, the sun threatened to come out, and they rode up to a creek. The Preacher helped Bo down, so gently Bo felt a little bad about what he'd been thinking during the singing. But not to any major extent.

The Preacher sat him down on the creek bank and helped him out of his clothes, easing him into the water. Which was cold, colder than Bo could have expected since he still wasn't used to hill country. But being in the water, having it flowing around him instead of coming toward him like pellets, the way it felt now was just fine. Lying there, floating, having it almost lift him up and hold him. That felt just fine.

The Preacher liked it, too. But first he rinsed the mud out of Bo's clothes and then he took off his own and did the same. After that, he sat down in the water beside Bo, the creek's current lifting up his round belly, and every so often the Preacher would let out a high-pitched laugh and splash water at himself, half getting himself clean, but mainly taking time and pleasure.

But he wasn't going to let it last. Just as Bo was getting accustomed to being comfortable, almost forgetting how bad his leg hurt, since the water was holding it, massaging the soreness, just about then the Preacher decided it was time to go.

Which seemed to Bo to be rushing, so he got out more slowly than he otherwise might have. By the time he'd hobbled back to his horse, the Preacher had their clothes already spread behind the saddles, where they'd catch the sun and be dry. And he'd put a gunny sack over each saddle to keep the leather from rubbing against skin.

"Why don't we just sit a spell," Bo said, "and after they get dry, just put them on then?"

"Pull on your boots," the Preacher said.

After they'd been in the saddle for awhile, wearing nothing but their boots and hats, their skin soaking in the warmth of the sun, the Preacher stopped in the middle of his latest song.

"We stop back there and wait, that leg of yours gonna stiffen up something awful. It'd take most half a congregation, getting you back on that horse. This way, you get stiff as a pine board, it'll be a pine board on top of a horse. Now this here song you're bound to know. You sing along, it'll take your mind off your troubles."

The land around them was lush, green hillsides in every direction. Not just green the way grass and bushes are supposed to be, but deeper, richer, almost too much of a good thing, like everything growing had soaked up more than it could hold, so the color had taken over the shapes, as though it wasn't just tagging along, the color had almost become the thing.

And everywhere there were birds, joining in the Preacher's singing, and if there had been justice, shaming him to silence. And dragonflies and butterflies, black flies that bit, and toward dusk there were mosquitoes. Which didn't seem to bother the Preacher. Maybe, Bo figured, they were all busy enough with his own skin, they didn't want to be distracted.

"Yessir," the Preacher said, stopping, letting his horse munch on the grass, "it sure looks pretty. It don't seem the same sort of thing, back there where it was chomping on your leg like it was hungry."

Bo wasn't sure what the Preacher was getting at. But the longer they stayed still, the more the blood pounded in his leg. Which may have been his only blood left, the only blood the mosquitoes had decided to leave inside.

"The land, boy, I'm talking about the land! It fools us, it lulls us in places like this. It makes us feel like we're in this thing together. Life, boy," he stood up in his stirrups and swept his hand across in front of him, "it's all around you. And in places like this, it seems like it's some kind of joint enterprise. It ain't healthy, boy, it lulls us."

Bo slapped at a mosquito, as a way maybe of suggesting he could be lulled more convincingly.

"It's hard to remember," the Preacher said, paying no mind. "It's hard to remember, boy, but we'd better, right 'neath the surface, doesn't really matter where, back there, here, right underneath us, there's that mouth still trying to swallow you, boy, letting you know you're somewhere you don't belong. Hardly matters where. It don't take long in some places to find out. Others, like here, it tends to make you forget. It ain't healthy."

"That's all very interesting, sir," Bo said, still swatting, "but why couldn't we have talked about it back there, sitting in the creek? Staying here, I'm starting to hurt bad and these things, they're trying to eat me alive."

"Didn't seem like the time, boy, seemed now was closer to it. Test some weight on that leg, boy. How's it getting?"

Bo tried, pushing down against the stirrup. It was all he could do to keep from shouting.

"Pretty near what I figured. You ever get down, we'd probably never get you back up. We'd best keep traveling."

Which they did. The moon was full, the air became cool, and the Preacher finally got tired of singing. Bo spent most of the time drowsing in the saddle, they were moving slow enough and he'd become accustomed to one-legged riding.

And even half asleep, Bo could feel the land changing, knowing it from inside as much as from anywhere else, the beginnings of light, grayness coming out of everything, blurring whatever shapes he was passing through. Except now his mind seemed to be blurring, too, and he was just leaving the barn back home, he'd harnessed the mule and was riding through half-light to the fields, feeling the light, the day fitting around him like something new, knowing all the time it'd be more or less like other days, except right now that didn't matter. This hour of morning wouldn't put up with that kind of sameness. If only for the time being, everything would simply have to be new.

And then his horse would swerve or shiver or slightly change gait, and Bo would be back riding one-legged through hill country, his body paining, he'd become deadened to that. But there was another hurting, one more distracting, because he was leaving something behind that seemed more real even than the barn and the mule and the smells of plowing. Because home was something you were born into, it was like looking up and seeing sky, feeling air and tasting fresh water. It was just there where it was supposed to be. What he was leaving now, back there at the ranch, was something he'd come to, something that was his, or could have been, or might yet still be. But whatever happened, it wasn't the same thing as home. Because it was something he could really lose.

But it didn't bear much thinking now. For whatever reason, good or bad, he was heading toward something else, drifting downhill, everything getting drier, browner. Not that he actually noticed, more like he was only moving through it, letting his horse meander behind the Preacher's. He'd long since decided they weren't ever going to get wherever it was the Preacher claimed to be going, he wasn't even thinking too much about the throbbing in his leg, just assuming it was a necessary part, like the flatness now and the dust, the sameness and the heat.

He wasn't even sure when the trail started looking like a road, not till he noticed scraggly buildings alongside and kids, mostly Mexican, glancing up at the two almost naked men riding by, before going back to their playing.

And then the road became a street, which wasn't much different except instead of kids there were dogs, lying motionless, not even looking up when Bo and the Preacher passed, or even wasting the effort of moving their tails.

And the street was different because it was so wide, not just a direction to move along, but a place with space enough to stop and not be crowded. So wide it didn't look like a street at all, more like a piece of prairie caught between two strings of buildings, as though the land inside couldn't quite make up its mind, so it had more or less reached a compromise.

The Preacher seemed to notice Bo was looking. "More land around here than most anything else," he said. "Might as well make use of it. Makes it easier to turn around a wagon."

More like two, maybe three, Bo thought, and all at the same time. But he didn't say anything, just kept on looking.

The street was empty, except for the dogs and the two of them. Everyone was staying inside, Bo figured, not because of the hour of the morning, but because that was the only place where there might be shade. For whatever reason, Bo was grateful. His hat and boots didn't make any difference, he felt naked.

The town looked that way, too. On both sides the buildings were dreary, made of wood, most of them unpainted except for maybe a sign across the front. And Bo could tell right off, the tops of them, even those without signs, were fake. Most of the buildings were one story, but all of them, even those with a second floor, had false fronts rising even farther, pretending to stretch higher, hiding the emptiness behind them. Which seemed strange. Since all the buildings were doing the same thing, nobody was going to be fooled unless they meant to be.

The Preacher stopped in front of a storefront that didn't look any different from the others except it had a sign on it saying SALOON. No swinging doors, no plate glass windows, just a two story, false-fronted building with a wooden sidewalk in front. Pushed up against one side, sharing a wall, was a store selling general merchandise. On the other side was a place that fixed saddles.

The Preacher tied his horse and helped Bo get down, and as soon as his bad leg touched the ground it buckled. So the Preacher held him up and half carried, half pushed him onto the boardwalk and through the open door. The Preacher's shoulder at first felt soft, a bit flabby, enough that Bo didn't want to lean heavily. Except the way his leg was feeling, it didn't leave much choice. But he found the harder he leaned, the firmer the Preacher's shoulder seemed to be getting.

Inside was dark and cooler. There were half a dozen tables pushed back against the walls, the chairs stacked upside down on top. Nobody else was around. The Preacher pulled down a couple of chairs and pushed Bo down onto one and lifted his bad leg up on the other. Then the Preacher walked over back of the bar, like he knew where he was going. He reached under and got two mugs and filled them up from a keg sitting with the bottles and glasses that lined a shelf on the wall behind.

The Preacher downed one mug without any waiting. And whatever it was, Bo figured it had to be beer, it was running out the corner of the Preacher's mouth and through the sprinkle of white hairs on his chest and over his little belly and finally down between his legs onto the floor. He wiped off his mouth with the back of his hand and let out a resounding belch. All in all, standing there in his hat and boots, it seemed a remarkable performance for a preacher.

He filled that mug again and brought both of them over to Bo's table. "Now you just put some of this down inside you and I'll roust up Sam." The Preacher walked through a doorway into a back room and Bo could hear him climbing some stairs.

Bo stared at the mugs in front of him. He had a terrible thirst, had it for some time now. But he hadn't been brought up to frequent saloons or partake of the substances within. And he was pretty sure this wasn't what folks had in mind when they'd sent him looking for Uncle Charley. But things would just have to be the way they had to be, Bo decided, so he picked up a mug and took a big swallow.

He knew real quick he'd just as soon drink tick dip.

He tried again. But it didn't taste any better. For the life of him, he couldn't figure why people went to the trouble of drinking such stuff. It tasted, and Bo was doing his best to be generous, it tasted just terrible. But it was cold. And wet. And in front of him. So he drank the rest, and it felt better in his stomach than it had in his mouth, there was that to say for it. Which wasn't much.

Then the Preacher was back, still wearing just his hat and boots, only now there was somebody with him. Bo tried to move fast, at least get his legs crossed, but with the sore one propped on a chair, the best he could do was grab his hat and drop it in his lap. Then get as much of himself as possible hidden beneath the table.

"Don't get yourself flustered," the Preacher said. "Sam ain't bothered by naked folk. Particularly when they're a young fella like yourself who's been pained."

Bo wasn't listening, because Sam wasn't what he'd expected. Not in the least. Not at all. She wasn't young, but then she wasn't old either, nowhere near like the Preacher. And she might not be what you'd call pretty, at least not at first, there was a worn look you noticed. But there was also something else, something that seemed to come from underneath the rest. And the more Bo looked at her, the worse he felt about her standing there, looking at him.

The Preacher didn't seem bothered one way or the other.

"You just sit real tight," he said, as though Bo could do anything else. Being behind the table wasn't much, but it was all he had. "You sit real tight, and Sam here will manage some breakfast. It's been awhile since I bothered to eat."

So she left and the Preacher went to the bar and refilled Bo's mug and then sat down at the table next to the other, the one Bo hadn't touched, and they waited. Only this time the Preacher didn't do any gulping, just sipped and hummed a hymn tune, and Bo felt the whole thing was all a little strange.

Sam finally came out of the back room, carrying two plates filled with fried eggs and slabs of steak, and put them on the table. Then she got a mug of beer and sat down herself. She leaned her elbows on the table and smiled toward Bo. "So you're the one who's looking for Charley." She shook her head. "Well, there'll be time," she said, taking a drink. The

Preacher still didn't say anything or even look up, only sat there wearing his hat and paying attention to eating.

After that, things weren't clear. It was as though Bo's tiredness had all come together, along with the food and the beer and being in a chair instead of on top of a horse. He remembered the Preacher and Sam helping him upstairs, and he remembered being grateful he was mostly unconscious. It would've been worse if he'd acted as embarrassed as he felt he should be, as he knew he was going to be once he woke up and thought enough about it. But they got him upstairs and into bed and after that Bo didn't know much about anything except that he was sleeping.

Then something was happening that felt good, but he was afraid to wake all the way up because he didn't want to face what it probably was, and when he finally had to, he'd been right. She was leaning over him, holding part of a cotton feed sack she was wetting in a basin of water. And she was washing him off. Everywhere.

He reached for the sheet.

She smiled and shook her head. "I'm almost done," she said. "The Preacher did his best back there on the trail. But men and being clean just somehow don't go all the way together. Even if they try, which isn't always usual."

She pulled the sheet up herself and smiled again and went out the door. It wasn't long before Bo was back asleep.

That was about all he did the next few days. The Preacher would come up and see him every now and then. He was back dressed now in his preacher clothes, the black suit and white shirt and little string tie. And he was all shaved and neatened. Enough so that if what Sam had said about being clean was true, he'd probably gotten some help.

Usually the Preacher didn't say much when he visited. Every time Bo mentioned his Uncle Charley, all the Preacher said was for him to get his resting done, they'd be time enough for that kind of talking later. Then he'd come over and look at Bo's leg, which had gotten bluish black where the ground had come together, but the swelling wasn't so bad. And the Preacher, who seemed to know, said all he had to do was stay off it awhile longer.

What made it easier, either Sam or the Preacher must have run across a room full of books, because every few days one of them showed up with a new one. The Preacher's tended toward long-winded ideas, which Bo could take for a time. But then he'd reach for one of Sam's and find himself wrapped up in castles and knights and every so often a quest.

What Bo liked best, though, was when Sam (her real name was Samantha, but everybody called her Sam. Except Bo. It didn't seem the right sort of name to call a lady), what he liked best was when Sam came up herself, usually bringing a tray of food. And Bo could tell that she liked being there, too, just to sit for awhile and talk.

But here he was flat on his back, no closer to his uncle and a lot farther from other folks than when he'd started. He looked down at his leg. There wasn't much he could do about that.

"You'll be gone from here in awhile," she said, coming in at noontime. "I'm going to miss being needed."

"I've liked it a lot, too, Miss Samantha. But my leg's been fine for days, and all I've been doing is looking out the window. Everybody seems to keep forgetting, the only reason I'm here, the Preacher's supposed to be helping me chase down my Uncle Charley. What good's it gonna do, just lying around?"

Sam smiled and put down the tray. "You can talk about that later with the Preacher."

"You know as well as I do, the Preacher's not going to tell me anything."

"Something the Preacher does like to say, hearing about something and knowing, as a rule, that's two different things," she said. "Besides, the Preacher's all through downstairs. He's off again on his circuit."

"Through downstairs?"

"That's something else you'll have to wait and find out about yourself. Till then, you'll have to make do with me."

"Okay, then you. You tell me. At least if you even know him."

She smiled. "Charley?" She stopped at the door. "Yeah," she said, "I knew Charley." Then she turned back around and left the room.

When she came back for the tray, she moved it over to a table instead, and sat down on the edge of the bed. "Since we're stuck here together," she said, "why don't you tell me something. About yourself. I hardly know anything at all."

He felt awkward. He was accustomed to talking, if talking was called for, mainly about what he was doing or what needed getting done. But once Bo got started, Sam didn't seem interested in those sorts of things. She'd stop him and ask questions, how he felt about the farm, what it was like being in a field all by himself in the early morning, plowing, how his mother liked it there. And when Bo without thinking answered his mother liked it fine, Sam wouldn't let him stop with that but kept asking. What did he mean and how did he know, and Bo would remember, there were times his mother would get mad, there'd be times she'd cry, there'd be times when she said she couldn't stand being cooped up on the farm one more hour and she'd get into the carriage and drive into town. But those times wouldn't ever last. When Bo thought of the farm, he'd mainly think of his mother.

"But what about him?" Sam asked.

"Who?"

"What about your father?"

It was hard to tell. It was hard to tell even when Bo was there. When his mother was mad, when she was happy, everybody saw it, she couldn't help but let people know. And how she felt mattered a lot to his father, you could tell. But about himself, it seemed like he didn't want things to show. "What he did, though, he'd tell stories. Right before my brother and I went to sleep, my father told us stories. Even mother would listen."

"What about?"

"Usually people he knew, places they'd been. We never knew if they were true. But it didn't matter. All the time we were listening, they seemed to be. And he seemed comfortable then, like he could talk about other people, even those he'd made up in his head, better than he could talk about himself."

It felt strange, talking about his folks as though they were just people. Still, it wasn't like gossip, Sam seemed to really want to know. And not just about them, about himself, too. How he felt about leaving them, how he felt about going back, having a life like his father's. That made him stop, the idea hadn't occurred to him. Now that it had, it was almost unthinkable. His father's life was all right. For someone who was his father. Which Bo wasn't, there had to be more.

"Like what?"

He didn't know. There had to be something. Then he wondered if his father had once felt the same way. For that matter, maybe still did. And without knowing why, Bo was remembering how he'd see them take a walk sometimes after supper, once things had gotten quiet. Most everywhere the land was flat, but a little ways back of the barn there was a rise, and they'd walk there together, not touching but looking close together, and then they'd stand there. While his father stared out over the fields, at what he'd just finished getting done, what was still left to do tomorrow, she'd turn and look away from the farmland, out into the distance toward where the sun was setting, making unbelievable colors in the sky. Sam let him remember, then she started again, asking about home. Only now he wasn't as sure as he'd been before about the answers.

But Sam kept on asking and answering got easier, but Bo couldn't help wondering why she kept doing it. It was almost as though she was trying to see into a different life, maybe so she could feel for a moment like she was there on the farm, too, she just needed a little help in her dreaming.

And the answering did get easier. At least till he mentioned Miranda. When he got there, Sam didn't push as much, as though she could tell the words were getting harder. After he told how the Preacher had pulled them out, she smiled and said, "How old are you, Bo?"

"Seventeen, ma'am, eighteen in July."

She looked at Bo and shook her head, as though being seventeen was like living in a world she had forgotten about and just now remembered.

"Almost eighteen," she said. "And it hasn't happened."

It wasn't a question. It was merely a statement of fact.

Bo could tell he was blushing, and he wanted to change the subject, but for the life of him, he couldn't think of anything to say.

She could. It seemed she had an endless supply of things to say that made Bo feel he ought to be someplace else. And at the same time Sam seemed like she actually was, or at least like her mind was, seeing things from somewhere distant.

"Well," was what she said, standing up, looking down at Bo, "I suspect at seventeen what a boy mainly wants the first time is just to get it over with."

Then to Bo's amazement, which to be truthful was more like horror, Sam raised her dress, then reached under it and matter-of-factly pulled off her drawers.

"You just relax," she said, as if he could. "Everything's going to be fine. No matter what you may be thinking, I haven't gone crazy. You just scoot over to the other side of the bed."

Bo couldn't have said anything if his life depended on it. Done anything either, but he didn't have to. Sam pulled down the bedcover and did the same with Bo's shorts. And by then it was clear, if Bo's thinking parts were stymied, there were others that didn't have similar problems.

Sam didn't talk, just got up on the bed astraddle him, her long calico dress draping down each side, and whether Bo intended it or not, it was finally happening.

"*Bo,* listen to me, please, Bo, *now,* pay attention, because I really don't understand. I thought you couldn't stay because you had to find your Uncle Charley. I don't understand, what has any of *this* got to do with your Uncle Charley?"

Oh lord, Bo thought, shaking his head, trying to make Miranda's voice go away.

"So it doesn't matter? All we talked about, it didn't matter, all that happened, you've already forgotten? That surprises me, Bo, maybe it shouldn't, but it does, Bo, it really surprises me." Only Miranda didn't sound surprised, she sounded hurt and angry. Then she did go away, or at least Bo stopped hearing.

When it was over, and it didn't take long, Sam had been right, what he mainly felt was relief. Things were fine, all parts were working, he could get on with worrying about other things.

And that's what he did. He got on with worrying about other things. Everything was fine, he knew that, yet still . . . He couldn't help feeling something was wrong. Sam could tell. "Don't even think about it, Bo, you just let it go." She was looking down at him intently, maybe even unsurely. "Just be glad you're out on the other side." She put her drawers back on and gathered up the tray. "Don't even think about who it was with. Treat it for what it's supposed to be. Past history."

She stopped before she went out the door. "And Bo," she said, "just remember. If this was back at the farm, people would say what I just did was awful. You remember. This isn't back at the farm."

She was different after that. More careful. She came up to talk, but she stayed away from subjects like Miranda. She seemed even more interested in life on the farm, in stories about Bo's father, particularly about his mother. She stopped sitting on the bed. Instead she'd sit in a chair by the window. She still seemed glad to be there, but she talked, she even listened like nothing had ever happened.

But it had. It didn't matter if Sam had said to forget about it, Bo couldn't. Folks just didn't do things like that back home. At least, not that he knew of. Finally, he gave up trying to understand Sam. Well, not quite gave up, that wouldn't be likely. What he did was more or less put it to the back part of his mind. There were enough troubles thinking about himself.

What they had done that day, it felt good, no ifs and buts there, about as good as anything Bo could recall or even imagine. At least in a way. And that was the problem. In some other way, in a way that was hard to get a handle on, it just wasn't as satisfying as Bo had hoped for. Sam had been so downright matter-of-fact, maybe even businesslike. No, that wasn't right. She'd been gentle, she'd seemed awfully friendly. But that was just it. When two people were doing *that,* you weren't *supposed* to be feeling just friendly. There was supposed to be something else, and it wasn't supposed to happen only between your legs. He hadn't put that into words before, but he'd thought it, or at least felt it somewhere deeper than he was accustomed to dealing with. And if his hopes had been wrong, if this was the way it had to be, then growing up wasn't going to be nearly as interesting as he'd one time expected.

Now that he thought about it, and it seemed kind of unnatural, but he'd felt more excited holding Miranda while she was climbing in the crevasse than he had when all that was happening with Sam. Matter of fact, given a choice, he'd rather be back in that crevasse with Miranda than back in bed with Sam, and he felt funny about that, almost unmanly. That wasn't the way it was supposed to be. Well, Bo said to himself, kind of shrugging inside. That happens to be the way it is. With me.

Of course, that may have been the way it was with one part of Bo. Just like before, other parts carried on differently. No matter how careful Sam was, no matter how much Bo had figured out about his feelings, every time Sam came in his room, parts of his body started getting ideas of their own. Most of the time Bo managed to keep such things to himself, but every now and then he knew it had to be showing, even through the bedsheet.

Finally, one day Sam stood beside his bed and looked down with a kind of exasperated smile. "Okay," she said, "so I wasn't fair. And maybe haven't been since. But you need to keep remembering, I was just trying to be helpful. And I reckon at seventeen, it's got to be confusing no matter what."

She sat down on the side of the bed. "So. What did you think? Was it what you expected?"

Then it was back the way it used to be. She wasn't being careful.

He tried to tell her, and when he was through she nodded. Bo could tell she was taking it seriously.

"I suspected as much," she said. "You see, Bo, maybe I wasn't thinking. At least not enough. But I really was trying to put myself inside your feelings, what it must be like, but maybe I stopped too soon and it wasn't fair. Because you didn't know, you still don't know anything about me at all. I was just this strange woman who was pulling down your undershorts. So no matter how much I was trying to help, it must not have been much better than if you'd been doing it with yourself."

"No ma'am," Bo said, "that's not true, and I never even thanked you. And you were right. About being relieved to be on the other side. That was awfully kind, Miss Samantha, and I do want to thank you."

Sam laughed and lay down beside him. She leaned on her elbow so she could look at him. "Do me a favor, Bo," she said.

"Yes ma'am."

"It hardly seems right, saying 'ma'am' to somebody you've been to bed with."

"Okay . . ." Bo paused, trying to decide.

"Sam," she said.

"Sam."

Then she was serious again. "So maybe I wasn't as smart as I thought I was. Still, if I was back there again, I'd probably do the same thing, because I'd probably still think it was the best thing to do. And so I'd be right back where I am, lying here worrying because you don't feel as good toward me as you did before."

Bo raised himself up. "But that's not true," except Bo knew it was. He didn't like admitting it, but a part of him did think less. Sam had done the best she could. But things couldn't be just in the *doing*, there had to be something else, something inside, the doing was just the way it got out. And there simply couldn't have been enough inside Sam for doing that. No matter what she was trying, what she was hoping to do. And there hadn't been enough inside him to justify letting her do it. So something in Bo had let her slip down a notch, and he knew that he'd slid, too.

"But that's not true, Sam, that's not true at all!"

"You want to believe that," she said, "and I like it in you that you do. But I grew up with the same sort of rules you did, I know they don't let go easily, if they ever do. But then you can't even know that about me, you don't know about me at all."

"I know enough," Bo said. "The rest doesn't matter."

"I suspect it always does," she said, "and even if it doesn't to you, it does to me. When I think back, it's like being another person. Unless it'll bore you." Sam didn't wait for an answer, only turned over and stared at the ceiling like she was seeing pictures. "Lord, Bo, when I think about it, it's like another person. Being young. Frilly gowns and dancing and champagne breakfasts after we were through . . ."

"You did all that in Texas? Even back . . ." Bo caught himself and stopped in time.

"What you're saying is 'even way back then?' Only your mamma taught you to be nice. But you're right, it was a long time ago. Before the war. And that's always been a long time, if it ever really was. In St. Louis. My daddy was a merchant, it wouldn't be proper calling him a storekeeper. Because it wasn't a store, it was more like a palace, two stories high, columns in front, all gleaming white. Just about everything shipped in. Other stores did that, too, but in Daddy's they weren't just shipped in from up North. Daddy got them from places like Paris and London, places if I'd ever gotten to see, they couldn't possibly live up to the pictures those names put in my mind.

"Mamma was a Southerner, her folks moved to St. Louis from Virginia, but they were city people. Grandmamma and Grandaddy hadn't ever lived outside Richmond, they wouldn't have known what to do with a plantation, much less a cotton field. So it didn't bother them much as it might that Daddy was a Yankee.

"If he was anything. And he loved Mamma so much I don't think he even knew she was a Southerner, she could have been an Eskimo, I don't think it would have mattered. Daddy was just that kind of person. Besides, I suspect he thought everybody connected to him was more or less European, stuck for awhile in a foreign country. And he did love to go back there to do his buying. If it hadn't been for the war, he'd have taken me. The war, and of course Blakely."

"Who?"

"Blakely. My husband."

"You're married?" What happened the other day was getting even more confusing.

"See? I said you hardly knew me. I was only seventeen when I first saw him. He'd just gotten out of West Point and looked absolutely beautiful in his new uniform, all those buttons shining and him standing so straight and behaving so proper." She giggled and sounded almost girlish. "If I'd only known then what I knew later. Of course, if I had, I probably would've fallen all the harder."

Bo discovered he wasn't enjoying hearing about Sam's being a girl and in love. But it didn't make any sense to be bothered, so he told himself he wasn't, and he concentrated on listening.

"Lots of folks, Bo, they'd look at my girlhood and say it was perfect. Never a worry about money. A mother and daddy whose biggest thing in life was taking good care of me.

"In most ways, I guess it *was* wonderful. My life back then, when I was seventeen." She smiled at Bo. "See, you're not the only one. Once upon a time I was there, too." She looked back at the ceiling, concentrating, as though she didn't want to miss any of the pictures. "No cares. Lots of sunshine. But, oh my lord, there were rules.

"You see, Bo, I was luckier than most girls, and I knew it. For one thing I was able to go to school, lots of girls didn't. But my folks were open to things like that, particularly my daddy. So I got to read some good books and even learn how not to get cheated when a clerk was making change. But you know what I learned most, Bo? I learned rules. How to act when I was being introduced to an older person who wasn't as important as my family, at least in the eyes of the city. How to be introduced to an older person whose money had been around longer. How to flirt with somebody and not be taken seriously. And how to flirt with somebody you wanted to pay real attention. The proper way to go into a banquet. What to do when you sat down after you got there.

"Jesus, Bo, you wouldn't *believe* the rules. It was like you weren't allowed to *breathe* until you knew the right way to do it. I actually envied the shopgirls in Daddy's store, who may have been poor, but after work they could take a deep breath and forget about rules. Or that's what I thought, you've got to remember, I was still awfully young.

"Then I saw Blakely. Blakely Jefferson Carter. And when I saw him, I knew why people made up stories about gods coming down on earth. When I saw him at that dance, I just went crazy." She stopped talking and when Bo looked at her, she was still staring at the ceiling, but she was smiling.

"He must have thought I was a silly little thing. But he must have seen something else, too. At least he came back."

"Back?"

"To St. Louis. The first time, he could stay only a little while. He'd been sent to one of those forts they built along the Oregon Trail to keep it open. But the first chance he got, he was back in St. Louis. To see me. It was then I first got to know him, maybe the first time I started knowing anything at all.

"You see, when I first met Blakely, he was a man in a handsome uniform at the fancy dress ball, and he seemed like a knight all ready to slay dragons, or maybe rescue a girl from some tower. And I wanted to be that girl.

"And I was. How many people get that, Bo? To have a dream and then have it happen? But he came back. He came back to see me. Which wasn't easy. Because to do it, he had to look through a lot of other things, like the lace and the fancy dress balls, even my being my daddy's daughter, he had to see on the other side of all that. And he did. I know that now. I didn't then. I knew later that all the things I was trying to get him to notice, what everybody else saw, he didn't have even the slightest interest in.

"So we got married, and then we danced. There were thousands of candles and we danced. And two days later we were heading west. Not to the Oregon Trail this time. Where there'd be new people passing every day, where there'd be endless lines of wagons. No sir, we were going someplace else, to a place called Fort Mason, in someplace called Texas.

"But it didn't matter where we were. As long as we were together. As long as it was outside St. Louis. Because as soon as our wagon left the city, it was like we had a clean sheet of paper to write our lives on. The land out there was so new, St. Louis rules couldn't possibly matter. There'd have to be new ones, but it wouldn't be the same, it couldn't be. Because whatever rules there were, we were going to be helping write them.

"But you can't just be anywhere, it has to be somewhere, so it was Fort Mason. And it was beautiful, too, although I suspect the way I was feeling, it wouldn't have mattered if it'd been a desert. There wasn't anything most people would pick out for special attention, nothing spectacular. But the fort was on top of the tallest hill." Sam smiled, remembering, seeing it on the ceiling. "Not that anyone would mistake it for a mountain. It went up gradual, but it kept on going, it seemed like forever, particularly when you were walking. And when you got to the top, up where the fort was, it was as though you could see all of Texas. Anyway, all that mattered, at least to me. Back then.

"And from up there, when you'd look out, it wasn't important which side, everything was rolling away, and all of it was green. Oh, there had to be rocks here and there, and in some places the grass was burned brown with sun. But when I think about it, Bo, it's all green.

"Lord, I remember those mornings, lying in bed, the wind coming through the windows and moving the curtains I had made, moving them back and forth, and every time I saw their whiteness blowing and then looked over and saw Blakely beside me or where he'd just been, and everything still cool and quiet, waiting for the fort to wake up and come to life, I couldn't imagine anything nicer than being married and in Fort Mason.

"I'd give a lot, Bo," and she looked over at him and seemed to be there with him more than since she'd started talking, "just to wake up some morning and believe I was back there. Just for a minute," she said, "even if it didn't last any time at all, I think I'd probably be happier than I've been any time since." She smiled, like she was making a confession. "Sometimes, before I go to sleep. Or when I feel myself waking up, I try to make it happen. Of course it never does. But you can't ever tell. Some morning. Any morning. Who knows, there's no way of knowing it won't." Then her voice moved away and she was back staring toward the ceiling.

"There weren't many of us living in the family quarters, most of the other married officers had left their wives back home, so things were usually quiet.

"Outside the fort, too. There'd be a raid every now and then, mostly for horses, but it didn't happen often. And when it did, people kind of liked the excitement. There wouldn't be many of them, and after they'd stolen their horses they'd disappear so quickly I don't think Blakely ever saw an unfriendly Indian the whole time he was in Texas. Things were about as peaceful as they could be. All the trouble seemed somewhere else, coming from back East where it was supposed to be civilized.

"It was like you couldn't get away from it. Even with the newness and the freshness all around us, that other world, the old one, wouldn't let us alone. It kept following, it wouldn't let us forget. Because the news kept coming after us. And when the letter came through from Washington, calling him back to fight, he did what he had to do.

"And I would have left with him, but the doctor and the other women at the fort, they said it wouldn't do. Blakely would have to travel too fast, across too much open territory, and it wouldn't be good for the baby."

"The baby?" Bo said. But Sam shook her head impatiently, like she didn't want Bo back inside her thoughts yet.

"I didn't argue," she said. "The war was far off, what was close was inside my belly, moving around, fighting wars of its own. I guess that mattered a lot more even than being with Blakely. Of course, if I'd known it would be the last time. But there wasn't any way of knowing.

"I was an army wife. I knew what could happen to soldiers. Except that wasn't real. It was something everybody, Blakely, my daddy, the other women, they all kept saying was a possibility, I had to think about it. So I did, but that was all, I just thought about it, the way you think about how someday everybody's got to die. You know it's true, but it seems an awful long way from getting up in the morning and cooking breakfast and doing whatever it is you've got to get done.

"And to be real honest, if I got to thinking about it and it started seeming too real, I had a way out that hadn't been there before. There was that baby kicking around inside, so even if something did happen to Blakely, and I really didn't believe it could, but even if it did, I still had the baby. It wouldn't take the place of Blakely, nothing could do that, but the world wouldn't be empty, there'd be somebody that needed me. That would let me need them.

"So Blakely left. I was going to follow. In an army ambulance, not because I was sick, that's the way most army wives traveled, mainly just a wagon with seats and a canvas top to keep you out of the sun. I was going to San Antonio, then to the coast for a boat to New Orleans, and then upriver to St. Louis. And when the war was over, it wasn't supposed to take long, that's where Blakely would find me. And the baby. It was all so simple and easy.

"Except nothing ever is, not when it's important. About halfway to San Antonio, maybe it was the bouncing around or the heat or I was worried more about Blakely than I wanted to think about, but that's not important. What matters is the baby started wanting to be born.

"There were other women in the ambulance, they did the best they could. But the baby was asking for more than it could handle, it wanted more than my body was ready to help it with. They got me to a little town. And that's where I met the Preacher.

"Or he met me. I don't remember much about what was happening right then. Mainly just the hurting and how hot it was, not just outside but all inside me, too. And when I was able to pay more attention, a real doctor had gotten there, an army one, and the Preacher was gone. But folks told me about him, that he was the one who had buried the baby. Not just said words over him. Dug the hole, put him in it.

"They said he insisted that even though I was crazy at the time and didn't know what was going on, he insisted they let me hold it. He said getting a little more bloody wasn't going to do me any harm, and God knows, I wasn't going to damage the baby.

"So that's where I stayed. For awhile. That's where I was when I finally understood how good my life had been up till then. I'd known that before, only not really. I knew other people probably didn't have it as nice as I did. But I guess I thought because I was me, I deserved being a little bit happier than other folk.

"Then I found out. First the baby, and the army doctor told me I wouldn't have any more. He didn't tell me to be careful, that I shouldn't have any more. He was absolutely clear about that. He said in getting the baby out, in trying to help it stay alive, they'd done things or things happened, so I didn't need to be careful. That was the only baby I was ever going to have.

"When Blakely found out, he went crazy. Not in his letters to me, they were still calm, they were comforting. But other people wrote, too. They said it was too much for him.

"Whatever it was, Blakely became a hero. That's what the newspapers said. That's what the little slip of paper said that came with his medal.

"What he really became was crazy. He did things he wouldn't have done if there'd been a son back home waiting for him. He went crazy and became a hero and got himself killed."

She got up and walked to the window. Then she came back and sat down on the bed again. The springs creaked, and she moved a bit to get comfortable. She didn't seem particularly upset by the story. It was like it was done with, like it really was completely in the past.

"But I didn't. I didn't become crazy, not for a second time. People expected me to. But I didn't. Not in the way they expected. I just went to sleep inside. There wasn't any reason not to. It didn't matter that I was in this little no-name town in the middle of Texas. I just went to sleep.

"People in St. Louis wanted me to come back there. I didn't see any reason to. My daddy went just about as crazy as Blakely. He did it in different ways and for different reasons, but it was just about as crazy. Maybe he wanted to prove he was a real Southerner or something. Nobody shot him, nobody had the chance. He got sick while he was still in camp playing at being an officer. So he got to come home and let my mamma take care of him. A lot of folks probably thought he was just trying to get out of it. But he fooled them. He died. Of course by then everybody was dying, the babies and the men, full grown and even older, ones who had come out on the far side of their lives and should have been left alone to enjoy it. Sometimes it seemed I was the only one being kept alive, as though it were a punishment.

"Not that I intended on changing that. I was asleep inside, I wasn't crazy. I'd go walking outside of town, and see all that empty space, and it would seem like I was linked up with it. It wasn't the greenness of Fort Mason. That was gone, it wasn't going to come back. Places, after all, they're really people, and Fort Mason wasn't going to come back. But there's more than one part inside you. And the emptiness all around me, out there on the prairie, it linked up with the emptiness inside, and that was better than being alone, there was something out there keeping me company. So I took my walks and I stayed.

"I had enough money to pay room and board for awhile, and when that was gone I could write and get more. I just didn't want to move. Certainly not back to St. Louis, to be around all the expectations and the rules and the fussings over. If I couldn't have Fort Mason, I sure wasn't going back to that. At least when I walked out on the prairie, I may not have been happy, but with all that emptiness, I did feel somehow at home.

"Then the Preacher came back and got me. He didn't ask me if I wanted to go, he didn't even tell me where we were going. He simply rode up one day while I was walking on the prairie. He got off his horse and just looked at me, didn't say anything, just looked at me and scratched his belly. Then he helped me up on his horse and led it back into town. I still remember like I was going through it again, him walking slowly in front, leading the horse, me sitting there, not knowing what was happening, but just having the feeling he knew what he was doing."

"Was he humming?"

Sam smiled. "Probably that, too."

"Then he brought you back here?"

"Then he brought me back here, and that's where I've been."

"You ever want to go back?"

"Where?"

"Back home."

"That's where I am, Bo. It's not Fort Mason, but it's not emptiness either. Because I'm scared of that emptiness, Bo, it makes things in me wake up that I don't need to know about. So this is as close as I need to get, I don't have to go anyplace else to get there."

Bo wanted to ask more, but Sam put her fingers to her lips and shook her head. But she did it gently, friendly. It wasn't like things had never happened. But everything else was back, close to being normal.

And Bo was healing. Except the better he felt, the slower it seemed. "The least you can do," he told the Preacher when he came back from his circuit, "is get me out of this room."

So that's what the Preacher did. He took him downstairs.

It didn't hurt as much as the climb going up. But by the time they got to the bottom of the stairs, blood was pounding so hard in his foot he expected to see it bursting out, spreading all over the floor. What he saw instead was sunshine, filtering through the dusty windows, making splotches wherever it landed. Then he noticed the half dozen or so men sitting, most in the shadows, as though any light managing to seep through was probably best avoided.

Some were drinking coffee. Others were drinking beer. The rest weren't doing anything but sitting. This time of morning, where Bo came from, someone holding a glass of beer was another sort of person. But the coffee drinkers didn't seem to mind. The main thing they were all doing was not talking.

The Preacher, looking comfortable in his shirtsleeves, not even wearing his tie, helped Bo across the room and sat him down in what seemed like the Preacher's corner. At least there was a stack of Bibles on a shelf. Next to those was a stack of playing cards. In boxes. With none of the seals broken.

The Preacher didn't say anything and he didn't join the others. He went to the bar and poured himself a beer, then sat down beside Bo. He didn't offer Bo anything. Which was just as well. Bo didn't want anything. Except maybe for his foot to stop hurting.

"Almost like home," the Preacher said, settling himself in with his beer. "Yours is what I mean. Except it needs a potbellied stove, maybe someplace next door where the women can be fingering dresses. But I reckon there wasn't much of this," he held up his mug. "Leastwise not next to the place they sold them dresses. You want something to eat?"

Bo shook his head and kept looking around. The Preacher was right. It could have been Abernathy's grocery. If, like the Preacher said, there'd been a little more of this and maybe a little less of that.

"These here are the daytime people," the Preacher said. "Town folk. About half taking a break from their storekeeping. Anybody needs them, they know about where to find them." He stopped and took a drink, not hurrying, like he appreciated the way it went down his throat. "Probably talking about the same as they'd be back where you come from. Except some here might be enjoying it a mite more, least for the time being." The Preacher waited a moment until he could belch. "Except they might better enjoy it somewhat less, before their pleasure gets too obvious at the dinner table."

The Preacher glanced around again. "Everybody seems accounted for," he said and wiped his mouth on his sleeve. "Let's take a walk, get that leg back to working."

Outside, it was so bright Bo had to blink before he could make out what he was seeing. Then he was looking down the street, away from the hills he and the Preacher had traveled through to get here. Where the buildings stopped at the far end, the street didn't hardly change, just broadened out, spreading across the horizon and becoming prairie.

"Well, boy," the Preacher said, "what d'you think?"

Bo had never thought about it, even now it was more of a feeling, but something didn't seem right. A town was supposed to be sheltering, comforting, a place to get inside of. Not like this, buildings simply sitting out there in the flatness, barely casting shadows against the heat and the glare from the sun.

Bo's leg was pounding, he'd had about as much walk as he wanted. But then the Preacher started moving. And since he was leaning on the Preacher's shoulder, Bo thought it best to move along with him.

They were walking down the middle of the street when without any warning the Preacher stopped. "Well, boy," he said again, "what do you think about it?"

Bo didn't know about what.

"The street, boy, the street!"

Bo took the weight off his leg and looked back at the saloon. "Long," he said. "It looks long. Especially that way, toward where we've just left from." He rubbed his leg. Toward where sooner or later they had to get back.

"You got to get it broke in," the Preacher said. "It ain't supposed to feel natural. What about the other direction?"

Bo wasn't sure what he meant.

"What we got here, boy, is a place sort of betwixt and between. Back of us, where we just come from, it's hills. Out in front, the other side of town, that's plains. Right in town, I reckon we get a little of both, depends on which way you're looking. You want to keep going?"

"I just said," Bo answered. "It ain't getting broke in, I'm getting recrippled."

"Well, what you think about sideways?"

Bo raised an eyebrow. "You mean walking?"

"I mean the street. In the sideways direction."

"I don't aim to walk over to the edges to find out."

"I understand, indeed I do. Because it's wide, Bo, it's wide." The Preacher started wandering down the street again. Bo gritted his teeth and followed.

"Yes, indeed, the street is wide, and not just in the walking, Bo, it's in the way you see it, too. Over there, on the other side, it looks pretty much the same this time of day. But at night it gets different, specially when the cowboys get paid. More than just different when a herd's passing through." The Preacher stopped and pulled out a handkerchief and wiped his face. He offered it to Bo. Bo shook his head. "What'd you think," the Preacher said, "about the folks downstairs?"

"I think I'd be feeling a lot better if I'd stayed with them. They seemed real comfortable sitting on those chairs."

"Just my point, boy, that's just my point, you'd have felt fine sitting down among them."

Bo didn't even give the Preacher's comment the credit of an answer.

"Now you think about it for a minute," the Preacher said.

Bo settled his weight on his good leg and just stared at him.

"Okay, sit down, go ahead and let that leg stiffen into a fence post, you go on ahead, sit down and let it just lie there."

Bo kept right on staring.

The Preacher stared back.

Then Bo sat down in the middle of the street and stretched out his bad leg in front of him and waited.

The Preacher looked at him kind of hard, then he sat down, too.

"You thought about it yet?"

"What am I supposed to be thinking?"

The Preacher raised up to a squat. "About how they seemed so *natural*. Some of them even drinking beer before the shank of the morning and you didn't even register."

"I registered."

"But you still felt comfortable. Because they seemed to be your sort, no matter where they were, what they were up to."

Bo felt silly sitting there. So he got up.

"All I was thinking about back there," he said, "was that I was sitting down. Someplace besides the middle of a street."

"Now across the street," the Preacher said, "things don't feel like that." He stood up and pointed. "Over there, when they come in, they're looking for something different."

Bo was interested. "Who? Like what?"

"Before you get done, I suspect you'll find it out. Right now, we're supposed to be walking. Make a turn."

"Which way?"

The Preacher didn't answer. So Bo turned down the next street he came to. The first block in that direction had houses. Then there was only prairie. But with ruts where roads must have been, and lots marked off with what once had been stakes, only now they were dried out and weather-stained, a part of the prairie. Except none of the lots seemed exactly the same size. Not enough different to bear much mentioning, only enough to make you look again to be sure.

"Folks expecting the town to start growing?" Bo asked.

"Not likely," the Preacher said. "There was a time, though, people didn't think twice before hoping. I reckon we all had dreams back then. Funny thing about dreams. You got to wake up before you figure out you were dreaming. While you're there, seems pretty real."

The Preacher turned onto a one-time road and walked alongside the empty lots. "Yessir, folks had it all decided, they had it signed, sealed, and delivered. This here had to be the spot. Right in the path of the biggest cattle trail moving out of Texas, so everybody heading north was bound to stop off and leave some of their money. Folks so sure they even named it Junction City. Yessir, Bo, it was going to be some town. And who knows, might have been, except for the fever."

"The whole town get sick?"

"That they did, only not in exactly the way you're thinking. Tick fever, boy, that's what made this town sick. Trail cattle, damned longhorns, no puny bug's gonna bother them. Any tick dumb enough to stick on trail cattle'd be fortunate finding blood enough to stay alive. Only stands to reason, given a chance, it'd move on to something else. And that's what they did. Leastways, that's what folks claimed. Up north, Kansas, Missouri, the farmers started blaming their sick stock on trail cattle, and they started telling Texas folk to take their longhorns and their ticks and anything else they might have and head them in some other direction. They passed laws, even got unreasonable and enforced them. So after a time, it was just as easy going some other way. Only problem, Junction City didn't happen to be that other way, it kept on staying right here."

"So these lots are going to stay empty?"

"I reckon so, boy, course some folks don't mind. The farmers and the ranchers around here ain't real crazy about the longhorns that still do come through. Course, there's others, townspeople mainly, they still got hope." He stopped and looked around him. "Specially them that still own these lots."

"I don't suppose it matters, they're going to stay empty. But why're they set out so strange?"

"Well, I'll tell you," the Preacher said. "You look out there across the prairie, you see one place much better than another to pound down a stake? What it is, boy, there ain't no plots of land out there. The only place where there's plots of land is in somebody's head. It's when you try taking something that's inside and laying it down on the outside, that's when things can start getting confused."

Bo already was.

"Just the way you're supposed to be," the Preacher said. "Not your time yet for anything else. But like I was saying, or getting ready to, back when more folks than now were still dreaming, we decided to set out the town real businesslike. Kind of get ready for the deluge. Except we didn't have anybody who'd ever done any surveying. So we got this fella passing through, said he had a cousin that had done some back in Georgia and he'd watched once or twice. We had us a drawing of what we wanted the town to look like, so we gave it to him and told him to have at it.

"Except what he did, what he used for measuring . . . You ever use rawhide?"

Bo shook his head.

"Well, it ain't bad when it's wet. And it ain't bad when it's dry. It's only when it gets itself both ways, you got yourself a problem."

Bo looked confused.

"Shrinks. You get it wet, it dries up and gets shorter. Which is okay, you're roping a calf. Measuring, you got a problem. The fellow doing it, sometimes he'd leave it out at night. Sometimes he wouldn't. Sometimes there'd be lots of dew. Sometimes there wouldn't. That's the trouble with maps. Lots of times they don't take into consideration the rawhide.

"So what we got here, it ain't quite what we had in mind. But come down to it, ain't much that is. So what we do, we just agree to go on living with it. You see, Bo," the Preacher said, "here in Junction City it's not exactly the way it was back home, where everywhere you look there's understood boundaries, you stay inside, you can do what you want and people'll leave you alone. It's not quite the same in Junction City, still we do give it a try. Here in Junction City, we got us a map, even if it don't fit real good. I reckon that's better than nothing."

The Preacher shrugged and looked out across the plains. "Which is kind of the way with the folks here, anyway. Most ain't had much luck following the maps when they were back East. So here in Junction City, we're kind of betwixt and between. Some say people come here when there's no other place they can go. But there's always some other place you can go. Here's where you wind up when there's no other place to go and you still want the comforts of people. You'll understand better, I suspect, once you get good and shut of us."

Bo figured that was his chance and so he took it. "That's what I've been wanting to get back to discussing," he said, "about getting shut and getting back started. You and Sam both, you keep acting like just being here's part of catching up with Uncle Charley. But neither one of you says why or how or what direction I'm supposed to keep chasing. So as near as I can tell, I'm not much closer than when I got started."

"You got to learn to walk, boy, before you start riding. When the time comes, I suspect you'll know it."

When they got back to the saloon, the same folks were still there. Except now there was one more, sitting in the Preacher's corner, his chair tipped back against the wall. The stranger didn't say anything, just touched his finger to the brim of his hat. Which was black, like his hat and his coat, like his tie and his boots.

The Preacher gave a sigh and went upstairs. When he came down, he had his coat and tie on, too.

Bo was standing out of the way, over by the bar next to Sam.

"What's happening?" he asked her. "This some kind of preacher's meeting?"

"Not hardly," she said. "Just wait."

The Preacher sat down at a table and motioned. Sam went behind the bar and came out with an unopened box of playing cards.

"Let the boy open them." It was the man in the corner. His voice was soft and somehow furry.

"His leg's kind of bad."

"Seemed to be walking when he came in."

The Preacher shrugged, and Sam handed Bo the cards.

"Spread them out," the man said, not like an order, more like he was passing the time of day. Bo looked at the Preacher. The Preacher nodded. Bo opened the box and spread the cards across the table.

"Not that way," the man said, still leaning his chair against the wall. "Face down, so all of us can take a look at the backs."

The stranger got up slowly and walked over. He moved lazily, but Bo could tell he was studying the cards carefully.

By now the Preacher was leaning back himself, his thumbs hooked in his vest, looking bored. "Whoever told you about me," he said, "didn't tell you enough. It ain't my habit to mark them."

The man didn't say anything, didn't even look toward the Preacher, just sat down across from him.

"Let the boy shuffle."

The Preacher just shrugged. "You know how?"

Bo sat down and started. But he was nervous, and the cards kept slipping. Then he felt a hand on his shoulder. "Take your time," Sam said. "You don't matter. That's the reason you're doing it."

By this time, the folks in the saloon had gathered around the table. More were drifting in the front door. Bo shuffled, clumsily, but he finished. The man nodded. Bo shuffled again. Another nod. Another shuffle.

The Preacher hadn't seemed to notice any of this. He was still leaning, his thumbs in his vest, staring at the ceiling.

Bo put the cards in the center of the table.

The man looked around the room. "You there," he said softly and motioned to a man in the front row of watchers.

The watcher leaned over and cut the deck.

That was when the Preacher looked down at the table.

"You got a thirst?"

The man across from him leaned back, too, and locked his fingers across his chest. He held them there for a moment, then without seeming to move them, he cracked all his knuckles at the same time.

"Not while I'm working."

"Makes sense," the Preacher said. "Samantha?" But he didn't need to finish. The cash box and a glass of beer were already on the table right beside him.

They started playing.

Nobody said anything, only what the game required.

The Preacher dealt.

The stranger dealt.

The Preacher won a hand.

The stranger won a hand.

It went on.

Bo got hungry. He got bored. But he sat there, and when the Preacher or the stranger motioned, he shuffled.

Then the stranger hit a streak. The coins started stacking up in front of him, but the Preacher didn't change his expression. He just reached into the cash box and kept playing.

Then there was a hand that neither one of them seemed to want to be over.

The stranger would raise.

The Preacher would raise.

Finally the cash box was empty.

"Sam," the Preacher said quietly. "Go get the spare."

Sam left the room and came back with a small bag. The Preacher put it on top of the pile in the middle of the table. The stranger picked it up and hefted its weight, then poured a little of the gold on the table and fingered it. Then he laid his cards face down, gently on the table.

He pushed his chair back and stood up, touched the brim of his hat, and walked lazily out the door.

The Preacher leaned back in his chair again, his thumbs hooked in his vest, and the crowd started buzzing. One of the watchers said kind of hesitatingly, "You mind if we take a look?"

"Looks like there's nobody left around who'd mind," the Preacher answered. So the watcher turned over the stranger's cards and whistled. There were three queens and two jacks.

"What'd you have, Preacher, you mind if I ask?"

The Preacher's cards were stacked neatly, face down in front of him.

"Don't have any idea, Walter, not even a notion. Never bothered to look. Sometimes, hurts a man's courage if he looks too close."

Bo just stared at the Preacher. Somehow the rules around here kept getting different. First there was Sam climbing into bed, and now the Preacher winning at gambling?

"Don't get yourself confused, boy," the Preacher said softly. "The two jobs, they ain't all that different."

Then the Preacher paused and looked at the ceiling, kind of whistling except there wasn't any sound more than the air coming through his teeth. "Knew a man once," he said and glanced at Bo like they were in on something together. "Liked to gamble, never done much before he met me, but he got real good. Said what he liked was just before everybody has to lay down their cards, everything else is over, but still nobody's had to show once and for all what they got. And nobody knows and everybody's waiting. He said he liked that moment even better than winning. Because right then you didn't care if it was only a game, right then it was almost unbearably all there was. It was like the not knowing cut a slice through time, and inside that slice everything was waiting, not even time was moving. So nothing outside even mattered. But he said none of them moments lasted long enough. So he stopped playing, said he reckoned he'd have to find those kind of slices someplace else besides card games."

Bo knew without asking that the Preacher was talking about Uncle Charley, but he was going to ask anyway, except he didn't have time, there were hoofbeats outside, and a man was rushing through the door.

"They're coming," was all the man said while Sam was pouring him a drink.

And they were, lots of them, both men and cattle. Except the cattle stayed outside of town. The men could hardly wait to get in.

The people who'd been in the saloon weren't there any more.

"They're at home," Sam said. "And they've closed their doors. They won't be back till the herd gets through."

They weren't missed. The cowboys came in droves. Maybe there weren't really that many. Maybe they just seemed to fill up the streets. With their noise. And smells. They'd been on the trail for awhile.

Most of them migrated to the other side of the street. They seemed to know where they were going, like they'd been there before. But some must have known about the Preacher. Only it wasn't him they were interested in. Or even the booze.

But the Preacher had rules. And he enforced them.

The men had to be reasonably sober. They had to be clean.

He made sure.

Before they could go upstairs, they had to visit a tub in the back room. It didn't matter if they said they were already clean. It didn't matter if they even looked like they were, which wasn't likely. First they had to go to the back room. And they had to bathe. Not just play at it, but get themselves clean. The Preacher made sure. Because he was watching. Bo tried not to. He tried not to think about any of it, while he carried water from the kitchen stove and poured it in, while he and the Preacher dragged the tub to the back door and poured the dirty water out.

But the Preacher watched and made sure. He sat, leaning back against the wall in his chair, holding a pistol across his lap. The men, one at a time, sat naked in the tub and soaped, looking sheepish, a little boyish, as the Preacher studied their progress, and they kept on until the Preacher nodded, telling them they could get up and get themselves dressed.

Bo was sitting on the floor next to the Preacher's chair, not liking at all what he was seeing, not even wanting to think about it, not wanting to but not being able to stop his mind from following the cowboy, whichever one it was, while he climbed the stairs, when he knocked on her door, but then his mind wouldn't go any farther. Without giving Bo any choice, his mind wanted to go somewhere else.

So what Bo was seeing, what he couldn't help seeing, wasn't the man in the tub anymore, or even the picture of him climbing the stairs, it seemed more like circling things that every now and then looked like long-ago schoolmates, but their faces were different, their shapes kept changing, melting into blurs that still kept on moving and making sounds. And the sounds were blurred, too, but he could understand, he didn't have to hear all the words to know what they were saying.

An hour ago they'd all been sitting in the classroom. Everybody still looked like they always had, the same faces that he'd flown kites and shot marbles with. They were all still, their shapes were no longer changing, and they were all taking turns reading. Everybody was doing it badly until Uncle Charley called on him. So he read, and then he forgot all about the people around him, where he was, he even forgot he was reading. A poem about protecting a bridge, dying and protecting a bridge, and he forgot about the classroom and his friends and even about his Uncle Charley. Until he was done and then he looked around surprised.

Uncle Charley didn't say anything, just looked at him. Then he said, "Fine." He said it quietly. "That was fine."

After that it was recess and he was outside and all the boys seemed to be around him, moving, "Fine," they were saying. "Teacher's pet sure did fine." Bo tried not to pay them any mind, he was still feeling the poem, protecting the bridge, but then he heard someone say, "Maybe that's cause his mamma reads books with Mr. Charley." And Bo was outside the poem now and throwing himself at the blur, trying to find which part of it had said it, but before he could someone was holding his arms behind him, and Chester Barnes who'd already been held back two years and was older than most when he started was standing in front of him and was saying, "Maybe that's what they do is get together and help Bo practice saying his pretty little poems. I reckon that's what they probably do."

Other voices were in the background and things blurred even more, but he knew Chester was going to hit him and that wasn't fair. He didn't mind fighting although Chester was too big and so he'd win, but that was all right. What wasn't, they were still holding him, crowded together like everybody wanted to be part of it and and he didn't want it to happen, not the way it was going to, but he knew Chester was going to do it and it was going to hurt, it was going to hurt bad, and there wasn't anything, there wasn't anything at all he could do.

Except all of sudden he was up above everything and looking down, everything on the ground looking small and far away, but he could see a group of boys with himself in the middle and a bigger boy getting ready to hit him, except he was up above now and looking down, and the people down there were so little and so far away, nothing could really hurt him, nothing could even touch him, they may have thought they could, but they couldn't, not the part of him that was seeing it all happen, down below, far away.

Then Uncle Charley came out of the schoolhouse and stopped it. He didn't say much, but he made them all go away and so Bo could come back down. It was only then that he wondered why Uncle Charley hadn't come earlier. He thought he remembered, right before he'd gone up above, when he'd been trying to find some way, any way out, he thought he'd seen Uncle Charley's face, maybe only for a moment, staring at him through the schoolhouse window.

Just then the cowboy in the tub suddenly rose up, soap and water dripping, and said,

"Shit."

The Preacher let his breath come out kind of softly, but loud enough so the cowboy could hear it, and know the Preacher had been through this sort of thing before and was wearied by it.

The Preacher let the front legs of his chair fall back to the floor. "If you are describing a need, my friend," he said in a resigned sort of voice, "there's a privy in the back. If you are describing a mood, the choice is yours. You may either go back and commune with your cows or you may finish with your bath."

"Shit," the cowboy said. "I ain't gonna be treated like no goddam baby. I'm a goddam cowboy, and I'm going upstairs."

The Preacher sighed and lifted his pistol.

"Son," he said, "I sure hate to do this. I really do." He cocked the hammer. "But I'm gonna be compelled to shoot either one or the other of your balls off. But I will try to be fair about it. Which one can you best afford to lose?"

The cowboy studied the Preacher momentarily, and must have decided it wasn't worth risking, because he sat back down and kept sudsing. Then he left and somebody else came in.

"Why?" Bo said. "Why do you let her do it?"

The Preacher thought, and then he said, "Who's gonna explain what a person needs, Bo, who has the right to figure it? Who has the right? For her," and he nodded his head toward the tub, "or even him?"

Much later that night, after the last bather, the last drinker had left, Sam came downstairs and the Preacher filled her a glass. She looked tired.

"How you doing?" the Preacher asked, and he was really asking, not just being friendly.

Sam smiled and shrugged. "Tired. A little sore. I've had my share of exercise."

"Why?" Bo asked. "Why do you need to do it?"

Sam looked at Bo, a look that was almost motherly, but one that also showed she felt strained.

"Why does it bother you, Bo? Does it make me seem kind of dirty?"

Bo didn't know how to answer.

"I'm tired, Bo. Come over to a table. Let's sit down."

Bo followed her, not liking what he was feeling, watching her body move in front of him, not wanting to think of her that way, not wanting to be just another man in the tub. But he couldn't help it. Right then she wasn't the person he'd once been in bed with. Something had changed. Her. Him, too, he figured. He wasn't sure he approved of either one of them.

"Sit down, Bo," she said, "and quit looking at me like that. I've had about as much of that today as I can stand."

Bo wanted to be somewhere else. How did they know, not just Sam, not even just girls and women, how did they always seem to find the parts inside you that you wanted to keep out of sight? Why didn't they ever see the other parts, not the ones you couldn't do anything about, but the ones you wanted to get in the open but somehow couldn't? How come folks never saw them? It wasn't fair, because if they could, they'd have to understand how the parts of yourself that you really liked only wanted the best for them, whatever it was, and then maybe Sam would feel better about things. Not the way she was feeling now.

She sat down and leaned her elbows on the table. "You may not know this, Bo, but the way you think about me matters. So try and understand what I'm saying. What we did together, you and me, it wasn't the same as what I've been doing all day upstairs. That's the first thing. The next isn't as easy to get into words.

"Up there," she nodded toward the stairs, "most of the people I was with, I was just their hand only it was shaped like a person. Except they think they're more of a man if it's me instead of their fist." Sam smiled. "And I suspect I can do things they don't know how to do yet with their fingers. But for most of them, I'm just something they can shove themselves into."

"Doesn't that bother you, that they're not even treating you like a person, you could be anybody at all?"

"Sometimes, Bo. Of course it does. But that's what they're looking for, Bo, that's the way they want it to be. But don't forget, Bo, sometimes I feel the same way, and so I don't mind at all.

"And there's other times, Bo, it's not really me they're doing it to. It's like the parts they're paying to use don't even belong to me, they're only attached by accident. They're a long way from whatever it is that's me."

Sam sighed and took a drink. "Besides," she said, "I can use the money."

"But doesn't it ruin it?" Bo wasn't sure how to say it. "Doesn't it ruin the whole thing when there're so many, when it's not just one person?"

She looked at Bo and smiled, like if she'd had the energy she'd reach over and muss up his hair. "Sure it does, Bo. Except that one person's got to be there, and you've got to be lucky enough to find him. And then you've got to manage somehow not to lose him." She got up slowly from her chair. "But it's late. And I've put in a day's work."

The next morning seemed terribly quiet. Bo got out of bed and looked out his window. The streets were empty, but that wasn't what he was seeing, his eyes maybe, but what he was seeing was a late afternoon, or maybe early morning, Bo couldn't be sure, but they were all sitting on the front porch, his mother and father and brother, himself too. And Davey was beside him, and he was looking at his father and mother who were sitting in chairs next to each other. But the space between them seemed more real than they were, as though the only reason they were sitting there was so Bo could see the space between them, the worn planks and then the railing and then the empty sky going on forever.

"But it doesn't have to be that way," Miranda's voice was suddenly saying inside Bo's head.

"Don't get too bothered," Bo heard Sam answering. "Keep on wandering around in your Daddy's pants while you've got the chance and enjoy it. There's plenty of time to learn better later."

The town was just an early stopover on the trail. The herd was already gone. Downstairs, the daytime folk were already back.

"Morning, Bo," the Preacher said. "Go fix yourself some eatings. Sam's gonna be sleeping a little late this morning."

Bo did, and when he got back, nothing was changed, nobody seemed to have moved. Except there were two new sitters. Actually, only one that was absolutely new. The other had been there before. Playing cards.

"Well, Bo," the Preacher said, leaning back in his corner, "It does appear like there are those who test the waters once and grow content. Then there are them who return daily to refresh themselves in the stream. Go behind the bar, son, bring me a fresh deck of cards. I fear my new friends would distrust those I keep by my side."

It was like yesterday, except for there being one more of them, and this time some townsmen sat in. The new stranger accepted the Preacher's offer of a beer, but he left it sitting beside him on the table. They started, playing hand after hand just like before, no one winning much, no one really losing. The crowd gathered, and Bo shuffled. The men, each in his turn, dealt. Nobody said any more than he had to.

Then they got to a hand where it was just the three of them, the townsfolk had dropped out quick, so it was just the two strangers and the Preacher, and they didn't show any likelihood of leaving. The money pile in the center of the table kept getting taller, it seemed like the strangers had come to town with an endless supply. Whenever it looked like they might be getting low, the new man, the really new one, reached inside his coat and pulled out his wallet and came up with more.

Finally the Preacher turned to tell Bo to get the extra money box, but Bo felt a hand on his shoulder. It was Sam, still looking tired, but now it was from so much sleep.

"Don't bother, Bo," she said. "I'll do it."

So the men kept right on.

Until it happened. The new man, when he reached for his wallet this time, his elbow hit his glass of beer, the one he hadn't so much as touched, but this time he knocked it over, the beer flowing over the table, heading for the money. Everybody leaned over to help, some to get the money out of the way, others to wipe up the flow.

The Preacher got up and went to the bar for a refill. Sam followed, and Bo did, too.

"Don't you see what they're doing?" Sam said softly, but with real concern. "As soon as that beer spilled, the other fellow milked that deck so fast, he's probably changed every card in it."

The Preacher took a swallow. "Oh, they look like fine upstanding chaps to me. I don't think they would stoop to such unsporting behavior."

"*Preacher?*" Sam said just as softly, but this time more urgently. "Is something wrong? Can't you tell they're fixing it so you don't have a chance?"

"Now don't you start worrying about the Preacher," he said and wiped his mouth with the back of his hand. "The Preacher has always been a fine judge of character."

The table was dry and the game resumed. The time finally came for the draw.

The Preacher put two cards face down on the table.

The strangers glanced at each other quickly, but they didn't change their expressions.

Then the Preacher threw the three cards he was holding into the center of the table.

"Well," he said, almost lazily, "I reckon I'll take three."

"*What!*" the stranger from yesterday said. "Are you *crazy*? You can't *do* that!"

"That so?" the Preacher said, still sounding friendly. "There some new rules slipped by me unnoticed?"

Then today's stranger spoke. His voice was quieter, colder. "I don't know just what's going on here, but whatever it is, it don't make sense. I think we should just each of us take our money and call it a day."

When Bo turned toward the man, he was looking into a drawn gun. "Except," the man said, "if there's something funny going on here today, more than likely it was happening yesterday, too. So just to be fair, that ought to make this morning's take somewhat larger."

Yesterday's stranger was leaning over the table, reaching for the money.

"Preacher?" The voice was soft and high, a man's voice, but somehow girlish. "Can I go ahead and blow his goddam head off?"

Bo and everybody else turned toward the door. A man was standing there, below medium height, young, almost a boy. His clothes were dusty, he'd obviously been riding. But Bo hadn't heard a horse. Whoever he was, he knew how to ride quietly.

Everybody except the three card players edged away from the table. The man in the door was holding a sawed-off shotgun.

"Well, hello there, Jeremiah," the Preacher said. "No need for violence. We were just having a little discussion about rules."

"Shit, Preacher, come on and let me do it."

"You're a good boy, Jeremiah. But there's no need. These gentlemen were just getting ready to leave."

And that's what they did.

As soon as the sound of their horses died away, Sam brought Jeremiah a cup of coffee, and he sat down, tired and looking disappointed. Then somebody asked what everybody was wondering.

"Well, I don't normally discuss a hand that's been finished, much less one that hasn't even been played. But I don't reckon those that had to leave early are going to mind."

He nodded to Sam. She turned over the cards the Preacher had thrown away. Two of them were aces.

Several folk took in their breath. "But Preacher," one of them said. "That don't hardly make no sense!"

"Sometimes," the Preacher said, "the wisdom of the world is but foolishness to the pure at heart. And sometimes what looks foolish to the pure at heart makes downright good sense to them that's been in the presence of wrongdoers."

He looked at the two cards he was still holding, then he placed them face up on the table. Both of them were aces, too. "You could say, being they were strangers, I just didn't want to be greedy. You could say that."

But nobody did. Nobody said anything.

"Well," the Preacher said, "look at it like this. A person don't want to distrust nobody. Because it can get habit-forming. It puts bad weight on the surrounding air. But there are times when, just out of curiosity, a person kind of wonders what *might* happen if he just *tries* distrusting. So I figured, now if I wanted to surely win a hand, and a big one, I'd want to make the other person feel right comfortable.

So I just *might* give him a handful of aces. Maybe around four. But if I *did* do that, I'd need some kind of straight flush to come out ahead. You understand that, Bo?"

Bo shook his head.

"Rules," Sam said, relieved now and at the same time irritated. "Made-up stuff. Full-grown men acting like one piece of cardboard's worth more than another one that's almost exactly like it."

"That's what a lot of life's made of, Bo," the Preacher said. "Pretending one thing's worth more than another. Sometimes makes things a lot simpler. But the rules, Bo, the rules say the only thing beats four aces is a straight flush, that's five numbers that belong together, all in the same suit. You understand suits, Bo? Not the kind you wear, the kind in cards?"

Bo nodded. He'd played card games. Just not this kind.

"Well, couldn't be a royal one, that's a run of the top cards. Because I'd have all the aces. So it had to be some kind of straight flush of lower cards. And it was pretty clear, it was downright definite, they couldn't hand out four aces and a straight flush on the same deal. Nobody was gonna believe that. So if they was gonna beat me, it was gonna come on the draw.

"But they had themselves a problem with how they planned to milk the deck. They didn't rightly know what I was going to do with my card number five, the one that didn't happen to be an ace. I might just hold on to what I had and not ask for any cards. Or for some reason I might just throw in the not-ace like I was bluffing, like I needed something, just to make the other folk more willing to keep on raising. So if they were stacking, they had to go two deep. You understand, Bo?"

Bo shook his head.

"Look at it like this. If they're going to win, they need—let's take a for example."

The Preacher reached out and flipped over what used to be the old stranger's cards.

"There they be," he said. "The four, five, six, and seven of spades. Now to make it work, he's gonna need either a three or an eight. So right now, he's got to have both ends open because he doesn't know what I'm gonna do. If I don't ask for a new card, then he gets the top one from the deck. If I throw my not-ace away, then I get the top one, so he gets the second one down. So he's got to be sure that the first draw fits on one end and the second one on the other."

"So you take two," Bo said. "That leaves him with nothing, just a lot of cards that add up to nothing?"

"Wrong," Jeremiah said in his soft voice. "You take three, as many as the game lets you, just so long as it leaves you with something. You can't never tell what they may be up to."

"Jeremiah's right," the Preacher said, "and that's pretty good for a man who don't play cards. I reckon a fellow don't need to, long as he's got practice in distrusting. What you don't know is how far the other folks have followed your reasoning. I don't rightly know what they might have figured out about what I'd figured out. That's what's good and that's what's bad about dealing with things that's human. You can't know for sure, but you got some idea what folks're capable of putting themselves up to. They at least *think* they got a reason, even if it seems truly strange to others looking on. So I just taken one step into what doesn't make sense, just to be sure."

"But you needed me behind you anyway," Jeremiah said, which was half a brag, half a question wanting an answer.

"Always need you behind me, Jeremiah, fact of life." He leaned over and patted Jeremiah's arm. "Always will. But now we're all getting comfortable, why don't you lean that shotgun against the wall and tell us what brings you back around?"

"Oh, I don't rightly know, Preacher." Jeremiah seemed shy about answering. "I reckoned it'd be nice, being around people who stay put for awhile. Reminds me that some folks might still be there next time I come around. And I guess it makes me feel good, figuring it'll be okay if I stay a spell."

Bo thought, he's talking about something like home.

"Where've you been, Jeremiah?" Sam's voice was gentle.

"Here, there," he said.

Sam kept looking at him.

"Back in the hill country, mainly," he said.

"Doing what?"

"Mainly staying out of the way of them that might get in mine."

"You been in trouble, son?" the Preacher said.

Jeremiah crossed his ankles and stared at the floor, then looked up at the Preacher.

"Nothing to speak of."

"Try."

"Over by Gulch Creek. Rounding up a few strays."

"Strays?"

"Strays."

"Somebody didn't agree?"

Jeremiah didn't say anything.

"Anybody hurt?"

"No sirree," Jeremiah said, looking the Preacher straight in the eye. "I promised you I'd try and I'm doing it. When the other folk decided they weren't going to slow down long enough and listen to reason, I just left. I didn't shoot nobody. I could have and I would have, but I didn't. Because I promised you and I'm trying. And it took a long time to leave. I had to tire out me and my horse and travel halfway to San Antonio before they'd say goodbye. And I could have saved myself the time and the tiredness and got me some stray cattle, too. But I promised I'd try other ways first, and so that's what I'm doing. I'm trying." He stopped as though listening.

"You done fine, boy, you're doing fine," the Preacher said. Bo could tell it was what Jeremiah had been waiting for. "How you been making out?"

"Not bad, Preacher, not that bad. I've managed myself a few uninterrupted transactions since the last time I been around."

"And Flake?"

Jeremiah grinned, like he was proud and didn't mind showing it. "Oh, he's back there, a couple of days behind maybe, but I reckon he's back there. That man, he sure wants to get caught up with me."

The Preacher sighed. "That's sure what it seems like. Although I'm not real sure what Flake would do with himself if he ever did. Seems like his job's more chasing than catching. But that does give us a day to make you feel a little bit at home, get you fed and clean and rested. First thing, you need to get that road off you."

Jeremiah sighed, too, and stood up and stretched, like he'd found where he'd been trying to get to. "Bo," the Preacher said, "you go back there with him and keep him in hot water."

Jeremiah's eyes narrowed as he looked at Bo.

"He's okay," the Preacher said. "He ain't gonna do nothing to you when you take your clothes off."

"I keep forgetting," Jeremiah said. "I keep forgetting where I am."

In the back room Jeremiah seemed nervous, fidgety. Like he wasn't in a big hurry to take his clothes off. He undid his gunbelt but didn't hang it from the pegs provided on the wall. He only stood there, holding a holster in each hand. The holsters were good leather, they didn't look old, just smooth and slick, most likely with wear. Everything else about Jeremiah seemed tired, his face, the way he carried himself, even his clothes. But the holsters looked like they'd been oiled, and not that long before.

Bo looked at him standing there, and suddenly realized. He's scared. He's shy about taking his pants off. Not like most of the other men Bo had poured water for, not like them at all, at least not to show it. He doesn't want to be naked.

"You do what you want," Bo said, "but if I was you, I'd wait till there was some hot water in the tub before I jumped in. If I poured it in right on top of you, it'd probably get you burned. Why don't you just sit till I get it kind of halfway filled up."

Bo could see Jeremiah relax. He still didn't hang his holsters up. But he did sit on a bench that ran along the wall, and he held his guns in his lap while Bo brought his bucketloads from the kitchen. And when the tub was about half filled, when Bo came back with the next bucket load, Jeremiah was sitting in it, and the water was already soapy. His holsters were on a chair, far enough away not to get wet, but close enough to reach for and not miss.

When Bo had filled the tub pretty close to the rim, Jeremiah cleared his throat and said, kind of mumbling, "Thank you, thank you kindly, I think that'll just about do it." Then he said a little louder, in his soft, high-pitched voice, but surer of himself, like he'd been practicing inside his head. "You're kind of new around here, ain't you?"

Bo put the bucket down and for the first time looked directly at him. "I reckon. Only just passing through."

"Where you heading?"

"Can't be certain. The Preacher's helping me locate my Uncle Charley."

All of a sudden, Jeremiah sat up and noticed. "So it's you that's chasing after Charley!" Jeremiah shook his head and grinned. "Well I'll be damned."

And then he was through. But Bo wasn't. It didn't make sense. Everybody he ran into seemed to know his Uncle Charley, yet they all seemed agreed on keeping him private. But that was all Jeremiah intended on saying.

The next morning Bo heard a knock on his door. He had grown up on a farm, so he knew about getting up early. But not that early. When he opened the door, Jeremiah was standing outside in the hall. Fully dressed. Even his hat on.

"Let's us go for a ride," he said, his voice like a whisper, although it really wasn't all that much softer than yesterday, speaking to gamblers and holding a shotgun.

Bo was still too groggy to know whether he wanted to go with Jeremiah or not. What he was sure of, he wished he was still asleep, but since he was already awake that wasn't a choice. So the easiest way not to have to make a decision was just to get dressed and go.

They rode out of town, away from the hills, onto the plains. Bo was still getting awake, but the morning air felt good, the going through it, feeling it pass around him, the horse under him loosening up, wanting to move, not even beginning to sweat. When Jeremiah stopped, Bo looked around. Every direction was the same. Flatness. Scrub grass going to the edge of the world, as though he could see where it reached the end and had to drop off.

Except things inside Bo's head didn't seem content with letting Bo enjoy the calmness. "You just keep looking that way," Sam was saying. "Only don't stop with the town, buildings trying to be what they're not, trying to reach higher than they were meant to, keep your eyes going till they reach hills on the other side, where there's water and grass, valleys where you can feel protected, maybe even hide."

"Course, she's right," the Preacher said. Bo shook his head, trying to get it clear, quiet, but the Preacher kept on talking. "You're out here on the prairie and look over toward Junction City, it seems nestling back in those hills. Kind of homey like. So it's all right for things, buildings, whatever, to be down to mansize, there's not so much need to try and be things you're not.

"But you just try looking from the other side, from them hills out toward the plains. Those buildings in between, they're the only things human in sight. And let me tell you, boy, they seem real puny next to all this space, all this flatness seeming like it ain't never going to stop. Looking this way, those buildings are the only things around seem to give any shape to all that emptiness. And up against that kind of emptiness, boy, you can't help feeling whatever you got, it ain't enough. So you got to reach for something extra, even if you have to cheat a little while you're about it."

"Get me some rocks," Jeremiah said, highly, softly, like he expected folks to be listening.

Bo was gratified for the interruption. "What kind of rocks?" he said, getting off his horse.

"Rocks," was all Jeremiah answered.

Rocks of any kind were hard to come by on the plains, but Jeremiah had stopped in the right place. Bo found a handful. He followed Jeremiah's directions and put them on the ground, a few feet apart. Jeremiah carefully stepped off a lot of steps, and when he stopped he told Bo to get out of the way.

That's when he started. At first Bo thought he was just showing off. But after awhile, he realized Jeremiah was working. Hard. Bo went back and stood beside him. Bo could hardly even see the rocks, some of them not much bigger than pebbles. If he hadn't put them there himself, Bo probably couldn't have found them.

Jeremiah would take out a pistol, starting with the one on his right leg, then after one shot he'd change. "I don't want to get partial," he said without being asked.

In the beginning, Bo thought Jeremiah just wanted an audience. It didn't take long to realize Jeremiah didn't care about that. What he wanted was somebody to go around picking up rocks. Even that wasn't so bad at first. The air was still cool, the exercise was helping his leg, and he was doing something a little bit different. Only it didn't stay different long. Bo was getting bored, and Jeremiah didn't show any signs of quitting.

In fact, he always seemed to know exactly what he planned to do next. After taking careful aim and shooting for awhile, he started doing it from the draw, slowly at first, then speeding up. Like before, he'd use one of his guns and then the other, but always from the holster on his right leg. "Other one's only backup," he said, pointing to the holster on his left. "That's just someplace to carry it." That was about all he said, except for telling Bo when to get more rocks and where to put them. Jeremiah'd practice, for instance, lying on the ground. He didn't actually hit many pebbles from there, but he did get close. Bo wondered about that, so he lay down, too. The grass was so high, he couldn't even see the rocks. Jeremiah had to be guessing.

But if he was, he was doing it pretty good. After that, he'd stand up and walk away, then he'd turn around and shoot. He didn't hit many this way either, but just like before, he didn't miss by much. Which seemed satisfactory to Jeremiah, because then he pulled a string of rawhide out of his pocket and tied both his pistols together. He'd hold them down to his side with one hand, and then he'd bring them up fast as though he was drawing from his holster. He kept doing it, it seemed like forever. "In case I got to use one of them," he said, "makes them feel like a feather."

After awhile, he stopped and rolled a cigarette and seemed contented, as though most of his work for the day was over, and yet it was still early.

"You see, Bo, about a lot of stuff, a person ain't got much choice." There was something proud in his voice, like it felt good to be explaining. "A lot of things, maybe even most, I ain't too good at. But using a gun, I found out early, I got talent. A fellow needs, he's got to have *something* he's good at. And when he finds it, it don't matter what, he's got to take it, he can't pass it up. For what he can tell, it may be all that's gonna come. So I kind of had to say to myself, maybe my something, maybe it's got to be a gun.

"Course, when you find what it is, that's just the beginning. It's like the Preacher and his cards. I bet you never seen him, I ain't except maybe twice. But sometime every day, he don't do it according to no schedule I can figure, he holes up someplace and works. Shifting cards around so fast nobody ever sees them, making cuts that look like cuts but ain't cuts at all, I mean working, doing the same thing hundreds of times, over and over and over, just in case he ever has the need."

"The Preacher? Practicing cheating?"

Jeremiah looked surprised.

"But then I forget," he said. "You're still new here."

Jeremiah went over to where they had left their horses, the reins looped over the saddle horns, letting them know they could eat their fill but had to stay put. He got a towsack out of his saddlebags, then he pulled his rifle out of its scabbard and came back to where Bo was standing. Jeremiah put the sack down on the ground, gently, and stood there with the rifle under his arm, the barrel pointing down, but more or less ignoring it, as though there were other things more important.

"But even being new, you best be kind of careful picking out words," he said. "There is cheating and then there is cheating." He cocked the rifle and examined the barrel, flicking off what might have been dust from around the sight.

"You see, Bo, when real gamblers sit around a table, they all know everybody's cheating, or leastwise doing their damndest. There's usually just too much money involved for only trusting in luck. Course, if they get themselves caught, there's trouble. But if you're good enough, you ain't gonna be caught. And if you are caught, that just means you ain't good enough, it means you ain't spent enough time practicing. The other kind of cheating, mirrors, spare decks, that sort of thing, that don't get no respect. But the other kind, the kind that takes practice, if you're good at that, it makes you something special."

"You mean, sitting around the table, *everybody's* cheating? Nobody's following the rules?"

"Well, maybe yes and then maybe no. This ain't back where you came from on a Sunday afternoon. If everybody is cheating, then I guess you could kind of say ain't nobody cheating. If nobody's following the rules, then that's what the rule is. So anybody that *does* follow them, they're the ones that don't understand the game. What you got to do is figure out which rules is being broken and why. And if you don't know how to do that, then you just don't belong in that particular game. Different places, there's different needs. There's got to be different rules. This ain't back where you come from on a Sunday afternoon."

Then he leaned his rifle against his leg and picked up the sack from the ground. He took out a roll of cloth and unwrapped it carefully and held out a gun. It looked worn, but it was clean and recently oiled.

"Used to belong to Charley," he said. "We'd come out here, this very place sometimes, and we'd practice together.

Lord knows," Jeremiah grinned, "when we first got started, he sure needed it. It wasn't long, though, he got good, he got real good at it." He rolled the gun back in the cloth and handed the bundle to Bo. "Go on," Jeremiah said. "You take it. I got no use for it, and Charley don't want it." So Bo reached out reluctantly and took it.

"No sir," Jeremiah said, still smiling as though he liked remembering, "about the time Charley got good, people taking notice kind of good, he just quit. Even left his gun behind, said he didn't care who took it, he didn't need it. He said, you get good at something like that, something people notice, that's all they tend to look at. And that's not so bad, Charley said, but after awhile, that's all you see, too, you keep paying attention to what other people see and you forget about looking inside. So he just all of a sudden took off his gun and left it."

Jeremiah wiped his hands on his pants, getting rid of the oil, but he didn't seem to be thinking about it. "What he told me, right before he left, he said that's what I was doing. If I could make enough noise on the outside, he said, then I wouldn't have enough time to be doing anything else except staying ahead of things that're after me. So I wouldn't have to pay any attention to anything that might be happening inside. And I asked him what was so bad about that. And all he said was, it depends. That's all he would say. Charley could be real uncooperative when it crossed his mind." Jeremiah shrugged and lifted his rifle and ran his hand alongside it. "I reckon," he said, "it takes all kinds."

Then Jeremiah sighted along the barrel and fired. A bird that Bo hadn't even seen fell lazily to the ground. But as soon as Jeremiah saw it was hit, he lost interest and was looking around for something else to practice on. Off in the distance, they both noticed a dog. Even from where they were, it was clearly a dog, not a coyote or something else wild. Jeremiah matter-of-factly took aim.

"Wait a minute," Bo said. "That probably belongs to somebody. Some kid's gonna miss it."

Jeremiah didn't say anything, just sighted and fired. The dog stopped like it was frozen, and then fell. "Whoever it belongs to," Jeremiah said, "had oughta take better care of it. You let something tame run around out here, it's likely to get hurt. What with snakes and stuff lying around."

He stopped talking, but kept looking into the distance, over the empty flatness of the plains. At first, Bo thought he was looking for something else to shoot, but Jeremiah left his rifle down by his side and kept staring out over the plains. "You don't want to go that direction," he said finally, as though Bo had just been suggesting it. "There's too much of the same, it ain't human. You get so lost out there, you can't never get back. Unless you got somebody following, sombody who's got a chance of finding you." Then it was as though he suddenly woke up and remembered Bo was with him. "Put that gun in your saddlebag," he said. "It's time we showed up in town."

When they reached the saloon, Jeremiah rode around back, and Bo followed. They tied their horses and Jeremiah slipped through the rear door and took a look into the front room.

"Who's the guy in the black suit?" he whispered back over his shoulder. "The one sitting there talking to the Preacher?"

Sure enough, there was yet another one. Bo shook his head. "Seems like every time I leave, somebody strange is sitting down when I get back."

"You go on in and find out. Then come here and get me."

As soon as Bo walked into the front room, the Preacher looked up. "You tell Jeremiah to come on in. Brother Bartholomew here don't mean no harm."

Jeremiah heard and followed. But when he sat down, he still pushed his chair against the wall so he could see what was happening all around him.

"Brother Bartholomew has just been looking over our town," the Preacher said, "and what he says he notices is, there don't seem to be no church. And he says that's what this town needs, it needs a church." And then he looked more directly at Bo's table and winked. "And maybe even a preacher kind of like himself to go in it. And so I've been telling him, as kind of a concerned businessman, I suspect a lot of us just might be interested. This part of the country's getting right civilized lately. It could be about time we got us a little church, might raise all our standards of behavior. Bo, why don't you go knock on some doors, tell everybody to come on over. Brother Bartholomew here wants to preach us a sermon. Besides, your leg there could use some exercise, since I suspect all you been doing most of the day is picking up little bitty rocks."

So that's what Bo did. And pretty soon the saloon was filled with townsfolk. After awhile there were even women and kids coming in, the men getting up from their tables and offering their chairs. When things had more or less quieted down, the Preacher got up and introduced Brother Bartholomew, then he sat down like he wanted to listen.

Brother Bartholomew was a big man, bear-like with a dark black beard, the sort of fellow if he described what happened in hell, you'd tend to believe him, and ask where he intended to spend eternity before you made up your mind yourself. But now he wanted to be friendly, you could tell he was trying. He looked around the room and smiled. You had to give him credit, he was trying.

He reached into his pocket and pulled out a deck of cards. "Now this here is the sort of thing you folks probably expect to find in a place like this." He smiled, almost like he was inspecting prey. "But even in a place like this, you can't run away from the Almighty. Because that's why He's the Almighty, because He's all places, all times, and All Mighty, even in a house like this, in the presence of whiskey and gambling, and even loose women."

He looked over to where Sam was standing behind the bar and smiled again, then kind of nodded his head and looked at the women who had come in just for the sermon, like they were all in agreement about such things. Only the women didn't change their expressions, except for one or two who looked over at Sam and smiled reassuringly.

Which didn't seem to faze Brother Bartholomew. "But even here, the Almighty is still just what He is, He's still the Almighty. Not even something as worldly as this deck of cards can keep him out, it's still His world, not yours, not mine, but it's His."

He fanned out a handful of cards and they were all face cards and all spades. "And even these cards has got what the world thinks is a king." Brother Bartholomew pulled out the king. "And it sure is pretty, dressed all up in robes and a crown. But we all know, this one may have the looks, it may have the fancy trappings. But there's only one that's got the real power." He pulled out the ace and slapped it over the king. "And that's what I'm talking about, brothers and sisters, when you recognize what's got the *power*, not just over some game between poor sinful creatures, but power over heaven, power over earth, power that controls every sparrow, every drop of *rain* that falls. It ain't our business to ask His reasons, it's our business to be grateful, there ain't nothing to do but, praise God, fall down before it.

"Yessir, brothers and sisters, even in something so ornery as a deck of cards, there's something to remind you, the Almighty's still watching. So when you sit down even in a den of iniquity, even in the valley, even some drywashed gully of death, you just remember, the Almighty's there, too, just a'watching. And that's the reason this here town needs a church. Now while you're thinking on it, let's all join together in a little hymn. 'Rock of Ages,' which all you folks know." He looked over his audience sternly. "And where did you learn it? You learnt it in a church house, because that's what it's talking about, the church, the rock of ages, all ages, young and old, men, women, children, alike. Now here's the pitch you start on."

He hummed a note and started out in a voice that sounded like it was used to leading. Everybody joined in on the first verse, and when he saw that everybody was singing, Brother Bartholomew himself stopped, but kept on keeping time, hitting his hand on the table in front of him. After the end of the first verse, he kept on hitting. A few people remembered the words to the second, so they kept on singing, but there weren't many who remembered, and even those didn't last long. As each person gave up trying, Brother Bartholomew nodded his head knowingly, like he suspected as much, and kept right on beating the table.

Pretty soon only three voices were left, and when Bo and Jeremiah and the Preacher got to the end of the second verse, Brother Bartholomew kept on and so did they, only when the Preacher realized that Bo and Jeremiah were doing all right by themselves, he let them go it alone.

It was amazing, the two of them standing there, both of them holding their hands in front of themselves, looking like choirboys dressed up to be cowhands, their voices sounding young and innocent. Then all of a sudden, Jeremiah's voice, without getting any louder, went up higher, into harmony, his eyes focusing on nobody, maybe not on anything, at least nothing anybody could have seen. But nobody was looking, nobody was making a sound. Even Brother Bartholomew stopped his slamming, and everybody listened to the sweetness of their voices. Jeremiah's, if anything, was the softer, but the way he moved it up and down, filling in emptinesses that nobody had even expected were there, it made what was supposed to be an accompanying seem like the melody itself.

When they were done, nobody said anything, not for awhile. Then the Preacher cleared his throat, not loud, not enough to really do much to the hush. But he cleared it just a little and stood up, leaning back on his heels, hooking his thumbs into the pockets of his vest. He looked over at Bo and Jeremiah.

"That was mighty pretty, boys, some of the prettiest singing I've heard in a long while. Started me thinking." He looked over the heads of the folks standing there. "Yessir, it started me doing a little thinking, that and what Brother Bartholomew was talking about. Yessir, that talking sure bears some listening to, but what I was thinking is, like with most things, there's lots of ways of considering it. Like this here deck of cards." He reached over and picked up Brother Bartholomew's deck that was still lying on the table.

"Yessir, I certainly agree there are lessons to be learned from a deck of cards. And Brother Bartholomew's right, you sometimes sure can't tell much about what something's worth just by pretty pictures and fancy clothes.

"Now here's this deck, fifty-two cards. You've seen 'em before, but look at 'em again, look at all the different shapes and pictures and numbers they got on 'em. And that makes some worth more, and some worth less. I mean, a trey ain't that much better than a deuce, but a trey's always gonna win.

And then look at these folks with faces, they look terribly important, all dressed up fit to kill, they make both the deuce and the trey look kind of puny. But this here one, the *ace*, lordy, he don't need to look any sort of way a'tall.

"Now you folks know all that, but what I want to ask you, what *makes* some cards more important than some others? Now you just think here a minute. What's each and every one of these cards made of? I mean each and every *one*? They're made of *paper*. You forget the pretty pictures on the outside, each and every one is exactly the same underneath. It's like Sam was saying the other day, it's just the game we're playing, it's only the rules that makes the difference. If we turned everything around and let the low hand win, the game would still be going on, there wouldn't be no real difference.

"But that's what I want to talk about, the game, and it was you boys' singing that got me started. Now you just look at them, ain't much difference in their ages, Jeremiah's a bit older, but listening to them singing, seems like the both of them know the same things about that song. Music like that just don't seem to come unless there's something making contact inside. And whatever that is, and it's a mystery, these two boys seem to share it.

"But, and this is important, it don't matter that down inside, somewhere so deep we can't see, these boys are enough alike to be brothers. The outsides of them boys has been stamped different. Here's Bo, I never met his ma and his pa, but I suspect I know them. Hardworking. Made Bo that way, too. But also taught him the way folks expected him to behave. He may have gotten mad at them at the time, but he probably knew, if he didn't then, he'll learn it someday, they were just trying to get him ready to go out and be a man. But I suspect he always knew they wanted him around no matter what. They knew he was sooner or later going to have to leave home, but he knew he'd always have a place to come where he was welcome.

"Then there's Jeremiah here. Look what's been stamped on him. He don't rightly know where he was born, all he remembers is living with kinfolks that didn't much want him in the first place. He remembers he had a ma, that's about the only thing that gives him pleasure about back then, he remembers and feels good that he had a ma, but it's only every now and then it's specific, most often it's more a feeling than a picture of something in his mind. He knows he had a pa, because you got to have one to get yourself born, but that's about all. What he remembers real good is that when he worked hard, nobody said much. About the only time he felt connected with the kinfolks he lived with was when they got started beating on him. Which was the sort of thing he got to expecting. When he woke up in the morning, there wasn't many questions about if, only about when. And even asking those types of questions stopped after awhile. After awhile, it got so it wasn't really worth the bothering.

"And so one thing kind of led to another. He hired out to work for a man who took a hankering toward him. At least treated him decent, which as far as Jeremiah was concerned was the same as treating him specially good. And I suspect he even listened to Jeremiah every now and then. And so Jeremiah started feeling toward this man like he was his father. Of course, the man didn't ask to be, he hadn't trained for the job, but a boy needs a father. And if the real one ain't available, he's got to go looking for the best one he can find. And under the circumstances, Jeremiah figured he'd found a pretty good one. Except this man he was working for was was having trouble with some other folk who had ranches close by, land, water rights, that sort of thing. And one thing kept leading on to another, till one of those other men killed Jeremiah's boss. And Jeremiah didn't go crazy or anything such as that. It only seemed natural, like his getting his beatings, that what he was supposed to do was go kill the man who had done it. So he did.

"And so one thing kept leading on to the next. Jeremiah, up till then, probably would've been happier singing in church than shooting a gun. But he found he had to keep on shooting it so he could stay away from that other man's friends, and he found he was getting pretty good at it and so he kept it up. And now one thing has led to another, so there ain't many places Jeremiah can go to, there ain't somebody already there gonna make him use that gun before he's done.

"Now let's don't just stop with Jeremiah and Bo here. Let me tell you about another young man I'm pleasured to know. Name's Rafe, though that's not too important. Lives with some folks I know, Bo does, too, a day or so's ride over the hills. Seems like his and Jeremiah's background started off pretty much the same. Both his folks dead, this time from Indians. But Rafe, just a squirt back then, maybe five or six, managed to hide himself away and get to the nearest neighbors and they took him in. Not the same thing as his real family, but they did their best, except they were getting to be old and wanting to go live with their grown-up kids who'd moved back East. So several years ago, when Rafe was about Bo's age, I knew a ranch that needed a hand, and so Rafe had a place to go, a place that wanted him and treated him that way. There's a man there that had wanted a son, now he's got one. And now there's a boy who's got a father he didn't even know was there, he doesn't have to go off looking for another one. And it's in a place where nobody's gonna shoot anybody else over getting to water.

"Now what I'm asking, what would have happened if Rafe's and Jeremiah's places been changed around? Course there's no way of knowing. Jeremiah may have had something inside him that would've had him practicing his shooting no matter what. And Rafe might have wound up drawing steady wages even if things had been different. There just ain't no good way of knowing. Cause neither one of them can or probably wants to go back and try it differently. But what went on back then was just pure luck. Neither of them little kids had much to say about what was happening to them. But I suspect it had a whole lot to do with what's happened since.

"Yessir. It's kind of like a game of poker. There's rules. They may not seem to make much sense. But there's rules. It might not seem to you that they're terribly fair, but if you want to play the game, you got to follow them. You might make them different if it was up to you, but it ain't. So you can't just decide right in the middle of the hand that two pair beats three of a kind, even if that seems to make a lot more sense to you at the time. Now you can go off and play that kind of game by yourself, except that tends to get lonesome. If you want to be in the game, you got to accommodate yourself one way or another to the rules.

"And then the cards get dealt. And if everybody's playing on the up and up, after about a thousand deals, everybody probably gets a fair shake and things even out. Except if it's the big game, the one where most things are bet on, like for instance the rest of your life, then maybe it ain't real fair that purely on the strength of the shuffle or the luck of the draw, one person gets good cards even from the beginning. He ain't done nothing to deserve it, still that don't change nothing. He's got 'em anyway, and there ain't a whole lot to be done about it.

"And Brother Bartholomew may know more about such things than me, most likely he does. But it does seem to me, just looking at the outsides of things, there's lots wrong with this here world we've been dealt. We look out there at what's around us and we got a fight on our hands and we ain't been dealt the right cards to deal with it. So if that's the only game we're playing, we've done lost before we get started.

"But that ain't the only game in town. We may lose in the long run, but in the short haul we got us a town and a room where we can come in out of the sand and the sun and sit around a table with each other while we look at those cards. That's the only reason we're playing, or it'd better be, so we can sit here and know that if somebody's done stacked the deck it's not any one of us around this here table. And so we can everybody feel a little bit for our neighbor, since we all got trapped into a game that ain't none of us gonna win.

"So the way I see it, it don't tell us much about a man, what kind of hand he's been dealt. What matters is what he does with it once he's got it. And so what this deck of cards tells me when I think on it, is not to be in any real hurry, making up our minds about a person. We might just be looking at the cards he got pure-dee by luck. Sometimes, if we take the trouble, we might find the fella with the low hand, one that ain't got a prayer of winning the pot, is playing a lot better game with what he has than the fella that for the time being seems to be raking in all the chips."

Then the Preacher sat down. Brother Bartholomew had been growing impatient, and now he got up again and looked out sternly over the townsfolk, who hadn't gotten impatient at all. This seemed to them like first-class entertainment.

"There's food for thought there, brother, not exactly according to gospel truth, but good for thinking on nevertheless. Except there's a danger there. Because everybody needs to remember, there's other things to do with our lives but think about cards and games and loose living. And no matter how low into sin we have fallen, there's a Good Book that tells us the rules we've got to follow if we want to sit in the presence of the Almighty. And the place we need to go to learn them ain't around some card table, it's in a church, a *real* church with a real *preacher* inside it. So folks can look at it and know there's some good people in this town that want to worship the Almighty in His own house, rather than associating with the ways of the world in some ungodly saloon."

"Well," the Preacher said, "I guess we do need all kinds. So, I'll tell you what we'll do. Every Wednesday, all the profits from this here house of sin, we'll let that go towards building your church. Course, that might taint the godliness of raising your building. Or you reckon the Almighty might see fit to welcome a little help from the unholy?"

Brother Bartholomew frowned. He seemed right on the verge of starting another talk. But he held himself in and smiled, although it wasn't a look that warmed you a whole lot.

"One of the wonders of the Almighty," he said, "He is able to find, even in things the most worldly, means to further the kingdom. Is Wednesday a pretty busy night, brother?"

"Since they'll be losing their money for a good cause, I suspect we can gather in a few folks. Now any of the rest of you, you want to help out the preacher?"

One by one, they came up and offered. Part of their profits, materials to build with, the hands with which to do it. There were some that hadn't thought much about it before, who now felt Junction City was one step closer to being a real town, one more step away from the frontier, that much closer to civilization.

But Brother Bartholomew didn't seem to want it made easy. There was a pond right outside of town, in the direction of the hills where the stream came from that fed it. That's where Brother Bartholomew called them together late in the afternoon, right before dusk, when things had started getting cooler. And most everybody came, there weren't a lot of competing attractions.

When everybody that was coming got there, Brother Bartholomew stood in front, his back toward the pond, and his voice booming louder than was probably needful.

"This is a grand day, folks, a grand day in the life of our little town. Before today, it was like a baby, trying to walk, stumbling, falling down, not even knowing where it wanted to go.

"But today, that same baby is standing up, learning to walk, getting ready to grow into a fine young man. Because today our town, and I say 'our,' yesterday it was only yours, but today it's mine, too, and what's more important, any day now it's gonna be the Almighty's. But it's a grand day, friends and neighbors, it's a grand day, because our town's gonna be a place, praise God, a place where our children are gonna grow up knowing there's rules for right and wrong, knowing there's an Almighty in charge. Yessir, because if a place is gonna be that kind of place, then that place has got to have itself a church, where everyone can look at it and know that this here town, on the edge of wilderness though it may be, not just balancing, brothers and sisters, nay *tottering* between savagery and civilization, that this here town has just decided to lean itself toward law, toward order, and not just any human versions, no sirree, praise God, but toward that hope, nay that faith, nay that *conviction* the Almighty's in charge, and that everything works for the good for them that obey the Lord.

"Now we're gonna build that church, praise God, we gonna do it, and I don't even bother to say God willing. Because I *know*, friends and neighbors, I *know* that's what God wants us to do and not starting tomorrow or next week, but *today*, this very day.

"So this is going to be a grand day, one that we ain't likely to forget in the life of our town. And what we need is something special to commemorate it, to stand as a living sign for our new beginning. So what we gonna do right now, right *now*, is take in our first member. What we gonna do is sing the first verse of 'Just As I Am Without One Plea,' and what I want you to do, what the *Almighty* wants you to do, whoever feels the call to be the first member, whoever wants to be known for doing that the rest of his life, the rest of this town's life, you just step forward. Now remember, brothers and sisters, there can't be but one tonight, because we want this to be special, so if you don't step lively, you gonna miss it, you gonna lose your once in a lifetime opportunity."

Then Brother Bartholomew began singing:

> Just as I am, without one plea,
> But that thy blood was shed for me.

Most everybody joined in. Most everybody, whether they could carry a tune or not, liked to join a singing if they knew the words. And even if they didn't, they could at least hum along with the tune. But apart from singing, most of them weren't especially big on joining. If they had been, they'd probably be living someplace else.

So when the first verse was finished and nobody had moved, Brother Bartholomew started into another one:

> Just as I am and waiting not,
> To cleanse my soul of one dark blot.

Nobody seemed to mind, some singers even added harmony. Well, that was almost true, *almost* nobody seemed to mind.

"We gonna be here all night?" Jeremiah half-whispered to Bo. "Ain't we done enough singing for one day?"

> Oh, Lamb of God, I come,
> *I* come!

Just then Bo felt something sharp poking into his side, not just poking, sticking, breaking through flesh and starting to hurt. By the time he turned around, he could see Jeremiah already putting his skinning knife back into his belt, and he also noticed that he, Bo, wasn't standing just exactly where he'd been a few seconds before. Because without knowing it, he'd jumped and was out a little bit ahead where everybody now seemed to be looking. Except for Brother Bartholomew. Brother Bartholomew wasn't content with looking, he was standing right in front, hovering and smiling, but a smile that Bo didn't find reassuring.

Bo looked back around to get Jeremiah to explain how it was only a joke and wasn't meant to cause any harm. But Jeremiah wasn't there. While everybody was distracted, Jeremiah had disappeared.

There wasn't any use to look for Sam. She'd stayed at the saloon. So it was all up to the Preacher. He was there, standing off to the side, but when Bo tried to get his attention, he just stood where he was, his hands stuck in his pockets, refusing even to meet Bo's eyes. Instead, he was looking out over the pond, his lips puckered up like he was whistling but there wasn't any sound coming out.

"Praise God," Brother Bartholomew said. "Praise the Almighty! Who has seen fit to shame the elders, to shame the fathers and the mothers by sending His spirit to the young. And that, brothers and sisters, is a signal to us, it will be the young of this community that will provide the energy, the will, the *spirit* to make our town the sort of place we want, that the Almighty wants it to be.

"So all you men, take off your hats. Cause this is a grand day, a holy day, this is gonna be our town's first real ceremony. So come on son, be proud. Don't be scared just cause the spirit seen fit to move you. You just come on and follow me."

Bo didn't know what else to do, so he did it.

But when they got to the edge of the water, Brother Bartholomew didn't even slow down, boots and all, he kept walking on in. Bo himself was slowing down a lot. Only he felt a grip on his arm, a hold that suggested there wasn't going to be much room for discussion. They got about waist deep, at least for Bo, Brother Bartholomew was considerably taller. Then Brother Bartholomew turned back to the townsfolk, but his grip hadn't loosened even slightly.

"Brothers and sisters," Brother Bartholomew was saying, "this here is a proud day indeed for our town. You just take a look at this fine young man. When this fine young man . . . what's your name, son?"

"Bo, sir."

"When this fine young man we all know as Bo comes up from this water . . ."

Bo looked down. Where they stood it looked pretty scummy.

"When this fine young man arises from the depths, he may look the same, he may seem on the outside to be just the way he's been all these years you've been around him. But he will have had his insides *changed!* Because he's been *moved* to enter the kingdom. His past has been washed away, praise God, and his soul will be washed clean.

"Now in the name of the *Father* . . ."

Bo felt his nose being squeezed between Brother Bartholomew's thumb and finger, he felt himself being forced down into the water. Everything all of a sudden turned brown and dirty, and then he was back up into the air, sputtering, but still back in the light and the sky and the air.

"And of the *Son* . . ."

And he was going down again, only this time he'd thought it was finished and so he wasn't ready, the water came as a surprise and he jerked his head away and felt the water coming into his throat, he wasn't ready and he felt trapped, choking, needing desperately to breathe. When he came up again, he got himself prepared, he didn't know how long this was going to keep going on, but he was getting used to it, from now on he was going to be ready.

But then, just as he was going under for the third time, there was a huge commotion and a splashing on the bank, and Bo saw two horses heading toward him.

But this didn't stop Brother Bartholomew. "And of the *Holy Ghost* . . ."

He felt himself going under, once more into the gasping, the choking, the being closed in. But then there was noise and splashing all around. The water was in turmoil and a horse was suddenly between himself and Brother Bartholomew and he was being pulled out of the water and pushed back toward a second horse, one that was being led, a horse that somehow seemed to be his.

Bo blew his nose between his fingers and tried to shake the water out of his eyes.

The man on the first horse was yelling something at him. "Get a move on!" Jeremiah was saying. "We ain't got much time. Flake's not more than a half a day behind, but the son of a bitch's heading in the wrong goddam direction!"

The Border

hey were heading out fast, which wasn't bad in itself, except Bo's pants were wet, well, all of him was, but the rest didn't matter, what mattered was the pants. And going fast over ground that wasn't smooth, somewhere between prairie and hills, as though the prairie had lost its flatness or the hills the greenness of their grass. But wherever they were, wherever they were going, wet pants rubbing leather was bound to make things sore before long. And when that happened, Bo was either going to be riding a lot slower or concentrating hard on wanting to.

But then Jeremiah was riding alongside him, yelling "Put this under your behind," holding out a croker sack, not bothering to explain. And it did make things better, but on the whole, Bo couldn't see a lot of benefit in being baptized.

Jeremiah seemed intent. Once the town was behind a hill, he raised up in his saddle and looked around. "I'll tell you, Bo," he said, "the Preacher's sure good to come home to, but it is some relief to be free."

Bo didn't say anything. He wasn't sure what being with Jeremiah might make him free from. But what he did know, and he knew this for certain, he didn't have any idea at all about where he was going or why he was doing it. Jeremiah seemed to. He acted like he had some purpose in mind that included Bo. Besides, the Preacher knew what Bo needed to be doing. He hadn't tried to stop them.

Right at the moment, Bo wished that he had. Being with the Preacher wasn't exactly the same as coming home, but at least it was like being with a grown-up, somebody who might take an interest in Bo's own well-being. With Jeremiah, he couldn't be certain. Jeremiah seemed to have lots of other things on his mind.

Like riding. Not full out, not enough to run down the horses. The horses, in fact, seemed to have the best of it. Jeremiah never bothered to ask Bo if he needed a breather. But at the very moment Bo was starting to wonder about tiring the horses, Jeremiah wasn't wondering at all. He reined in and said, "They've had enough. Let's give them some rest."

So they got down and started leading. Methodical, like Jeremiah knew what was needed, like he'd been doing something similar before, having to move fast but steady.

And doing it alone, or at least with folks who weren't big on talking. Or maybe this was the way you were supposed to do it. Whatever it was they were doing. Finally, though, Bo had to ask. "Hey, Jeremiah," he said, " I hope I'm not talking too loud, but where we going and what we plan to do once we get there?"

Jeremiah didn't say anything at first. All Bo could hear was Jeremiah's horse every now and then swishing its tail, Bo couldn't figure out why, there wasn't anything to fan away, except maybe some of the darkness.

"It ain't too loud," Jeremiah's voice came drifting back, soft, high, and surprisingly clear, there wasn't much else to get in the way except the sounds of the horses' hooves and the two boys' feet hitting against the ground.

"It ain't too loud, nobody around to hear it, maybe some coyote or rattler or something that's probably just as glad knowing, so they can get out of the way.

"That ain't it," Jeremiah said. "It's just you ain't likely to understand once I try to tell you."

"Why don't you give me a try," Bo said. "It looks like we got time to spend anyway. I don't plan on getting mad and riding away, since you may be the only person in the world who knows where I'd be riding away from."

"Oh, there's others, this here's a trail all right. It's just you ain't been here before, there's no way for you to know it."

"Then how do you ever find it the first time?"

"They's ways. That's not what we was talking about.

"What we're doing," Jeremiah said after awhile, "we're going after Flake."

Bo wasn't going after Flake. He was supposed to be going after his Uncle Charley.

"Seems to me you don't know what you're going after," Miranda's voice said. "Seems to me all you're doing is going away *from.*"

"You don't worry about nothing," Rafe said. "You go on doing what you're doing. I'll take care of things back here."

"You can keep listening to those young'uns jabbering," the Preacher said, his voice sounding calm, like nothing much mattered. "It breaks up the quiet, kind of like hymn-singing. But you change directions now, you're gonna be giving up on parts of yourself you ain't even tried yet."

"Who's Flake?" Bo said. He remembered the name from back in the saloon, but that was all. "And how come he needs going after?"

"Well, as a matter of course, he don't. As a matter of course, it's him that usually does the chasing. Except every now and then he makes a mess of things that I got to straighten out."

They walked on awhile longer.

"That doesn't help," Bo said finally.

"Well, I don't know how to go about it. It ain't the sort of thing a fellow gets a lot of practice talking about."

"You sure used me for practice before."

Jeremiah didn't say anything.

"Pebbles, rocks," Bo said. "Watching you shoot dogs."

"This here," Jeremiah said, "is kind of different."

For the time, that's where Jeremiah left it. He was out there in front, Bo figured, looking straight into blackness, trying to think things through. Sometimes walking helped. Sometimes doing something you could do without putting your mind to it made the thinking through easier. There was something about the rhythms of walking, Bo had done enough plowing to know that. Of course, he hadn't been looking out into darkness, he'd been looking at the rear end of a mule.

But he could still smell it, the hot fresh-turned dirt, the sweat of the mule beside them in the shade, the breeze that hadn't seemed to be there while they were plowing. It felt good, the heat, the tiredness, everything felt good, helping his father now that he was old enough, his mother sitting there laughing, opening the lunch bucket she'd just brought with her. He could still feel it, their being together, feeling that his mother's being there was a part of the resting, part of the reward for a morning's work. He could still feel how close to everybody he was, even his little brother playing a ways off, building something with clods of dirt, then knocking them down and watching them fall.

"Ranger," Jeremiah said.

"Here?" Bo said. "Close by?"

"No. Flake. Flake's a ranger."

Bo didn't say anything.

"He's a good one, too," Jeremiah said. "It's just he sometimes gets confused. But that ain't all his fault either.

"Back twenty miles or so, prairie side of town, I turned north, he went south. He missed my trail, that ain't like him, his mind must have wandered."

"Missed your trail? Was he trying to catch up with you?"

Bo almost ran into the back of Jeremiah's horse. Because Jeremiah had stopped and was facing him, his voice was coming straight back toward Bo.

"Well, hell *yes*, he was trying to catch up with me, what the hell you *think* he was doing?"

Bo decided to be quiet. It wasn't the sort of question that was looking for an answer. Pretty soon, Jeremiah's horse started up again and Bo kept on following.

"Like I told you, Flake's a ranger, and he's a good one, except when his mind kind of wanders. So it's his job to catch me. That's the rules. He has to go on some other jobs naturally, but every time that one's done, he heads in after me again. Been doing it for a couple of years now." Jeremiah laughed softly. "Son of a bitch, damn near got close a couple of times, too."

"What's he chasing you for?"

"Cause he wants to catch me," Jeremiah said quietly.

"Then if he took a wrong turn, what're we doing riding all night so we can tell him about it?"

"Cause it's nice knowing he's back there. When he's out doing another job, I make sure I stick around kind of close, then once he's through, we can get started again."

Jeremiah's voice had started coming from higher up, so Bo mounted, too, but Jeremiah's talking hadn't slowed, it was as though he hadn't noticed any change.

"There ain't nobody else ever gone near to so much trouble, just trying to catch up with me. So I don't want nothing to happen to him."

Bo was beginning to have a hard time figuring out who was chasing who. "Like what?" he asked.

"Like them Mescan horse traders right down that trail Flake just happened by accident to get on."

"What's the problem with Mexican horse traders? Why would they cause anything to happen to Flake?"

"Because they trade somewhat different from the way some folks do. Flake might get a wrong idea, he might think, being a good ranger, he ought to look into their business habits. Worse than that, them Mescan horse traders might see him coming and it might be them that get the wrong idea and do something to him before he figures out about it."

"How do you know all this, Jeremiah?"

"Let's just say I do some horse trading myself every now and then. Let's just say me and them Mescans have had us some business dealing not that long ago, and so I got a pretty good idea where they are and how they tend to do business when they get there."

It was almost daylight when they got to a small stream, not so much running as oozing down a shallow ravine. But the horses seemed to know how to make the most of it.

"So what would Flake do if he caught up with you?"

"Just what I said, he'd try and take me in."

"Would you let him?"

"You crazy?"

"Then what would he do?"

Jeremiah grinned. "Try to shoot my ass off, I suspect."

"What would you do, would you try to shoot him?"

"You think I'd let a man try and kill me?"

"Then if the two of you both wouldn't be bothered by killing each other, why are we going through all this trouble?"

"See, Bo, I told you, there's no way you're going to understand. You're still trying to figure it out like you're back there in town. No, that ain't it, either, like you're back in your town, wherever that is. What you got to understand is, me and Flake, we're in this thing together. It's like there's a connection, and it wouldn't be playing the game right if we didn't hold up our end of it. If we quit just because he caught up with me, it'd be like playing by the rules right up till the end and then saying it wasn't worth playing in the first place. It'd be like we'd been lying all that time before. Hell, Bo, I'd lose all respect for Flake, he didn't shoot me if that was the only way of doing it. He'd feel the same about me. Except if someone's gonna kill Flake, it's got to be me, it can't be no Mescan horse traders. That wouldn't make no sense at all."

What worried Bo, he was beginning to understand.

So they rode, moving over the land like it didn't matter, like it was there just to let them get someplace else. Riding with the Preacher had been different. The Preacher had paid more attention. He may have talked like he was fighting some kind of war against it, but at the same time he gave it more respect, he seemed closer to it.

What Bo and Jeremiah were doing was riding over it. They'd been feeling the sun for awhile when Jeremiah stopped on the crest of a ridge and pointed. Bo followed the direction of his finger and saw a sliver of dust heading straight toward a solid canyon wall.

"Son of a bitch," Jeremiah said finally, pulling on his reins, jerking the head of his horse around so it could go down a path Bo hadn't even known was there. "The sorry son of a bitch is riding right into it."

Then for the first time they started riding hard, really hard, cutting a diagonal toward where the rider, Bo figured it had to be Flake, was heading. When Jeremiah reined in again, he let Bo get alongside and then jerked open Bo's saddlebag and pulled out Uncle Charley's pistol.

"You know how to use one of these things?"

Bo nodded. "Kind of," he said.

"Boy," Jeremiah said, "you are getting ready to learn."

They kept riding hard, but by the time they saw the lone horseman again, Bo knew they'd never catch him, not before he got to a pass that led, Bo could see it now, through and then out the other side of the canyon. And Bo could tell, even from where he was riding, the pass was perfect for somebody who was lying around waiting.

"Shit," was all Jeremiah said and used his spurs.

Bo didn't have any idea what was getting ready to happen. The only thing he knew was the sound of hooves and the cocoon of dust they seemed to be carrying along with them, but most of all the movement, the excitement of the race, of the just getting there. What would happen next, he'd deal with that when it happened.

Suddenly he heard gunfire. At first it seemed to be going away from them, then it was coming back in their direction. Jeremiah slowed, just long enough to take stock of what was happening.

"He's heading back this way," he shouted, "and they're coming after him."

Bo and Jeremiah were off again, but this time Jeremiah had his pistol in his hand, holding it alongside his horse's neck while he leaned over low, helping them get there faster. Bo did the same. Whatever the next thing was, it was getting ready to happen.

"Pull up!" Jeremiah yelled, and Bo followed, his horse half sliding down a shallow arroyo, but deep enough they wouldn't be noticed. When they were there and had turned back around toward whatever was passing, Jeremiah shoved his pistol into his holster. "Use your rifle," he said, pulling his out of the scabbard, sighting along its barrel.

Then they were coming, the lone horse stretching for all it was worth, its rider as low along its neck as he could get, seeming almost connected to it. The other horses weren't far behind, about half a dozen of them, their riders sitting up straight, not seeming so intent, more like they were enjoying it. But pounding away with the ends of their reins, yelling at the top of their lungs. Some of them were already shooting, but at that speed they weren't likely to hit anything except maybe themselves.

"Now!" Jeremiah shouted, and for the first time in his life, Bo tried to shoot a man. And for the first time in its life, Bo's horse felt a gun fired from off its back, and it wasn't about to wait for what was going to happen next. Bo's horse whinnied and snorted and took off like a bullet himself, but this time straight for something more familiar, like his nearest cousins.

Which happened to be ridden by Mexicans now past Bo and moving on ahead. Which of course was fine with Bo, who was pulling back mightily on his reins, trying, if he couldn't stop, at least to slow down his horse's progress. He might as well not have bothered. His horse had long since decided, whatever else might happen, whatever explosions were yet to be, he was going to be in the presence of sympathetic minds.

Bo had only thought he was going fast before. Now he was flying, heading straight for the middle of the Mexicans, and all he could do was hold on.

Somebody up ahead must have noticed. Bo saw heads turning, he was that close, he could clearly see the Mexicans craning around and acting confused.

The least Bo could do was look dangerous, so he shot his rifle, more or less pointing it straight up, over his head, which made his horse leap through the air, not even a hoof on the ground, and when he finally did touch earth, he was moving even faster.

But Bo's shot did make the Mexicans take notice. In fact, almost as though they'd practiced so they could do it like a dance, they all wheeled around to face whatever it might be that was coming up behind them.

And Bo still couldn't get his horse to stop, so he did what he'd seen Jeremiah and the man out in front do, he leaned over his horse's neck, trying to become part of it. If a gunshot had made his horse go faster before, Bo decided, now was a good time to go faster again. He was leaning over, pointing his rifle, it would be saying too much to claim he was aiming, but he was pointing the barrel, and so this time the noise was coming a lot closer to his horse's nose and so the horse thought whatever it was that had been after him before was right now just about ready to catch up.

Which was what Bo himself seemed to be doing. Except that the Mexicans were turned around now and Bo was heading straight into the bunch of them, and the closer he got the more confused they seemed to act. So Bo kept on shooting and his horse kept right on running and when it became clear he wasn't going to pull up, jump off, or get to cover, the Mexicans didn't know what to do. And when they finally decided, it was like before, like they had practiced it, wheeling around all together and heading off in the direction they'd just been coming from, only not shooting as much now and going a little bit faster.

And Bo's horse never even slowed, it still had plans to catch its distant kin. Except there was another horse coming in from the side, Bo couldn't tell exactly from where, cutting suddenly in front. Bo's horse was so surprised it couldn't decide whether to swerve out of the way or stop or jump straight up in the air, so it did some of all three, and it was all

Bo could do to stay on. But he did, and that seemed to settle his horse down, or at least make him stop. So it just stood there, trembling a little and blowing, ready to take off again as soon as it seemed practical.

The man on the new horse was just sitting, too, looking lean and used up. But right now he was mainly curious.

"What the hell?" he said matter-of-factly, like it was a real question, and did some more looking.

"Hell," he said, this time like he was answering. "You ain't much more than just a kid. Son, don't you know you could get hurt, doing stuff like that?"

Bo didn't say anything. He was still trying to catch his breath.

"Where'd you come from, anyway? And who in hell taught you how to chase Mescans?"

"Mainly my horse," Bo said, looking back toward the arroyo.

"Not that I ain't grateful. Name's Flake. What you looking around for?"

"Mine's Bo. Friend of mine. His name's Jeremiah."

"Oh," the man said, "that kind of fills in the picture. Ain't you a little young to be riding with the likes of him?"

"I don't do it regular. What I'm really doing is trying to find my uncle. Jeremiah was just kind of helping out along the way."

"There ain't many uncles these parts, not that I know of. He got a name?"

"He's called Charley."

If there was a flicker in Flake's eye, that was all. "Guess we'd best be going," was what he said.

"You hold up a minute," Bo said. "Why should I just ride off along with you?"

"Beats me," Flake said. "I never could figure why folks stayed so bothered about keeping up with Charley. Lord knows he could be an ornery cuss. But I reckon none of us could figure out a way to help it."

"You mean *you're* going to take me to my Uncle Charley?"

"Well, I wouldn't go so far as to say that. Hard to know, any given time, just where Charley keeps himself. But I reckon I could ride along with you part of the way while you're looking."

Bo still wasn't sure. He thought about Jeremiah. He'd take advice from anywhere he could get it.

"Maybe I should go see if things are all right with Jeremiah. By myself. If you don't much mind."

"You leave Jeremiah be. He done what he come here to do."

"You mean, look after you?"

Flake looked around at Bo sharply, almost as though something had bitten him. Then his eyes went back to usual, like they were staring out at something even he couldn't see yet, but he just might be the first to notice once it happened.

"Yeah," he said, "that, too."

Bo could tell by the sun they were going south. Over hills and down hills, and still there was another one ahead. But not like the ones he'd ridden over with the Preacher. Those had been heavy with green. These were white, covered with limestone, crumbly but not sharp, Bo could tell by the way his horse was walking.

The land looked dry, it sounded dry. But it wasn't. There were streams, not even that, only trickles, but most often close by, never deep or wide, but they always seemed to find low places to travel through. If there were trees, for some reason they were always on the top of hills.

Flake wasn't a lot of fun to ride with. Of course, he didn't hum like the Preacher, which in itself was a blessing. But it was like Bo wasn't there. Everything Flake did, it seemed practiced, something he didn't have to think about, and whatever it was, it was something that didn't include Bo. It wasn't that Flake was unfriendly, only his practices didn't make much allowance for somebody else.

Like whenever they stopped for water. Flake wouldn't say anything, he'd just stop and get off. His horse knew what was happening. Without any hurry at all, it would look around, sniff at the water, and start to drink.

Flake would squat down and stare into the trickle, like he was looking for something he didn't expect to find. Then he'd take off his hat and put his hand into the water like a cup, scooping and then dumping water onto a bandanna he kept wrapped over the top of his head. The bandanna could use it, it was dirty enough. Still, given Flake's general condition, Bo was pretty sure his purposes didn't have much to do with washing.

But Flake would do that a time or two, then he'd drink some himself, but only a little. Then he'd remember Bo and glance around and smile, mainly just crinkling his lips, like he really wanted to look friendly, only his face wasn't quite used to it.

So when Bo and his horse drank, they didn't waste time. Flake might forget about them and be over the next hill before he remembered. And Bo and his horse drank deeply, as though they both had a feeling that water stops weren't going to happen real often.

Bo had already decided to forget about food. But just when the sun had moved away from right overhead, Flake stopped and pulled something out of his saddlebags. He handed Bo half of it. Whatever it was looked as though it had been dead a long time.

Flake didn't say anything, just started eating. So Bo started, too. The best part, Bo figured, was it didn't taste like it looked. As a matter of fact, it didn't taste like anything at all. The worst thing was, it was almost impossible to chew. But after awhile, after they were back riding up one hill, down the other, it became kind of nice, having something to do.

They moved out of hill country, down to flat land filled with grass. Not like the plains, where you could see ground between where the grass was growing. The grass here covered like the floor of a house. They rode steadily over it, and Bo decided Flake not only didn't eat, not really, you couldn't call all that chewing really eating. He also hadn't done a whole lot of thinking about sleeping.

Then Flake pulled out his rifle. He didn't dismount, just aimed it toward some bushes where Bo could see something moving kind of raggedly, like it couldn't decide whether or not it was in a hurry.

Even after Flake shot, Bo still didn't see anything, but when they got up to whatever it was Flake had been aiming at, Bo could see that at one time it had been a turkey.

"You hungry?" Flake asked. "You ain't, we can leave this 'un here and ride on awhile longer. They's bound to be more."

Flake sounded like he was serious, so Bo didn't even answer, he got off his horse.

Flake did, too, and built a fire. Bo unsaddled the horses and hobbled them close by a stream, not just a trickle this time, but a real one, while Flake made coffee and cooked turkey.

Bo was so hungry he was eating the smell. When Flake finally said it was ready, Bo took the hunk of meat Flake gave him and ate it quicker than he'd been taught was proper. Which was a mistake. His mother must have known something she hadn't told him. Because as soon as the piece of turkey hit his mouth, Bo gagged and choked and even when he spit it out he was still coughing.

All Flake did was laugh, at least the laugh was trying to get up from his stomach and out his mouth, only Flake's face still wasn't in practice, it was like a dam holding back a river, the laugh couldn't quite get through.

"Water," was all Bo could say as he was moving toward the stream. He pushed his head in, not just his mouth, but as much of his face as he could manage. Once his mouth had cooled down, not a whole lot, but at least where it was bearable, he went back to the campfire.

Flake was still trying to laugh. "What they is," he finally managed, "what the Mescans call *chil-ee-pi-keen*, little red devils, grow down in this part of the country, them turkeys love 'em, eat as many's they can find. Most folks figure, eating them peppers, the turkey'd be too hot. Like them birds done figured out a way to keep from getting themselves shot." He bit into another hunk of meat. "But those folks is wrong," he said. "You want some more?"

Bo shook his head, but when he went back to his first piece of turkey, he took it slowly. He bit gently, and he managed all right, at least for the time. During the night, though, he did feel an occasional need to locate the bushes.

But before that, sitting around the fire, Flake got more talkative, like he hadn't been used to company and was just now thawing out. "Kind of funny," he said, looking into what was left of the campfire, "running into them Comancheros."

Bo looked confused.

"Folks call them that cause they do business with the Injuns. I been hearing they was around, that they was even doing a little business with your friend Jeremiah, one reason I was following him, hoping I'd run across me some horse thieves. And here they were, just hanging around waiting, hoping they could get rid of me. Might've done it, too, hadn't been for your tomfoolery."

He took a drink from his coffee cup. "They gonna wish they'd gotten it done."

"Why?" Bo asked, pretty sure of the answer.

"Because I know where they're heading. I hadn't planned to fool with them, not back in their home place. Except that was before they got started making things personal."

"So you're going after them?"

Flake nodded. "It'll be more or less on our way."

"Toward Uncle Charley?"

Flake shrugged. "Hard to say. But I suspect we'll run across somebody or other that might be helpful."

"So you're not going to take me to him," Bo said, not really asking, it was like he already knew. "You're only going to pass me on to somebody else."

"They should have just headed on home," Flake said. "They didn't need to make it personal. But it'll be more or less on our way."

"You know who they are?"

"Course I do. They work for a Mescan named Salazar, one of them folks that calls themselves a general and has what he says is an army. Which means he's a horse thief. He sends his cut-throating devils up here ever now and then so he can get himself enough pesos to keep on being a general down where he lives. They usually got some crazy Injuns hanging round. I don't know what they give 'em, firewater or what, but when they start coming at you, you don't rightly know what they gonna do. Truth be told, I can't figure where they was this morning.

"But folks shouldn't ought to make things personal. They was on their way home, there wasn't no need waiting around, doing things to me. But once they did get that idea, they should've done it right, they most surely should have done it right and got it over with."

"You mean you're going to cross the river?"

"How else you think I'm gonna get to them?"

"Can you do that?"

"I wouldn't have a horse that couldn't swim."

"That's not what I mean. Across the river, that's Mexico, that's another country."

"What I got," Flake said, "is a letter from the guvner of Texas that says, being a captain of the Rangers, one of my lawful jobs is getting rid of cut-throating cattle thieves. How I go about getting it done, this letter don't say a whole lot about that."

"Just us?"

"Nope. Gonna get us a troop."

He stopped as though the talking were over and it was time for sleep. But he stood up and wandered down toward the stream. When he got back, his hat was still dry, but there was water dripping from under it, down his face and the back of his neck. He was the only man Bo had ever seen getting ready to go to sleep with his hat still on his head.

Bo figured it wasn't any of his business.

"You wake up in the night," Flake said, "you see my hat ain't on, it fall off or something? You wake me up. You don't touch me, you just say something. So I can wake up and put it back on myself."

"Sure, Flake," Bo said. "I can do that."

Neither of them talked for awhile, so Bo felt they really were going to sleep this time.

"You want to know why?"

"Sure," Bo said. "I want to know why."

"What it does, it keeps the flies away, out of my head."

"You mean out of your hair?"

"Head. Ain't got no hair. You wanna see?"

Bo did what he was supposed to do and said yes.

"You wait," Flake said. "I'll get some more water, I don't want this here bandanna sticking to the top of my head."

Flake went out into the darkness and came back with water dripping again from under his hat.

"Here, boy, over by the light."

Flake squatted down by the fire and gently lifted off his hat. Then he carefully unwrapped the bandanna. What Bo saw looked mainly like raw meat that had been aging awhile. Pus was oozing here and there. In a place or two Bo thought he could see bone.

"Ugliest thing you ever seen, ain't it?" Flake said as though he still found it remarkable. "I try and keep it wet, so nothing don't stick to it."

Bo just kept on looking, but Flake didn't seem bothered.

"Well, it's a long story," he said, wrapping his head back in the bandanna, putting back on his hat, getting ready to tell it. "What it is, I been scalped."

"Happened back maybe six, seven years. I was already rangering, but I didn't have nobody to chase for awhile, so me and Si Carpenter, Ben Hood, boys that lived over near Painted Canyon, the one over by the Brazos, we were out there rounding up strays. It got lunch time, so we tied up in a pretty little place, trees, lots of shade, stream running through it. We was gonna sit a spell and eat some of the vittles Ben's wife fixed us, Si wasn't married, he'd tried a few times but nobody'd have him." Flake tried to laugh. "Lord he was homely. Been bald even when he was younger. Tried to make up for it with this scraggly beard that come out another color than his eyebrows. I mean it was like he was downright designed for staying lonely.

"Well, we was sitting there jawing, finishing off with a smoke, when right out of nowhere, there was kind of a thud and Ben let out with a yell and a mouthful of cussing and by the time our minds took it all in, there was an arrow sticking out his leg and we was already pulling him back behind a tree.

"There'd been talk of some Injuns passing through, but that's all they usually do, just pass on through. So nobody had thought much about any of 'em still being around.

"Course, we was thinking right smart about it just then. There must have been maybe a dozen of 'em, not whooping a whole lot, just going bout their business. They didn't seem to have any guns, at least not at the time, but they knew what they were supposed to be doing with them arrows.

"And us, time like that, you don't worry much bout what's gonna happen next, you're too busy figuring out what's going on at the moment and we figured we was doing okay. Ben was hurting something awful, but he could still manage a rifle. And we figured any three Texans worth their salt ought to be able to take care of a handful of redskins.

"Except about half of them devils managed to get themselves back the other side of them trees and they come up from behind us. And what we found out real soon, them was the bastards that had the rifle. And whoever it was that had it, he wasn't no expert, but he knew enough to cause damage. First thing I know, there was this explosion back of my head and a stinging in my neck and there I was lying face down on the ground. For awhile there was a kind of quietness. It didn't hurt none at all, matter of fact, I couldn't feel a thing. What I learned later, the bullet went in the back of my neck and come out my throat, didn't hit much of nothing, except it messed up some kind of nerve in there that was supposed to let me know when I ought to be hurting. So, far as I could tell, my head didn't even belong to me, I couldn't even tell it was there.

"Except I could move it. I knew it was moving because my eyes could see different things, even though I wasn't feeling it at all. And I still couldn't hear nothing. But when I turned my head sideways, I could see plenty. They must have figured I was already dead, cause them devils had rushed up around Si and Ben, about half of them tending to each, and it was right then that the hearing came back, and it was like waking up in a storm. All there was everywhere was noise, and most all of it was screaming, and it wasn't coming from the Injuns. I knew what was happening, I just hoped they'd killed them first. You couldn't be certain. It appeared like they was mean ones.

"I was hoping they'd been so busy with what they were doing, they hadn't noticed I'd done any moving. After that, I just shut my eyes and acted like I was dead. Truth be known, I wished I was, that would've made what was getting ready to happen a lot more pleasurable.

"They must have finally got finished with Ben and Si, the screaming ended kind of abruptly. They must either have finally killed them or they'd passed out. Or something. So they came over to tend to me.

"I was hoping like hell I wasn't gonna start pissing in my pants or nothing, I ain't ashamed to tell I was surely scared enough, but things were bad enough even with them figuring I was already dead.

"Which they did. They jerked my head back and saw the hole in my throat and then slammed my head back down on the ground. I spect it hurt, like I said, I couldn't feel nothing, so even when they started in on the scalping, I didn't so much as flinch. All I heard was a sound like somewhere far off there was thundering and then a tearing, like someone was ripping up cloth, maybe in the next room. And then I felt damp all over and sticky, down all over my face, and now I was truly scared. Because it might get down into my nose and start me to choking. Then they'd know, and then I'd be in trouble.

"But I was able to keep on being dead and they started taking off my clothes. And I just thought I'd been scared before, because right then I didn't know exactly what else they planned on cutting off. But the thieving devils only wanted my clothes, they didn't plan on leaving anything behind they could take along with them, and it was about then I must have passed out. When I woke up, they was gone and I figured I was still alive, at least for the time being. I was naked but I had stopped bleeding. There was blood all over and I could tell I was gonna start hurting real soon and I wasn't sure I wanted to be around when it started happening.

"First thing, I had to find out for sure. I knew what I was gonna find, but I had to do it anyway. So I dragged myself over to where they were. They were naked, too, with both their throats cut. The devils must have decided the hole in my throat had done the job good enough without their having to waste any more effort. Then I looked down at Ben's head and figured that's what mine was looking like. Si's looked fine. His head was too bald for them to bother. What they done instead was scalp his face.

"I didn't have time to feel nothing about them, not right then. What I wanted was to pass out before the hurting got good and started, so I figured while I was able I'd better drag myself over to the stream, which was useful because as soon as I got there, and it took some doing, I found out I had a terrible thirst.

"I reckon it was the hurting that made me come to. I don't know how long I'd been out, the sun was pretty low when I woke up, but I didn't rightly remember where it had been when I'd passed out. But it was the hurting that made me wake up. Like nothing I'd ever gotten close to before, like there wasn't anything else in the whole world but the hurting.

"Except there was, I could hear them buzzing. The blowflies had found me, and after they'd done that, they discovered my head and then they'd gotten downright beside themselves with joy. Because they'd found themselves a nest for their eggs that was better than they'd ever dreamed. Or at least they thought they had. You know about blowflies?"

Bo shook his head.

"It don't take them eggs long to hatch once they find a good place for laying them. They're real little, you can hardly even see them when you're looking. And what comes out is worms that like to eat, and what them worms like to eat best is meat. And at the time there was some real available.

"So what I did was pull myself over to the water and get as much of my head in it as I could without drowning myself, and when the water hit it, my head or what was left of it felt like it was gonna explode, but after awhile it didn't make any difference, it was hurting so bad a little bit more didn't much matter.

"So I was lying there, one eye kind of under the water, which was strange, like I was looking out on two different worlds, one on top and the other down underneath. And at first the world on the bottom was kind of blurry, but after awhile my underwater eye saw stuff moving around me. After all that had already happened, I didn't much care what it was, except I was curious.

"So after I got my underwater eye focused, I saw that I had laid myself down where there was a school of little bitty minnows, and once I had gotten in and got still, they'd all come back to investigate. And near's I can tell, what they did was poke around where my scalp had recently been, all the time I could feel things brushing up against it, and what folks told me later, when I had finally dragged myself to where there was people, somehow or another the top of my head was almost unnaturally clean, like it had been carefully picked through, but softer than any person, even a doctor, could have done it. So what I figure, them minnows must have saved my life. They must have nibbled away at anything up there that might have made things get worse, they must have eaten up things that probably would have finished me. Leastwhile, something must have happened, I ain't seen nobody else that's been scalped and can still talk about it.

"What Charley said once, it was like I'd risen up from the dead, naked and bloody as a baby. So maybe I ought to do something new, he said, instead of chasing horse thieves from one place to another. But I told him somebody had to do it, so it might as well be me. Besides, I know better than most people how it's supposed to be done."

Bo felt seriously mixed about changing the subject, but he had to take whatever chance he could get. "How'd you know my Uncle Charley?" he said. "What was he like when you did?"

"That ain't part of the story, which anyway is just about done. When I came to I started crawling. We'd passed a little ranch that first morning, wasn't much more than a lean-to, and it felt like it took forever to drag myself back there. Matter of fact, I don't even remember when I did it. They said they found me passed out in front of the door."

"But what about Uncle Charley?"

"Folks ask me sometimes if it hurts much, and what I tell them, I guess I'm pretty much used to it. But I got to be careful. There ain't much up there," he pointed to his hat, which was still dripping water, "that's going to help me out if I happen to fall off my horse or something. One good lick and I'm a goner. I got to be a little careful, even slapping at skeeters. Lord knows what'd happen, I fell on a rock." He made his laughing sound and then was silent. Bo looked over and saw he was staring into the campfire, at least what was left of it.

"Only thing is, I ain't told this to many folks, only thing is, sometimes when I ain't expecting it, sometimes when I'm doing other things, I get the strangest kind of dreams."

"What about, Flake, what kind?"

"Wish I could say, boy, but I don't know how to. Just strange, that's all, just strange. Charley says I ought to pay more attention. He says there might be a world in there I don't know nothing about, maybe I'm lucky I can get to it so easy. But what I told Charley, I got enough to do looking after things in front of my eyes. I can't spend too long worrying about what's going on behind them."

Then he made sure his hat was fixed firm on his head and he lay down on his blanket and before Bo could ask him anything else about Charley, Flake was snoring so loud Bo had a problem dropping off to sleep.

When Bo woke up, Flake was getting the fire back going, and the water was already dripping from underneath his hat. He fixed coffee and they ate what was left of the turkey, which Bo was getting used to, he only headed for the stream maybe once. And even then, he was able to do it slowly.

After that, they rode.

The land had changed into real cow country, where the grass wasn't just covering the ground, it was growing stirrup high. And when a breeze blew, it shimmered into waves, rolling gently, humming soft. About midmorning, Flake all of a sudden stopped and stood up in his stirrups, looking out over the flatness, listening hard.

"I think we're getting ready to find them Injuns, the ones that stick to them Comancheros," he said quietly. "I think I want to get over there to that grove of trees."

Bo hadn't even noticed, but in the direction Flake nodded was a stand of trees, looking solid against the blowing grass.

Then Bo could hear it himself, somewhere in the back of his head, or maybe just almost feel it, the nearest thing to a shaking of ground underneath them. But by then, they were off, going fast, heading for the trees.

Which turned out to be pecan trees, you didn't have to look up at the limbs, all you had to do was listen to the crunching while the horses walked over those that had fallen on the ground.

"You think they saw us?" Bo asked when they had gotten down and tied their horses.

"When you're dealing with them kind," Flake said, "you don't wonder about think. You're pretty much stuck with know."

Bo didn't ask what to do. He was just watching, getting ready to listen.

Flake pulled out his rifle. Bo did, too.

"Here they be," was all Flake said.

Bo could see them, now. About a dozen of them, circling about on their ponies, still a long way off, staying just out of rifle range.

Bo looked hard. Then he thought he'd noticed something.

"Flake?"

Flake grunted.

"They don't have rifles?"

"Nope. Them Comancheros ain't dumb. Give them red devils rifles, they'd wipe out them Mescans same as look hard."

Flake seemed to be thinking. Bo hoped he wasn't going into another of his spells of daylight dreaming.

It was hard to tell. He just might have been. He was walking back and forth slowly, making the pecans crunch underneath his boots, like that was what he was really doing, crunching pecans instead of looking out toward where the Indians were still circling and trying to decide, Bo figured, how they were going to go about killing them.

Then Flake gave what for him was a laugh and walked over to his horse and felt around in his saddlebags. He pulled out a long strip of rawhide and began cutting it into shorter pieces.

"Now what I want you to do," he said, handing Bo some rawhide, "is tie a piece of this real tight at the bottom of your sleeves, same way with your britches." Then he laughed again, only this time it was getting closer to the outside of his face.

Bo stared out at the Indians. He looked over at Flake.

"You awake?" Bo said.

Flake laughed again. He seemed the happiest Bo had seen him.

Bo took the rawhide and started tying. Flake did, too.

"You done?"

Bo nodded.

"That's good. Now start stuffing."

Then Flake started scooping up pecans and pushing them down his pants, all the way to where rawhide tied the bottoms.

Bo looked out at the Indians. He looked over at Flake. Flake was still concentrating on his pants.

Bo shrugged. Flake had found ways of staying alive a lot longer than Bo had. It was just that Bo was getting more and more curious about how he'd managed to do it.

Bo started stuffing, too.

When they'd finished with their pants, they started in on their shirts.

The Indians were off their horses. Bo thought every now and then he could see some movement in the tall grass.

"Flake, I think they're creeping up this way," he finally had to say.

"Course they are," Flake said and tried to get his rifle up to his shoulder, but he couldn't because there were too many pecans inside his shirt. So he kind of held it out in front of him and shot in the general direction Bo had just pointed. Or that's what Bo thought he had done. He must have been more careful or a whole lot lucky, because Bo heard a yell and kind of a mashing-down sound out in the grass.

"You about done?" Flake said.

Bo looked over. Flake seemed more than twice his usual size, like some kind of bulging-out monster, not just fat, huge, not even close to being human, like something out of a nightmare right after you'd eaten too much supper.

Bo looked down at himself, and figured he probably looked about the same.

"All right," Flake said, "let's do our hats. Then let's us go for a little walk."

"Out there? Where they're hiding in the grass?"

All Flake did was try to grin, then he was stuffing pecans in his hat. So that's what Bo started doing, too.

They started walking. Or at least trying to. There were so many pecans in their pants, they couldn't really bend their legs, but had to stretch them out stiff-kneed.

The Indians were a lot closer than Bo had expected. Flake was out in front, so the first arrow hit him. Bo could hear the pecans crunching where it bounced off. Flake looked around and tried to laugh.

"Keep your head down, boy," was all he said. But he pointed his rifle out in front and shot. Bo thought he heard something fall down again, somewhere out in the grass.

Bo shot a few times himself, with arrows all around him coming faster. Then the arrows stopped.

"Don't shoot for a spell," Flake yelled. "Let's just let them keep on looking. Let's just us keep on walking."

So they did. They got so close they could see Indians down in the grass, squatting there just staring, not quite knowing whether to make a rush or to turn around and run like crazy.

"Make some noise," Flake said, and started gobbling like a turkey.

Bo decided to be a crow.

The Indians decided to turn around and run like crazy.

Flake tried to laugh and reached into his shirt where the arrows had been bouncing.

"Here, boy," he said. "Let's us eat some pecans."

They rode all day, slept some of the night, then got up and kept riding. They came to a rise and Flake reined in and nodded straight ahead. Down along a narrow river, more or less nestled in a bend, there was a town. From where they were it seemed quiet and clean-looking.

But that was from where they were. Closer in, Bo could hear yells, most often sounding like curses. And back there on the rise, the wind must have been blowing some other direction. Because the closer they got to town, the more it seemed they were heading toward an outhouse. The smells were everywhere, like it was water and they were in over their heads and trying to swim through.

Back where they'd been riding, the air had smelled good, the grass had been thick and high and green. But the only street in town was cluttered with horse leavings and human trash. And the little air that was moving didn't cool the skin, it only made sand demons, whirling about in the middle of the street. Almost every store was a saloon and all of them could stand some working on.

Flake rode to the other end of town, which didn't take long, and stopped in front of an adobe hut that had thick walls and bars on the windows. "You try and stay close," was all he said and dismounted.

Inside, there wasn't much, a table with papers spread over the top and a chair behind it, the only place to sit that Bo could see. A couple of jail cells were in the back, with their doors all the way open. There was also a man lying down on the floor, over in a corner. When he saw Bo and Flake, he got up and belched.

He was a big man, tall, with his belly drooping over his belt, like it wanted to get all the way down so it could rest on the floor. He slumped into the chair and grinned. There was a dark hole in his mouth where front teeth used to be and where now some tobacco juice was dribbling out, a little way down his chin.

"Hi, there, Flake. What you doing, back in town?"

"Sorry bout bothering you, Elbert, got me some business."

"That so? Sorry to hear that. What's it gonna be this time?"

"Raising me a troop."

"That so? Sorry to hear that. What you gonna do with it, once you do that?"

"Take care of some Mescan horse thieves. Heard they was holed up, some ranch close by. Got me a letter from the guvner, gonna get rid of 'em. Once for all."

"That so? Heard something bout that ranch myself. Cept, what I heard, it might be cross the river."

"Heard that myself. Could be the same one."

"Probably not, Flake, most likely not. This one I heard about, it was across that river between us and Mexico."

"Guess you're right. Must be a different bunch."

"Probably so. Say Flake?"

"What you want, Elbert?"

"You bring your book?"

Flake went outside to his saddlebags and came back with a ragged stack of papers sewed together like a book.

"Yep," Elbert said, "you brought it."

Flake handed it to Bo. "Here, boy," he said, "can you read this?"

Bo did. It was a list of names, all of them men.

"You got any?" Flake asked when Bo was through.

"Well, hard to say, who's here, day in, day out."

"Let me change the way I was asking. You got any book folk here you want getting rid of?"

"Well, you put it that way, I did see ole Shorty Baker around little earlier this morning. Might still be, probably up at the Kick of the Mule. Could be wrong, hard to say who's around, day in day out."

Flake started to leave, and Bo turned to follow.

"Say there, Flake."

"What you want, Elbert?"

"You sure ole Johnny Foster ain't on that list? Boy, why don't you look just one more time?"

Bo did and shook his head.

Elbert shook his head, too. "That's real bad, that's a shame."

"Why you say that, Elbert? Who's Johnny Foster?"

"Fellow showed up, day or so back."

"What's he done?"

"Well, when I'm doing my rounds and stop off at the Mule, he's usually there, too, leaning on the bar, sometimes even right beside me."

"What's wrong with that, Elbert?"

"Farts. The bastard farts. Real loud, too, right there in the saloon. Real close. Where I'm trying to drink my beer. Ruins my mood. Don't smell nice, neither."

"That's a shame, Elbert. What's he done so he might get on the list for next time?"

"Hell, Flake, everybody's done something. Fella keeps farting all the while you're trying to drink your beer, he most likely done something, most likely real bad. You tell those folks back in Austin, put him in their book next time. Hell, Flake, everybody, even me and you, we all bound to done something sometime."

"I can't promise nothing, Elbert. I can't never tell what they gonna do over in Austin. But I'll see what I can do."

"Much obliged, Flake. Good luck with them Mescans."

"Flake?" Bo said when they were back on the street, standing next to their horses.

"Yeah, boy."

"I don't understand."

Flake didn't say anything, just mounted up. Bo did, too.

"The book. About the book."

Flake took off his hat and loosened his bandanna where it had been sticking.

"Goldurned guvner's idea. Got a committee up there in Austin. Every once in awhile, they send us this here book where they list folks they can agree is outlaws. Man's name in the book, we can arrest him. Hell, we can shoot his ass, he don't even have to be doing nothing at the time. But his name ain't in the book, even though everybody knows he deserves killing, maybe even worse, we can't do nothing. We got to wait till we catch him up to something."

Flake was satisfied with his bandanna. He started his horse walking up the street toward where the saloons were.

"What about the other way?" Bo asked, moving alongside him.

"What you mean? What other way?"

"If there's a name and it doesn't belong there. If somebody's made a mistake?"

"Ain't likely. Like Elbert says, most everybody been guilty of something. Them whose names ain't there, probably just lucky and ought to be grateful. Out here, we don't need no book, pretty much a waste of time, we could just pick most anybody and splatter 'em upside some wall. I spect right before they passed away, they'd have figured out why we done it, even if'en we couldn't."

Bo didn't say it very loudly, but he felt like he had to say it, not like a question, more like a fact. "It doesn't hardly seem fair."

"That's what the guvner thought. So now we got us this book."

"Yessir," the Preacher said, "it's just what I told you. You get dealt a hand and you're stuck with it. Someone else gets to write the book."

"And this here book," Rafe snickered. "It don't help much, being able to read it."

"What you need," Jeremiah said, "is knowing when to ride fast, when to slow it down. What you need to know is places you can come home to."

They dismounted outside a saloon with a sign painted over the door that made you think you were looking up the rear end of a mule. Flake pulled a shotgun out from behind his saddle.

"Here we are, boy. You leave your gun here, but you go ask if there's a Shorty Baker inside. Then you tell him there's a ranger named Flake outside and he can consider himself called."

"That's all?"

"That's gonna be enough."

When Bo got inside the door, it was like he was walking through vats of stale beer. There were about half a dozen men standing at the bar, maybe that many scattered around tables. In a couple of corners there were men stretched out snoring. Everybody that hadn't passed out was already staring at Bo before he was halfway in.

Bo cleared his throat. "I'm looking for a Mr. Shorty Baker. Does anybody know where he might be?"

A huge bear of a man straightened up at the bar. Once he stretched all the way out, he seemed almost to reach the ceiling.

"What you want, boy? What you think you want with this Shorty Baker?"

He didn't give Bo a chance to answer, just walked up and grabbed Bo by the front of his shirt. "I say what you *think* you want, cause what I *got*, you don't want no part of."

For some reason, Bo wasn't even scared. He didn't have time to think why, although it had something to do with Flake's being just outside the door. And for some reason he also didn't have time to think through, he knew he'd a whole lot rather be lined up with Flake than with Shorty Baker. Or whoever this was about to lift him off the floor.

"Are you Mr. Baker?"

"You damn right. You done found *Mister* Baker. Now what you want with him?"

He was leaning over Bo. Even with the beer smells all around, Shorty Baker's breath broke through and smelled terrible.

"I'm supposed to tell you there's a ranger outside named Flake and you're supposed to consider yourself called."

The blood in Shorty Baker's face seemed suddenly to go someplace else. He let go of Bo's shirt and started pulling his gun up and down in his holster, not like he was loosening it, getting it ready for use, but like he couldn't figure out what else to do with his hands. And all the while, he was looking around the room, moving his head back and forth in little jerks.

The men at the bar moved back away, and Bo could tell Shorty Baker was trying to decide something. Then he seemed to have made up his mind and started at a trot toward a sort of desk that was almost but not quite against a far wall. There were lots of shelves built in, like boxes in the post office back home, and Shorty Baker must have decided it was tall enough to hide behind, even for a man as tall as him.

What Bo saw right off, what Shorty Baker must have forgotten to take into account, was that the desk was tall all right, but so were its legs. And when Shorty Baker got behind it, you could still see him from the knees on down.

Right about then, Flake walked through the door carrying his shotgun. Bo started to say something, but Flake shook his head, except he wasn't just shaking it at Bo, he was looking real quick around the room. When he got to the desk, his eyes stayed fixed on it. Then his face moved like he was trying to smile.

He pulled back both levers on his shot gun and aimed it real carefully at Shorty's knees.

He fired one round and Shorty let out a yell and his legs weren't there anymore and when the rest of him showed up where his legs had just been, Flake fired the other barrel before Shorty Baker's body had even hit the floor.

"Some of you folks clean up that mess," was all Flake said and headed for the door. When he got there, before he went out, he turned back around. "Do it kind of quick. Then gather up the rest of the boys over to the store. I got business that's gonna need some help."

When they were back outside, Elbert was across the street, leaning against a porch post, picking his teeth with a broom straw. "What if it hadn't been Shorty Baker?" Bo asked while they were walking over toward him.

"Was it?" Flake answered.

"Yes. But what if it hadn't of been?"

"Then he shouldn't of been hiding behind the goddam furniture."

"Yessir," the Preacher said. "The world never gave no promises about being fair. What you need is a place to go to, where you can sit around the table out of the sun, and everybody agrees on the rules."

"That just may be, Preacher," Jeremiah said softly. "But just in case, I think I'll carry a gun."

"If you had any sense," Miranda said, "you wouldn't be where you needed to be asking such questions in the first place."

"You best head on over to the Mule," Flake told Elbert.

Elbert didn't move. "Something left for me to do?"

"Naw. Just looks good having local law around. Makes it seem more official."

Elbert straightened up and more or less dragged himself in the direction of the saloon. Flake started reloading his shotgun.

"You think there's gonna be more trouble?" Bo asked.

"How the hell should I know, boy? Round these parts, it don't pay, do too much thinking. You liable to get your ass blown off."

When they went inside the general store, a group of men was already waiting. And by their smell, Bo decided they'd all just taken a bath in beer and then pissed in their pants.

The first thing Flake did was ask for Shorty Baker's gun. Elbert handed him a gunbelt. Flake took out the pistol and threw the rest of it over to Bo. "Here you go, boy. Stuff the pistol Jeremiah gave you into that thing."

Bo was reaching out when he realized he hadn't said anything to Flake about a gun from Jeremiah. So either the hole on top of Flake's head was getting unnatural information, or things were going on that Bo didn't know about.

There had to be a connection, everybody seemed to know what was happening next, the Preacher had waited for Jeremiah, Flake knew about Uncle Charley's gun, like he wasn't just moving place to place, but he was moving from person to person. As though there was a plan, but if there was, what? And even more important, why?

But everybody was so busy Bo didn't even bother to ask. He figured nobody was going to answer him anyway. So Bo took the gunbelt and was about to put it on, except Flake shook his head. "It ain't the time, boy. Wait till you need it. Which ain't now."

Flake looked around him. "I reckon this here's enough. Okay, boys," he said, not raising his voice, "I guess you've done heard, I need me some help. I don't care where you been or what you was doing when you left there. What I care about, there's some cleaning up that needs done around here. They's some Mescans been stealing cattle, which is bad enough. But now they're starting to act like they're Injuns and take horses. A man can live without a cow, can't ride no cow. Taking a horse, that's something different."

He reached over into a barrel, took out a cracker and chewed it while he looked around the room. "I can pay you a dollar and a half a day and food. You got to use your own horse, gun, and ammunition. You got to do what I say do and you can't do what I say you ain't gonna do. And if I ain't said nothing, you can do as you please, but you fuck with me, I'll kill you.

"I'm going out for a spell," he said, "take me a little walk. When I get back, those of you interested be here ready to ride. What I mean is ready and able to ride. I don't care none about sober. All I care about, you be able to act sober. If you planning to stay drunk, you stay doing it right here, we getting ready to have other things on our minds sides drinking."

Flake brushed the cracker crumbs off his hands. "Come on, Bo," he said and walked out onto the street.

"*They're* gonna be rangers?" Bo asked.

"Yep."

"How can you tell them apart from the folks you're trying to catch?"

"They ain't Mescans."

"I know. I heard you. But I mean after you're done with the Mexicans, don't rangers catch outlaws?"

"Yep."

"Then how can you tell them apart?"

"Got me a book."

Flake put his shotgun back into its scabbard. "You look at it this way. It ain't often you get to do what you want, particularly if it's slaughtering and killing, and people thank you for it, hell, they pay you. Usually what them in there like to do, decent sorts want to throw you in jail. For folks with special needs, a place like this feels right good.

"What else you got to consider, I ain't necessarily interested in what you folks back home might call justice. I ain't even real bothered if folks break the law. Most of the laws ain't ours, anyway, they come from Austin where they're all sitting around, suitcoats and ties and fancy-smelling handkerchiefs, they don't know shit what goes on out here. If they want their kind of laws followed, let 'em come do it themselves.

"Except that ain't what I'm paid for. If two fellows wearing guns want to kill each other, if they ain't ready for it, they oughtn't be wearing guns. So long as folks keep their killing and stuff to themselves and don't bother decent folks while they're doing it, that ain't my concern. Course, Mescans and Injuns, that's different, they ain't civilized."

Bo shook his head. "That just doesn't seem like the rangering I read about back home."

"Most things ain't."

Flake went back in the store and started picking out provisions, the storekeeper and Bo sorting them into stacks and shoving them into large cloth bags. By the time they were done, a crowd of men was pushing through. Bo didn't have to look up, he could tell by the smell. Almost all of them crowded up to the counter, buying ammunition and tobacco.

They had guns everywhere, not just one or two in holsters, but stuck in their back pockets, crammed under their belts, anyplace one would fit. And where a gun wouldn't go, there was usually at least one knife. Some had them on thongs around their necks. Bo wondered they could walk, they were so loaded down.

Flake told them to line up so he could look them over. Bo moved back against the wall, and from where he was standing, if you were just looking, if you didn't know any better, it was hard to tell anybody apart, Flake or those lined up in front of him, at least in any way that was important. Bo knew who he was with, and he was glad of it. But to a stranger, looking on from the outside, it'd be a hard job choosing.

While they had been out by themselves, it was as though Flake was different. Maybe it was because a long time ago he'd stood by a stream and stared inside his own head. Or maybe it was when he was lying in the water, staring eyeball to eyeball with fishes. But now that he was back in town being a ranger, standing next to the lined-up men, it was hard right off to keep remembering the difference.

He threw out a few who were too drunk to even complain, and then he pulled a rumpled sheet of paper out of his back pocket.

"Now I know for a fact, there ain't none of you here can write."

The men looked sheepish, but they didn't say anything.

"But I suspect most of you got a name, whether it's the one your Ma and Pa gave you, that ain't my worry. But you come up here, one at a time, and tell this boy somebody's name and he'll write it down and you can put your X beside it. And if you're too drunk for putting your X, you're a mite too drunk to ride."

So that's what they did, one by one. Bo listened and did his best to get it down on paper. Most of them that had looked so mean acted like schoolkids while they made their X's, biting their tongues, working hard, trying to get it right.

When they were done, Flake took the list. "Where's old Miguel?" he said.

Elbert had come in during the signing. "What you want with old Miguel?"

"I need somebody that speaks Mescan I can trust."

"His cabin, I reckon," Elbert said. "He tends to stay out of town. When he comes in, some of these boys have a hard time telling one Mescan from another."

"Why're we going after somebody else?" Bo asked.

"Like Elbert says, it's hard to tell one Mescan from another. Course, far's I'm concerned, it don't make much difference, but them folks in Austin get bothered. So I need me somebody can tell which ones belong around here and which ones don't."

"Who's old Miguel?"

Flake tried to laugh. "Bout the only good thing them thieving Mescans ever did for me, back when he was younger. Lot younger. Miguel had a real pretty wife. Some of the thieving kind from across the border, they thought Miguel was talking too much with the sheriff. Might even be discussing some of their raids. Hell, the sheriff back then, he was just like Elbert is now, he didn't care what the Mescans do, long's they stayed out of his town. And Miguel's the type minded his own business, taking care of a few goats, tending his garden and his pretty young wife. He was the last person in the world to get involved in such stuff as that.

"Well, some of them thieving kind of Mescans got drunk one night and they rode over the border and did some things they shouldn't have done to Miguel's pretty young wife. She never quite got over it. Miguel ain't either. So he likes to go hunting ever now and then for them thieving kind of Mescans."

It was just a shack, some rock and adobe, but mostly brush that was dried, stacked, mashed together and buzzing with whatever life found it comfortable. Miguel was waiting outside when they got there. An old man, brown and wrinkled, with a mule standing close by, saddled and untied. Its only movement was an occasional twitch of its head to avoid the flies.

"I am ready," he said and got on his mule.

"Which way?" Flake asked.

Miguel pointed.

At first it was only grassland, flat, but not quite endless because there were trees, most of them scrubby, only a lot of them were tall enough to get in the way of the sky. Then Bo could tell it was becoming a road.

Flake slowed down. Miguel nodded. Soon Bo could see a man walking, coming toward them. The man paused, looked behind him, but made up his mind and kept coming. Then he thought better and left the road, going catty-cornered across the grass. Flake and his men didn't hurry. They just left the road, too, and met the man, making a half-moon around him.

Flake looked at Miguel. Miguel shrugged and got off his mule. The man, clearly a Mexican, stared at the Texans around him. Bo looked around, too, and he wasn't surprised the man was scared. Flake's rangers weren't pretty at their best, and now they were all grinning and waiting for something to happen.

Miguel walked around the man slowly, not talking, only staring. He asked a few questions in Spanish. The man was nervous when he answered.

Miguel didn't say anything else, just got back on his mule and started back to the road. Flake and his men followed.

Bo rode up beside Flake, and before he could ask, Flake just said, "He belongs around here."

"But how can you tell?"

"Can't. Miguel can. Makes it his business to know."

Travelers became more frequent. Some were going one way, some were going the other, but Miguel did the same with everybody. If the traveler wasn't walking, Miguel would tell him to get down off his horse or his mule or his cart. Then Miguel would walk around him while the rangers looked on. If it was a cart, sometimes there'd be other people, maybe a family, in it too. Bo could see fear in their eyes as they looked up at Flake's rangers and then back at their father or husband or whoever it was standing there on the ground with Miguel. Miguel would ask a few questions, get some answers. Then he'd get back on his mule.

Until the rider of the black horse. Bo could tell right off, even from a distance the black horse was different, bigger and more powerful in the haunches. It just looked prouder than the ones they had met before. That was the way the horse and the rider both came toward them, not nervous, just steady, like they owned the road at least as much as the next fellow.

When Flake and his rangers got to him, they made their usual half-moon. The rider, dressed in campesino clothes like everybody else they'd met, didn't say anything when Miguel talked to him. He simply got off the big black horse and stood there while Miguel walked around him. Then Miguel started asking more questions than usual, they started coming faster, until he wasn't even waiting for the answers. Then he became silent and looked at Flake and nodded. One of the rangers giggled.

Flake pointed to the men closest to him. The stranger's expression didn't change while he watched them get down from their horses. But what he saw couldn't have been helpful. Flake's men were all grinning wider now, and one of them who was off his horse even did a kind of square dance step and hopped up in the air. The stranger looked back at his horse and took a step toward it, but there wasn't enough time.

Flake's men grabbed him and tied his arms behind his back with a strip of rawhide. Miguel pointed to a nearby tree. The ones still on horseback rode slowly over toward it, taking the riderless horses with them. The rangers on foot followed, shoving the stranger along. The one that'd done the dance step occasionally gave him a kick in the seat of his pants. Bo could still hear somebody giggling.

Miguel took his time getting back on his mule and riding to the tree. When he got off again, he took a thick rope from his saddle and slowly unlooped it, examining it closely while it straightened out. When he was satisfied, he tied a noose in one end and put it around the stranger's neck. He threw the other end over a branch halfway up the tree. The stranger was staring straight ahead. Bo couldn't tell from his face what was going on behind it.

Miguel looked up at Flake who was still on his horse.

"Ask him where the ranch is," Flake said, "and how many men Salazar has with him."

Miguel asked him in Spanish, but the stranger just kept staring straight ahead.

Miguel looked up at Flake. Flake nodded. Miguel handed the free end of the rope to one of the rangers on foot. Miguel didn't say anything, just measured with his thumb and first finger the space of about an inch.

Two rangers pulled on the rope, raising the stranger off the ground the distance Miguel had measured. They held him there, and then Miguel nodded and they dropped him.

"Ask him again," Flake said.

The stranger still didn't answer.

They raised him again.

Then they dropped him again.

After awhile the stranger answered.

When he'd finished, Flake simply nodded to Miguel and rode away. When Bo followed him, Flake stopped and turned his horse around, facing back toward the tree.

They watched as Miguel had the men on the ground lift the stranger, almost limp by now, up on Miguel's mule, using the rope like a pulley, until they had him standing on the saddle. Then Bo could see that Miguel was saying something to him. Then he was talking to his mule. And the mule started walking slowly.

The man knew what was happening. Bo could see him trying to keep his feet on the saddle. Then on the mule's haunches, finally kicking toward the mule as it left him, as though if he could just keep contact with living flesh there still might be hope. But the mule kept going, slowly, steadily, until the man's reaching out, his kicking was not only hopeless but made things more painful. Then the man reached up, grabbing the rope above him, trying to take the strain off his neck. It worked for awhile, then his arms started getting tired. Before they had straightened out, Bo turned his horse around and started back toward the road. Flake went with him.

"You didn't need to do that," Bo said.

"I didn't. Miguel did."

"You let it happen."

"If a fellow does what I want, it wouldn't be right, not doing the same for him. It's what folks call fair trade."

Flake took off his hat and smoothed out his bandanna.

Miguel came up to them, back on his mule, leading the black horse. Flake looked over at Bo. "You want it?"

Bo shook his head.

"No reason not to," Flake said. "Better mount, I suspect, than the one you're on. Fellow over by the tree, he ain't got no use for it."

Bo glanced at the men gathering around. Then he looked back at Flake. "I reckon not," Bo said. "I like the one I've been riding. It reminds me of home."

They kept riding south. They passed more walkers but didn't bother to stop. Flake must have decided he knew all he needed to know and besides, the rangers were getting restless. Soon they were riding through small towns, nobody around but Mexicans, peaceful places, kids playing in the streets. At least at first. By the time the rangers were close, everybody got inside and stayed there, like they knew enough about Texans not to be curious.

The rangers didn't make any trouble, they were too busy getting to the river. Except when they got there, it was shallow and muddy, not much to look at even for a river. Except this one wasn't just a river. If it hadn't been there, a person wouldn't know where he was, which side was Texas, which one was Mexico.

As it turned out, Flake wasn't much interested in distinctions. He gathered his rangers around him and didn't talk loud, everybody was listening.

"Okay, rangers," he said. "I got a letter here, signed by the guvner. It says for us to get rid of cattle thieves, not even to mention throat-cutting horse thieves, that are pestering our peace-loving citizens. Now this here letter don't say nothing about crossing rivers. It don't say we ought to, it don't say we ought not. So I reckon that leaves it up to my sense of what the right thing is to do.

"Now the more I think on it, I don't see no reason a piece of water that wouldn't get your knees hardly wet, why that should stop us from getting done what the guvner of Texas wrote us to be doing. Or maybe some of you boys see the reason, it could be I've missed something."

Nobody said anything. Somebody behind Bo giggled.

"I figured you boys was about as puzzled on that as I was. Far as I can make it out, rivers is rivers. Now you boys listen. What Miguel tells me, our friend back there says Salazar's ranch is about a mile or so the other side. Says there's look-outs and lots of rifles." Flake's face made an effort to laugh. "I suspect, though, the folks holding them ain't quite so mean as some others that's close by."

The rangers near Bo didn't say anything, but they grinned.

"Now since there's more of them than us, we can't be real particular. We'll be coming in fast. Anything moves, you shoot at it."

"You mean everybody?" somebody asked.

Flake didn't even answer.

People started checking guns, loosening pistols in their holsters, making sure they could reach their rifles. Bo could tell the rangers were getting eager, they jerked their reins almost like they were mad, they couldn't sit still on their horses. It occurred to Bo, they didn't care what they were doing it for or who they were doing it to, they just wanted to go across the river and kill people.

"You want to put your gun on now?" Flake asked him.

Bo shook his head.

"You may have cause to use it."

"I've got a rifle, if things get close I can reach it."

"You rather stay back and just watch?"

Bo shook his head. "I already rode this far."

The river looked hot and thick with mud, and it only came halfway up the horses' legs when they crossed it. Nobody was hurrying, nobody was talking, but Bo could feel the tightness all around, the eagerness for letting go.

When they got to the other side, Flake held up his hand to stop them.

"Miguel," he said, "we gonna be over yonder under them cottonwood trees, case there's a passer-by. You ride on ahead and ree-co-norter. We'll be here when you get back."

So Miguel left while the rest of them waited. Even under the trees, it was hot and the flies were out. The smell of horse sweat was all around, Bo liked that. But there were other smells, too, the usual ones coming from the men, dirt, stale beer, the dried-up piss. But something else, too, something like he'd smelled back on the farm when a bull got wind of a cow just getting in heat, not something you could really describe, but you knew for sure it was there. And it was here, all around him.

Miguel came back. He and Flake talked, and then Flake motioned for the men to gather round him. "Bout a mile away," he said. "There's a couple of lookouts, but everybody else seems quiet, kind of see-ess-ting. You boys ready to ride?"

Flake didn't wait for an answer.

The ranch was a long, low adobe house with some corrals and a few outbuildings. Flake didn't say anything, just dug his spurs in and headed off at a gallop. Bo stayed close to him. Everybody else was doing the same. About halfway there, Flake reached for his revolver.

All of a sudden, there was noise everywhere. The rangers were yelling, screeching, making noises Bo hadn't even known existed, like sounds that had been trapped inside, waiting a long time to get out.

Bo felt the excitement, too, until the first shot. Then things were happening inside a haze. He knew the outside was moving fast, going by so confusingly he couldn't keep up. But inside he was swimming slowly underwater, through the heat and the cries from the buildings, some of them coming from women, a few maybe from children, Bo couldn't really tell, what with the sound of gunfire, the pounding, the galloping. And for the first time, blood.

When Uncle Charley had killed the alligator hunter, Bo had been back at the farm, he'd never seen anybody shot before, and he didn't see much of it now. Not at any one time, only a blur of spurting blood, insides exploding out the backs of people, or the fronts, depending on which way they'd been running.

It didn't take long. Flake sent men into the buildings to make sure nobody was hiding. Then after a few more shots, it was over. Miguel, in the meantime, had ridden up and was talking to Flake. Bo couldn't hear what he was saying. But he could hear when Flake turned around and spit hard, he could hear it hit the ground.

"Shit," Flake said. "Wrong goddam ranch."

He looked around. "Hey, boy, you!" Bo thought he meant him, but Flake was pointing to one of the rangers. "You ride back to town. You tell the sheriff to get a telegraph off to Austin. Tell them we're doing fine. We just ran into a little resistance on the outskirts of the ranch, but nothing we couldn't handle. What we're going to do now is take care of the ranch itself. We oughta be done and back on the other side before any guvments get involved."

The ranger looked disappointed. "I druther get some fighting done first, same to you."

"No, it ain't the same to me. I got to let the guvner know we done killed some Mescans on this side of the river. He's got to hear it from me fore he does from them, so he can have some kind of story made up to tell them."

"I still get paid the same?"

"You still get paid the same, now get the hell out of here."

Then Flake turned and talked to the whole group. "We got to get riding. I spect they done heard the shooting at the other ranch. I spect they're getting ready. So let's get on with it."

Then they were riding, traveling as fast as they could through the tall brush. Bo kept up, doing his best not to think about what they'd just done, occupying his mind with what he was already doing. As near as he could tell, nobody else had to make much effort.

The brush suddenly cleared out in front. Flake raised his arm and everybody stopped. The ranch was up ahead, looking about like the other one, except there was a low brush fence surrounding it. Nothing was moving anywhere.

Flake pulled out his rifle. He aimed it toward the middle of the fence and fired. There was a scream and some loud sobbing, and then the whole fence erupted in gunfire.

"I figured they'd be waiting," Flake yelled. "Now give them assholes some moving targets!"

The rangers started out at a gallop, leaning low, with reins in one hand and a pistol in the other, not firing yet, saving ammunition, but even above the sound of the galloping and the gunfire coming from the fence, Bo could hear the high-pitched yells, the horrendous screechings of the Texans.

Then they started shooting and Bo felt lost again in the noise, but it wasn't like before, now everything was moving impossibly fast, both inside and out. They were up to the fence, jumping over it, down beneath him he could see the frantic faces of the Mexicans, not knowing which way to run so just staying put, looking up at the Texas devils who were flying overhead.

Flake and his rangers kept going, still riding low, some of the men had pulled out fresh pistols, but they were more interested right now in not being good targets, because people inside the house had started firing.

The rangers shot back, but it was hard to tell if anything was accomplished. Then they were suddenly on the other side of the ranch, and they were out of range.

Flake looked around. "How's the damage? Everybody here?"

The man Bo had been hearing all day giggled again. "Got me a sore hand, I reckon."

He held up his left hand. A bullet had taken off his little finger. "It shore do hurt," he said while he wrapped a bandanna around it, which didn't do much to slow the spurting blood.

"Bo," Flake said, "you got any piss in you?"

"Sir?"

"I said, can you get down and take a piss. We're liable to need our canteen water."

So Bo got down and pissed. Then he did as Flake told him. He gathered up the mud made from his water and packed it over the hole where the man's finger used to be. Then he tied the handkerchief over it.

"There," Flake said when Bo was done. "Good thing it was your left hand. You're still gonna be able to shoot."

"Hell, yes," the man said. "I shore am gonna kill me some Mescans now. They gone and got me mad."

"You boys ready?"

Nobody said anything.

"Then let's go."

With another whoop, they were off. Except this time, when they were just about up to the ranch house, all of a sudden there was gunfire coming not just from in front, but every direction imaginable. Everything was terribly confused, but Bo could see Mexicans on horseback coming at them from all sides. The Texans were wheeling around, firing as fast as they could. Bo could see people dropping off, but it was hard to tell who, there were Mexicans mixed in everywhere, on horseback, lying on the ground, everybody yelling and cursing and shooting. And without any warning, Bo felt his horse falling. All he could think of was, who the hell would want to shoot my horse, it wasn't hurting anybody.

But he didn't have time to think. He was already jerking up his leg on the falling side to keep it from being caught under his horse, and without even asking for it, a picture flashed in his mind, he must have seen it in the newspaper back home or in some friend's dime novel, he wasn't allowed to read such stuff himself. But wherever he saw it, there it was, a beleaguered buffalo hunter, crouching behind his fallen horse, using it as a shield against hordes of attacking Indians.

By the time Bo and his horse hit the ground, Bo was lying flat, pushing so hard against his horse's belly he seemed to be hugging it. Bullets were flying everywhere, some getting close, but none of them hitting Bo or the horse either.

Then one got real close, almost grazing the horse's skin right over where Bo's head was hiding. The horse raised up and suddenly seemed to realize where he was and what was happening. As soon as he did, Bo's horse decided he needed to be someplace else and got shakily to his feet and scampered off to where things might be a little quieter.

So that's how Bo found himself. Lying on his side out in the open with horses galloping all around, bullets flying everywhere and kicking up dust.

But another horse was heading straight toward him. He couldn't tell who was on it, but right now that didn't seem to matter. You might as well be killed by one side as the other. But even without thinking, Bo started rolling to get out of the way. Then he noticed that a hand was pointing toward him, and it was empty, there wasn't a gun filling it. So almost out of reflex, Bo raised up to grab it, then felt himself still rising, being lifted until he was sitting on the horse's haunches, back of the saddle. And it was only then that Bo realized the rider wasn't a Texan.

They were moving fast, the dust was floating around almost solid, there were shapes darting through it, but none of them seemed to be Texan. Then he saw Flake, riding hard and yelling, telling everybody that understood English to back off, get out of the way, leave it to somebody else. Bo didn't even try to figure out what was happening, because whoever it was carrying him stopped, elbowed him off and left him standing.

He looked around. He was on an outcropping of rock, overlooking the action that was happening out front in the dust. The other Texans, at least a goodly number, were there, too, sitting on the ground or on their horses, just looking. They seemed kind of dazed.

Bo sat on the ground himself and waited. He figured sooner or later someone would tell him what was happening. All he could see out in front was a wall of dust with every now and then somebody riding through a quick clearing of air, with guns firing and the yelling, even when it wasn't meant to be words, still Bo could tell it was in Spanish.

Then Flake was sitting beside him, not talking, just sitting beside him and sucking on a blade of grass he'd found somewhere and watching what was going on inside the dust.

"Flake?"

"Well, what it is," he said, pulling his hat down tighter, "we got ourselves involved in a little civil war."

Then he stopped and pulled another piece of grass out of his shirt pocket.

"Not a real big one," he said. "Just a little bitty one."

"But who was it that grabbed me? Why did he do it?"

"Bo, son, there is lots of things you ain't ready yet to understand." Then he stopped talking, just sat there sucking his grass and looking on.

Finally, the dust started settling. Flake got up and turned around to the other Texans. "You folks get yourselves ready," he said, adjusting his holster, "just in case the wrong side might have won."

A horseman rode through a clearing in the dust. When he got a reasonable distance from them, he swept off his hat. "Señor Flake," he called out, "it is over, and justice has prevailed!"

"Come on, son," Flake said. "I want you to meet somebody."

Bo could tell that the two men were suspicious of each other, yet they also seemed friendly. Careful, but friendly. "Son," Flake said, "this here is Señor Mendez. He's the one that gave you a ride. We'll find your horse later."

"We have heard about your bravery attacking the Comancheros," Señor Mendez said. "I could not let such courage be wasted on the vermin of Héctor Salazar."

"Sorry we couldn't help out, Mendez. But my men sometimes can't tell one Mescan from the other. Probably wind up shooting everybody, which you mightn't have taken too kindly."

"Do not worry, my friend. My men are capable of handling the like of anyone who would follow Héctor Salazar."

"Well, is it finally over or did he get away again?"

"Ah, I am sad to say, that once more, at the final moment, he had the wisdom to run like the rabbit. So," Mendez shrugged, "another day."

"I got to get this boy's horse," Flake said, straightening his hat.

The dust had settled completely now, and Bo could see his horse a little ways from their rock, standing by a cottonwood tree and grazing contentedly, like he was at peace with the world. In fact, after all the gunfire and the horses, everything seemed strangely quiet. If it weren't for the dead bodies lying around, the wounded horses occasionally wheezing, it would have been like nothing much had happened.

"Don't bother," Bo told Flake. "I'll go fetch him myself."

When he brought the horse back, Flake and Mendez were talking, saying things Bo couldn't make out. They stopped once Bo got close, but Mendez seemed to look at him differently. By this time Flake was directing his attention toward his rangers, who were lying around on the ground or sitting on edges of rock and all of them staring greedily at Mendez's Mexicans.

"I suspect we'd best be going," Flake said, "before one side or the other gets restless. You want to take the boy?"

Take the boy? Without even asking if the boy wanted taking? Did everybody think he was just something they could keep handing around, as if his own opinion didn't matter? And besides, Bo was getting less and less sure about the company. Mendez shrugged, and Flake turned around to his horse. Just as he did, Bo's horse flicked its tail at a horsefly, but caught Flake's head instead.

"Shit," Flake said while he was falling, his head bouncing a couple of times on a stony edge before settling down like it had just found a pillow.

"Ah, Señor Flake," Mendez said, slowly mounting into his saddle. "He was a good man. Come. Now we must go."

"You're just going to leave him here?"

Mendez shrugged and flicked his reins.

Bo sat there on his horse. But that didn't seem to be of much use, one way or the other.

Mendez's men had emptied the corrals of Salazar's horses and cattle. The bodies were left lying as they were. Everybody seemed in a hurry to leave, but Mendez waited until Bo was alongside him. "Ah, Héctor Salazar," he said once they had started riding.

"But what about Flake?" Bo said, still looking back toward the ranch.

It was like Mendez hadn't even heard, but was still waiting, expecting him to say something else. Bo felt foolish, confused, he said the first thing that came to mind.

"So why were you fighting? Was it for the cattle?"

Mendez looked genuinely surprised. "Fighting for cattle? Who needs cattle? We took the cattle because they were there. We would look crazy if we just left them. But no. Nobody would fight for cattle when we can cross the river and get them from Texans. We would be very stupid to fight our own brothers merely for cattle."

"Then why are you doing it?"

"We will talk more of this later. Now we have another river to cross." And there was, right in front of them. Mendez rode to join several of his men by the water's edge. This river was wide, but even from a distance Bo could see shrubs that couldn't have been tall growing in the middle of it.

"It is like life," Mendez said when he came back, but he wasn't looking at Bo. His eyes were intent, studying the river.

"It looks very simple," he said. "All we must do is ride through it. But it is not simple at all. Underneath the muddy water, it is not simple at all."

Bo's horse was edging toward the water.

"No, hold him back. Underneath it is not simple at all."

He called one of his men over, and pointed upstream, saying a few words in Spanish. The man answered, pointing lower down, not too far from where they were waiting.

Mendez looked a little longer. Then he shrugged and motioned for the man to go ahead downstream.

"The sands, they shift," he said, still not looking at Bo, only at the river. "From the time we crossed this morning, maybe because we crossed, the sands will have shifted."

The cattle stopped at the water and acted unusually nervous, as though they knew something.

"They can smell it," Mendez said. "Underneath the muddy water there are sands that sink. The water is not deep. But the sands don't seem to know any bottom."

Mendez's men were urging the animals into the water, but they wouldn't go, they kept waiting at the edge. One of the men got off his horse and tied a rope around his chest. He gave the other end to the man beside him and leaped on one of the unsaddled horses. Then he rode alongside, driving the horses and cattle farther out into the river.

"We never know," Mendez said. "We cross the river all of our lives, but we never know. The sands shift. And if we make a mistake, the sands hold very tight and very, very slowly you sink." Mendez shrugged. "It is like life. Sometimes there is nothing you can do."

The animals were almost to midstream. Then they stopped. "*Madre de Dios,*" Mendez muttered, glancing upstream to where he had been pointing earlier. Then he shrugged.

The man who had ridden into the river lowered himself very gently into the water and lay as flat as he could, floating on the surface. The men on the bank pulled him back slowly to land. But the cattle and horses, once they were in the water, kept going until they were jammed against the ones in front. Then the sands caught them. The horses just stood there, trying to lift their hooves, looking around wide-eyed. But the cattle immediately began braying, long mournful sounds, flowing from the river like a continuous wave.

Mendez spoke briefly to his men, who didn't act happy about what he was saying, but seemed resigned to it. They had come prepared. Some pulled large cloth sacks out of their saddlebags. Others untied long machetes from their saddles.

Mendez now was back beside Bo. He sighed. "It is very sad," he said. "But there is nothing we can do. We cannot save them. It would be shameful to waste the meat."

The horses and cattle formed an almost solid bridge to the middle of the river. The men with the machetes walked upright across the animals' backs until they had reached the end of the bridge. Then they began cutting away flesh.

Bo had only thought the earlier sounds had been unbearable. And the river now was no longer muddy, although the horses and cattle tried with a new desperation to escape the sands.

"If they could pull free," Mendez said, "we would not mind. We do not enjoy this."

"But couldn't you at least kill them first?"

"Of course. But if they fall into the water, we lose the meat, the sands will only take them sooner, then everything is waste."

It was like a bucket brigade. The men were lined up from the shore to the farthest animals. The ones with the machetes gave the flesh to men behind them carrying sacks. The full sacks were passed backwards from hand to hand until they were piled on the bank. While the full sacks were going in one direction, empty ones were being handed in the other.

The animals, even with their sides slashed away, were still almost alive. They swayed back and forth, keeping on their feet as long as they could. Then they fell sideways into the river, into whatever space had been opened by their already collapsed neighbors, stacking up against each other, many of them still moaning as the sand caught their bodies, making the water swirl as it pulled them under.

"And you were worried," Rafe said, "about hurting their titties."

Bo ignored him. There was too much suffering outside to pay any attention.

When it was over, the men slung the full sacks over their horses' haunches, back of their saddles. The horses must have been used to it. They were skittish but followed their riders' directions. When one of the men held up a sack for him to carry, Bo shook his head and looked at Mendez.

Mendez merely shrugged.

Toward nightfall, they came to another river. But for this one, they didn't even slow down. Mendez waved, at first Bo couldn't figure out to whom or for what. Then he saw, almost hidden behind some boulders, a man with a rifle. Bo looked. There were more, behind clumps of bushes, lying lazily along the banks of shallow ravines.

"Ah," Mendez said. "We have come home."

The hacienda was behind a ring of cottonwoods, which may have been there as a windbreak, but after the morning's attack, Bo suspected there were other reasons as well. Something to get behind. To slow down horses.

"Of course, no one has ever gotten so far," Mendez said. "If someone is mistaken enough to try fighting Mendez on his own island, we simply wait for them at the river. But no one is usually so foolish. Héctor Salazar, perhaps once or twice. But the river would slow even the bravest. To which, of course, Héctor Salazar is not even close."

"Why do they have to cross the river here? Why don't they just come up from behind?"

"They could do that," Mendez said, "but it would solve nothing. It is like life. What you see and understand at one moment means that other things are outside your vision. What you cannot see, the river becomes a little drunk here. It makes bends so crazy, the river almost meets itself where it has already been. It is as though it has decided that it has come too far and now it wants to go backwards. The bend here is so great that it makes us almost an island. And what nature did not finish, Mendez and his men did. We made ourselves into an island, to get to us you must cross the river. Charley once said the only rivers I pay any attention to are the ones I make on my own. Perhaps he is right. Other rivers are more difficult to understand. But come. We are all weary."

There it was again. "Uncle Charley?" Bo said. Except Mendez had ridden ahead, and Bo was too tired to keep asking.

As they rode to the hacienda, he noticed field cannons among the cottonwoods. Mendez's home was like a fort. There were two large buildings, looking about the same from the outside. Most of the men, after they had seen to their horses, went into the largest. Mendez motioned for Bo to follow him into the other one.

He wasn't prepared for what was inside. It was the fanciest room he'd ever been in, fancier even than the lobby of the hotel back home, and bigger.

"The furniture, the chandeliers, the piano, they all come from France. There were some very tired people who brought them. Come now, let us clean ourselves, then we must eat."

An older woman dressed in black led Bo upstairs, into a high-ceilinged room with a washbasin and a large, canopied bed. Bo had never seen any of the rooms in the hotel back home, but he was pretty sure they couldn't measure up to this one.

After he'd washed and brushed off his clothes, he went back downstairs. The old woman was waiting. She led him into another room, just as fancy as the first, another chandelier, all the candles lit. The longest table Bo had ever seen was covered with all sorts of glasses and dishes. Mendez was already sitting at one end. There was a woman sitting at his side, beautiful in a way, but Bo figured from how she was sitting, back a little from the table, looking stiff and not talking, he probably wasn't going to get to know her very well.

Mendez was busy chewing, but he motioned for Bo to come sit next to him on the other side. As soon as Bo did, before he could reach for any of the plates himself, from out of nowhere there were girls about Bo's age dishing things out and pouring into his glass.

Mendez motioned for him to drink up. He did, and it wasn't awful, but for the life of him, Bo couldn't figure why anyone who hadn't just been told to would ever want to drink it.

"That also came from France," Mendez said. "We do not drink it very often, but tonight, in honor of defeating Héctor Salazar and of course, also your visit . . ."

Instead of finishing the sentence, he raised his glass and took a large swallow. Then he reached for the bottle in front of him and filled his glass. He didn't put the bottle down, but began talking rapidly in Spanish to the woman sitting next to him. She smiled tightly and shook her head. Mendez pointed with the bottle toward Bo. Bo shook his head, too.

Bo wasn't sure he'd like to eat that way every night. But there was an awful lot of food, and some of it wasn't bad. He only hoped it had gotten to the table some way different from the beef they'd probably be eating tomorrow.

After they were through, Mendez wiped his mouth and walked over and kissed the woman lightly on the top of her head. She smiled, but that was about all of her that moved.

Bo followed Mendez into the big front room. One of the girls who'd been serving Bo was in there doing the dusting. When Mendez passed her he put his arms around her and squeezed. She laughed and straightened up and squeezed back. But neither of them said anything. Mendez kept on his way to wherever he was going. The girl went back to her dusting. Bo figured it was a different sort of family.

He followed Mendez into another room, much smaller than the others he'd been in. There were leather chairs and bookcases filled with books. Mendez motioned for Bo to sit down and then filled two small glasses from a decanter on a low table between their chairs. He opened a box and held it out toward Bo. When Bo looked in the box and shook his head, Mendez took out a cigar himself and held it under his nose and inhaled deeply before he lit it. Then he sat for a moment and enjoyed the cigar, almost lost in the clouds of smoke surrounding him, seeming far away and separate.

Bo was tired, he was sleepy. What he saw when he looked into the smoke wasn't Mendez, the shapes in the clouds made other pictures. In the ones Bo was seeing, the grown-ups were all sitting on the front porch drinking lemonade, Uncle Charley and Uncle Charley's mother on the cane-bottomed chairs, both of them sitting unnaturally straight. Bo's mother was on the porch swing. There was plenty of room beside her for his father, but he was standing, leaning against one of the porch posts. Bo was playing with Davey in the front yard, not really playing, he was too old for his brother's idea of games, but Davey probably couldn't tell Bo was pretending.

It was the way a lot of Sunday afternoons had been before. Except it was different. Nobody seemed to be having any fun. The grown-ups were talking, but not acting like they were doing it because they wanted to. Bo's mother called him to go back to the kitchen and get more lemonade and when he'd come back and refilled their glasses, his mother motioned for him to sit next to her on the swing and he did. Then she put her arm around his shoulders and pulled him toward her. Only being there wasn't like it usually was. Not soft and comforting, the nearest thing to a snuggle a boy his age could allow himself. This time she felt stiff, as though she was holding him like some sort of support, almost like a protection. Except Bo couldn't tell whether it was for her or for him. But whatever it was, it wasn't anything that gave him pleasure. So he moved away and went back down into the yard and played some more with Davey.

"Well, at least you must drink," Mendez said through his cigar smoke. "The brandy also has made its way from France."

Bo took a sip. At first it seemed sweet and then it turned to fire. He managed not to gag or even cough, but he wondered what people lined their throats with so they could enjoy such stuff. Or why they wanted to. Then, just a little after it hit his stomach, he was beginning to understand.

"Ah, Héctor Salazar," Mendez said. He drew on his cigar, then sighed.

"If it wasn't for the cattle," Bo said, "then why were you fighting?"

"Ah, Bo, it goes much beyond mere fighting. That is what one does in cantinas. This was one skirmish in a war."

"A war? That was supposed to be a war? A war about what?"

Mendez shrugged and sipped his brandy. "Why must a war be about something?" He held his cigar in front of him. "Of course, with Héctor Salazar, there are reasons. He himself, actually, is the cause of it.

"When we were young, Héctor Salazar and I, we were from the same village. And though when we were boys we fought over games and then later over girls, we were still *amigos.* We even joined the same army."

"The same army? There was more than one army?"

"Naturally. If there is more than one general, there must be more than one army. Our general was General Pablo Ostrada, an animal if there ever was one, I would not wish him near the ugliest sister of even my worst enemy. But he was good to fight for. There were fine fiestas and he shared what we won."

"Won?"

"Women. Money. In our battles, in the wars."

"Oh."

"We were doing quite well. Pablo finally decided that we now ruled our own state. So we should conquer one of those next to us. And if we kept on doing well, he had dreams of one day conquering all of Mexico." Mendez raised his hands, the cigar in one, the brandy glass in the other. "Who knows? It has been done before. Even I have been close." He laughed. "At least much closer than the animal Pablo.

"So we marched into the next state. Their general was General Oscar Hernandez. Pablo should have known better. Hernandez, if he wished, could be an animal, but most of all he was a general. Besides that, he had many, many more men. Pablo had not told us that. Perhaps he had not known. But we quickly found out.

"I was with the artillery. We had only two cannons which we pulled with mules. I was in charge of one of them. Our army formed two long lines, the infantry and the artillery in front, then the cavalry with their lances in the back. We were supposed to fire our two cannon when Hernandez's men came toward us, then the infantry was supposed to charge. Then, like an angry wave, the cavalry would roll over the enemy, driving them into the ground. That was Pablo's idea of strategy.

"I was in the artillery, Héctor Salazar was behind me, about as far as you can throw a coin, in the cavalry. It was quiet, we were waiting, there was no time to get ready when we finally saw them, more men than we could imagine, and this was only the beginning of them. We had no more chance against them than a candle in a storm. They would crush us, ride over us as though we were pebbles in a courtyard. There was, of course, only one thing to do."

Mendez waited.

"What was that?" Bo asked.

"Well, of course, I turned my cannon all the way around, began shouting 'Viva Hernandez' and started firing in the other direction, which was of course where Héctor Salazar was waiting. I do not think he has ever forgiven me."

"What happened?"

"We won."

"You mean Pablo won after all?"

"Of course not. General Hernandez. I was now a soldier with General Hernandez. And then one thing led to the next, and now I am General Mendez, who has just fought a battle with General Héctor Salazar."

"But what are you fighting *for?*"

"Fighting for? To keep General Héctor Salazar from winning, of course."

"But don't you have to be fighting *for* something? So things will be different somehow if you win? How can just winning be enough?"

"Listen. It is simple. I will explain. The world is a rotten place. There is much suffering, there is great unfairness, and if I know that and do nothing, my soul will die.

"But I also know, that is the way the world is. It is not going to change because I wish it. So if I fight, and if I win? The world would still be the same. Only I would be the person in charge. And since I cannot change the world, the other people who know that it is rotten, at first they will be disappointed, then they will be angry. And so I will have to fight someone else who wants the world to be better.

"And of course I would fight. Except now it would be different. Before, I could think I was not like the others who had won and then failed. Now I would know better. A man cannot change just because he wishes it. And so I would fight, but now I would know I am pretending. Then I would die lying not only to others, but to myself. So if you win, you make everyone your enemy, even yourself.

"Charley says this is just foolishness, he says it is merely avoiding having a cause. But Charley pretends not to understand. I have a cause. I wish to avoid unhappy endings, and the only way to avoid unhappy endings is, of course, not to lose, that would be worst of all, but also not to win. It is better to live somewhere between, where endings are postponed."

"When did he tell you this? My Uncle Charley?"

Mendez held a finger in front of his face and shook it. "So. Do not ask me why I want to win. I have no such desire. But General Héctor Salazar? About him I am not sure. He may be foolish enough to wish victory, and General Héctor Salazar is not even a good man. So?" Mendez shrugged and drank. "It is my duty to frustrate his desires.

"Now." He leaned back in his chair. "I have answered your questions."

Bo could feel the brandy swirling in his head. "No sir," he said. "I need to know about my Uncle Charley."

"Ah," Mendez said. "That is a different matter."

"Different how? Why won't anybody talk to me about my Uncle Charley? I don't know any more than when I started."

"Do not be so certain. But what you ask is impossible. No, not impossible, even Charley makes mistakes in his friends. But it is unlikely. Your uncle talks very little about himself. And he picks friends for whatever reasons he chooses them. But one of the reasons, certainly not the most important, but a reason nevertheless, is that they, too, speak very little about your Uncle Charley. If a person wishes to learn about your Uncle Charley, he must find out for himself." Mendez reached again for the decanter. "But you will be leaving tomorrow in a direction I think might be helpful."

"With you?"

Mendez shook his head. "That would be unwise. Here, I am an honored man. By passing over a muddy river, I become an outlaw. It is, of course, absurd, a river is only a distance of water.

"But it is amusing. If I go too far on one side, I am in danger of losing my freedom by being thought a bandit. If I go too far in the other direction, I am in danger of losing it by becoming a hero. It is better, I think to stay where I am on the border.

"So in this, as in many things," Mendez said, "I am but an interlude." He puffed on his cigar for a moment. Then he asked, almost as if it didn't matter, "Have you been much around cattle?"

The Plains

By most folks' standards, Bo hadn't drunk terribly much the night before. But when he woke up, all of it seemed to still be in his mouth. What he wanted was a glass of cold milk, maybe some biscuits and a slice of ham. What he got was a cup of coffee and an egg covered with hot sauce. At least it made the brandy taste go away. Maybe later he could eat something to take away the hot sauce. Maybe that was why people ate in Mexico. To get rid of what they'd eaten before.

Mendez was waiting in the study. When Bo walked in, Mendez put down the book he was reading and motioned for Bo to follow. Their horses were already waiting, saddled, just outside the front door.

It was early enough not to be hot, and the air felt good while they rode through it. Bo merely followed Mendez, he didn't pay much attention to direction. That's what he'd been doing now for awhile. Not just Mendez, of course. First, there'd been the Preacher, then Jeremiah, Flake, and now it was Mendez. Wherever his Uncle Charley was, this couldn't be the shortest way to get there. There was bound to be some kind of connection, some kind of plan. Or maybe there wasn't. Maybe Charley just had an unusually large circle of friends. But Bo somehow tended to doubt it.

They didn't ride long before they got to a corral. It was fenced in by a hedge of prickly cactus, with cattle shuffling about and a man bending over a campfire inside. Bo got down and dragged the gate open, and Mendez rode through. He stopped beside the man but didn't get off his horse, only nodded toward Bo. Then Mendez rode back past Bo, out through the gate, and disappeared in the direction they'd just come from. It caught Bo by surprise. Although by this time, he found himself thinking, it probably shouldn't.

The man who was kneeling didn't look up from the branding iron he was holding in the fire.

"Close it," he said.

Bo did.

"You going to just stand there?" He looked up without smiling. Bo saw that he was Indian.

Bo caught and held the cattle while the man did the branding. And while he was holding, he tried to study the stranger, to figure out why this particular one was going to be next, to get some hint about where this one was supposed to fit in. But there wasn't the time, not even to wonder. The stranger worked quickly, Bo had to pay attention even to stay up. Quickly, but not hurriedly. He just never seemed to slow down.

Bo had seen branding irons before, except never any like this one. It looked like a straight iron rod with only a slight hook at the end, but the man used it like magic.

There were brands on the cattle already, different ones, most of them not even nearly alike. But the man took the iron and without even seeming to think, he turned them all into one of his own, an elaborate design of zigs and zags that was interesting to look at but didn't seem to mean anything at all.

Bo and the man worked without talking. The animals complained a lot, but after yesterday at the river, Bo hardly seemed to notice.

There were a lot of cattle and they worked steadily. It was into the afternoon before they were through, when the man walked unhurriedly over to the hedge and came back with a canteen and two slabs of some kind of meat. He handed one piece to Bo and then squatted down and began eating the other one. Bo had been working hard. He was hungry. He didn't care what it was.

At first the meat seemed almost as hot as Flake's turkey, but then it turned suddenly mild, bursting out with tastes Bo hadn't ever experienced before. He looked up to ask the man what it was they were eating, but before he could the man answered.

"Armadillo," he said. "I had to do a lot to it. So we could swallow it without throwing up."

Bo looked at all the cattle milling about. "But why not just eat . . ."

"Because my people need beef. I didn't come down here to take it from their mouths. Come. It's time we got started." He straightened up and headed toward the far end of the corral where his horse had been standing all day, untied, chewing every now and then on the prickly hedge.

Bo picked up the branding iron and caught up with him. The man took it from him and smiled tightly. He ran a finger along its curve. "It's called a running iron," he said. "With it you can be an artist. With any other iron, you are confined to one shape, to only one pattern. With any other, the iron controls you. With this one the shape comes from within, and most things are possible. With this one," he said, "you can become an artist." He flung the running iron into the hedge. "But then," he said, "it's always dangerous being an artist. Others don't understand. Where we are going, if they found me with this, they would more than likely kill me. Perhaps you, too. It's always been a problem, being an artist."

They herded the cattle and began driving them north toward the border. When they got to the river with the drifting sand, the man looked first at the carcasses still left swaying in the water, then made a growling sound in his throat and spat on the ground. "We should be confused," he said, "about who we call animals." He looked quickly up and down the river and pointed to a spot upstream. They crossed without trouble.

Bo had herded cattle before, only never this many. But he caught on quickly, mainly by watching the man. The man seemed to know what the cattle were going to do before the cattle were sure about it themselves. He never seemed to be in a hurry, only watching, and when a cow acted like she wanted to wander off on her own, he was already there, waiting, where she had intended to go. Bo watched, too. And before long he was seeing the signs, although he couldn't have told you what they were, only that he seemed to know.

The man noticed, too. Once when they were riding near each other he said, "You're doing well. You are learning to think like a cow. Only smarter."

"That's probably right," Rafe said. "You just stick with your cows, farm boy."

"There's things even dumber than cows," Jeremiah said softly like it was a threat.

Bo told both voices to hush, he was busy. Besides, if the Preacher had been right, it was only a matter of luck that he and Rafe and Jeremiah hadn't been each other. And although he was pleased it'd turned out the way it had, the least all of them could do was be quiet and stay friendly.

That night, Bo and the man took turns with the cattle. "You don't need to ride," he said. "Sit on your horse and listen."

Bo did. The cattle stayed lying down, stirring, grunting, but mainly sleeping. Later, the man rode out to meet him, and handed Bo another hunk of meat. It looked different, but tasted pretty much the same.

"Prairie dog," he said. "Lot harder to catch than an armadillo. Then you've got to do even more things to it."

They sat their horses together while Bo finished eating, then the man said, "Go sleep."

"What about my horse? There's nothing around for tying. Should I hobble him?"

"Hobbles." The man spat on the ground. "A horse should know that he can walk." The man handed Bo a length of rope. "Unsaddle," he said, "and tie this end to the bridle. On this end tie a knot, a big one, and bury it in the ground. If your horse pulled it straight up, it'd come out. But your horse doesn't know that. The rope is long, and he'll pull from an angle. Then he'll finally give up and eat grass."

That was all. The man turned his horse and rode away.

Maybe, Bo thought, that was what they were doing with him. Give him enough rope, just not too long, maybe he'd get tired of wandering this way and that and finally go home. But he was smarter than a cow, he was smarter than a horse, too. Sooner or later he'd learn enough so he could pull free.

When the man gave him meat the next morning, Bo didn't even think about asking, he just ate. The man seemed relaxed, as though riding night herd had calmed him.

"Excuse me," Bo said, "maybe I shouldn't ask you, but it'd be a lot easier if I knew something to call you."

The man was stretched out on the ground, leaning on his elbow. "You've got to be careful," he said. "When you've got a name for something, next thing, you think you know what to do with it. But what you need to remember, you're traveling with me for only two reasons. Not because we are friends. Only because your help is useful. And because you belong to Charley."

"I belong to Charley?"

The man stood up. "Of course. When someone cares, the other one belongs." He got back into his saddle. "I belong to Charley, too." Then he stopped and after a moment he smiled tightly. "Or maybe it's him that belongs to me." He straightened up in his stirrups like he was ready to leave. "It'd take you too long to learn, and then you'd mispronounce it anyway. Bobby Joe will do."

They crossed the border the next morning. Bobby Joe glanced over the cattle who were shuffling about, drinking in the muddy, shallow water. Then he got down and filled his canteen. "You do it, too," he said. Bo dismounted and squatted by the water.

"Don't worry about the mud," Bobby Joe said. "The earth is clean. Water, earth," he said, drinking from his canteen, "we're a part of it already. Drinking them together won't make us any more so. Or any less.

"It may look only like mud here," he said. "But it comes from mountains." He pointed upstream. "Far that way, hundreds of miles, the mud that we're drinking now was once the side of a mountain. Because it's by itself now and washed free from its neighbors doesn't make it any less the part of a mountain.

"Drink up," he said. "Enjoy the mountain."

Bo drank. It didn't taste like a mountain. It tasted like muddy water. But he thought he understood.

Except all the time Bobby Joe was talking, Bo wasn't only standing by the edge of this muddy river, he was back home, sitting on the bank of the creek that ran through the pasture behind the barn. Davey had taken off his clothes and was playing in the water, scooping up handfuls of mud and making something, Bo couldn't be sure what, but it must have fitted in with whatever Davey had in mind, since he'd been doing it awhile and didn't show any inclination to stop.

Bo was more or less staring into space, keeping an eye on Davey like he was supposed to be doing, except Davey was old enough now not to need watching and they both knew it and suspected their mother did, too.

So Bo wasn't paying much attention, it caught him by surprise when his mother and Uncle Charley walked up behind him. It didn't suprise him that she was there, when she had time she liked to walk. And it wasn't unusual for Uncle Charley to be with her. This was the summer he was helping Bo's father with the farm. But usually when two people are together, they make some kind of noise, talking or laughing, letting each other know, even if nobody else, that they're there. So Bo was surprised when out of nowhere they were standing there together.

Neither one of them said anything, but Uncle Charley stared at Davey for awhile. Then he walked, boots and all, into the creek and squatted over the shallow water. He spent a moment studying what Davey was doing with the mud. Then he reached down to the bottom and picked up a handful himself.

"I read a story once," he said quietly, which didn't surprise Bo. Even when he wasn't in the schoolroom, Uncle Charley was always talking about something he'd read, something you might want to know. And most of the time he was right, Bo did. "One of those that didn't quite make it into the Bible, but it might have. It was about Jesus when he was a little boy, just like Davey here, making shapes out of mud. Except Jesus was making little mud people. Course, maybe Davey is, too, it's hard to tell when it's not you who's doing it. But when Jesus finished, he didn't play with them much, he put them on the bank and let them play together. Then he let them go, and they ran away. And the story says that the boys and girls out there with Jesus were amazed, which makes sense. What the story doesn't say, though, what I've always wondered, is what happened to those little mud creatures after they'd run out into the world, once Jesus was done playing with them? What'd they do next?"

He stood up and let the mud he'd been holding slide off his hand, not paying any attention as it sank back shapeless into the water. "Sometimes, when folks tell a story," Uncle Charley said, "they leave the best parts out."

"You talk like Uncle Charley," Bo said.

Bobby Joe stared at Bo. Then he smiled. "To sound like a white man isn't usually a good thing. But sounding like Charley? I guess I can live with that."

"Why?"

Bobby Joe waited.

"Why do you sound so much like Uncle Charley?"

Bobby Joe smiled, but only his lips changed, not even his eyes. "That's a good question." he said. "At least it's better than why I don't sound like an Indian. So. This much. No more?"

Bo nodded.

"When I was a boy, I learned what I needed to know, not only to be one of my people but some day to lead them. Then people came whose skin seemed sick, who looked like they were strangers to the sun. And they didn't just look it. They acted that way, not just strangers, enemies, they didn't want to be something the sun shined on, they wanted to be the sun itself. Above, controlling everything beneath it, the land, the people. Me.

"I didn't want their knowledge. I didn't want that kind of power. But if they weren't going to control me, if I was going to help my people, I had to understand their knowledge, their kind of force. Even though I had already learned all I wanted to know, I still had to learn things that I'd need to know."

"You went to one of our schools."

"He was a good man. He called himself a Quaker. He came to where we were spending the winter and said we'd help each other. I would help him learn our language better. He'd help me learn his. The two of us. And we were both good students, we stayed together a long while. But he finally said he didn't have any more to teach me, I should go to something called a college. I asked him which one was the best. He said probably a place called Harvard. I asked him if I could go there. He said probably not, but that he knew people, he would see. He did. I went."

Bobby Joe got back on his horse.

"So now I know," he said when Bo was riding beside him. "Now I have knowledge I don't want, that I wouldn't need if I had lived in my grandfather's time. But if the knowledge that I do want is going to survive to my grandchildren's time, I've got to understand your people's world. I have to know how to survive in the company of strangers."

"What happened to your teacher?"

"The man who was a Quaker?"

Bo nodded.

"He was killed."

Bo looked at Bobby Joe.

Bobby Joe looked straight ahead.

"Just because we are all the same color doesn't mean we're all alike," he said, and rode off after some straying cattle.

The further they traveled from the river, the more Bo recognized semblances of a trail. By late afternoon, when they stopped beside a small stream not too far from a stand of cottonwoods, the trail was firmly fixed, clear enough for a herd of cattle to know the direction they were intended to go.

Bobby Joe pointed to another trail, less marked, but clearly there, joining the one they had been traveling. "We'll wait here," he said.

"Wait?"

Bobby Joe didn't answer.

Bo took the first shift, although Bobby Joe's eyes were open when Bo left, and Bo suspected Bobby Joe relieved him sooner than was fair. Bo wasn't going to argue. He unsaddled and was asleep as soon as his body settled on the ground.

He woke almost as quickly, surrounded by squealing, squalling, mooing, and braying. At first he thought Bobby Joe was in trouble. Except it would have taken something catastrophic to get that much noise out of a herd no bigger than theirs. But after he had jumped up, already holding his saddle and reaching for his horse blanket, he smelled fresh coffee, then he looked toward the herd, then he looked again.

Somebody had done a loaves and fishes, the way he'd read about in the Bible, only this time it was with cattle. Instead of the hundred or so he'd been with in the middle of the night, now there seemed to be thousands, and all of them stirring up a racket. And horses, some with men on top. Strangers.

Bobby Joe didn't seem bothered. He was sitting by the campfire watching coffee boil in a skillet. He poured Bo a cup, then stared back into the fire. Bo was getting ready to ask, when Bobby Joe shook his head.

Two men rode up to the edge of the camp, stopping far enough away to let Bo and Bobby Joe see who they were. Bobby Joe filled two more cups with coffee. The men got down and stretched and walked over to the fire. The tallest stranger was about as old as Bo's father, but bigger and with a face that looked like leather.

"Morning, Mr. Joe," he said when he took his coffee.

"Morning, Mr. Staples," Bobby Joe answered. Then nobody said anything, until the three of them—Bobby Joe wasn't drinking—finished their coffee.

"Beg your pardon, Mr. Joe," Mr. Staples said, "but them cattle, they look a little wet." Which meant they'd come across the river and were more than likely stolen.

"They got brands."

"Don't doubt it," Mr. Staples said. "Don't doubt it a'tall. But I suspect you already threw it away?"

Bobby Joe didn't even answer.

"This your help?"

"Yep," Bobby Joe said. "He's the one that's looking for Charley."

Mr. Staples didn't say anything for a spell.

"That so," he said finally.

"How far you going this time, Mr. Joe?" Mr. Staples said.

"Same as before."

"That's fine. You help out my bunch. My boys'll help with yours. Seems like your kinfolks don't cause so much trouble, you being along."

"Like everybody's," Bobby Joe said. "Some behave decent, some don't. Some have their reasons."

Through the afternoon other herds kept coming in. But Mr. Staples's herd didn't just have cattle, he'd brought along a chuck wagon. And toward late afternoon, that's where everybody who wasn't riding settled down.

They sat on the ground around a big campfire, eating pork and beans, cornbread, drinking black coffee. Bo felt comfortable. The cowboys were talking about earlier trail drives, about storms and river crossings and stampedes. Right in the middle of a sentence about a man-killing horse, a man said quietly, "Smith's Golden Peaches."

Then all of them, it didn't matter if they came from different ranches, they started saying all together:

Picked only from the finest trees,
Picked only at the ripest moment,
Packed only in the purest water
With just the right amount of sugar added.
We do it right
Because our customers expect it,
And we expect our customers to stay our customers.
If you have any complaints, just write
Smith's Canning Company,
St. Louis, Missouri.
Sixteen ounces.

Then the cowboys kept on talking about the man-killing horse. Bo looked over at Bobby Joe. Bobby Joe only smiled.

When the story of the man-killing horse got over, another cowboy started in about a horse that wasn't a mankiller, at least not intentionally, but he might as well have been, because he wouldn't buck you off, that would have been too easy. What he did was keep you on, but every time you bounced up in the air, he'd be coming up, too, meeting you hard when you were coming down, and so you stayed on but you weren't good for much thereafter. Then without even pausing he said quietly, "Wilson's Canned Tomatoes."

And everybody started in together:

> Packed in water and just a little vinegar.
> The right amount so you can taste
> The real tomato flavor.
> Not too much water,
> So we can give you more
> Of the best tomatoes
> You can buy in a can.
> If you hadn't opened it yourself,
> You probably wouldn't believe
> They weren't fresh.
> Wilson's Canned Produce,
> Chicago, Illinois.
> Thirty-two ounces.

Then they were quiet except the cowboy who'd been talking about the bucker. "Yessir," he said, "that horse sure had a belly full of bedsprings."

When there was a pause, a cowboy who was sitting close to Bo cleared his throat. "You got it all wrong."

Everybody looked at him.

"Wilson's Tomatoes," he said.

Several of the cowboys started talking at the same time.

"There ain't no way we got it wrong. We been sitting in the bunkhouse staring holes through them cans all winter."

"What's your problem, fella, you saying we can't read?"

"What you been doing, boy, sleeping with sheep?"

The cowboy they were all looking at got up and went to the chuck wagon. "They got them a new can," he said when he got back. "New picture," he said holding up an unopened can. "Right underneath, they done added something. See right here. It says now, right before 'packed in water,' it says 'our finest quality.' So you all got it wrong. And now," he said grinning, sitting back down, "looks to me like I've done won and you folks got a little more learning to do. So you fellas can decide amongst yourselves which one is gonna take my place riding night herd, cause it ain't gonna be me."

Bobby Joe got up and motioned for Bo to follow. "Let's take a look at our bunch one more time. They're probably not used to so much company."

All the cattle were mixed together, but Bobby Joe's were more or less in the same vicinity. Most were already lying down. He looked them over and seemed satisfied. "You've got to be careful not to let them get too close," he said. "They lie down too close together, one of them'll swish its tail, catch the next one on the nose. Get it spooked, we got us a stampede. But they look peaceful, you get some sleep. I'll see after things here for a spell."

Next morning at breakfast, Bo decided he was going to like having a chuck wagon. Not that Bobby Joe's hot sauce wasn't good. It was just nice being able to taste something else, knowing what it was you were eating by how it tasted, not just by the way it felt against your tongue. On the other hand, considering some of the things Bobby Joe put his sauce on, it might have been just as well not having to think about knowing.

After they finished breakfast, Mr. Staples called everybody round the campfire. "The herd ain't all here yet," he said. "Probably won't be till nightfall. But those folks that's going to keep them cows staying happy, you ought to be settled in.

"Now most of you already know, we're going a far piece. We got us a government contract to take this herd all the way to the Blackfoot Reservation. We're not talking about railhead here, we're gonna leave that way behind and keep going. We're talking five months, we're lucky.

"Now most of you been with me before, so you know what I'm getting ready to say. But there's a few of you signed on for the first time, you listen close. Back when I was a boy, I read about captains on ships, the big ones that went out on the ocean. I wanted to be one of them captains, because what I read, once those ships left land, that captain he was the king, he became God. Now I ain't saying this prairie's some ocean, and you ain't gonna be riding no boat. But once this drive leaves right here, there ain't but one captain and I'm it.

"What I'm saying is, I don't care what you think is fair. I don't even care what you think is right. Although you can tell me in private and if we're not in a real big hurry and your voice sounds polite, maybe I'll listen. But when I say something, you're gonna do it.

"Where we're going, there ain't no law yet. So if you can't deal with somebody telling you what to do, you just head right out there all by yourself, and you're going to be about as free as you're ever gonna get. Course, you're also gonna be about as by yourself as you've ever been. Or will be again, you get lucky and live through it.

"But you go with this herd, every step you take, all of a sudden you got law. Because you got me. And you don't like it, you got freedom, you got the freedom to get up and leave. But you do it right now. Once we start, you gonna finish. We got three thousand head and we got twelve riders not counting me, and we gonna need every last one, and we gonna need them all sober. So starting right now, you got private whiskey, get rid of it. I ain't saying we're gonna be five months without none. But when anybody drinks it, we all drink it, and I'll be bringing it in from wherever I just bought it.

"We gonna get real mad at each other at times. And some of you gonna want to take it out on somebody. And if I say it's all right, then you can beat the living skin off each other. Just so long's it's after your night herding and you both can saddle up next morning. But anybody pull a gun except me or Mr. O'Gonegal," he pointed to a stringy silent man, the one who had ridden up with Staples to their camp, "you gonna be left a long way from nowhere carrying a saddle. You keep remembering, all these horses they belong to me.

"We gonna pick out the ones you want just in a minute. But before we do, I got one more rule to lay down." He looked over at Bobby Joe. "Mr. Joe here is Indian. I ain't got no more use for Indians than most of you and I suspect I've got lot better reasons. But Mr. Joe here is our guest. He won't be with us the whole trip, but while he is, I don't want no trouble. You're gonna find he's probably the best rider in the bunch and you're gonna miss him when he's gone. I've even tried talking him into going the distance. He says he's carrying his cows up to some Indians along the way, I've told him we're heading for Indians too, it don't make no difference which Indians get what. But he don't see it that way. So what I'm saying to you. You give Mr. Joe any trouble, then it ain't his problem. It's just become yours.

"So let's get on down to business. The remuda's got enough for twelve mounts a hand. We're gonna start choosing based on how long you been riding my brand. Mr. O'Gonegal and me, we've already picked ours. So you all get a choice, then we start over again. Except I reckon it'd only be polite to let Mr. Joe get in pretty early."

Bobby Joe didn't say anything. Just shook his head so slightly that probably most people didn't see it.

"Mr. Joe says no. So we'll do it the usual way."

"What about the boy?" O'Gonegal said.

"After everybody else."

"Each turn?"

Bobby Joe shook his head again.

"Don't think so," Staples said. "After the rest of us get all done." He looked around. "Where's Smith?"

"Rounding up some strays," O'Gonegal said.

"Well, we might as well get started," Staples said. "He don't know enough about horses to help much in the choosing anyway. Make sure you boys pick at least one that looks like a swimmer."

The solid colors went first. Bo was left with a lot of paints. "Don't worry," Bobby Joe told him later. "That's white man's thinking. They think paints come from inbreeding, so they aren't good cowponies. My people use them all the time. You simply ride them a different way. I will help."

"You, boy!"

Mr. Staples was looking at him.

"Me?" Bo said.

"You see any other boy around? Come over here."

He pointed toward the herd. "Three thousand head out there," he said. "One thousand of them steers. What you reckon that says about the rest of them?"

Bo wasn't sure what kind of answer Mr. Staples wanted.

"I reckon that means the rest of them are cows," he said.

"That's right, boy. And why you reckon God made them cows?"

"I don't know, sir. Except maybe to make more of them."

"More what, boy?"

"Cows, steers, more of themselves."

"That's right, boy. Calves. Now I don't want to cause any confusion here about what your mamma and daddy taught you about God, but on this cattle drive I'm taking his place. God's, I mean, not your daddy's. And what I say is, on a cattle drive the reason God should've made cows is so we can make 'em cover distance, so we can sell 'em, so somebody else can kill 'em and then lots of other folks can eat 'em. So as far as a cattle drive's concerned, God made a real mistake when he invented calves. You get my drift, boy?"

"You don't particularly like calves."

"Well, yes and no. Can't have cattle less we got calves. But where they belong is back on the range, not on a drive. They can't keep up. Then their mammas want to drag back, stay with them, take them off the trail and hide them. Calves are fine in their place. Which ain't on a trail drive, where what cows is supposed to do is keep moving."

Bo was getting the drift more than he liked. "Mr. Staples, sir, why are you telling me this?" he said. "I mean it's something I hadn't thought much about and I appreciate learning, but why are you telling me about it? I mean, right now?"

"Well, son, everybody on a drive has got to pull some weight. And you weren't exactly born herding longhorn cattle. So what you're gonna do is ride drag. You know what that means?"

Bo shook his head.

"Talk to me, boy, don't just shake things around."

"No sir."

"It means you ride behind, even if we spread out five miles, you be sure you're behind."

"Yessir."

"But your job ain't gonna be hurrying up lazy cows. Somebody else'll be doing that. What's gonna happen once we start moving, maybe even bedded down tonight, them cows is gonna start fulfilling that other god's purpose. But the god you're talking to now, the one that's gonna be in charge of the world for the next several months, he don't need the results of that other god's purposes. You get my drift?"

"You want me to kill the calves."

"That's right, boy. Once we start moving, some of them cows gonna drop calves right in the trail. What you're gonna do is wait for them and when you find them you're gonna shoot them."

"I didn't come here to shoot calves."

"You forget where you are, boy. When I tell you to shoot calves, then the reason you came here is to shoot calves."

So that's what Bo did. On his first day as a trail hand, while the rest of them were riding herd, what Bo did was shoot calves.

But in ways a lot harder to put into words, it was different traveling with Bobby Joe. There was a lot Bobby Joe wasn't saying. But it was clear there was a place he wanted to go and he believed he had a good reason for getting there. Which was a change from the rest of Bo's most recent traveling companions.

Jeremiah, he didn't have much choice, he was running away from something. But Flake and Mendez, at first they seemed a lot different. Still, they both seemed to be moving this way and that, they didn't seem to know where they were, which side they were on when they got there. Bobby Joe at least acted like he knew where he was going and had a reason.

For the moment, though, Bobby Joe was usually up with Mr. Staples, riding point, one of them on each side of the herd. They rode a little bit behind the lead cattle, letting them think they were going where they were going because they wanted to be doing it. Most of the other cowboys were riding swing, spaced out behind Bobby Joe and Mr. Staples, far enough away from the herd so they didn't seem to be pushing, but close enough to persuade any wrong-thinking cow into staying with the crowd.

Back behind all of them was the man riding drag, and Bo could tell right off this was the worst of the regular jobs, where all the dust was and more of the work and most of the cussing. But Bo got the dust of even the drag rider. There were others even behind him, the chuck wagon and the wrangler with the remuda, the extra horses. But as far as Bo was concerned, he was the tail end.

Only the dust wasn't the main problem. Bo simply wasn't used to killing things, not if they weren't bothering the barnyard animals. And of course he'd gone hunting for things to eat. But he didn't think of that as real killing. This was.

What he did was simply ride behind and wait. It never was long before one was left behind. The mother would be standing there with the just-dropped calf, licking it a little, looking tired. Bo would get off his horse and hold his pistol to the calf's head. Bo had grown up on a farm, he wasn't particularly sentimental about animals. But he still didn't look at the mother while he was going about his job.

As soon as he'd shot, as soon as the mother sniffed around the body a bit, bawled a bit, she would usually shake her head and turn around, then make her way back to the herd. The chuck wagon would get there and the cook would look over the calf to see if it was of any use. More often than not, the cook would shake his head and move on. Then Bo would drag the body off the trail, more a courtesy to anybody following than anything else.

And right at first Sam would say something like, "It's not so bad, Bo, they can go right back into the herd, cows aren't blessed with long memories."

And Rafe would chime in, "Seems to me, farm boy, it did take you awhile and you did have to travel some distance, but you have finally found you a job that suits you."

Then the Preacher would say, "Drag it on out of the way, boy, and keep going. It don't hurt the baby none."

By and by, Bo got more used to it. It was even becoming routine. Until the time he got off and was about ready to shoot and cattle started showing up out of nowhere, charging toward him, and not out of the herd, but wild-looking creatures coming from a patch of nearby brush. They had their horns lowered and they were coming hard. Bo fired his gun in the air but that didn't even slow them. Then he shot directly at the one in front, but either he missed or he hit it in the wrong place or the cow just decided not to notice.

Bo started for his horse, but he wasn't sure he was going to make it, when all of a sudden, for the second time in the last few days, he felt himself lifted onto the back of somebody else's horse. And for the second time the hand that reached down to get him wasn't white. Only this time it wasn't brown either. This time it was black.

As soon as Bo was on horseback, the wild cattle slowed down and looked confused. The black cowboy doubled up his rope and slashed at them with it a few times, then they turned around and moved off into the brush they'd just come from.

"Thanks," Bo said and started to slide off the horse.

"I wouldn't do that just now," the man said. He wasn't a whole lot older than Bo, maybe in his twenties. He talked slow, as though he was being careful. Bo stayed on and they rode to Bo's horse, who was grazing not too far away.

"Once you hit the ground," the cowboy said, "don't be real slow getting back off it. Them things that just left, they've never seen a man who wasn't on a horse. They don't know what it is. They see something they don't know what it is, they set about getting rid of it. I reckon when they see a person riding, they think it's all the same animal and so don't bother. You get on foot, any of them wild ones around, you're liable to be in for trouble."

"I'm glad you happened to be passing by," Bo said, "but where'd you come from? I thought there was only one fellow riding drag and you're not him."

"You sure of that?"

Bo nodded.

"How come you so sure?"

"Well," Bo hesitated.

The man smiled. "I suspect because nobody said the man riding drag happened to be black. Don't you worry. I know what color I am. And you're right, I ain't riding drag. You know what the lowest job in a cow outfit is?"

"Yeah," Bo said. "Shooting calves."

"You could be right, but real close is being horse wrangler. So it makes sense that's what I got. I was back with the chuck when I saw what was happening. Reason I knew, same thing happened to me right after we got started, before you joined up. This is my first drive, too, us newcomers got to stick together."

"For a fact, it sure was convenient sticking to the back of your horse, Mr. . . ." Bo remembered that Mr. Staples had mentioned the wrangler's name when they were choosing their horses, but for the life of him he couldn't remember.

The cowboy frowned. "Some advice, boy. Out here you don't ask information. You wait and see if it's offered. And if it ain't, you learn to do without. The name's Smith."

"I'm sorry." He meant it. "I heard it said but couldn't think of it. My name's Bo. And I do appreciate your being there, Mr. Smith. I'm grateful."

The man smiled. "There ain't no 'mister,' not to somebody riding the same end of these cows as I am. The name's Smith."

A lot of the time Bo felt by himself, but there wasn't any worry, all he had to do was follow the herd. For that matter, all he had to do was be sure he kept breathing. Because if he tasted fresh air, he'd know for certain he was lost. But even if he was by himself, even without the herd, there'd be no problem. At least here where the ground was soft, where the untrampled grass was thick, the trail was like a road, packed down by the thousands of hooves that had already traveled over it. In some places, the trail was worn down so much the cowboys riding swing were high above it, as though there was a smooth dry river bed down beneath, flowing slow and steady with cattle.

Bo was down in the riverbed with them, doing his job but staying on horseback now, shooting, throwing a rope around the carcass's feet, and then dragging it out of the way. When there weren't many births, he'd help out the man riding drag, wearing a bandanna over his mouth like a mask to keep out some of the dust, riding along easy, making sure the tail end of the herd stayed part of the flow. Or sometimes he'd drift farther back and chat for a moment with Smith or help herd the spare ponies.

Smith had to stay busy with the remuda, getting horses ready for the next shift, even when the regular hands came in for their meals. But when he could, he got back in time to sit for awhile with Bo. Before long, Bo began to suspect it wasn't him Smith was trying to be friendly with. It was Bobby Joe. And Bobby Joe, for reasons of his own, wasn't being particularly helpful.

One evening after supper, it was still light and before Smith could join them, Bobby Joe motioned for Bo to follow and they walked a little ways from camp. "Look around," he said. "You notice anything different?"

Bo knew Bobby Joe wanted an answer.

"More light?"

"The land," Bobby Joe said quietly. "You noticed the land?"

"I've been riding drag," Bo said. "I've been noticing the rear end of cows. The land I'm familiar with starts off flying in the air and winds up somewhere in the bottom of my throat."

"This isn't riding drag. What do you see?"

"Dirt," Bo said. "Lots of grass."

"But what do you really see?" Bo didn't know what Bobby Joe wanted him to say, so he didn't say anything.

"I'm serious," Bobby Joe said. "Not what you know is out there. When you look, what do you see?"

Bo was confused, but he looked.

"It's the sky," he said. He was surprised he hadn't noticed it before.

Bobby Joe nodded.

Bo looked at Bobby Joe carefully to be sure he wasn't being made fun of. Bobby Joe's face stayed serious. "Keep going," he said. "Tell me about the sky."

Bo decided not to try to figure out what Bobby Joe was up to. "You look straight ahead to see it," he said. "No matter which way, it's there, not just over you, it's straight ahead."

"Yes," Bobby Joe said, not teaching, just saying it matter of fact, "here the sky isn't above us, it is all around. We're walking inside it."

"I'm used to hills," Bo said quietly, "and even if there's none of them, I'm used to having things broken up at least by trees, having things make shapes up against the sky."

"Look more carefully. That also happens here."

"You mean way off there, the buzzards."

"You notice them more here, probably because there's not much to get in the way. They're almost always around, because they know to wait, it's bound to happen. It's only a matter of who it is and where."

They walked awhile longer.

"Feel the grass," Bobby Joe said without pausing.

"What?"

"Feel the grass."

Bo started to squat on his heels.

"No. While you're moving."

They began walking again. At first Bo was aware only of the wind blowing over the flatness, and the occasional buzzing of some kind of bug. Then he heard the grass under them, the dryness, the sense that it was cracking under their feet with each step.

"It sounds different," Bo said.

"What else?"

"Back where we made up the herd, when you walked on it the grass felt soft, like it was lying down. Maybe it came up later after you passed, but right at the time it felt like it was staying down."

"And here?"

"Like it's ready to snap back up right under you."

"Does it?"

They kept walking. Bo paid attention. "Some does, some of it comes right back up."

"What else?"

"Color," Bo said. "It looks dried out. Back there, several days ago, all you could see was green. At least off the trail. When you weren't behind cows."

"What else?"

"You can see the ground."

Bobby Joe nodded. "Back there, all a cow had to do was stand and eat, move a little this way, move a little that way. Back there was standing grass. This," he motioned to the clumps in front of him, "this is traveling grass. It doesn't come to you. You have to reach for it. But once you do . . ." He squatted down. "Go ahead," he said. "Taste it."

Bo reached for a handful. But when he pulled, the grass wouldn't let go of the ground. He tried again. It still held.

Bobby Joe smiled. He didn't do it often. "It looks weak. In its dry little patches, all by itself. But don't be mistaken. It is not ready quite yet to surrender. I've even seen its roots break plowshares. It may look helpless here on the surface. But it has had to learn to live without rivers and the rain, so its strength is underground. Here," Bobby Joe broke off a blade above ground. "Taste it."

Bo did. It tasted more or less like grass.

"I know," Bobby Joe said. "It does to me, too. But there's something in it that gives cattle strength, as much, maybe more than back where it's thick, where it's green." He shrugged. "The real god of cows, not the one of trail drives, he must know something about the god of grass that we haven't gotten our hand around." He smiled again. "At least, not yet."

Bobby Joe looked back toward the camp, the trail running beside it worn into the ground, seeming as permanent as the prairie itself.

"Staples says he's home only when he's on the plains. But he doesn't mean that. If he were really on the plains, he'd be answering to a different god. What he means is when he's on the trail. That's something different. It's people like Staples that make trails, trails aren't a real part of the plains. They're only a way of bringing along what we say we've left behind."

Bobby Joe didn't talk any more, only turned and started toward camp. Bo still wasn't quite sure what Bobby Joe was up to, but while he was walking across the grass, feeling it beneath him, while he was passing through the evening air, feeling the sky all around him, Bo wasn't as confused as he might have been. The Preacher had talked about the world being more or less against you. Whatever there was outside, you needed to be on your guard, you needed to be ready to fight against it. You might not need to, but it shouldn't come as too big a surprise if you did.

Bobby Joe was saying something different. Out there on the prairie, Bo had felt a part of it, not the way Sam said she had, like something that joined up only with her emptiness. There was a different kind of connecting as well. Because when he was pulling on the grass, the strength wasn't just in the grass, it was in his arms, too, some flowing down, some rising up.

Bo couldn't say the Preacher was wrong, his leg was still too sore for that. But something had happened out there on the prairie, nothing he could exactly get into words, but it made Bo feel that the Preacher couldn't have been altogether right, either. And maybe if he paid more attention to his tasting, something might even happen there, too. But whatever he'd felt out on the prairie, once he got back to camp, it was gone.

Occasionally a town appeared more or less out of nowhere, seeming foreign and temporary, out of place, like it was only anchored for the moment in its sea of grass. The herd would pass close, but that was all. Usually Staples would leave O'Gonegal in charge while he and the cook paid a visit to replenish supplies and find out any news that might be of interest. This time he also brought back a couple bottles of Old Crow.

"Can't risk you boys getting carried away," he said. "We still got too much work ahead. But this should help you sleep through the night." He took a burnt stick out of the fire, then measured off each bottle into six parts and marked them. "Cookie, you're in charge here. Anybody gives you trouble, you send them to me. Those of you on night herd, you get yours once you come in."

The hands immediately started ragging the two cowboys who were stuck with riding the last watch, the one between two o'clock and four when sleep was always the best and night herding the worst. There wasn't any blanket to come back to, there wasn't any extra sleep stretching out ahead. Once they got done herding, it was time to begin the day. And now besides that, having to wait for their Old Crow.

"Bo and I don't need any whiskey," Bobby Joe spoke up. "We'll do the last ride."

They went to the remuda to pick horses. Night horses were special. They had to be good-natured and gentle, slow to get excited. Even so much as snorting might cause a stampede. They had to be almost able to see in the dark, so a good night horse was special. And since no one had expected Bo to ride nights, he hadn't been given one.

"Don't worry," Bobby Joe said. "There's one in my string. I'll keep the one I'm already on."

When their turn came, they rode slowly to the bedding ground. "All you do," Bobby Joe said, "is ride in a circle, not too close in, you one way, me the other. Then we can be on two sides, looking in both directions."

"Am I supposed to sing or anything?"

Bobby Joe smiled, Bo could hear it in his voice. "Probably not," he said. "You might get them stirred up. But if you start getting sleepy, use this." He reached over and handed Bo something. "Chewing tobacco. I borrowed it from the cook."

"What for? I don't chew."

"It's not for chewing. You get sleepy, chew just till there's spit, then rub some juice in your eyes."

"You serious?"

"Rub some in your eyes. It'll keep you awake."

"I don't doubt it," Bo said, and decided against getting sleepy.

The air was clear, and nights on the plains were always cool. It was never perfectly quiet, some cow was always muttering in its sleep, snorting, getting itself readjusted. But after a time that simply became background, like the sound of the wind blowing, a part of the silence.

And not knowing where it came from, Bo felt overpoweringly lonely. Like it was something coming from the outside, covering him, making it hard to breathe. And in ways he hadn't thought about before, he felt surrounded by the miles and miles of emptiness, nobody to reach out to if he needed it. And it surprised him, but he felt like way down he needed it now, at least to know he could. Maybe he'd needed it all the time, except in the daytime he didn't have to think about it. He could keep himself from knowing he needed it, since there was nobody to reach for if he did. At least nobody he could be sure would reach back.

But even in the night, especially in the night, he couldn't let himself think about that. It wouldn't do any good, it'd get in the way. There was work to be done. Even in the night there was still work to get done.

Except not much. So what there was, he made himself pay special attention to. Once or twice a cow got up and started to wander, but Bo found he didn't have to do anything. On its own, Bo's horse slowly headed it off, turning it back to the bedding ground. Only once, about halfway through his shift, without knowing it was happening, Bo started nodding. He could tell he was somewhere between being awake and asleep, but it was hard to tell which was nearest to winning, he could only feel that there was sleep all around him, slowly oozing toward the center, at any moment ready to take over, and maybe it was late at night, he couldn't tell, he'd already been asleep, but somehow now he was awake. And he saw his father standing there in the dark. Not doing anything. Just standing and looking down at Bo in his bed, probably thinking he was still asleep. And Bo didn't want to be any more awake than he already was, so he didn't let on he wasn't. And Bo's father reached out as though he was going to touch him. But he didn't, he stopped when his hand was almost there. Bo could see it not moving, stretched out in the dark. That was all Bo could remember. He must have fallen back asleep. But now Bo broke through, he was awake and out the other side of his remembering. Because he wanted to know. Right now, out riding herd in the middle of strangers, he wanted to know if his father, standing there in the dark, had finished, if he'd reached all the way, if there in the dark he'd touched him. Except now it was too late. And it wasn't fair. It mattered. He had a right to know.

And then suddenly the whole horizon seemed to light up, a sort of flickering glare that for a moment brightened the far edge of the world, like a burning seen through smoky glass. Then it was over, things were dark and back as they'd been.

Except they weren't. The cattle sounds were different, wakeful and more restless. Then there was another sound, a melody like he'd never heard, a language, if that's what it was, totally foreign, drifting across the prairie, changing it for Bo as much as the heat lightning. The cattle must have felt that way, too, because they soon settled back down. The singing stopped, but the prairie still didn't seem the same.

The next morning after breakfast, Mr. Staples called all the hands that weren't on duty around the fire. "Got some news yesterday," he said. "All the trailherds that've passed this way, they've had a little trouble, the unnatural kind. Nothing big, except everybody has lost cows. They've found the carcasses, buzzards seen to that. But seems like there was other kinds of vultures that got there first.

"What they do, they look for drifters and when they find one, they don't even take meat, just hide and tallow. Makes them loaded real light and hard to track down. If they get a dozen head from every herd that passes, by the end of the season they got themselves a wagonload. Mr. Peters, you on drag today?"

"Yessir."

"You let maybe a dozen cattle get sort of left behind. Accidental, just in case someone's watching, like you had come up front to tell me something and didn't get back quite in time."

"You're going to just *give* them some cattle?"

"I don't like wasting cows," Mr. Staples said. "Mine or anybody else's. Mr. Beauchamp."

"Yessir."

"You let the drifters fall back, maybe wander a mite. Then bring most of them on in, only let some keep drifting. Make it look natural, but I don't want to lose any more than I have to.

"Mr. Joe. You follow those leftover cows. Do it quiet-like. When somebody meets them, you come get me. Fast."

So not too much farther down the trail, Mr. Peters came riding up to point and stayed long enough for the drag to spread out, to let some of the stragglers fall behind and start drifting. Mr. Beauchamp, who was the last flank rider on one side, was watching and in a moment he started after them. But Bo could tell, even if Mr. Beauchamp looked in a hurry, he was too good a cowboy to need that much time.

When Mr. Beauchamp came back, about half a dozen head were still drifting, and Bobby Joe was drifting with them. He wasn't gone a long time.

"Find them?" Mr. Staples asked.

"Found one."

"Shoot him?"

"Wasn't my cow."

Mr. Staples nodded. "Good. O'Gonegal, Tillis, you stay with the herd. The rest of you, come with me." He turned to Bobby Joe. "All right, Mr. Joe, take us to him."

"The boy, too?"

"The boy, too. He might learn something."

Bobby Joe headed out across the prairie toward a slight rise you wouldn't notice from far off. But you did riding toward it, because even though you were covering distance, you didn't keep seeing more prairie in front, only more sky.

When they were getting close to the top of the rise, Bobby Joe stopped. He motioned for them to split up and circle. They pulled rifles out of scabbards, and nobody said anything. Nobody needed to. They rode slowly, quietly over the crest, and then they were on him. He was kneeling down beside a dead cow, but starting to turn around, looking frozen for a moment, his hand dropping a skinning knife and starting to reach for his holster, stopping on the butt of his gun. Then he let his hand fall back to his side.

The cowhands moved up slowly. When they got to a comfortable speaking distance, Mr. Staples came a little closer.

"Boy," he said. "Get down, go take a look at that brand."

Bo did, walking carefully. Up close to the man and the cow, he smelled something different, hard to put your hand on and describe. But when he thought about it later, when he remembered seeing the man's eyes, darting around, trying to find something, Bo figured for the first time he'd smelled not just being scared. He'd smelled fear.

Bo looked up and nodded.

"All right, mister," Staples said. "Here's your chance."

"I just got here myself," he said. "This was the way it was when I found it."

"And you just happened to check on the cause of death. Holding your skinning knife."

The man didn't say anything.

"Where's your friends?"

He still didn't say anything.

"They'll come looking," Staples said. "Boy, get back to your horse and get your rifle."

Bo did. "If this fellow even looks like he's taking a step I didn't tell him to," Mr. Staples said, "you send him straight on to hell where he belongs."

Mr. Staples got off his horse and walked toward the man. The others, except for Bobby Joe, did the same, making a circle around him, standing between him and the cow.

The man was looking around the circle now, his head jerking this way, then that. "Look," he said, "ain't you even gonna take me into town, put me in a jail? Ain't you gonna even give me a trial?"

"This ain't town, fella. You want town justice, you better stay there. But while we got the time," Staples said, "let me explain the kind of justice you're getting ready to get. This here is my cow. You knew it was my cow. You took it. If you had been smart enough or strong enough and could've got away with it, then it would have been your cow. But you didn't and it ain't. It don't just belong to me because I own it and got a bill of sale to prove it, it belongs to me right now because I've got more men than you and they'll do what I say and all you got is yourself.

"And what I say is killing a cow that belongs to me and then leaving his meat and bones out here to rot don't just make me mad, it makes me sick to my stomach. So when your friends come looking, I suspect they're going to feel somewhat bad themselves, they might even think longer next time somebody else's cow starts wandering. You, Matthews, Beauchamp, tie this fellow up, hands, feet, but make sure he can lie down straight.

"You, boy. You can put your rifle down, he ain't likely to do anything, the shape he's in. Come on over here."

Bo did.

"You ever do any skinning?"

The man let out a whimper.

"Don't you worry about that," Mr. Staples said. "We gonna leave your skin on. I wouldn't much care to look at your insides. Well?" He looked at Bo.

"Yessir. Squirrels, pigs, rabbits, things like that."

"Never done a cow?"

"No sir. Watched it done."

"High time you done a cow. You see where our friend has already got started working on that cow's throat?"

"Yessir."

"Well, you take his skinning knife and keep it moving on down, just stop somewhere around the middle of its belly."

Bo knelt down by the cow and put the knife in the opening that was already there. The knife was sharp, it moved easily, like it had been planned for speed.

The farther down he cut, the more of the cow's insides started spilling, blood, organs, guts, Bo had enough trouble just trying to stay out of the way, he wasn't trying for precision. When he was about to midbelly, Mr. Staples said, "That's enough, boy. Wipe your hands on the grass and get away from there.

"All right, fella, you listen, this is gonna interest you. One of these boys here is gonna take his gun and he ain't gonna hit you hard, you just ain't gonna know what's going on right afterwards. That's the reason I want to explain it to you in some detail.

"Once you're good and asleep, some of these boys is gonna take you and shove you headfirst up into that cow. And they ain't gonna stop shoving till your nose is breathing cowshit. Now what I'm real interested in, though I've got too much else to do besides staying around to find out, what I'm interested in is what's gonna happen once you get inside.

"Now I see two possibilities. Either you gonna quit breathing because your nose is shoved up against something too close, and that's okay, I wouldn't mind that. But what I'd really like if I had any choice in the matter, is for you to wake up after awhile and just lie there, all nice and comfortable, not being able to move, but knowing exactly where you are. And likely to stay there till your friends come along, whenever they do. Either way, I think they gonna get the message I'm trying to send."

It looked as if they wouldn't even have to knock the man out. He was gasping for breath, like he was trying to store it up. His face was pale and covered with sweat. Mr. Staples let him be that way for awhile. Then he motioned to Mr. Beauchamp. The stranger pulled against his ropes, although he seemed to know they weren't going to come loose. Mr. Beauchamp stood in front of him so the man could see it coming and hit him over the head with the barrel of his gun. It made a hollow-sounding thud and the man crumpled over, but he had a hard time falling because of the ropes.

"Okay, boys," Mr. Staples said, his voice calm and quiet. "Let's get it done."

Afterwards, they rode back to the trail more slowly even than they'd come. Mr. Staples was in front by himself. Back behind, the cowhands rode mainly in pairs, sometimes more. Bo was riding with Bobby Joe.

"Is that the only way to have done it?"

Bobby Joe thought for a moment. "It was one of them."

"Would you have?"

"Don't know. Probably wouldn't have thought of it."

"But if you had."

"Probably not. I suspect there're other ways."

"But you didn't say anything about them."

"Wasn't my cow."

That night, sitting around the campfire didn't feel so comfortable as usual. Once Bo got through eating, he went back to the remuda looking for Smith. He found him sitting outside his makeshift corral, a waist-high triangle of rope looped around sticks Smith kept in the chuck wagon just for that purpose. The horses could get out any time they had a notion, except they'd been around ropes too long for any such notion to come even close to their minds. But Smith was staying there anyway, just in case one of them that ought to know better decided differently.

Bo sat down alongside.

"You want to talk about what they did to that man?" Smith asked after awhile.

Bo shook his head.

"Then what you want to talk about?"

"Most anything."

"That's a lot of territory."

"Then let's talk about you. We been around each other long enough for that?"

Smith chuckled. "Boy, you're determined to get yourself killed. But I reckon we've been together long enough for me to want to." Then he stopped, like he was thinking where to start. "It's not that unusual," he said finally, but his voice was different. It was soft and had lost some of its drawl.

"What isn't?"

"My being out here. Lots of us are. You ever heard about GTT?"

"Sure. When folks from other places get in trouble and leave, people just say they've gone to Texas."

"And why do they say that?"

"I suppose people think there's not much law out here, so it's a way of going someplace and getting out of trouble."

"That's right. But it's also a way of starting over. There's not many places you can do that, begin again, get rid of what's past. Course, it's still there inside you. But as far as the outside's concerned, once you get into Texas folks kind of figure your history started about the time they just met you.

"Now, that's got its bad side. You get a lot of folks running that most of us might feel happier if somebody caught. But there's also some that's running with good reasons on their side.

"Like my kind of folks. Some of us ran away even before the war. But even those of us who didn't, who didn't start moving till the fighting was over, it didn't make any sense to stop back in your part of Texas. We might've been free on paper, the war had done that, but it wouldn't have changed the way we'd be treated, not in your part of Texas, except maybe make it even worse. So some of us had to get out here on the prairies before it started feeling free. And even here, you don't get real friendly with white folk. But you do your work and stay out of their way, most folks treat you like a man. So there's usually one or two of us on every drive. Mostly it's only a cook or a wrangler, but sometimes it's a regular hand. I'm not that unusual."

"But you said it was your first drive."

"That goes further back. You ready to listen?"

Bo nodded.

"Well, I reckon I had some hard times owed me. Up till the war, life wasn't all that bad. Both my mother's and daddy's family had lived in Philadelphia, seemed like forever. Somewhere along the line there'd been slaves, but it was so far back nobody hardly remembered.

"But none of us was ever allowed to forget what it meant to be free. My daddy was a preacher. My mother's daddy was, too, so was her granddaddy. But the main thing they all seemed to preach, staying free meant fighting for it. And they told us over and over, the best weapon we had was our learning. So my daddy and granddaddy used to almost have fights themselves about which one was the best to do the teaching. And while everybody was arguing, my mother didn't say anything, she just had my brothers and sisters and me turning the pages of our books. By the time my daddy and granddaddy reached a truce, we knew about as much they did. Or at least we thought we did.

"I was the oldest, so I was supposed to be a preacher, too. I wasn't real happy about it. I wanted my world to be bigger than a churchyard. But I suspect I'd have given in if it hadn't been for the war.

"Like I told my daddy, if I was going to tell my kids about freedom, I'd better be able to say I'd done something about it when I'd had the chance. What I didn't say, he could start one of my brothers practicing to be the preacher.

"So I found a black regiment that was being made up. I hadn't ever even held a gun, but I found out I was a fast learner, and not just from books. It didn't take long before the white men in charge decided I was 'officer material,' and made me a sergeant. That meant I could take what they told me and tell it again to everybody else.

"Our regiment did fine during the war. Starting off, our job was mainly to build and clean up things. The folks in charge didn't believe a black man wouldn't turn and run when the fighting got tough. But toward the end, they gave us a chance and we showed them. We showed them we could stand there and get killed as good as anybody.

"But that wasn't the real war for me. Mine came after that one was over. There wasn't any reason for me to leave the army. Somehow being a preacher had even less appeal than it had before. I'd tried doing instead of talking, and I liked it. I liked even more feeling needed, not just by a church of black folk, but by the whole country, whatever color they happened to be. Except after the war it was different. While it was still going on, people around us may not have liked it that we were black, but we happened to be on the same side, we were all trying to kill the same people. But after the war, that changed. We got sent to Texas.

"A lot of us went down there. Some of us to fight Indians, or to chase down outlaws, or maybe to build roads. My regiment was sent to patrol the border.

"Looking back, it seems kind of funny. Here we were trying to protect people who hated . . . that's the wrong word. They didn't hate us, we weren't human enough for that. They despised us. And here we were working to protect them from brown-skinned Mexicans who the white folk more or less stole their land from. Or when we weren't doing that, we were trying to save them from brown-skinned Indians who the white folks not only stole their land from, they were going about killing just to get them out of the way. And there I was again, like back on the plantation, still siding with what might as well have been the same white folk.

"I didn't like it, but I could live with it. Because while we were doing it, we were the army. What color our skin was didn't matter, what people saw most was the blue we were wearing. It was the between time, the off-duty time, that gave us our real troubles.

"Those same people we were keeping safe, when we'd pass them on the street, you could tell they wished they were on the other side of the street, or better yet, they could elbow us out of the way. But about all they could do was whisper 'nigger' once we got past.

"Of course, it didn't help much that somebody in their family, maybe it was even them, had just spent several years shooting at folks in our kind of uniform. And it didn't help that folks like us, folks they'd gotten used to ordering around, were wearing it. What was strange, I was still white enough inside my head to know how I'd of felt myself, if all of a sudden some field hand started telling me what to do and what was worse, I had to do it.

"I imagine they'd have been happy just forgetting all about us, so long as we kept going out on raids and getting ourselves killed for them. Or if they could've kept us out of town, quarantined us at the fort when we weren't on duty, but they couldn't do that either. What they could do was make us feel uncomfortable when we did come to town, and they managed to do that. They got real good at doing that.

"We learned we had to come in groups. A black soldier riding into town alone, it got so everybody knew he wasn't coming back. They let us find a body the first time, just to make sure we understood what was happening."

"Weren't there courts and jails? We've got them, even in Texas."

Smith laughed. "Yes, indeed, there were judges, mostly from the outside, and even if they weren't, most likely they'd sided with the North. You can figure how that set with the folks in town, don't even think about a jury. But let's say there was a judge, who was going to testify? You put everybody who wanted to shoot us in jail, you'd have to find one big enough for most everybody in town.

"So we learned to go places in groups. Now, I wouldn't say we didn't add something to the problem ourselves. Some of us been on bottom so long, I suspect they took pleasure from being in charge awhile. So there were a few of the troops that got out of hand. But most of us had spent long enough finding ways to stay alive, we went on being careful. But the troops sure didn't mind letting people see those uniforms, reminding folks about the war, who it was that won it.

"Naturally most of the trouble happened in saloons. That's when both sides got so they didn't think so well as they might have. One night, it was after a patrol chasing Mexican horse thieves that we almost caught but didn't, when we got back to the fort some of the men wanted to go into town. There were enough of them and one, a man named Carrol, was the careful type. He'd see to it that nobody got into unnecessary trouble.

"I wasn't there. But I could piece it together later. They all drank awhile, then some got tired and wanted to go back to the fort. Others didn't, and I suspect Carrol tried to talk everybody into either going or staying, only it didn't do any good. So Carrol looked around the saloon. It seemed peaceful enough. And if he stayed, there'd be four of them, he figured that ought to be enough.

"So some left, some stayed. And just about when even those were ready to go, this group of cowboys who'd been drinking somewhere else, a lot more than they should have, came bursting through the door.

"And I wasn't there, but I have been enough other times, I can hear it pretty well. The cowboys walked in and saw who was standing at the bar. And one of them said, 'Well, lookey who we got here,' and grinned. Then the rest of them, they grinned, too.

"That's the way it would start. Somebody'd say something like, 'Bartender, I sure hope you ain't letting none of them niggers drink out of the bottle. I might be pouring out of it next and God knows what might happen to my mouth. Hell,' he'd say, 'maybe even my hand.' And my men at the bar probably wouldn't say anything.

"Then another white man would keep it going. 'Course, if they did,' he'd say, 'ought to make the next drink from the bottle a lot cheaper.' 'Cheaper, hell,' somebody would say. 'Bartender'd have to pay somebody to take it.' 'Yeah,' another one would answer. 'Get better money for bottled piss.' 'Well, that depends.' 'Depends on what, Sam?' 'Depends on whether it's white piss.' And then they'd all laugh.

"But my men would just stand there, facing the bar, acting like they didn't hear. So the cowboys would start in on something else. 'Them sure are pretty uniforms, don't you think so, Joe?' 'Yeah, right pretty. Sure is a shame weren't more niggers wearing them during the war.' 'How's that, Jim?' 'Hell, Sam, if we could've fought more niggers, we'd have just won that thing.' And on it would go. And Carrol would be looking at the faces in the mirror behind the bar, looking real careful, making sure none of our men was thinking about doing something stupid.

"And when Carrol felt they'd stayed long enough so it wouldn't look like they were being chased out, he would turn to the other soldiers and say something like, 'Well, gentlemen, that's enough pleasure for the evening. We've got a job to do in the morning.' And then, without so much as turning to the cowboys, who'd be sitting at tables behind them, they'd head for the door.

"And then one of the cowboys would say in a kind of quiet voice, 'Hey, nigger, don't you turn your back on me.' Then louder. 'Hey, nigger boy, you hear me? You turn around, face me when I'm talking to you. You turn around and face me or I'm going to teach you some goddam manners about how you act around white people.'

"And then one of the cowboys, probably one who was drunkest, would say, 'Why don't we do that, do it right now?' And he would pull a gun and try to shoot at the floor beside the soldiers as they walked toward the door. But he'd be too drunk and instead of the floor, he'd hit one of our men in the foot.

"My man would have yelled. I would have, you'd have done it, too. But things were tense, there was a gunshot, there was a scream, and all of a sudden when Carrol and the men turned around, reaching without thinking for their guns, the cowboys were already shooting.

"One of my men got away, got back to the fort. He was shot up pretty bad, but he lived. When the cowboys were tried, the bartender testified that the trooper's being shot was an accident, and then the cowboys were only acting in self-defense because my men were going for their guns. All of them got off, free and white like the day they were born.

"So we waited awhile, till some of the tension wore off. Then about a dozen of us rode into town. There was room at the bar, and we stood there. Real soon there was even more room at the bar, because everyone else had left.

"Then it started again. The usual sort of baiting. Maybe it was even some of the same ones that shot Carrol and the men, I didn't know, I didn't care. I was looking in my men's eyes in the mirror, too, and although it looked like they were paying attention to drinking, they were really looking at me. And every one of them was drinking with his left hand, I'm surprised none of the cowboys noticed. I suppose they were having too much fun.

"When I nodded, we turned and started firing. When we finished there were only three of us left. There weren't any of them.

"We knew what it meant. All of us had our horses packed and waiting. If we were anywhere close to there by morning, we knew we were going to be just as dead as those folk in the saloon, only their friends would make sure it'd take us a whole lot longer getting that way.

"We all rode together for an hour or so, just in case something happened and we needed the firepower. Then we stopped and doctored each other, changed clothes and split up. The last thing we wanted was for somebody to spot three black soldiers riding together. As far as that went, it wasn't going to be too comfortable now for any black man, not just one of us, to be seen in a uniform. But we all figured it couldn't be much worse than it was before. Might even be better. I suspect it was going to be quieter in a lot of bars, at least for a time.

"Anyway, I rode for awhile. For a long while. Then I became somebody named Smith. Out here, your name gets to be whatever it is you want to call yourself. And for about the first time in my life, I realized the advantages of white folk not being able to tell one nigger from another. And then I became a cowboy." Smith grinned. "Or at least a horse wrangler. Which is almost the same thing."

He stood up and looked down at Bo. "Now, boy, you know why out here it ain't polite, asking personal questions."

"How about just one more?"

"Boy, you just trying to get yourself killed?"

Bo shook his head. "Where you going? Nothing specific, only kind of in general."

"Hard to say, Indian country maybe. I think I'd probably feel comfortable there. I didn't know it back when I was chasing them, but us and the Indians, we have a lot in common. Maybe I'll try that."

"Why not stay on the range? You're free enough here."

"I've considered it. But you look around. Out here, there ain't many of nobody. But of those that is, how many black folk you see? Back there at the campfire, how many black, how many white? When I sit down back there, I'm not Smith. I can't even be a name that's not mine, I'm just the nigger. Even sitting right here, away from anything, there's as many of you as there is of me."

Bo felt awkward. He'd never thought of himself as a "them." But it crossed his mind, he'd never had to before.

"I'm learning, Bo," Smith was still talking. "These people around me, they're not my kind and I sure as hell don't want to be theirs."

And Bo wanted to say, "But I'm not either. Where am I anyway? Back there at the chuck or out here by the remuda?" But he didn't know how to say it. And looking at Smith's face, hearing the seriousness in his voice, he figured any way he'd say it would sound too easy.

"So if I stay here," Smith said, "I'd have to get real accustomed to being lonely." Then he wiped his hands on his pants like he was through. "Now that's enough," he said. "You go get some sleep."

"One more thing."

"Boy, you're truly gonna need somebody around looking after you."

"One more thing."

"All right. What?"

"Do you know my Uncle Charley?"

"Do I know who?"

"I just wondered."

They were out on the high plains now, and they made good time. Later there was going to be a problem with water, first in getting it, then later getting across it. But right now, the hard rivers were still out in front, and there were small ones enough to keep both the men and cattle comfortable.

They'd traveled this way a day or so, each one pretty much like any other. Then one night something happened, no one could quite figure out what, since the cattle were full with water and good grass. It could have been really out there, a coyote, or simply something in the dreams of a single cow. But one thing led to another. When the next cow heard the first one, maybe that reminded her of something she probably should have already been worrying about, and so on it went. Anyway, they all got up and started scattering. Nothing major. The cowhands got them turned and got them milling, going in a circle that gets tighter and tighter until they pretty much stop themselves. Once they'd settled down, they grazed some, and then bedded and that was it.

Still, the next day Mr. Staples wanted the herd counted. It didn't take long, everybody was practiced at it. The cattle were walked slowly through the wide end of a funnel-shaped rope corral, so when they passed out the the other end they had to go between Mr. Staples and Mr. O'Gonegal who were sitting their horses, each holding a long strip of rawhide with knots in it. Every hundred cattle, they would ease their hand down to the next knot.

They had done it before. They agreed down to the single cow. So they both knew that eight or nine were still out there somewhere. A couple of hands stayed with the herd and started them moving along the trail, but the rest of them, Bo included, spread out to bring the wanderers in.

It didn't take long. All but Tillis and one cow got back to the herd in half an hour. When he came back, Tillis rode up to Mr. Staples. "You'd better see this," was all he said. Then the two of them rode off in the direction Tillis had just come from. It didn't take them long to get back, either, and even though Mr. Staples's face seemed calm, it was taking an effort.

"Tillis, you and Beauchamp watch the herd. The rest of you come with me. There's something you need to look at."

They could see it from a distance. Where there should have been only grass heading straight to the end of the world, instead there were two long, skinny parallel lines, stretching across the horizon, with skinny posts going up and down every so often. Except when they looked at it longer, they saw it didn't really stretch that far. They could see where it made a corner and started off in another direction.

Mr. Staples stopped when he felt everybody had seen it. "Don't look like much, does it? Let me show you boys something."

He jerked his reins, which was unusual, all he normally did was just kind of pull them to whichever side he wanted to go and give a nudge with his knees.

Everybody followed, and they saw it, too. First only a dark spot lying against the fence. Then the closer they got, it became a cow, one of theirs. Then it became a cow that not only was dead, but a cow that was ripped into shreds, turned almost into ground beef. There was blood all over the ground. It didn't look like it had died in a hurry.

"I want you boys to take a good look at that wire, go ahead, get down. Go ahead and take a look at it."

They all did. Except for Bobby Joe.

Mr. Staples glanced over.

"I've seen it before," Bobby Joe said.

Bo looked at it. Flimsy strands of wire, probably cheap to buy and not too hard to string. And along each strand, barbs, little strips of wire with pointed ends. But when they worked together, they could kill a cow.

"You want us to tear it down?" O'Gonegal said.

"No," Mr. Staples said, noticing the direction the fence took. "Not here. Let's get back to the herd."

The cattle had been moving slowly, grazing, getting a little thirsty. They could go a lot farther without drinking, but they wouldn't like it. When everybody was back, Mr. Staples called them around him.

"Boys," he said, "I know how you feel about fences. But I want you to keep your shirts on for awhile. As near as I can figure, pretty soon we're going to find another part of that same fence, only it's going to be between us and water.

Before we do anything that might get out of hand, I want to find out, whoever it was built that thing, how he feels about watering."

Sure enough, it wasn't long before they saw two lines of the same kind stretching across in front of them. "Okay," Mr. Staples said, "this time Wilson and Martin stay. The rest of you, let's go."

They rode closer. When they were almost there, a man seemed to rise up out of nowhere from behind the fence, big, wearing a long-sleeved winter undershirt and carrying a rifle. Bo could see steps behind the man, going down straight into the ground. There was also a gate in the fence, but so narrow, if they were going through, the cattle would have to do it single file and slow, to stay away from the barbed wire.

When they were in earshot, the man said, "Morning," not even trying to be friendly. Staples touched his finger to his hat. "Nice bunch of cattle you got over there," the man said without moving his eyes from Staples.

"Bout three thousand head," Staples said. "Taking 'em to Montana, gonna feed some Indians."

"Kind of you," the man said. "Suspect they'll be grateful."

"Don't doubt it," Staples said. "Except just now, I've got a problem."

"What's that?"

"There's this fence in my way."

"Sorry about that. Except on this side of the fence, it happens to be my land, all recorded and legal, so it's my right to fence it. But it don't go far either direction. Shouldn't be much bother getting round it."

"That's not exactly my problem. I recollect that there's a water hole I need inside of those fences."

"Wouldn't surprise me. Different circumstances, I'd say you're welcome to it. But these ain't them. Look over yonder." He motioned over his shoulder. "I'm gonna make crops out of that land. So I'm gonna feed people, too. Me and my family first, later other folks, maybe even some of those Indians you're worried about. But this is dry farming here, mister, real dry. I'm gonna need that water."

"Maybe I should make myself clear," Staples said, both of them still sounding polite. "I'm not worried about Indians, and I'm not worried about farming. What I'm worried about is cattle, and mine need water. You may have got paper and you may have got fences. But I was watering here before it crossed your mind this hole ever existed."

"That was then," the man said. "This here is now. If it was only your cows, that maybe'd be different. But there's too many coming through. I let every herd drink here, wouldn't be water left to even grow flowers. Sorry, mister, you got to go around."

Staples simply nodded his head, and then almost every cowhand was holding a rifle. "I'm sorry, too, mister, but I reckon I'm coming through. Things like water, it's hard to see how a person owns them, specially when other folks have a need."

The man raised his rifle, too. "That's right easy for a man to say, he's just passing through. Those of us who plan on staying, we got different considerations. It's my land, mister, and you shoot me down, you'll be committing murder. But some of you won't have any worry about getting hung, before I'm done I'll get at least one, maybe two or three of you myself. You'd best take your cattle around."

"Don't talk to me about laws," Staples said, calm-voiced. "You go down your fence a ways, there's a cow hanging on it. That cow didn't die easy, mister, it was butchered."

"Then you should have kept it away from my fence. It won't take long. After awhile, they'll learn."

"I ain't got awhile." Staples just looked at the man for a moment, as though he were sizing him up.

"I consider myself a fair man," he said finally. "Tolerant, too, considering what I could say about a man who'd use something as infernal as this fence of yours. But I'm not taking that into consideration. I'm simply meaning to be fair. You've got my cow down there. It's sure as hell slaughtered and pretty near skinned. You're bound to have a family. That'll put some meat on your table. It ought to pay for the wire I'm getting ready to cut and the water my herd's gonna drink."

The man didn't say anything. His face didn't move.

"Where's those crops you're talking about?"

The man still didn't say anything.

"Jesus Christ, man! Can't you see I'm going through here? What I'm trying to do now is find out where your fields are so I can keep my cows away from there, so I don't do them any damage."

He still didn't say anything.

"Okay," he pulled out the wood ax he'd brought from the chuck. "You ain't gonna shoot nobody. You got a family in there, it ain't worth the risk." He turned to Bo. "Looks like you're the only one that's not holding a gun around here. Get yourself down and cut us a hole through this wire."

A woman ran up the steps that went into the ground. Her face was almost black from the sun.

"Bertram!" she called out, "Don't let him do it, don't, for God's sake, don't let the boy do it!"

"Look, lady," Staples said, "we're not going to hurt anything much. All we want is a little water."

She didn't even look at Staples, just at her husband.

"They want to do it," the man said. "I ain't gonna help them."

"Go ahead, boy," Staples said.

Bo walked up to the wire right next to the gate. He knew how to use an ax. He should have. He'd had enough practice back home on the farm. He hit a blow at an angle, where the wire was attached to the post.

There was an immediate twang, a singing sound, and Bo felt a searing across his chest, not just a slash, but a ripping. Instinctively, at least he didn't remember thinking about it, he threw himself up and away, as though escaping the strike of a snake.

"I told you, Bertram, I told you not to let him do it. You knew what would happen." Bo realized he was lying on the ground, the woman had his head in her lap. A man was bending over him, and his father's face came close, caring, pained, wanting to reach out, and Bo felt relieved, he could relax now, everything would be fine. But the face wouldn't stay still, its shapes kept changing, sliding into something else, until it was his Uncle Charley's. Only now farther away, he wouldn't quite come into focus, smiling but not offering comfort, as though saying this isn't any way to find me or anything else you left home looking for, lying here safe, waiting to be cared for.

And the faces kept merging back and forth until they settled into just one, and it was Bobby Joe's, and this time it didn't have any expression at all.

Then there was another face beside Bobby Joe's, only this one was different, he'd seen it only once before, on the other side of a barbed wire fence.

"My God, Sarah, how was I to know? He's the only one all summer that's known anything about using an ax. How was I to know he'd cut through it that way, first try?"

"You all right, boy?" Staples was still on his horse.

"Yessir, Mr. Staples. I'll finish with the fence in just a minute."

"You stay right here," the woman said. "Bertram," she said, "you finish opening a hole there. And you tell him to keep his godforsaken cows away from our crops."

Bertram had already pulled some wirecutters out of his back pocket and was carefully cutting away a portion of the fence.

"Can you ride, boy?"

"Yessir," Bo said. "I'm all right. Least I'm gonna be in maybe a few minutes."

"Are you sure?" Bobby Joe spoke for the first time. "If you want to ride, I have something in my bedroll that'll make the hurting easier."

"Look, mister," the woman said, looking up at Staples, "I don't know who you are and I don't very much care. But he's not much over being a boy. And he's hurt."

"Lady, I appreciate your sympathy. But when somebody signs up with me, I don't care what his age is, right then he stops being a boy and starts being a man."

"He didn't sign up with you," Bobby Joe said quietly. "He signed up with me." He turned to the woman. "Are you offering to keep him overnight? A sleep indoors will do him good. He can catch up with the herd in the morning."

So the lady and the man named Bertram helped Bo to his feet, down the steps that led into the ground. But by this time, Bo didn't care where anybody was carrying him, so long as it was someplace he could try and find a way to keep his body from hurting so bad.

When he woke up, it was dim all around and cool. But out a doorway off to the side, bright light was edging around a hanging buffalo hide. He tried to sit, but there was a rippling of pain across his chest, not bad, but a warning. So he lay back and touched where the hurting had started, and realized he wasn't touching clothes, but skin, his own and it was greasy.

"You awake?" The voice was gentle and cheery. He looked in its direction. His eyes were getting used to the light, he could tell she was standing by the opposite wall doing something over a stove, wearing a man's beat-up straw hat.

"Yes ma'am, and I appreciate the rest. But I'd better be getting back to the herd. I feel a lot better after lying down."

She laughed. "Yes indeed. I noticed how much better you felt when you tried sitting up. You just lie there awhile. It's all settled with your Mr. Staples. You're staying here for the night. You can catch up tomorrow. With all them cows, they ain't gonna be moving real fast."

"Did they do any harm to your crops?"

"Lordy, no. Bert planted them back a ways so the cattle wouldn't get near them coming through, unless somebody made a special effort. Most of the herds have been right considerate about that."

"Then why make all the fuss out there by the fence?"

"Well, Bert, that's my husband, he says we got to get them used to it, we got to get them thinking about how this is our land, not theirs. And he says, we're gonna win, it's just gonna take some time, all we got to do is wait them out, wait till there's more of us, and he says there will be, all we got to do is wait."

"So you don't really care if they use your water?"

"Well," she said, "that's a horse of a different color. We need that water. We don't get enough rain here to trust it growing anything, except maybe some more of that grass out there you can't get through with a pickax anyway. So we got to carry our own water to the crops. Up to now, it's all right, there's plenty for your cows and our crops both. But Bert says it can't last, not when other folks like us start showing up out here. Sooner or later, Bert says, there's gonna have to be a reckoning. We just ain't got enough collected on our side quite yet. So for awhile, we got to wait it out. You ever been in a dugout before?"

"No ma'am."

"Well, look around. I hadn't either. But it is truly a wondrous thing."

By her tone of voice, Bo couldn't tell whether she meant it or not. But he did look around. Somebody had tried hard. Everything looked about as clean as it could be. The dirt was packed solid. In the middle of the room there was a cloth rug and a plank table with four cane-bottom chairs. Over in a corner was a sewing machine sitting on a packing crate. There was one other bed, a wooden platform with some buffalo robes on it, Bo figured his was more or less like it. There were magazine pictures fastened somehow to the dirt walls, only Bo couldn't make them out in the dimness. A lantern was on the table but it was unlit, the only light came in through the door. He couldn't make out much about the ceiling, either, it seemed mainly a dark bramble.

"Yessir, it's a wondrous thing. But it'll do for awhile. Bert says someday there's gonna be railroads all over the place. Then we can get some lumber shipped in, costs a fortune by wagon. Till then, though, it's not so bad, kind of cool in summer and not all that cold in winter. And when one of them tornadoes hits, it's about the safest place anybody's gonna be.

"Course, there's problems. When one of them herds came through month or so back, calf got scared, ran away from her mamma, right over the roof. I was standing here by the stove, all of a sudden there was this bawling animal slap dab beside me."

"Through the roof?"

"Certainly did. All that roof is, there's a lot of bush thatching and a little hay covered with dirt packed down. Which does okay except when it rains or some calf tries running across it. Someday I'm gonna grow flowers on top, right now Bert says we can't spare the water. In here, there's usually a piece of canvas stretched across, except I'm letting it get some sunning outside. That's why I'm wearing this hat."

"That's why you're wearing a hat?"

"Sometimes things fall down, most of it's no bother, but every now and then it's a tarantula." She laughed. "Once or twice what dropped was a rattlesnake. I don't know who was scared most, me or that snake."

Bo all of a sudden was less comfortable. He looked more carefully at the dark clutter over his bed.

The woman laughed again. "Don't you worry. They come over here to get near the chimney pipe. They like it because they get warm, but then they get drowsy and forget to hold on. They're not gonna bother you over there. Now. That's done." She put a lid on something. "I reckon it's time to take another look at them cuts."

When she came closer, Bo saw she was younger than he'd thought earlier, maybe because what he'd noticed before, out there in the yard, was how the sun had darkened her face. But in here where everything was dim, he could see that if it wasn't youngness, at least there wasn't age underneath.

She reached for a can on a shelf dug back into the wall. "You're gonna be fine," she said. "You jumped back just right. If a person's not careful, that wire can go a long way toward doing real damage. I don't even like Bert to be handling it. But here, let me wipe some of that grease off and take a look."

She took a rag and carefully wiped Bo's chest clean. While she was looking at the cuts, she kept talking, as though to take Bo's mind off any pain she might be causing. "Yessir, this is gonna be in pretty fair traveling condition come morning. That stuff your friend, the Indian-looking fellow, gave me to mix with the buffalo grease, it's gonna make a real difference, I think you're gonna be just fine. Here, let's smear more on and then you lie still and let your strength come back just a little."

So Bo lay there, hearing the woman doing something over by the stove, listening to the buzz of insects over his head in the ceiling, not really sleeping, not really awake. Then he must have truly been asleep, because without his knowing when they came in, there were more people in the room and a lot more noise. A man, the one who had been holding the rifle, was standing above him.

"How you doing, boy? That was a nasty cut you took. Let me take a look." He seemed different from out in the yard, almost like somebody you'd want to know.

"Seems like Sarah's done you okay. Where'd you learn to use that ax, anyway?"

"Home. On a farm."

"Figgers." All the time, the man was looking closely at the cuts, sometimes pulling them apart to see inside. "How come you roaming around with those fellows. You trying to be a cowboy?"

"No sir. I'm looking for my uncle, my Uncle Charley. I don't suppose he's been around here?"

"Not that I know of. What makes you reckon that?"

"I don't know. Just seems everywhere I go, that's where he's already been."

"Well, he must've skipped us. But you'll be back on your way soon enough. Mandy, you and Sammy come over here and say howdy, what'd you say your name was?"

"Bo."

The boy was about five, the girl a year or so younger. They came over and hid behind the man's legs.

"This here is Bo," the man said. "He's a farmer, too."

Bo got up for supper, even though they tried talking him out of it. But he'd been too long out in the open, he'd almost forgotten what it was like, sitting around a table, being with a real family, if nothing else, just to hear a blessing before eating.

Bert finished first and sat there, studying Bo for a moment. Bo wasn't sure what he was supposed to do while Bert was looking, so he busied himself, wiping up some pot liquor with a biscuit. Finally Bert said, "Don't you worry too much about your friends, they're decent enough folks for cowpeople. There's been a lot worse than them through here. Besides, it won't be long, everybody's going to be better off. Us, them, everybody, they wait long enough."

"Excuse me," Bo said, there wasn't anything left on his plate, he had to say something. "Excuse me, but I'm not sure I understand."

"Well," he said, "it's like this. Folks like us, like Sarah and me, we're going to win. Because we come out here to stay, we've got a stake in the land, we're not just traveling through. And there'll be more of us, lots more, like the grass out there, kind of puny-looking on the surface, but tough. We're gonna beat the weather, we're gonna beat the heat, and we're gonna win over bunches of cowboys holding rifles. By hook or by crook, boy, we're gonna make this land into something that didn't even exist before we got here.

"Of course it may not be Sarah and me. We may have to go back East, start over on her daddy's farm. But there'll be other folks like us. And sooner or later, our sort is gonna win. Then there's gonna be churches and schools, and a lot more stretches of that barbed wire. And your friends are gonna have to find a different way of doing business."

"But I thought you said everybody was going to win, even them."

"Yep. Course, they don't know it, but they're gonna be better off, too, only they'll have to change some. Once our kind get set up, other things'll have to follow. Like railroads. There won't be any reason, driving cattle all the way to places like Abilene or Dodge. Once there's enough people who plan to stay put and buy things, no reason there can't be railroads right down here in Texas. Then folks like your friends, they can raise cattle and quit worrying about how they get along on the trail. Only thing they'll have to bother with is getting them all pretty and big and fat. Won't be any reason to worry about keeping them that way."

"You mean no more trail drives?"

Bert smiled. "I know. Everybody wants to be a cowboy," he reached over and ran his hand through his son's hair. "Riding herd up the old Chisholm Trail.

"But life's gonna change. It ain't so exciting, living out here, fighting tornadoes and dryness and the being lonely. It'd be more interesting always riding off into nowhere, leastways Sammy thinks it just might. And I suspect even Sarah here gets bored at times, sharing her life, day in, day out with a farmer."

Sarah looked over and smiled, as though such an idea had never crossed her mind. Except Bo could tell by Bert's face, it wasn't the first time it'd crossed his. "But times are gonna change," Bert said, "and it's people like us that work hard and stay put that's gonna matter in the long run.

"Life's gonna change. And Sammy's dreams are just gonna have to change with it. Once everybody gets used to it, not just us, everybody's gonna be better off. Particularly my friend Sarah here." He put his arm around his wife's shoulders.

"Yessir, before we get through, we're gonna have this place set up fit for a woman like Sarah to live in. May take awhile, but we're gonna do it. Your friends can handle somebody like me, I know it and they do, too. But it doesn't really bother me much. Sooner or later, there's gonna be lots of us. We're gonna be just like that grass out there, tough and stringy and sprouting up everywhere. And they're just gonna have to get used to it."

Mandy and Sammy slept on the other side of the room in a bed just like the one where Bo had been. Where he still was. No matter how Bo argued, Bert and Sarah wouldn't hear of him sleeping on the floor in his bedroll. "You could use a night off the ground," Sarah said. "You're gonna have more than enough of it when you get back with the herd. You take advantage of what you got, now that you've got it."

They took some blankets and went up the stairs to the outside. "Where it's nice and cool," Bert said. "Besides, it'll be good to get away from kids awhile." He patted Sarah on her bottom, but she took his hand away and said, "Don't do that," except she was smiling.

The next morning there were biscuits with wild bee honey and lots of milk. Both Bert and Sarah looked pleased with themselves. Bo himself felt awfully sore. Sarah rubbed more of the buffalo fat medicine over his cuts, which made them feel better, but it also made his shirt stick to his chest.

"You sure you want to leave so soon?" Sarah said. "You're more than welcome to stay till those things get healed."

"No thank you, ma'am," Bo said. "That's kind of you, but I'd better get back with the herd. If I don't keep up with them, I wouldn't know where to go next to find my uncle. Bobby Joe, the one with the medicine, I think he knows something about it, I'd better stay up with him."

But it wasn't just that. Bo knew now what Jeremiah felt like, leaving Junction City. It was nice for awhile, staying someplace that reminded you of home. But then you missed being outside, you started feeling closed in, and not just by walls.

Bert had gone up the steps to look at the sky. When he came back, he was shaking his head. "You better stay here, boy. That sky out there is twister weather."

"Twister?"

"You never been around twister weather?"

"Tornado," Sarah said. "These here dugouts aren't good for much, but they're the best place when one of them twisters starts moving around. You better stay awhile."

Bo hesitated. "Are you sure one's on its way?"

"Hard to say, can't be sure of much around here, except too much sun and next to no water. The sky makes it look awfully likely."

"You're going out into it?"

"Got to. Lose a day, the land's liable to start winning."

"I reckon I'd better keep going, too, but I appreciate the offer. And I thank you for putting me up."

"Least we could do. Just wish you'd let on earlier you knew what to do with an ax. Then maybe you'd be able to get some air between your skin and that shirt. But you come this way, you drop in."

The herd's trail was easy to follow, until after awhile it got too easy. And even though it was empty, Bo kept remembering the dust, seeing cows sniffing over bleeding babies. He moved away, close enough not to lose direction, but far enough to seem like he wasn't just riding to get someplace, so he could feel the plains stretching out all around him.

"Be careful about that, Bo," Sam said. "Don't let all that emptiness make connections."

"That's not just emptiness," Bobby Joe said. "It's strength if you know where to look for it."

"Where strength is," Bert said, "it's inside me, you, anybody else that's willing to work at it, to put fences around all that emptiness, make it grow things that ain't even occurred to most folks that pass on over it."

"What all you folks better do is quiet down," the Preacher said, "and start noticing them clouds up there that's getting ready to blow everybody just about half way to kingdom come."

The sky seemed heavy and ragged, pressing down hard on the land. Everything was quiet, even the wind that seemed always blowing over the prairie. Bo felt better once he caught sight of the herd, when he was near enough to hear the mutterings of cattle, although they sounded more restless than usual for this time of day. Still, the plains seeemed more comfortable once he could hear them. He waved to Smith as he passed the remuda, and looked for Bobby Joe to tell him he was back. But Bobby Joe wasn't where Bo expected to find him. Instead of being at point, he and Staples were on the flank, talking. When Bo rode up, Bobby Joe acted like he'd been there all the time.

"Go bring the men," he said, without moving his eyes from the sky.

"You boys ever been in a twister?" Staples said when they got there.

The men looked at each other nervously. Even their horses seemed edgier than usual.

"Me neither," Staples said. "And maybe we still won't have the privilege. But Mr. Joe thinks there's a good chance we're gonna have something to talk about before the day gets over. Okay, Mr. Joe, you tell us what we need to know."

Bobby Joe talked quietly, like he was explaining that you ought to put a slicker on if you noticed it was raining. "The first thing," he said, "we got to find someplace to put the herd. There's a place off the trail up a ways, it's not exactly a valley, but it's lower than anyplace else around. If we need to get there at all, we'd better do it now. In a hurry."

The men started to leave. "One other thing," Bobby Joe said. "Twisters move funny and they move fast. If it hits you broadside, you're done for. But there's a circle of wind around a twister. If it looks like the funnel is heading for you, ride straight into the circle of wind. Not the funnel. If you hit the funnel, if it hits you, somebody else rides your horses in the morning. Except the one you're on. Nobody's ever gonna find that one. But don't forget. If it's coming toward you, don't try to outrun it, because you can't. The only way to be sure it won't hit you broadside is to take charge yourself. Ride straight into that circle of wind. Now get those cattle to where they belong."

The cattle were restless, wanting to mill, but now wasn't the time. The cowboys kept straightening them out, heading them toward the depression Bobby Joe had told about.

Things now were even stiller, the air heavier and becoming dark. As soon as the cattle moved into the hollow, they started bedding down, getting themselves low to the ground, as though somehow they knew. But it wasn't like at night, they didn't just lie there, all the time they were bellowing. They lay there like they knew, whatever it was that was going to happen, they couldn't stop it. All they could do was lie there and bellow, helpless and waiting.

Bobby Joe and Bo were still up on the prairie, getting the last ones in when they saw it. At first they just sat there, watching it coming toward them like it had a plan all its own, moving one way then the other, every direction except a straight line.

It got close. Then it got closer.

Bobby Joe's voice stayed quiet.

"Okay, Bo, you know what we got to do."

"What about the rest of these cows?"

"Leave 'em. We got something else to get done. *Now!*"

And so they did it. Almost like a race, spurring, leaning low over their horses, heading straight for the whirlwind. It wasn't easy, the funnel kept moving, they had to chase it down.

"Not in the middle!" Bobby Joe yelled. "Hit it off to the side!"

They were going fast, and when they got there, it was like smashing through a brick wall, except every brick was its own different wall, not just staying there waiting, but coming out after you. And the noise, roaring oceans of sound pouring over them, and all around them things were moving, cows flying through the air, doing somersaults, managing maybe one bleat, two, before they rose up higher, like they had been jerked by a string. Then there was even Mr. O'Gonegal, still sitting on his horse, flying, a strange, disbelieving look on his face, his horse pawing, racing, moving up higher and then away.

And they were out of it, on the other side, like it hadn't even happened.

"Is that all?"

Bobby Joe looked at him curiously. "Don't you reckon that's almost enough?"

They rode back to the herd, where the wind hadn't so much as gotten close. And so they got back on the trail and kept going, as though nothing had happened at all.

That night, before bedding down, Staples and Bobby Joe counted.

"Eight cows and Mr. O'Gonegal is what I got," Staples said. "What about you?"

"I got the same," he said. "We came out pretty good."

While they were counting, Smith was talking.

"He won't listen," Smith was saying.

"He listens," Bo said. "He doesn't let on. But he listens."

When Bobby Joe got back, Bo didn't want to, but Smith had asked, and Smith had gotten to be close.

"He can't understand," Bo said, "why you can't be friendly."

Bobby Joe started to smile, then he looked at Smith. "Good reason why I should?"

"You look around," Smith said. "All these white folks. They've got the same use for you they've got for me. There's color on both our skins, that's reason enough for them. Ought to be reason enough for us."

"Only thing is," Bobby Joe said, "it's not."

Bo had planned on helping with the horses, but after Bobby Joe left, Smith seemed irritable. So Bo headed for the campfire instead. He didn't mind. On the trail, everything kept moving and changing. But the chuck wagon and the campfire seemed to stay put. Cookie made sure there was always a pot of coffee resting on the coals. And although Bo didn't particularly like the taste, it still made him feel good to see it there. And at night, everybody who wasn't on night herd sat around the campfire and talked, lied, told stories.

Except Bobby Joe, who would sit out of the light, looking on, listening. And Smith, who usually was back with the horses. Except for tonight. After he'd looked over the remuda, he seemed to have changed his mind and wanted company.

Everybody was already edgy. They weren't used to being chased by things coming out of the sky. They weren't accustomed quite yet to O'Gonegal's leaving.

By the time Smith poured himself a cup of coffee and sat down, nobody was talking. Then Beauchamp said, mainly to fill up the quietness, "You lose any horses, Mr. Smith?"

Smith seemed happy somebody had talked to him. "They don't know anything's even happened." Then he chuckled.

Bo hadn't heard him be that way before, sounding the way he thought white people wanted him to. It turned out not to be good enough.

"Where I come from," Tillis said, "niggers say 'mister' when they answer white folks."

Staples immediately broke in. "This ain't where you come from, Tillis. This is a trail drive. Anybody draws pay from me is as good as anybody else till he shows me different. That what you're doing, Tillis, you showing me different?"

Tillis wasn't listening. "I draw pay and do my job. Which ain't listening to some uppity nigger sitting around, acting like a white man."

"All of us got feelings," Staples said, "but they don't do nobody any good on a trail drive. You want to have opinions, you wait till we get the work done and get these cattle sold."

"What I heard, he ain't only just a nigger, he's a goddam yankee nigger to boot, I ain't paid to put up with that."

"Mr. Smith," Staples said. "Maybe you should go tend your horses."

Smith got up to leave.

"I didn't say I was through with you," Tillis said.

Smith didn't pay him any attention, only kept going.

"Listen, nigger, I'm talking to you," Tillis said and reached toward his waist, maybe for his pocket, maybe for his gun, nobody could tell for sure, certainly not Smith. And Smith couldn't afford to be wrong.

Bo didn't even know Smith carried a gun. He still didn't know where he'd hid it. Wherever it was, Smith found it in a hurry. There was a flash and Tillis wasn't standing where he'd just been.

Bobby Joe moved quickly. He had Smith by the arm, getting him out of there, away from the campfire where the men were gathered over Tillis, all of them hoping what had happened hadn't, hoping that everything was going back to being the way it'd been before supper, but knowing it wasn't.

Bo went with them. Bobby Joe was helping Smith saddle a horse. "Where you plan on going?" Bo asked.

"Someplace a far piece from here."

"There's a trading post, day's ride up the trail," Bobby Joe said. "Ask them for directions to Zeke Butters's cabin. His wife'll put you up for a day or so. They'll help you get started someplace up North. You're not going to be real welcome for awhile along the trail."

"Where you plan on going?" Bo asked again.

"Away," Smith said. "From white folks."

Bobby Joe stared. "You stay clear of Indian Territory."

"People that's not white, they need to stay together."

"You listen, Smith, you head North. You stay away from the Territory."

Smith didn't answer, but jumped into his saddle, not even touching his stirrups till he was riding out of sight into the dark.

"If he's still at Zeke Butters's when you get there," Bobby Joe said, "you make sure he goes back North."

"How'm I supposed to do that?"

"That's not my problem. He's your friend, not mine."

Bo hadn't expected it to be so lonely without Smith there to turn to. Except Bo kept hearing Smith interrupt the cowboys when everybody was sitting around the campfire. He never had done that when he was there. And he sure wouldn't have said what Bo kept hearing him say. So in a funny way, Bo was more aware of Smith's being around now that he was gone. But it didn't make things any less lonely.

Then one morning, Bobby Joe woke him up early. "It's time for us to leave," he said. "Each of us has places to go."

While Bo was saddling up, Bobby Joe gave him directions to Zeke Butters's, how to find a place called the Thicket.

"We'll see each other again," he said. "Zeke will lead you to me. First I've got to deliver my cattle."

"Why don't I go with you? Two horses could handle the herd better than only one."

"My horse can manage fine alone. I'll be waiting when Zeke brings you."

It felt strange. And lonely once he left, the first time in a long while he'd been riding alone. And all around was only space, flat, endless, nothing between Bo and the sky.

The Thicket

He rode on steadily, till evening when he knew he was getting there. Bobby Joe had said the land would start rising, then there'd be a draw taking him deeper into a canyon.

It was still daylight when Bo started downhill, feeling the air getting cooler, which was natural anywhere on the prairie with the coming on of night. But this was different, somehow sharper. The smell was richer, heavier, almost like the piney woods back home.

Then there it was ahead. An absolute wall, green, tangled, trees of every kind growing all directions, vines weaved around and between, a mass so thick Bo didn't see how a dog, not to mention a man on a horse, could get inside, or go anyplace even if he did.

Besides that, it didn't belong. After all that emptiness, things now growing everyplace, as though life was trying to fill all the spaces, even if it meant pushing other things out of the way.

"Don't let it," Sam said. "Keep holding to what you've got."

"How're you going to know what's there?" Bobby Joe said. "How're you going to know what it connects up to, unless you push on, farther inside?"

"Don't worry about what's all around you," Staples said. "That just gets in the way. Find a trail, if you don't find one, make it. Then you'll know where you are. You're not lost in some Thicket, long as you're on the middle of your own trail."

"Whatever you do," the Preacher said, "I suspect you'd best get doing it before nightfall."

Maybe he'd taken the wrong draw. Maybe there was another one he'd missed or hadn't gotten to yet, one where there was a road at the bottom or at least a path. He rode closer, slower, looking along the green wall for the chance of an opening.

It wasn't much when he found it. Some branches pulled apart, some vines not quite blocking the way. And even if it was a trail, and a poor excuse if it was, Bo couldn't tell how far it might go, it seemed to disappear before it got started. But Bo had need of a trail. It was the best he could do.

And if it was a trail, it wasn't a straight one. Inside the Thicket the sun was almost blocked out. Any rays that got in didn't much matter, filtering down crazy-quilt through layers of branches and vines and leaves, making whatever trail markings there might be even more difficult to see.

Bo could feel life all around him, and not only the standing-still, growing-just-in-one-place kind. There were noises, bird callings, insect chirpings, and somewhere off a ways the rustling of things through leaves. And it was getting dark, not just inside the Thicket, outside, too, the rays making it down were getting dimmer. Bo wasn't happy about spending the night on the ground, ground like this where everything seemed alive, but there was no way he could follow this trail in the dark. If that's what he was doing, following a trail, not the meanderings of some wild cow, not just the paths open spaces made in his mind.

Finally there wasn't enough light, he couldn't keep it up any longer. It didn't seem to make much difference where he was going to sleep. Everything looked about the same. At least he'd move off the trail, just in case it was a trail, in case it was traveled by things curious about strangers.

He was off his horse, getting ready to unsaddle. When he heard somebody laugh. It sounded out of place, he'd been so long without hearing a voice, it scared him more than the Thicket sounds he didn't recognize.

"I reckon you'd sleep more comfortable inside a house. But then there's all kind of folk, it's up to you."

Bo laughed, too. He could barely make Smith out, leaning against a tree, almost lost in the darkness.

"Been waiting," Smith said. "I knew somebody was on the way. You been driving birds crazy all down the trail for least an hour. So hurry it up, let's get on in, there's snakes in these woods. I'd just as soon be able to see if they're not there."

So Bo remounted, and Smith walked ahead, leading the way. "You just missed Zeke," Smith said. "We were out looking for wild pigs, we could use a little bacon, when all of a sudden Zeke looked around and started laughing." Smith laughed himself. "You just wait till you hear Zeke start laughing. When he finally got himself stopped, he said to me, 'You go tell the Missiz I'll be back after while.' Zeke pointed down to a pile of droppings. 'Tell her,' he says, 'I've found me a bear that's new around here, else he'd know better than get this close to Zeke Butters's cabin. You tell her I'll be back once I get done, we'll eat us some bear meat.' That's the last time I saw him. I looked around, he was just gone. When I told Mrs. Butters, she only laughed and shrugged. I figured he'd be back for supper, but she said only maybe. Or it might be next week or next month, she'd long since stopped wondering.

"So it's just us and her and the kids. I figured I'd stay round awhile, make sure she gets along all right. She said it wasn't necessary, she was used to it. But I said I figured I'd do it anyway. So we've been waiting for you."

They went along for a minute or two. Then Smith stopped. He turned around like he'd been wanting to before but hadn't thought it proper. "Anybody follow you here? Anybody coming after me?"

Bo shook his head. "Only me. Once you were gone, things got back to normal. Tillis wasn't somebody a lot of folks were bothered by missing." Bo looked around. "Besides, this seems a good place to be if somebody was looking."

"Maybe. But you got here. I got here. He could have told somebody else, too."

"I suspect there's no cause to worry."

Then unexpectedly like a sudden sunrise the tangles and underbrush, the linked-together trees were gone, there was a clearing, more than that, there was something that had been cleared. There was grass for a ways, then it was dirt, hard and red that looked clean from sweeping. There wasn't need for a fence, the Thicket took care of that, but a woman was waiting where there might have been a gate.

Mrs. Butters was tall and gaunt, with a mouth set like it wasn't used to talking. But when she smiled, Bo could tell it wasn't unusual.

"We've been waiting," she said. "You come on inside."

Back home they'd have called it a dogtrot house, two rooms with a roofed porch running between, so if a dog took a notion he could trot right through. Except the dogs back home, Bo remembered, usually never quite made it through, only about halfway to where there was shade. That's where Mrs. Butters stopped, too.

Bo could tell it was built solid. Thick beams, filled in with mud caked so hard there couldn't be much difference between it and the wood.

"It's all center cut," Mrs. Butters said, "heart of pine. When Zeke finally gets around to doing, I'll give him credit, he gets it done."

She cupped her hands to her mouth. "Hey kids!"

They came running from all sides, five of them, the oldest and youngest were both girls, the boys were scattered in between.

"You done with chores?" It was directed to no one in particular, but they all answered.

"That's fine." she said. "We can get on with the introductions. This here is Mr. Bo. He's a friend of Mr. Smith. He's also kin to Uncle Charley."

Mrs. Butters must have noticed Bo was paying more attention. "We just call him that, at least the kids do. It got kind of hard to keep calling someone like Charley 'mister.' Now, you kids, get yourselves straightened out."

They all lined up in what must have been chronological order. "Okay, that young lady over there is Genny. Zeke named her Genesis since she was the first, but that didn't last real long. Next to her, that's Eck. Same as before, started off as Exodus, only I didn't like the sound of that. Zeke does all the exodusing we need around here. Then the middle boy, that's Levi. Then the little fellow . . ."

Bo interrupted. "You named him Numbers?"

"No," Mrs. Buttons said, "but it shows you been brought up right. It was about then I started getting pushy. We call him Dute. But with the baby," she pointed to the little girl, "well, that's when I finally put a stop to it. Before Zeke even got a chance, I said her name's gonna be Ruth. That comes from the book, too. All we got to do is skip a few chapters. So this here's Ruthie. Now we've got that done, let's get ourselves inside."

The floor must have been center cut, too. There wasn't any give walking across it, just the solid sound of your feet.

The room they were in had a pot-bellied iron stove and a table with oilcloth on it. There were several chairs around it that looked storebought and a couple of benches that probably started off as nearby trees. There were a couple of small tables, too. On one there was a Bible and an almanac. On the other was a glass holding magnolia blossoms, which must have been picked carefully and then left alone, because they were still all white, without even a speck of brown.

Then they ate, good fresh potatoes and tomatoes and turnip greens, all washed down by clear-tasting water. He looked around at the kids, Eck and Dute and Ruthie and the rest. It seemed almost like home, sitting around the table, listening to Mrs. Butters tell the kids to get on with their eating, quit playing with their food. Telling, not scolding, as though this went on most nights and everybody, Mrs. Butters included, wouldn't be quite happy if something got in the way of having to do it. It seemed almost like home, but not quite. Because Bo seemed somehow far off, as though he was outside looking on, as though he almost but didn't quite belong.

When everybody finished, Mrs. Butters shooed the kids out, telling the older ones to get busy, to start getting everybody ready for bed. But she didn't need to, since everybody knew what was expected. Then the grown-ups stayed sitting and drank coffee, at least that's what she called it, and Bo wasn't about to ask questions. Only it tasted a good bit different from what he was used to at the chuck wagon. It seemed strange, without thinking, that was what he was comparing things to, as though that's where things were done right. Whatever this was, it tasted as though a lot of it had come from Mrs. Butters's garden. Except after he drank some, once he quit expecting it to be coffee, it started tasting, well, maybe not real good, but it was satisfying.

Mrs. Butters seemed to feel comfortable sitting with company, still Bo could tell she was only half listening to what anyone was saying, herself included. Then she got up and went into the other room, and they could hear her talking, higher up, like she was in a loft.

"Prayers," Smith said.

"I know you came hoping to find Zeke," Mrs. Butters said after she came back down. "And now you're stuck because he ain't here. But it won't be long, he'll be back. You're young," she said. "It ain't gonna hurt you to wait.

"I should know," she laughed. "I've done some waiting myself." She was looking off, as though she could see through the walls. "It gets lonesome, but then that's sometimes the way even if Zeke's here. Besides, I got the kids."

Bo let his gaze follow hers, letting it rest when it came to the same spot on the wall. His mother, too. She got lonesome, too. There was too much work on the farm for a lot of socializing, there was too much work pure and simple. It couldn't be helped, that was the way it was on a farm. But once every week or so, Bo's mother would take the wagon and meet other women, they called it their sewing circle. His mother laughed and said she was afraid there was a lot more talking than sewing. But Bo's father said that was fine, you could sew by yourself, you needed other folk to talk to, and once a week wasn't too often talking with folks of your own kind. Sometimes they met at their farm, but since most of the women lived in town, most often they met there. And Bo remembered a night, he hadn't even known before that he'd seen it, his mother was out later than usual and his father was waiting, sitting at the kitchen table beside the lantern. He had one of the books Uncle Charley had loaned Bo's mother, and he was studying it, like he was trying to understand.

"Truth to tell," Mrs. Butters said, as though she'd heard herself complaining, "I'm better off than most. He built me this house. He didn't settle for no dugout. Even after the walls, he wasn't going to stop with no dirt floor. He done it right. My kids live in a stouter house than they'd have in the middle of most towns.

"And he brings in food. Sometimes there's a spell between deliveries, but he brings it in. So that means whatever he's doing out there, he's still remembering what's back here, he never forgets to bring food."

She looked around, as though she'd forgotten Smith and Bo were there. Then she smiled.

"I guess I get to talking. It's not often I'm around grownups. Even with Zeke, it's not quite the same. It's like he'd be just as happy talking with one of his dogs or some possum up in a tree. And he never was much good at listening, less it was to some other animal."

"Doesn't sound like much of a life," Smith said, "working, keeping a home ready so someone can just drop by whenever the mood strikes him."

"I thought about leaving," she said, "except not much. I guess I'm like Zeke that way. Maybe we even belong together, although that's an idea that takes some getting used to. I can't go out there and wander in the Thicket the way he does. But I like its being there. Even when you can't understand it, I still feel better knowing it's close. It's like having kids, they're out there, too, filled up with life, and you're part of them, whether either of you like it or not."

"Ma'am?" Bo interrupted. "Seems to me it wouldn't be so bad growing up here. So long as there's family, and kids enough so you wouldn't get lonely, and there's food." He thought for a minute, then he went ahead and said it. "And somebody like you."

Mrs. Butters smiled. "That's nice, Bo, I'm glad you said it. But times, every now and then, it gets hard.

"I remember back in Mississippi, Zeke and me were just getting started. Life was good and we both had family. But when it looked like Zeke had either killed or made friends with all the bears in the Delta, he couldn't help getting restless. I didn't know where we were going. But Zeke had somehow heard about the Thicket. Maybe one of his animals told him.

"I didn't believe a word of it. Still, it wasn't so bad while we were traveling through land that looked the same as where we come from. That gave me hope. But when we hit the plains, flat for as long as you could look, then something went out of me. It didn't seem like any kind of life I knew about had ever lived there. Or was in a hurry to get started.

"Zeke, though, he never seemed to mind. He'd shoot this thing, he'd shoot that. Being with Zeke, you weren't going to get hungry, though you might get somewhat tired of meat. That's the reason I made sure about bringing seeds. You got to remember, I didn't know where we was going.

"So I brought along a bag of seedcorn. I figured it might turn out to be the most important thing we were carrying, if you didn't count the kids and mules, maybe the chickens. I didn't know then there was going to be all these wild turkeys. But Zeke laughed, he wasn't much for things you had to plant yourself, still isn't. He laughed. But I figured that seedcorn was likely to come in handy."

Mrs. Butters laughed herself. "Then I saw that old rooster, a mean old thing, even back in Mississippi. Now that we were traveling, we'd let him out when we stopped, he wasn't about to go anywhere, he was too ornery for that. So we'd let him out to find bugs and stuff, and then one day I could see he'd found something for sure. And whatever it was, he was eating it harder than I'd seen him do much of anything in awhile.

"Then I saw what it was he was eating. The seed bag had sprung a leak and my corn was dropping out, not fast but steady, and that rooster thought he'd died and just gone to heaven.

"Which he was getting ready to do, or wherever else roosters tend to go. But one thing sure, when he got there he wasn't going to be eating my seedcorn. Because I grabbed that rooster and snapped its neck and even before it finished flapping, I had its craw open and got my seedcorn back.

"Good thing I did. It grows right nicely in the Thicket. Never did learn to miss that rooster.

"But while we were getting here, I sure did miss seeing trees. We could have been going over the exact same ground again day after day after day. You sure couldn't tell any difference from looking. Nothing but grass and grass and the next morning there was still more of it. It was like we hadn't been traveling at all. But then one day, out in the middle of all that flatness, the bottom just dropped out, not even a sign, everything like a tabletop and then it was as though we had walked straight off the end of the world. Except down below was what we'd been looking for, there lay the Thicket.

"No way it should have been there. It was like God and Zeke had gone into cahoots to make it. More game than you could put a dent in, water, trees to build with, for deer and bear to hide behind and after awhile, wild hogs running everyplace. We brought some with us, they were tame at the time, but when Zeke took a good look at the Thicket, he said, 'Let 'em go. With all this around,' he said, 'I ain't planning to feed no hog. Besides,' Zeke said, 'be more fun to catch them.'"

"That may be Zeke's idea of fun," Smith said, looking over at Bo. "But you keep away from them. Them suckers are mean. I thought I wanted a little pork, so I set out to catch me some. What I caught was a tree limb, real fast and glad to find it. More than likely I'd still be there if Mrs. Butters hadn't got worried, come and got me."

"Carrying a shotgun, too," she said. "Mr. Smith is right, them pigs has got mean. But they're just part of the Thicket. One way or another, we've all gotten used to it. I reckon I'd miss them if they went someplace else."

"So in the whole Thicket," Bo said, "there's nobody but you?"

"Well, me and the kids, and somewhere there's Zeke. But nobody close enough to bother us."

"What about Indians?" Smith asked. "Isn't this pretty close to the Territory?"

Mrs. Butters shook her head. "Zeke says it's something about spirits, but he didn't say what. He ain't much for explaining, only when it suits him." She smiled. "There are times I do get lonely for grown people, I have to admit it, but I reckon if I was somewhere else, I'd get just as lonely for the Thicket. It's like there's no way a person can win." But the way she said it, she didn't seem too unhappy.

"Ma'am?" Bo said.

Mrs. Butters waited.

"I like it here, too, but I'm kind of in a hurry to find my Uncle Charley."

Mrs. Butters smiled and shrugged kindly. "Things come and go in the Thicket," she said. "Sometimes it's hard figuring why. Zeke somehow seems to understand such things, you'll just have to wait till he can help you." She got up like the evening was over. "There's one thing you can count on about Zeke. He's always going to be leaving. But sooner or later, he's always going to be back. Whatever they are, he's got his reasons."

Bo was accustomed to early rising. But by the time he woke the next morning, it seemed everybody else had put in a half-day's work. "That's just fine," Mrs. Butters said. "You been traveling."

She put a plate of corn bread in front of him and covered it with cane syrup. "You want milk or some coffee? But I best warn you, the cow's been eating clover."

"Milk'd be fine, I don't much care how it tastes. The people I've been with don't seem able to swallow much else besides coffee."

By the time he got done, Mrs. Butters had left and Smith was back inside, sitting across from him, drinking more coffee. "What we got to do now," he said, "is get these folks something to eat that'll stick to their bones."

Smith got each of them a wide-brimmed hat and a gunnysack, then they started off through the Thicket. Even close to the clearing, the trees were thick, shutting out light, but the ground underneath stayed clear. Soon, though, they were closed in by vines and bushes, some of them taller than Bo. He probably couldn't have chopped his way through with an ax.

Of course, he didn't have to. Smith seemed to know where he was going. "It happens," he said. "Following around after Zeke, it kind of rubs off."

Bo was enjoying the morning, flowers growing everywhere, the good clean smell of earth, damp enough to feel springy but nowhere close to being mud. Then something different was in the air. It didn't smell bad, you didn't necessarily want to get away from it. Only it didn't make you want to get any closer, unless you had to be going there.

But it got worse. A sharp smell, like if smells were tastes, it'd be bitter. Or if they were sounds, they'd be getting shrill. Then even bitterer. And shriller.

"Smith?" Bo said.

"Pigeons," Smith answered.

Bo wondered why he hadn't heard it before, their wings making a thick blurring noise, but inside that thickness there was a moving up and down, always solid but never quite still.

"It'll get louder," Smith said. "Smellier, too. But Mrs. Butters wants pigeon pie."

Bo could see light ahead, a strange in-between kind, as though it had gotten free of the trees, only there was still something in the way of the sun. It was a clearing all right. But when they walked into it, the sounds were deafening. The air was filled with whirring pigeons, none of them ever still, but so many they took the place of sky, their mewings never quite drowned by the flapping sounds of wings. There were trees scattered across the clearing, but you couldn't really see them, because they were submerged, the limbs, even the trunks, beneath thousands and thousands of pigeons.

What you could smell was pigeon shit. Everyplace. Piled up, almost to the bottom tree limbs. "You follow just where I walk," Smith said. "And I don't mean almost. I mean exactly."

Smith walked carefully around the edge till he got to what seemed a slight ridge. Then Bo saw it was really a pathway made of felled trees, leading out toward the center of the clearing.

"Well, at least Zeke's bridge has stayed above water," Smith said. It was made out of single trunks laid end to end and looked slippery.

"Now you listen, boy," Smith said, "you fall in that stuff, you liable to drown. I don't know if it's possible, I never heard one way or the other. But you fall in, it's gonna take me maybe a second or two deciding what I plan on doing about it. And even if I decide to do the right thing, it might already be a little late. So do your best to move careful, you hear?"

Smith started out gingerly and Bo followed, going sideways, half walking, half sliding, and doing it slowly. They came to a tree limb sticking straight up, so they could both stop and hold on.

"Them birds sure been keeping themselves busy," Smith said, allowing himself a deep breath now that it couldn't interfere with his balance. "When Zeke and I put these trees down, we laid them right on top. And they're already just about covered. I bet this time next week you won't be able to even see them. Zeke says there's walking logs down underneath all over this clearing, he can't even remember where. How you doing?"

Everywhere Bo looked there were oceans of pigeon shit. "I'll be fine," he said, "only you don't need to get in too big a hurry."

"Consider yourself lucky," Smith said. "I was following Zeke. He was prancing cross here like it was a downtown boardwalk."

It took forever, but they finally got to the first up-and-down tree. "What Zeke said . . ." Smith moved over a little so Bo could reach the trunk. It felt slimy, but Bo didn't care, it was something to hold on to. "What Zeke said, never stop at the first tree. The birds, the big and fat ones, they somehow know to go farther in. The only birds left here are sickly, kind of scrawny ones."

Bo wasn't in any hurry to let go. "Why don't we all just develop a taste for scrawny?"

"She'd know. Even trying, we won't get them fat as Zeke does. He's got her spoiled. Anyway about pigeons."

So they started off again. And all that Bo could think about was every step he took, he was going to have to take it again going back. Carrying a gunnysack full of pigeons.

Even at the next tree, Smith didn't slow down. At the one

after that, Bo didn't ask, he just stopped. Smith must have figured out that Bo meant it.

"All right," he said. "First you lean against the tree. Then you locate a fat one. But be careful. Sometimes they don't take it too kindly." Smith reached up quickly and grabbed a pigeon and stuffed it into his gunny sack. All in one motion.

"Go ahead," Smith said. "She needs two bagfuls."

So Bo did. He leaned against the tree, half wondering why they were being so careful not to fall in since they were getting smeared all over anyway from the sides of the trees. He looked up, right above him, trying to locate a bird Smith would consider plump. But he didn't do it quite fast enough. The gob some pigeon just then released splattered squarely on the bridge of his nose, and without thinking he reached up to wipe it away, then thought better just in time and grabbed for the tree. Smith didn't say anything because he was laughing.

So the next time Bo didn't look straight up, only glanced from under the rim of his hat, and then grabbed for a bird like Smith had done. Well, almost like Smith had done. What he forgot, the one he grabbed for was a bottom limb bird, there were lots more higher up. And what dropped from up there came to rest on what was lower down.

So when Bo reached up for the pigeon, expecting to hold on to birdflesh covered by feathers, what he got instead was slick and damp and slimy. So his hand slipped, he missed the belly, he only caught a wing. And the pigeon, somewhat surprised itself, started flapping the other one, trying hard to get away.

Bo knew later he should have just let it go. There were plenty more pigeons even on that limb, ones that weren't moving, just sitting there looking on. He didn't need this special one. But he only knew that later. At the time, he held on. To the pigeon. Not to the tree. It was only when he realized what he'd done, then he let go.

The pigeon could fly away. And did. Bo had a similar, maybe even a bigger need. His feet were slipping and he could see it coming up at him, getting closer, oceans of slime, and pretty soon he was going to know all about it, how it really smelled, felt, even what it tasted like.

He took a deep breath, he didn't know how far down he'd be going, how long he'd be staying there, when he felt his shirt jerking backwards, choking him hard, and Smith was pulling him slowly back to the tree. Smith never did say anything about it, probably because then he would've had to stop laughing.

That night they ate pigeon pie. At first Bo wasn't too sure. When he looked over at the birds cooking, all he could think about was the way the slime lake had smelled, how he'd expected it to feel. But after the first few bites, he didn't exactly forget about it. But it didn't seem to matter much anymore.

After supper, they followed the kids outside. A couple played toward the edge of the clearing, but the rest stayed near the porch, feeling better close by the grown-ups.

"Yessir," Mrs. Butters said, settling in her chair, "there's a heap of pigeons out there. I been out there enough times to know. But that ain't nothing next to the hoppers."

"Ma'am?" Bo said.

"Grasshoppers," she said, "right after we first moved here. Zeke was convinced it was like in the Bible, there was some kind of reason, but he wasn't convinced enough to do anything about it. He'd found where he wanted to be, and hoppers or not, plague or whatever, he wasn't going to be pushed out.

"But lord, they was something. You couldn't hear somebody talk, even right up next to you, the whirring got so loud. And it wasn't just bothersome, it could make your ears truly hurt.

"When Zeke first started seeing 'em, he seemed to know what to do. He started boarding up windows, stuffing rags under the doors. So we were pretty safe inside the house. But outside, lord, they were everywhere. All over the trees, finally even the house, like it was painted top to bottom with hoppers. And a good bit of the time they covered the air the same way, like the clearing here was a jar stuffed full as you could get it, you could hardly get from one side to the other. It was like you were swimming through hoppers.

"You couldn't hear that you were walking over them, not at the time, the whirring was too loud for that. But you could feel it, they must've been two, three layers thick, lying all over. Zeke had taken the stock into the Thicket, where he figured the hoppers wouldn't be so heavy, and he was pretty much right. But one of the dogs wouldn't stay in the woods, he tried to follow Zeke back to the house, then he stood outside whining, pawing at the door. Only by then the hoppers were too thick and I could see it paining him, but Zeke wouldn't open the door. Next day, after the hoppers had left, least those that weren't still on the ground, the dog was lying out near the edge of the wood, blood dried all over him. What we figured, the hoppers got so thick they covered up his eyes, got into his ears, he kept pawing at them, scratching at them, but it didn't do him any good. Then he tried to run away from them, and almost did. But we figured, before he could get to the Thicket, they covered up his face and he couldn't breathe, they finally just buried him under, he finally just got drowned.

"They must have done it to themselves as well. The ground was covered with dead hoppers. We had to sweep them away. And the trees, all those close by the clearing, not a leaf left on them, like it was middle of winter in a place that stayed cold. But a little ways into the Thicket, things were just like they'd always been, thick and green like it's supposed to be. There ain't much you can do to the Thicket, not for long, there's just too much life out there. Can't no hopper stop it, not even a million."

The next morning Smith said he hadn't come here for rest, he was staying to help Mrs. Butters, and he figured it was time to get her some bacon. It wouldn't be any problem, Smith said, there were hogs everywhere, running wild, mainly acting mean.

"Razorbacks, Zeke calls them. In summer, when berries turn scarce and the acorns are all gone, they start getting gaunt, backs all humped up and sharpened, like the edge on a razor. That's what Zeke says, the ones I saw looked mainly fat. And ornery.

"Get yourself a rope," Smith said. "What we're gonna do is lasso us a hog."

"You ever do this before?"

"Nope," Smith said. "Which way you want to go?"

"Which way's easiest to find hogs?"

"Them devils are everywhere. You just pick."

They took their ropes and rifles and started out in a different direction from yesterday, but if Bo hadn't known, he couldn't have sworn to it. Once inside the Thicket, they were swimming through the same greenness, flower smells coming so dense it was like they were solid, pushing back against them while they were walking through.

"Don't you forget," Smith said, "these hogs got one tusk on top and they got another on the bottom, and either one'd ruin you for life."

"How bad we want hog meat?"

"What you do," Smith said, "you don't ever run from one. Shoot him, climb a tree, but don't you ever run from it. No man alive can outrun a hog."

"Any hog that mean," Bo said, "it's bound to be trouble eating. You real sure we need tough meat?"

"We don't plan to kill it, not just yet. When we find it, first we're going to rope it. If we do it with two ropes, we ought to be able to handle a hog. Then we're going to bring it back to the clearing, put it in the pen and fatten it up. This one ain't for us. I don't know when Zeke's gonna get back, it may be after I'm gone. So if we don't get hog meat, sooner or later Miz Butters is gonna try. But if you want to back out, one rope ought to manage."

Bo shook his head. "Let's go get us a hog."

Before long they heard a thrashing in the bushes ahead. Smith motioned Bo to be quiet and loosened out some rope. Bo did, too, and followed after him carefully. There it was right in front, too oblivious or disdainful to notice, or just more interested in some blackberry vines he was rooting in. Smith pointed to a nearby tree that had reachable limbs, and Bo nodded.

They edged up slowly. Smith held up one finger, then two, and right after he held up the third, both lassoes were heading through the air. As soon as they hit the pig's neck, it let out a squeal loud enough to rattle pots back at the cabin and made a leap Bo wouldn't have thought possible for an animal no bigger than that, and with two men on the other end of two ropes. Bo figured it couldn't last long, but for the moment the pig was winning, pulling them helter-skelter through the Thicket, all the time squalling mightily. Bo was lucky, the hog was pulling him straight into a sticker tree, so he had to let go. But Smith was still holding on. That is, till the whole Thicket seemed thrashing about, the whole sky seemed filled up with squeals.

And so there they came from every direction, what looked like hundreds, thousands—who wanted to count?—more hogs than Bo had ever even thought about, and they all seemed to be heading for him, and not a one was looking friendly.

Bo didn't care what Smith had said about running, he turned and headed faster than he thought he could back to the tree. He had to do it fast, because he heard something behind him and it was gaining.

"You, boy, get out of my goddam way," Smith said as he passed on by, picking up speed.

They'd had a head start, which was a good thing. Bo could feel a tusk graze his boot just as he pulled himself up into the tree. When he and Smith had both found a limb and gotten some breath, Bo looked around. The hogs were still there, none of them seemed inclined to leave, in fact it looked like more were still coming. As though, now that the danger was done with, now that their fellow hog had been relieved, it was time to hang around and have a party.

Except they didn't seem in a real joyful mood, they kept squealing and grinding and banging their tusks together like they were getting them good and sharp. A few of them, most likely disappointed they'd been cheated out of a fight, started in on each other, ripping and slashing and snorting, only none of them kept it up long.

"Okay, Smith," Bo said. "What're we gonna do now?"

"Just for the moment, we're gonna stay here in this tree. Where'd you leave your rifle?"

Bo pointed. It was leaning against a different tree, back where they'd started getting their ropes ready.

"Mine, too. Zeke forgot to tell me about taking it with me. Or maybe he didn't forget, maybe he just thought he shouldn't have to, anybody who wasn't a damn fool wouldn't need reminding."

Most of the pigs were settling in, raking up pine straw, lying down, content on staying right where they were. In fact, Bo could see young ones now, some no more than babies, playing around, first on the edges, but now coming on into the group.

"Watch this," Smith said. He broke off a small branch and threw it into the middle of a gathering of hogs. They immediately started up again, squealing and gnashing about.

"Why'd you want to do that for?" Bo said.

"You watch. Zeke told me about it, only I haven't had any reason before to see it."

What they did, at least the ones that must have been mothers, was round up all the little pigs in a hurry, get them into a circle. Then the grownups started piling up around them, over them, the pile all the time getting bigger and bigger, higher and higher, till it grew almost the size of a small house.

"I'll be damned," Smith said. "Not much chance a wolf or cat has, getting inside of that."

"Much less you or me. If for some reason I can't figure we wanted to. But what're we gonna do? They might decide on staying here a month."

"Well, sooner or later I suppose Miz Butters will come looking."

"That'd be just great," Bo said, looking at the hogs, thinking about her stumbling in and being surprised.

"Well," Smith said, "Zeke said there was something you could do, except I can't work up much enthusiasm about it."

"We've got to do something. What'd Zeke say?"

"He said the only way to handle a hog if something had happened to your gun is just walk right up and kick him in the nose. Says most of the time just once will do it, then the hog gets out of the way. He didn't say what happens the rest of the time."

Bo stared at Smith to make sure he wasn't joking. He decided he had to be.

"No, I ain't joking," Smith said. "Zeke may have been, but I'm not in that kind of mood right at the moment. Cause if Zeke *was* joking, there just may develop right here a very wrong relationship between man and hog."

Smith eased down till he was almost on the ground, being careful to stay on the side of the tree away from the pile of hogs that were still giving shelter to their young. Most of the hogs weren't paying much attention anyway, but there were still two left between Smith and the rifles. Even now that he was on the ground, Smith didn't move hurriedly. But one of the two hogs did, coming straight for him. Bo could see Smith kind of sigh, and then draw back his leg like he was aiming real careful and then letting it rip.

The hog let out a howl and scampered backwards, but by now the other one was coming. Except now Bo had climbed down, too, and just as the other hog got to Smith, Bo was running hard, not even slowing down when he felt his boot hitting the snout, almost lifting the hog in the air, and Bo was still running, grabbing at his rifle. But Smith already had his own and was turning around, not bothering to take much aim, only not firing toward the pile either. Even so, Bo heard one hog squalling in a different tone and then the others were running, this time in the right direction, the ground under Bo was even shaking. Bo fired, too, but he did it in the air, and he probably didn't need to even do that. The hogs, all except the one Smith had shot, had fully decided to leave.

"Well," Smith said, looking at the one on the ground, "he's not likely to get much fatter, but we do have us our hog."

They spent most of the afternoon taking care of it. Mrs. Butters told them how. Cut it up, she said, throw the pieces into a barrel of water so the blood can get all soaked out.

Then they put the pieces into another barrel of cold water to soak all night. Tomorrow, she said, they'd take the hog parts out, add some salt, then pack it all down inside another barrel. Later, after the brine got good and thick, there'd be pickled pork and collard greens. But for now, Mrs. Butters said, they'd done enough for one day.

So in the cooling down of afternoon, they were sitting out on the porch, feeling a breeze come through the dog run. The kids, their chores finished for the time being, were doing whatever it was they felt like. Genny and Eck, the two oldest, had tattered almanacs and were practicing their reading. Levi, who was maybe about eight—Bo still hadn't gotten their ages quite straight, but Levi was somewhere in the middle—was sitting out in front, digging in the packed-down dirt. Dute and Ruthie, the two youngest, were out at the edge of the clearing, halfway up a sapling tree, letting the breeze make them sway back and forth. It gave Bo the feeling of home.

Then Ruthie screamed. Bo and Smith were up at the same time and running toward the sound. They didn't know what had caused it, but they hadn't heard anything like it coming from Ruthie before. They hadn't got started good across the clearing when Bo felt something, he couldn't see it, but he felt, heard it go by close to his head. He dove to the ground, and right behind where he'd just been, now there was an arrow quivering, its shaft halfway down into the hard dirt.

Bo didn't bother to look where it had come from. He rolled to a crouch and ran zigzag to where the barrel of pig was sitting. There wasn't much room, because Smith was already behind it. They both were breathing hard.

"We got to get them kids," Smith said softly, in between catching his breath.

That's when they first saw the Indians. Not real clearly. It was like they just wanted Bo and Smith to see enough to know they were really there. About a dozen, staying close to the ground, surrounding Ruthie and Dute's tree.

"Keep your heads down!" It was Mrs. Butters. They looked back toward the house. The other kids were inside. The shutters were already closed, leaving only portholes just big enough for rifles and aiming. There was a muzzle sticking out of one of them.

They felt the bullet going by them, kicking up dust out near the tree.

"We got to do something," Smith said.

"What?"

"Hell, Bo, how do I know?"

Then they saw it. An Indian, on the far side of the tree, pulling himself up onto a bottom limb. When he was halfway to the kids, Mrs. Butters shot again, but the tree was in the way, she missed again.

Then she had to stop. The Indian was holding Ruthie. She was screaming, not the loud surprised way she had at first. Now it seemed to come from some sense of terror so deep inside her it was like somebody else's. And she wasn't struggling, just screaming.

He lifted her, then let her drop into the arms of an Indian standing just under the tree. They seemed to be treating her gently. Forcefully, but gently.

Then the Indian in the tree went for Dute. It took longer. Dute was still climbing. That was the only way open for him, so that's where he meant to go. And if the tree had been built different it might have worked. If he could have gotten where the trunk or one of the branches was so slender, so fragile that it would support the weight of a boy but not a man, maybe it could have worked. Though in the long run, Bo didn't see how.

The Indian caught up while Dute was trying to dodge his way out onto a limb. But once he was caught, Dute started fighting with a silent desperation. He stopped worrying about holding on, about the possibilities of falling. He was kicking, gouging, trying to make every part of his body that had an edge to it hit against some part of the man who was trying to hold him. He kept it up even when he was in the air, being dropped to the Indian standing on the ground waiting.

"Maybe we could edge the barrel up close, stay behind it, use it like a shield?"

"What you plan to do when we get there?" Smith said.

"Maybe we ought to go back and get our rifles first."

"We're sure not doing much good here."

Right when they'd decided, they heard Mrs. Butters. Her voice wasn't excited. It sounded grim and determined, but not overly loud. "You boys be careful, but get yourselves back in here. I'm going to do some shooting just to keep their attention. You get around to the back and get there down low and fast."

That's what they did, running low, while she shot over their heads, not hitting anything, but getting Bo and Smith to the back of the house where there was a small door, right next to the ground, just big enough for a person to scoot through. Above it was a porthole with a gun sticking out. As soon as they got there, the little door came open and they slid themselves inside, right by the legs of Genny, the oldest, who didn't even look down from the barrel of her rifle.

Bo and Smith didn't say anything until they had their rifles and found shooting places looking toward the front yard.

"What're we going to do?" Smith said once he'd gotten positioned.

"I don't know," Mrs. Butters said quietly. "I don't know yet what they're up to."

"What is it usually?" Bo asked.

"There ain't no usually," she said. "Most of them think the Thicket's filled with spirits, sacred animals and such that don't want messing with. They figure anybody fool enough to live here, they'll get taken care of by things a lot scarier than themselves. Those out there, they must be strangers, worship different spirits. I don't know what they want. I only know what they got."

"Maybe we should try to get around in back of them?" Smith said.

Bo didn't look back from his porthole. "It'd be worth a try."

"You'd just get yourself killed," Mrs. Butters said. "Zeke, maybe. Zeke might could do it. But those devils out there, they know more about such things than you do. You'd just get yourself killed, you wouldn't even know where to go. Look out your hole. Where you figure they are?"

Bo kept looking. All he could see was the Thicket, dense, impenetrable, the same as it always was.

"We can't just stand here," Smith said.

"What else you got in mind?" Mrs. Butters said.

Neither Smith nor Bo had any answer.

Then they started hearing it. Screams that started off more like whimpers, then they got louder and stayed that way.

"Mama," Genny said, still looking out her porthole. "That's Dute."

Mrs. Butters didn't turn her head. "You kids be quiet. Try not to listen."

Eck turned around and stared. "Mama, that's Dute out there. We've got to go get him!" He started for the crawl hole.

"You get back here, Eck." There wasn't any maybe in her voice. "You're just thirteen years old. You expect ever to be fourteen, you stay inside this house."

He did as he was told. He sat in a corner and Bo could hear him trying to stop crying. Levi, the eight-year-old, sat in a different corner, simply not understanding, probably not wanting to, just wanting it to be over.

Bo stared out his porthole. An hour ago the world was good, people were happy. And now there was nothing but screams, still steady but getting tireder. Then they stopped. A minute earlier Bo wouldn't have believed that silence could have been worse than the screaming.

Bo didn't see who did it. It happened too quickly. But all of a sudden Dute's body was lying in the clearing. Naked. Bloody. Clearly dead. All Bo could think about was Ruthie.

Then he saw her. They all did. Two men brought her to the edge of the clearing and ripped off her dress. She was too scared now even to scream. At least at first.

One of the men took a stick, it didn't look terribly pointed, just sharp enough, and started scraping it across her body. It didn't take long for the blood to start showing. It looked like it would be a long time before they were through.

"Mama." Genny had long since left her post. Smith without saying anything had taken her place. "Mama, you saw what happened to Dute! Go ahead and shoot. If you hit Ruthie by mistake, what'll it matter? At least it'll be over."

Mrs. Butters didn't take her eyes away from the barrel of her gun. "I'm thinking about it, Genny, I'm thinking."

"Let's go, Bo," Smith said quietly. "I'm not gonna want to live with myself if we don't."

"You stay right here," Mrs. Butters said. "We're probably going to need you."

Then as suddenly as she had appeared, Ruthie was gone. Nobody saw where, only that the clearing was empty. The only sound in the Thicket was the raucous call of a crow, somewhere distant, overhead.

Inside the cabin, nobody moved. "We may be here for awhile," Mrs. Butters finally said, without looking away from her porthole. "Sooner or later, like it or not, we're gonna have to eat." Still, nobody moved, until Genny stood up and got everybody a slice of pickled pork, but nobody except Levi ate any. Then it got dark.

"Okay," Mrs. Butters said. "Whatever it is that's going to happen, it's about ready to get started."

She was right. Pretty soon there were some sparks, then there was a bonfire just at the edge of the Thicket. The light flickered across the clearing, making the darkness seem to be dancing.

"You folks get ready," Mrs. Butters said. "I suspect some of them have already moved in around us."

Nobody said anything about Ruthie.

Then there was a man, seeming huge in the light of the bonfire. "Don't anybody shoot," Mrs. Butters said. "He's holding onto something."

They could see it was Ruthie. She was naked, bloody, and the man let her go. Then she was alone, there was only Ruthie standing in front of the bonfire. She started toward the house. She took maybe a dozen steps before she fell the first time. She got up and took maybe a dozen more. She moved slowly, her face older by ages, frozen in concentration.

Bo tried to see through her eyes, but he couldn't. He couldn't even guess what she'd been going through back in the darkness. But he could imagine something of what she was seeing now. Home, her mother. Except it was a blank wall, shut up windows with rifle barrels sticking out.

Then she started screaming. But it was different. There were words this time. Or at least a word. For the first time Mrs. Butters seemed to flinch. The screams didn't stop.

"Mama," she screamed over and over again, trying not to fall, wanting only to get closer, to get behind the walls.

"Ruthie!" Mrs. Butters's voice sounded calm, stern, as though she was giving instructions about chores. "Ruthie, you listen. Go around to the back. We can't let you in the front. You've got to go around to the back."

But Ruthie didn't stop, didn't stop screaming or change her direction. Her progress was slow but it was steady.

She made it to the front door. They could all hear her, it wasn't exactly pounding, it was too weak for that, but they all heard and Bo expected everybody heard it the same way he did, sounding like thunder. The only thing louder in the world was her screaming.

And through it all, there was Mrs. Butters's voice. "Ruthie, honey, we can't open the door. You've got to crawl a little bit farther. You've got to get around to the back."

"Goddammit," Smith said, "this is goddam crazy. I'm opening that door."

"You get close to that door and I'll shoot you." Her voice still seemed calm. "Why do you think they let her go? You open that door, they'll be in here with us. All of them. I don't even care much about you. Or Bo. Or for that matter, about me. But I've got three kids left in here. And maybe, just maybe, one outside. But I know I've got three left in here. I'm going to salvage what I can."

Smith turned back to his porthole.

Ruthie kept pounding, Mrs. Butters kept talking to her, "I'm gonna take care of you," she kept saying, "but you've got to go around to the back."

Finally the pounding stopped. Everybody in the house, without saying anything, suddenly became tensed by the silence. Then they could hear her stumbling down the steps, around the corner, toward the crawl hole in the back.

"Okay," Mrs. Butters said. "Everybody get ready. When we open it, they're gonna be there, too."

They were. Ruthie got about halfway through. Smith had her arms, trying to help, when there was a pulling from the other side, dragging her backwards, and another arm came in from the outside, reaching for Ruthie's waist, and then suddenly there was a gush of blood, a hand was by itself on the floor and Ruthie was in the room, the crawl-hole door was closed. Everybody turned and looked at Levi who was standing there crying, holding an ax.

Then things were still for awhile. Mrs. Butters doctored Ruthie the best she could and held her, even after her crying quietened and she finally fell asleep. "We don't know how long we're going to be doing this," Mrs. Butters said. "We'd better start taking turns."

Everybody knew what she meant. Nobody wanted to sleep. Except it wasn't a time for inclinations. They had a job to do, so Bo and Mrs. Butters and Levi stayed awake first.

Things kept on being quiet. When Bo woke Smith up to take his turn, Bo said, "You think they're still out there?"

Smith stared at the wall, not really looking at it, as though he was trying to shut out what was close by so he could stay tied down to some other part of his mind.

"Them," was all he said.

Then he said it again.

"You keep remembering," he said, "they ain't after me. They may get me, but they ain't after me. It's you folks they're after."

"What're you talking about? They aren't after me, I mean not personal, at least no more than they're after you."

"It ain't me," Smith said, "that's taking their spirit lands."

"What's wrong with you, Smith? I don't want anybody's land, theirs or anybody else's, you know that."

"That could be true. But you got lots of similarities with them that do."

Then he turned away and went to a porthole.

When Bo woke up, it was morning and Smith was sitting at the table drinking coffee. The door was open. The kids were sitting on the floor close to it, looking, but not wanting to go someplace where there wasn't a roof over them, a door between themselves and the outside.

"You good awake?" Smith said.

Bo stretched and got up from his blanket and walked to the door. The sun was shining hard. Birds were sounding like they usually did. The Thicket was acting as though yesterday hadn't happened.

But Ruthie was back there sleeping, probably still hurting, feeling it even while she was sleeping, hurting not just in her body, probably even in her dreams.

"Nothing's happened," Smith said. "They're gone. And Zeke's been back."

"Been?"

Smith nodded. "Long enough to bury Dute. Now he's gone to kill some Indians."

"How'd he know to come?"

Smith just looked at Bo and then turned his attention back to his coffee.

Bo got himself a cup, too, and they sat there, not saying anything, just drinking, doing their best not to think.

"Where is she?" Bo said.

"Out by where he dug the grave, back of the house a ways. Inside the Thicket."

Bo walked outside and got a pan of water and splashed it on himself as best he could. He'd at least like to look presentable. Then he went to find her.

She was just standing there looking. Bo walked up beside her, and he just stood, too. It wasn't a time for talking. Then she walked over to a tree trunk that had fallen. She sat down, her back to the mound of fresh dirt, looking now into the Thicket. Bo sat beside her. She seemed content to have him there, another human presence to share her grief in the middle of such relentless, unquenchable life.

Bo sat for awhile, and then he left her. He could feel she wanted to be left alone now, as though she needed time to see differently, to take in that Dute was part of the Thicket in an unaccustomed way.

Bo walked away quietly. But then he turned and looked back. She was still sitting there, not moving, so still she seemed to merge into the Thicket surrounding her, as permanent and as fragile as life itself. He walked a ways farther, feeling the greenness coming at him from every direction. When he turned around again, he had lost her. But he knew she was still there, sitting quietly, breathing in the smells of the bushes, the trees, the freshly turned earth.

When Bo got back to the house, Smith was ready to leave.

"Why now?" Bo asked.

"Zeke's back, she won't need me."

"But he's already gone again."

"He won't be long."

"I thought you felt good here, it's like you belong."

"Maybe that's what I'm afraid of." He cinched his horse and was strapping his gear behind the saddle. "What you don't understand," Smith said, "maybe I was on the wrong side last night."

Smith was right, Bo didn't understand. Not at all. He didn't even want to pretend.

"Don't listen wrong, Bo, I got no stomach for these kinds of killing, I'm not talking about that. The folks here, Zeke and Mrs. Butters and the rest of them, they're not the ones who're taking away the land and the buffaloes and the hunting grounds, they're not the ones putting up fences. But the rest wouldn't come unless they hadn't got it started. So they're part of it, even if they don't know it, even if they don't want to, they're part of it.

"And those Indians last night, they may have been crazy on liquor or just crazy in the head naturally, but whatever their reasons, even if they don't know it, they're part of it, too. Except on the other side, they're saying you can't just come in here and say this land is yours. It wasn't put here to be owned. So I've got to leave. You understand now?"

"No."

"Then you're not listening. Because it's the same sort of people who think they can own land that think they can own me. Like the land. They think I'm something that can be bought and sold, too. Just like the land."

"The war's over."

"That's what you think."

"Where you going?"

"Same place I've been all along."

"The Territory? Even after last night?"

"Whatever they were doing, trying to do, they weren't doing it to me," Smith said. "They won't be my people, but it'll be close, it'll be nearer than this."

"How're you even going to know where to find it?"

"I talked to Zeke. He told me to wait, told me if I waited he'd take me there. But I need to go. If I stayed much longer, I might forget which side I'm supposed to be on."

So Smith left. Then Zeke was back.

He wasn't at all what Bo had expected. He wasn't sure what he had expected, but Zeke wasn't it. He looked like some kind of elf, maybe a leprechaun, like in one of the stories his mother had read him and Davey. When Zeke walked in the door, Mrs. Butters looked him in the eye, and all Zeke did was nod. Just once. Then as far as Zeke seemed concerned that was all there was to say about Dute and the Indians.

That first day, they tried to get back into routines. Everybody spent a lot of time tending to Ruthie. But besides that, it was like they'd decided that the only way to deal with yesterday was to make today seem like most of the others, the ones they were used to. Zeke spent it on the porch, studying the edge of the Thicket.

At first Bo thought he just didn't talk much. Then he realized that wasn't it. He just didn't listen. At least not to people. Not to words. He heard other sounds, he seemed to pay them close attention. Just not to words. When he talked, it was like he was simply giving sounds to things going on in his head. And when he was done, that's where he went back to.

Mrs. Butters busied herself with household things. But Bo felt she was looking inside herself, too, only she was probably seeing different things.

The kids did their chores and stayed near the house.

That night on the porch after supper, nobody was saying much until Mrs. Butters asked Zeke if he was staying.

"Awhile," he said. "Maybe I'll give Bo a look at the Thicket fore he heads on up to the Territory."

"The Territory?"

Zeke didn't answer, only kind of snorted, which Bo figured was a laugh, except it sounded like Zeke was blowing his nose and needed to.

Zeke didn't answer, at least not Bo's question. "Boy," he said, "you ever see a man jump out of a barrel? I mean, just standing there, inside a barrel and then jumping clean out?"

"No sir," Bo said. "I don't think I ever did."

"Don't *think!*" Zeke said. "Son, if you'd ever seen it, most likely you'd remember. Martha," Zeke said, "we got us a barrel? This is something the boy might remember."

Mrs. Butters answered quietly. "I don't think so, Zeke, the only one we've got is half full of flour."

"Well, let's get it emptied. This is something the boy

might want to remember. What's traveling around good for, you don't come back with things you want to remember?"

"Not tonight," she said. "If you want it emptied, you do it yourself. I'm going to bed." She gathered up the kids, sent them on their way, and then she went to sleep, too, lying on the floor beside Ruthie's bed.

Zeke didn't seem to notice, only leaned back a little more in his chair. "Well, you'll just have to imagine it. But I suspect it's the sort of thing you'd probably want to remember."

It wasn't so bad in the daytime. There was enough usually going on, you didn't have to think much about things that had already happened, that might happen again. He and Davey slept in the attic, it was more like a loft than a room, but it was theirs, it felt like a world that belonged only to them. Bo was trying to sleep, just like he was now, but he couldn't and he didn't know why, except that home just didn't feel the same anymore and then he realized that Davey was crying, not loud. It was like he was trying not to but couldn't help it. Bo called over to him and the crying stopped. Bo called again, and there still wasn't any answer, as though Davey was pretending to be asleep. So Bo got out of his bed and went across the room and lay beside Davey and waited.

"I miss Rooter," Davey said.

"But you knew we had to kill him, that's why we had him. We've had to do it with other pigs before."

"I know," Davey said, and trembled a little as though he wanted to start crying again and he wouldn't let himself. "But somehow this time it wasn't the same." He sniffed, clearing up his nose, and turned his head even farther away from Bo's. "It doesn't seem like anything is anymore."

Bo didn't answer, there was nothing he could say or do. Except just lie there until he could tell Davey was really asleep. Then he got up quietly and went back to his own bed.

"You want to find honey," Zeke said, "you got to find yourself some bees." He held up and studied one of his shoes, stout, heavy, freshly cleaned of the mud and gunk it'd carried the day before.

"A man's got to be careful about shoes," he said. "If he's considering walking, shoes is about the most important thing there is."

Light shone through two holes in the shoe, one on each side, a little back of where Zeke's toes were going to be.

"Oh, that," he said, seeing that Bo had noticed. "That's so the water can get out. Hand me them buckets."

Bo did, two of them, empty, their handles tied to each end of the same rope. "You take that other one," Zeke said, slinging his two over a shoulder.

Bo's bucket didn't have a rope, but it had a lid on and wasn't empty. "You carry that there rifle," Zeke said. He picked up the ax, the same one Levi had used the day before yesterday. The stains were still on it.

The sun today was everywhere, the same way it had been yesterday, the day before, so strong it seemed to push its way through branches where there should have been shade.

"I seen 'em the other day," Zeke said. "Bees. Doing their drinking. On my way back home."

They walked, Zeke heading straight through the Thicket, finding moving space where it didn't seem possible. Then he started talking again, like there hadn't been a pause. "Lots of folks, they try to find 'em near where they get their honey, around berry bushes and flowers, tallow trees and such. You can do it that way. Water's better."

They kept walking.

"Reason is, they usually head for water, close to their tree as they can find it. You locate where they drink, you can start looking for where they live."

They kept on walking.

"Following them from where they get their honey, though. Lord, that can be a piece."

Bo was getting used to it. He wasn't even waiting. Whatever Zeke planned to say, it would come in due time.

"Course, it's not always the case. I seen bees drinking long ways away and there's water right nigh their tree."

Bo didn't mind. It got so that Zeke's voice, when it did come, was like the Thicket's other sounds, a bird you'd hear and then it'd be gone, only to come back again later.

"You see, what I figure, it ain't just the water. Bees, they don't like real water, what they want is damp ground. They want something they can be standing on, doing their drinking."

It blended in with what had been there before, the rustling, the buzzings, and the birdsongs.

"Course, it ain't just that. They want water, that's for certain, but it's like they're drawing something else out of the ground, too, like they pick that particular spot cause the ground's adding something to what it is they're getting. Sometime what I figure, it ain't the water, it's the land we need more understanding about."

Bo wasn't paying much attention, so he didn't know why, but all of a sudden he was remembering the alligators back home in the bayou, strange beings looking as though they'd come from different times, or stayed on through all of them.

But Zeke was discussing bees. And about things in the Thicket, Zeke was more than likely right.

They were on a path. Bo didn't know what had made it, pigs, deer, maybe even people. But it looked like it was used. It had to be, Bo figured. Otherwise, the Thicket would have covered it almost overnight. However it got there, Bo was grateful. He trusted Zeke, no matter what direction. But he still liked being on a path, going the same way other people or things had already been.

It was as though Zeke was listening to Bo's thinking. "Pretty soon now," he said, "we got to head back through the Thicket. Where them bees drink, it's a ways off."

Bo shrugged.

"I spect you like this here path better," Zeke said and snorted. "I spect you worried bout snakes and spiders and such."

"Should I be?"

"You bet," Zeke said.

They walked some more.

"Course you don't need to worry bout what's off the path."

"Why not?"

Zeke snorted again. "Cause right now you need to be worried bout what's on it. Paths is just there to make folks feel better. Except when you got your eyes working right. Then it's about the same. For instance, why don't you mosey on over to that rock over there." He pointed toward a ridge of red clay running head high. On top of it, near where they were standing, was a medium-sized rock.

"Why don't you just go over there and pick up that there rock."

Bo figured Zeke wouldn't do anything truly harmful. He wasn't sure, but at least he figured. Still, he stood in front of the rock awhile before reaching.

There was a glint in Zeke's eyes. "Go ahead, boy, I reckon you figure we're safe, being we're still smack dab in the middle of this here path."

Bo gingerly raised up the rock. As soon as he did there was a rattling and the smell of sour cucumbers. But before he could smash the rock back down on the snake, Zeke had it by the tail end, swinging it around his head, Bo having to duck so he wouldn't be hit by the other end, all the time Zeke snorting away as though he'd just done something wonderfully clever. Then he snapped the snake like he was popping a whip, and the head sailed off into the Thicket, and almost without a pause in his motion, Zeke flung the rest of the snake after it.

Zeke was beside himself snorting. When he finally quieted down, he took a deep breath and Bo thought he was getting ready to start again, he'd just temporarily run out of air.

"No sirree, beasties like that, boy, they're gonna be all around you, just a matter of knowing which rock to look under."

Bo wasn't interested in looking. But he did regard the rocks, the fallen trees, and the bushes he passed with considerably more respect and distance.

"This way," Zeke said without even looking back, leaving the path, pushing his way into the Thicket. "Never owned a compass," he said. "Got one inside my head. Don't even think about it, I just follow where it tells me to go."

"Has it ever been wrong?"

"Yep. You be careful now. It's usually the second one they bite." And then he snorted and didn't slow down.

"Right here," he said.

It didn't look different from anywhere else they'd been, not even a clearing, just a spot in the middle of the Thicket, everything dense, still growing and green, buzzings of different sorts, but not even the sign of a bee.

"Over there," Zeke said, pointing to a stump. "You take your bucket over there."

Bo did, the ground so damp it was sucking on his boots. He set the bucket on the stump. "I reckon you better open it," Zeke said. "What you got is the bait."

"Bait?"

"How you reckon on coursing bees less we find them? And the secret is, boy, we don't find them, we kind of let them find us."

Bo pried open the lid. Inside was a liquid, not quite clear, but not far from it, and smelling sweet.

"Sugar water," Zeke said. "With just a smidge of honey. You don't want it real thick. Bees'll get stuck in it, all smeared over, they won't be able to fly. They'll drown happy, but they shore will drown."

Zeke took a swig of the sugar water and spit it all over the brush close by. "Don't just stand there, boy, spray them bushes."

Bo did, until the two of them had spat bait on all the branches near at hand, but that still left the bucket half full.

"What we do, boy, we want them to come down, we got to get their attention. They smell these bushes, they think they've found what they're after. Then they're gonna find that bucket and have a sudden change of mind." He snorted, but only at about half force this time. "They're like most folk I know, they ain't even close to figuring out what it is they're really looking for. So somebody's got to help them a mite. And when they do manage to find it, they'll go on thinking they got it done all by themselves. Which is fine with me, long's we get to eat their honey. Now you get some twigs and float them down inside, on top of what's left of the sugar water."

Bo did, not even bothering to ask why.

"That's what they're looking for," Zeke said, looking into the bucket, "this here sweet stuff. But they want to be standing on something while they're sucking it all up. They ain't dumb, least about some things here and there. They know they can get drowned in too much of a good thing."

"Now what?"

"Take them two," he pointed to the empty buckets. "Bang them up against each other, hard like. You got to get their attention."

Bo did, the clanging seeming unnatural among the everyday sounds of the Thicket. But it worked, at least something did. A few bees drifted down out of nowhere, most of them drawn to the bushes where Zeke and Bo had sprayed. A few still didn't seem satisfied, they buzzed about till they came across the bait bucket. Before long they were joined by a sizable number of their friends.

Zeke snorted, almost softly this time. "They're all inside, storing it away. Watch. It's about this time they'll be heading home."

Sure enough, they were coming out, circling, as though they were considering directions.

Bo was ready to follow, but Zeke motioned him to stay put. "People who talk about something being straight as a beeline, they ain't coursed a whole lot of bees. What the beasties will do first, they'll circle around, looking for the easiest way to get where they're heading. And what they know, what most folks don't, the quickest way to get someplace ain't necessarily on a straight line. It all depends on what gets in your way. Like them longleaf pines over yonder."

Zeke pointed to a stand of more than usually tall trees. The bees, only buzzing black dots by now, were flying alongside the timber, skirting around.

"What we'll do is go straight through," Zeke said, "come out the other side. Then we'll see which way they truly mean to go. Hard to be real sure, right off."

Zeke seemed able to find a path where Bo knew for certain there wasn't one, as though he carried one along with him, opening things up a ways in front. But when Zeke got a few steps ahead, the Thicket seemed to move in behind him, leaving Bo feeling what it would be like being lost, feeling the Thicket closing in around him, like direction didn't have any meaning, there wasn't any this way or that, not even a whole lot of up and down, everything was tangled, filling every space no matter how it had to twist to get there. There was just too much of it.

Then they were out on the other side of the stand of pines. And sure enough, the bees had changed course. Zeke pointed up and snorted. Which was the last time he seemed concerned about the bees. Once they got walking, he even started slowing down.

"Zeke?" Bo said when he noticed, "you sure this is really the right way?"

Zeke's head jerked around. "Depends. What's certain, it's the direction that's gonna get us honey."

He waited awhile. "Course, we ain't out here mainly to get honey."

"Then why're we messing around with bees?"

"Cause we're gonna get us some honey. We just ain't mainly gonna do that. But to do what we're really doing, we've got to have them bees."

Bo was finally getting impatient. "Then you tell me. What're we really doing?"

"What we're really doing, boy, is walking. Through these here woods, this here world that's around us, walking and looking and feeling and smelling. And we need them bees so we can have us a reason for doing it, so we can have us a direction to be heading in. But now that we've got it, boy, it's time to slow down. Slow down, boy, let yourself walk through the Thicket."

So that's what Bo did. And it was like Zeke was pointing things out, though he wasn't, he didn't seem to be paying Bo any mind. But it was like something or somebody was causing Bo to look at things differently, shades of colors, smells of flowers, whole walls of orchids. And after awhile the animals. At first just sounds, a scurrying and crashing and the quieting down of birds. Then Bo got to noticing, a squirrel here and there, a porcupine in the distance. Then off in the shadows a pig, a solitary deer. Finally through an opening in the undergrowth, a mother bear, her cubs struggling to keep up, heading fast in the other direction.

"Start looking," Zeke said.

"I have been," Bo answered.

"No you ain't, you been seeing. What I want you to do now is start looking."

"For what?"

"For a tree, one that looks like maybe it's hollow. Or one with claw marks. We ain't the only animals that's got a liking for honey."

Of course Zeke didn't need any help looking, and they both knew it. Even while he was talking, he was heading straight for a tree. The closer they got to it, Bo could see black dots coming and going.

"Now, boy, whatever you do, leave off slapping at them. They ain't gonna do you no harm, less you start knocking them down and pushing them every which way."

Bo looked skeptical.

"Here, you take this." Zeke handed Bo a homemade match and a rolled-up rag of cloth, maybe a foot long, a couple of inches round. "When we get to the honey, you take this and light one end. The smoke'll help keep 'em out of your way. You wait here." Zeke walked up to the tree like the bees weren't even there. He reached down and took a handful of moss from the Thicket floor and stuffed it in the bee hole. The bees on the outside seemed confused. Bo could only speculate about the attitude of any others.

"That's good," Zeke said. He handed Bo the axe and stood back like he was mainly an interested bystander.

"Cut her down," he told Bo. "Just don't hit where it's holler."

Bo had felled trees before, except there hadn't ever been any bees inside. He tapped along the trunk, making sure he found a place that was solid. He wasn't anxious for early encounters.

The tree was pine, the wood was soft, it wasn't long before Bo had the tree on the ground. He figured a grown-up couldn't have done much better.

Zeke grunted. "Shows what happens, you keep your ax sharp. Here, give 'er to me."

Zeke took the ax, then banged it against the tree until he'd located both ends of the hollow. Bo could hear the bees buzzing more loudly inside. Zeke just snorted. "They ain't real smooth-natured, is they?" And he banged again.

He chopped about halfway through, just above and below where he'd figured the hollow to run. "Now, boy," he said, "you'd best set fire to that smoke rag and come here with them buckets."

Then with just a few strokes, Zeke split out the section between the earlier cuts, opening up the hollow, and the bees came out swarming.

It didn't matter what Zeke had said. When the bees came roaring around him, Bo started swinging away with his smoke cloth. But there were too many of them, he finally threw the rolled-up rag away, toward what looked like the biggest bunch of them. He hit Zeke instead, who seemed a little surprised, but Bo didn't have time to bother, they were landing everywhere, on his face, in his eyes, there wasn't much else to do but start waving and slapping. As soon as he did, he remembered again what Zeke had said, and he was learning the reason why. The more he slapped, the more they seemed coming at him, in his hair now, he was moving too furiously to have more than one or two stings, but it was early yet and Bo knew he was outnumbered.

He started running and the bees started following. But water in the Thicket was never far off, so at the first sign of a creek, Bo dove in. It turned out to be mainly mud, so Bo slid a ways, getting good and burrowed in, but the water was still deep enough, the bees lost interest before Bo had to start breathing.

After he'd brushed himself off the best he could and got back to the tree, Zeke was sitting on the ground eating great hunks of honey, bees flying all around, walking across his face, resting in his beard. Zeke only stopped eating long enough to blow some away from his mouth, and when he saw Bo up close, he snorted and offered Bo a huge gob of honey. Bo shook his head and kept his distance.

Later, that afternoon at the cabin, Mrs. Butters matter-of-factly rubbed tobacco into Bo's bee stings and went back to Ruthie's bedside. In everything else, Genny had become head of the house. Everyone was quiet, the kids looking as though they were only gradually getting used to what had happened, what still might. But they did eat a considerable amount of honey. When Zeke brought a bucket of it over, even Ruthie smiled.

Still, everything was a lot quieter than normal. Except, of course, for Zeke. Now that he'd finished what he'd figured was his job with the Indians, it was like nothing had happened.

"What'd you expect me to do?" he said out of nowhere to Bo. "I can't do nothing to bring the boy back."

They were sitting on the porch. Zeke was still licking honey off his fingers.

"It's a fact," he said as if he were answering some question Bo had forgotten to ask. "It makes the difference. Back in Mississippi, fore I knew any better, I tried to have me a hive right out the back door, it'd be there anytime I wanted. Attracted some fine wild bees to live in it, too. They liked it. Ought to, lot better place to live and make honey than the trunk of some tree. And they'd leave and go back to the same woods, right where they'd been before they set up with me. Then they'd come back and make their honey. But it never was the same. The taste, it was somehow different, just not as rich on the tongue. It was like you needed to taste the wildness, and it just wasn't there. No sir, it ain't worth arguing, you need some wildness to get it done right." Then he licked his fingers a time or two more and joined Mrs. Butters inside.

The next morning, Zeke was back on the porch when Bo got up. Ruthie was sleeping quietly, and so was Mrs. Butters, still sitting on the floor, resting her head on the pillow near Ruthie's. The other kids, Zeke said, were out in the fields doing chores.

"As for us," he said, "we'd best be getting you back on the road. Charley ain't gonna come looking for you, least not in any way could be expected. So we'd best get you heading toward him."

"You know where he is?" Bo was back getting accustomed to sleeping indoors. He wanted more warning before giving it up. It wasn't that he'd forgotten about chasing after his Uncle Charley. It just seemed that everybody wanted him to do it at their own convenience. "Why now?" he said. "Why not tomorrow? Or yesterday?"

"Because it's today that I feel like it."

"You're *sure* you know where Uncle Charley is? You're not just taking me around to someplace because you think I ought to go there?"

Zeke just kept staring out into the Thicket.

"You've known it all along," Bo said. "Even when you were wandering around in the Thicket without me, you knew it even then."

Zeke only snorted. "I reckon I ought to give Martha a little surprise. Go in there, get some of her lye soap, let's go down to the creek and get presentable. Little enough I can do before leaving."

It was true, when you got close to Zeke you knew for certain he was there. It wasn't that he necessarily smelled bad, he just smelled, well, different.

They went inside the Thicket to a small stream, clear running and cold, where they stripped down and soaped. Bo was rinsing off when Zeke looked over at him.

"Never could figure it," he said, "why a person wants to do that."

"Do what?"

Zeke was already dressing, still lathered and unrinsed from the neck down. "Wash it all off," he said. "Way I do it, once I work myself up some sweat or next time it rains, I get myself another bathing without wasting any effort. Never could figure it out, don't reckon I ever will."

The leave-taking from Mrs. Butters was short, almost like it didn't happen. They both seemed used to it. She didn't even ask for how long.

"You don't worry none about meat," he told Eck. "I'll be back fore you run out."

They left, Bo leading his horse because of the overhanging branches. Zeke, for a long time, just walked. Bo didn't mind. The Thicket felt different from the way it had when he'd first come. He could handle the silence.

Without breaking stride, Zeke raised his rifle and fired into the air. There was just the sound of the shot and a slight fluttering of wings. Zeke didn't bother to explain. He left Bo standing there, holding onto his horse, while he went off to the side, away from the path, deeper into the Thicket. He came back carrying a bird, not just any bird. It was huge, big as a hawk. But it wasn't like any hawk Bo had ever seen, with its black and white and red splashes. And its long whitish tail. Bo thought it was beautiful, except for where the stomach was missing because of the bullet.

Zeke looked pleased with himself. "Ever see this sort of thing?" He didn't wait for an answer. "So big, folks call 'em godamighties. Leastwhiles, they do if they see 'em. Not so many around as they used to be. What it is, and you could tell if you ever heard it, is one hell of a big woodpecker. Get one of these folks on a holler tree, make you want to stuff a wad of moss in your ears. They get to be lonely sorts of birds. You want it?"

Bo shook his head. Zeke flung the woodpecker into the Thicket.

"That's all?" Bo said. "You're not going to eat it or anything?"

"You ever taste woodpecker?"

"But then why shoot it?"

Zeke thought for a minute. "I reckon cause it was there. And it was me that saw it."

They walked on, and Bo was glad to be submerged again in the Thicket, paying attention to things that were still alive. It didn't make any sense. Someone like Zeke would be lost outside the Thicket, but here he was killing it off in ways that wouldn't come back. It was almost like he was doing it to himself.

"I don't think much on things like that, never could," Zeke had started talking again, just like he hadn't ever stopped. "Can't help it," he said. "Reckon I'm kind of like a panther. A bear or something. I can think ahead about getting something to eat, I figure I'm bound to get hungry. Or I can try thinking about what a panther or bear's going to do next while I'm chasing it. But outside of things like that, I can't seem to concentrate on what's happening tomorrow. Or what got over yesterday. Too much going on right now. Can't help it. Reckon it's built in."

Bo could almost understand. He couldn't help thinking about tomorrows, he had a job to do. But he could look around and see life going on in every direction, and he was a part of it, his breathing, his walking a part of everything that was moving, changing, getting ready to happen not later today, not sometime tomorrow, right now in the Thicket.

They got to what Zeke called a creek, but to Bo it looked like it had just about worked its way into being a river. "It's right deep," Zeke said. "You'd best get on your horse. That way maybe the top of your head'll keep dry."

"What about you?"

Zeke snorted and walked straight into the water, holding his rifle over his head. "Adds a little weight," he said as he was leaving. "Helps keep my feet close to the bottom."

Zeke kept walking and the water kept deepening, up to his knees, then his waist, his shoulders, and still kept right on coming. Pretty soon all Bo could see was the rifle, just barely above the water. Then it all happened backwards, head, shoulders, waist, and finally Zeke walked out onto the far side.

"What you waiting for?" he said.

"What I tell you?" Zeke said when Bo and his horse had joined him. "I said leave that soap alone, sooner or later it'd come in handy. Though it does seem wasteful, getting clean twic't and it still the same day."

They camped that night at a clearing. Zeke had seemed to be aiming for it, speeding up a little to beat nightfall and looking satisfied when they got there. Bo couldn't quite see the reason. The ground was flat, that would be comfortable, but it was also soggy, kind of damp.

"What we got here's a stomp," Zeke said, as though it explained things.

When Bo didn't react, Zeke said it again, "A stomp, boy, don't you know what a stomp is?"

Bo shook his head.

Zeke let out his breath. "Boy, you best be glad there's folks leading you around." He began studying the ground for firewood. Bo hobbled his horse and started helping.

"Okay. What's a stomp?"

"Where things come to get away from muskeeters."

"Why here?"

"Cause they ain't no muskeeters."

Bo looked at him, waiting.

"Hell, boy, I don't know. Something in the ground, how the hell am I gonna know? But there ain't none here, and as far as sleeping goes, that's near enough to what matters. Here, you grab the other end of this."

Zeke was pointing to a heavy log, what once had been a good-sized tree.

"What do we need something this big for? We're only going to stay here one night." Bo hesitated.

"Aren't we?"

"I ain't here to discuss it, boy, grab ahold of your end."

Bo did, and they carried it back to the middle of the stomp. Once Zeke had gotten the smaller stuff burning, they rolled the log on top of it. Bo wasn't asking any questions.

They squatted down on the damp ground, drinking water they had gotten from a creek close by and eating food Mrs. Butters had fixed them. "Makes a man feel foolish," Zeke said, "out here in the middle of everything, still eating woman-made food." But he didn't slow down his chewing.

When they were through, Bo got ready to spread out his blanket. "Don't be getting in no hurry," Zeke said, standing up and stomping out most of the fire, leaving the big log not really burning but still glowing. "You get on that end and when I kick my end, you do yours, do it quick, boy, and don't burn your boots."

They kicked the log back and forth, moving it around until Zeke seemed satisfied. He pulled a tattered blanket from his pack and spread it out where they'd been rolling the log. "Now, boy," he said, "throw down your blanket and lay on it." Bo did, and where the ground had been damp, it was dry now and warm, like the heat from inside the earth was seeping up to them, through them, and only then spreading out over the Thicket. Bo was tired. He was ready for sleep.

Zeke wasn't. "Boy?" Zeke said, just as Bo was drifting off. "You think, boy, maybe I'm a little strange?"

Bo woke up. It was the first time Zeke had ever said anything of this sort. He wasn't sure how to answer. "I don't know much about strange," Bo said. "Could be that different's better."

"Sometimes," Zeke said, "I think myself strange. Like I almost make it to being human, then just stop a little short of getting there. I know it ain't my fault, a man's got to be what he is. If it's nature, he ain't got any more choice than a pig or a panther or a bear. But sometimes, usually only when I'm around folks, almost never when I'm out here in the Thicket, I wonder how it feels to be them. And then I start feeling bad, I start feeling real bad. Like I'm not hardly a person at all."

Zeke stopped a moment, and Bo could feel the quiet weighing down heavy. "Once or twic't," he said, "I got to thinking, if I can't be no more of a man than this, I ought to just stop being at all. That's when I got to get back to the Thicket, get back around bears and panthers. Ain't no animal that'd think that way. Charley, sometimes he'd do the same thing. He'd have to get away from people, get away from things that think, or at least things that think such things."

It seemed to Bo that everybody kept knowing a different Charley.

"It ain't that I don't want to grieve for Dute," he said, "to be able to feel like Martha does. I know it's the human thing, it's just that I can't seem to manage it. I liked the boy, I truly did, if I could do something to change it, bring the boy back, I surely would. But since I can't, I just don't seem able to keep my mind on grieving. There's so much out here that's still alive."

Bo knew Zeke didn't want an answer. Which was fortunate, since Bo didn't have one.

"Boy?"

"Yessir?"

"You want to stay on? We got room for another fella now. Even if we didn't, the Thicket's always got room for more. We'd be proud to have you. I know for a fact Martha feels the same."

"I thank you," Bo said, "not just for the offer of staying, but saying that about yourself, about how you feel." He thought a minute. He wasn't used to talking like this. Usually what he did was listen. "But I look at it this way. You belong here. Because you're the way you are, you kept looking till you found the Thicket. It's almost like the Thicket is what's inside you pushed all the way out. Or maybe what you are is the Thicket pushed in. I don't know and I don't think it matters, but what does is that you kept on looking till you found the right place.

"But I'm not sure it's the same way with me. About the Thicket. I'm still on my way looking, I'm just passing through. I've still got to find my Uncle Charley."

They were quiet for a moment. Bo looked over to see if Zeke had gone to sleep. "He's been here, hasn't he?"

"Yep."

"Is he still?"

"Nope. Just like you. Passing through."

When Bo woke up in the morning, the leftover food from Mrs. Butters was on the ground beside him. Zeke was gone. Bo knew he was awake, except it was like a nightmare that was real. He was by himself and the Thicket seemed to be stretching up higher all around, reaching out farther, ready to take even the smallest open space and make it a part of itself, even the edges of the stomp seemed closing in toward him. With Zeke around, with somebody, anybody, there always seemed to be somewhere to go, some place to move to, now there was nothing but Thicket, nothing but twists and tangles, getting ready to swallow him. There was too much of it, there wasn't enough space to breathe in. And what made it scarier, the Thicket wasn't just getting ready to drown him, it was connecting up with something inside him, too, just like the prairie, except this was even more frightening, this was something he couldn't breathe in, and he wanted the voices inside now, anything to fill up the space, to keep the Thicket from getting in, but the voices wouldn't come, there was too much of everything else, too much was trying to happen.

That's when he saw it, a small pile of sticks, an arrow made of twigs right beside it.

As the day wore on, as Bo and his horse kept pushing through the Thicket, sometimes he wasn't sure whether the broken branch was a sign or just happenstance. But usually there was another one not too much farther along and if there wasn't, he backtracked till he found one he was sure of, and then he looked for something else that was certain.

And as the day wore on, he got better at it, his eyes seeing quicker what didn't belong, being able to pick out of all the confusion a direction. He had been wrong, Bo told himself. Zeke wasn't just a reflection of the Thicket. He was something added to it. Even with the parts of Zeke that Bo didn't understand, that Zeke didn't either, as long as Zeke was in the Thicket, there was a direction.

Toward midafternoon, the land started rising, the air got cooler, there were fewer brambles and more distance between trees. Then it ended. Just like when he'd come in, there was a ridge, only this time he was traveling up toward it. It was high, but not quite so high as on the other side, Bo had been climbing gradually for awhile now. There was a path. It looked freshly made. Bo could see two sets of tracks, one going each way. The boots that made them looked the same, but Bo couldn't be certain.

When he got to the top it was late afternoon. There was a stand of trees that went straight over the ledge. Bo led his horse through it, coming out on a view that was too huge for Bo to take in. Instead it seemed to reach out, surrounding him, pulling him into it. Mesas, canyons, arroyos, grotesque mounds sculptured by winds, long since battered by ancient seas. Treeless, except for occasional scrubs near the tops of mesas. Everywhere, different shades of brown and red and yellow glowing in the late afternoon. And endless.

"Indian Territory," he said almost aloud.

He looked for signs. He didn't find any, so he went back down the path to the last one. That one was definite. He looked carefully all the way to the top. There weren't any others. Zeke must have stopped at the rim of the Thicket.

He looked out into the emptiness, and it was the summer his father had been kicked by the mule. That was the first time he'd seen Uncle Charley outside of school, when he hadn't been a teacher, just a regular person. His father could work some, but not much and so Uncle Charley was coming out almost every day to help. It was summer, so Uncle Charley was freer than most men, and one day after work he took the swing Bo's father had hung from a front yard tree, he'd hung it down low so Davey could swing on it, but Uncle Charley climbed the tree and untied it and he and Bo took it to the barn and knotted it to a beam in the loft, so if you swung hard you could go out the loft door, high up where they pitched hay in from the outside, from the wagon in the fall. Your feet were on the loft floor when you started, but then you were out the open door and swinging through the air, nothing under you at all, which wasn't so bad while you were going up, leaning back, pulling hard against the ropes, all you could see was the sky. But coming back was different, it felt all the time like you were going to fall out frontwards, so you held on tighter. You could see the ground blurring beneath you, but you couldn't see what you were rushing back towards, the loft door seemed so narrow in your mind, so easy to miss, and when you finally felt the loft floor back beneath you, coming with a jolt, Uncle Charley said do you want to do it again, and you felt you had to say yes, and then he pushed you harder, made you go even higher, come back even harder. After supper, Bo's father had Bo untie the swing and put it back in the front yard where he said it belonged.

Bo looked farther out ahead. At first it seemed only a wispy cloud, then it was smoke, slender and rising slowly.

"You got to know where you're going, boy, what you want to do when you get there," Staples said, "before there's any trail to be following."

"There's trails inside yourself you don't even know are there," Bobby Joe said. "They may lead nowhere, but how're you gonna find out till you follow them?"

"I ain't doing nothing," Zeke said. "I'm just walking."

Indian Territory

He was soon buried by canyons, closed in by buttes, and the farther he rode the more bewildering the world became. But he could always see the sky. And ahead, traces of smoke or cloud or whatever it was he was following.

It was close to night before he found it, a fire on top of a mesa, flames making contorted shapes against the twilight. There weren't any trails. He gave his horse free rein.

It was full dark by the time Bo reached the top. While he'd been climbing, the fire had been hidden behind the rim. But once out on flatness, Bo knew the flames weren't there just to guide him. They were there forcing him to see.

Behind the fire, not close enough to burn, a tall stake had been driven into the ground. Hanging upside down from the top was a naked black man.

Bo made himself not think, he didn't want to feel anything until he'd made sure. It wasn't impossible, it might be somebody else.

He made sure. He found where the arrow had gone in, where it had come out. Whoever had removed it had done so respectfully. There wasn't much ripping, and it was the only sign of injury. Everything else was intact.

"He was a brave man. But he refused to listen."

Bo jerked around. Bobby Joe was sitting cross-legged, just outside the range of firelight. But now his pants were made of skins, and his hair fell in long braids over his chest.

"It happened before I got here. But it wouldn't have mattered."

"Why?" was all Bo could say. "Why did it happen at all?"

"I told him before he left the cattle, I told him to go back to people he knew. I wasn't here, but I can tell you what happened, I could have told you when he left the cattle, he got to the edge of the Territory, and he thought he was free. He took off his clothes, saying to whoever was out there, his skin might be like the color of night and theirs more like sun-hardened earth, but still they were joined because they both had escaped the paleness of those he was leaving behind. So he rode into the Territory naked, yelling he was their brother, he had finally come home. Whoever saw him must have figured he was either monstrous or crazy or a little of both. But whatever they considered him, they knew he was different and that meant he was dangerous."

"You couldn't have helped?"

"I wasn't there."

They both were quiet. When Bobby Joe spoke again, his voice was gentle. "What he didn't understand, what you need to, here in the Territory there's not just one kind of people. Some of us will be friendly, some of us are frightened, all of us have reason enough to be angry. And a few won't have to feel much at all, they just know anything that acts too strange needs getting rid of.

"But they did the best they could, they left his hair. It reminded them of the kind on buffalo. They have to kill it to live, but they have great respect for the buffalo."

"It didn't have to happen," Bo said. "Your reasons aren't good enough."

“They’re not mine,” Bobby Joe said. “I only found them.”

Bo didn’t answer. He kept looking at Smith, as though if he stared long enough there’d be something he hadn’t noticed, something that would make things all right.

“People come to the Territory,” Bobby Joe said, “because they think they’re looking for freedom. What they don’t think about, once they get here, it’s not just themselves that are free, other things are too, things happen they don’t expect, that they maybe don’t want. But that’s the sort of thing you find if you’re looking for freedom. If that’s not what you want, you’re better off staying home.”

Bo wasn’t thinking about freedom. He was still staring at what used to be Smith. “Then I’ve gone far enough,” he said. “Nobody asked me if I was interested in freedom, they just told me to chase down Uncle Charley. But I reckon he can look after himself. It’s about time I started back home.”

“You can go where you want to later,” Bobby Joe said, walking to his horse, waiting on the edges of the firelight. “But now you need to come with me.

“Home,” Bobby Joe said, mounting barebacked. “I’ll show you home.”

Bo didn’t move. “What about Smith?” he said.

“We’ll leave him here. They treated him with dignity. We won’t interfere.”

“The buzzards?”

“He won’t feel them. They need to eat, too.”

The next day they traveled steadily. And the next. Their trail, if there was one, seemed to twist as much one direction as the other. Toward noon of the second day, the land changed, it became rolling, with more scrub, a few more birds. Up ahead there were trees and the outlines of a small muddy river.

"You'll see houses," Bobby Joe said, "but they're empty. Don't touch anything. Everything here is sacred. Besides, there might be germs."

It had been a village. The earthen lodges were still sturdy. The trees provided shade and would keep back the wind. It had been a good place to live.

"In summers," Bobby Joe said, "we'd hunt buffalo. We'd leave, carrying our tepees with us. But when we got done, this is where we'd come back home to."

Bo looked out over the village. It seemed like it had always been quiet, lying there in the sun.

"You lived here?"

"Except when I was at school. When I came back, this was where I came back to. By then there weren't as many buffalo. Hunters, white men who only wanted their skins, slaughtered them by the thousands, leaving them lying in the sun until you couldn't ride through the hunting grounds because of the rot.

"Your government thought that was fine. If anyone objected, your government explained that if the buffalo were killed, then the Indians would starve. Or do as they'd been told and live on reservations.

"My village didn't have any desire to do either, and I could help them. I knew the other world, I could act like a white man. So I did. I arranged to buy cattle or I found enough wild to keep us from being hungry, and we weren't doing badly. We were even raising our own.

"Then I came back from one of my trips. I was happy. I'd found more wild stock than usual. I even thought I'd seen signs of new buffalo wandering close to our range.

"I came back, and my village was gone. The hogans were still there, the people hadn't left. But the village was gone.

"Where the sickness came from, we were never sure. A visiting trader or a villager who had been among whites, it doesn't matter. By the time I got back, only a few were still alive. The children who weren't dead by then were screaming with hunger. Those of us who were left tried. We nursed and we fed, but it didn't matter.

"We had thought we were safe. We thought, no, we knew. Our home was not just a village, it was a joining of something in us and something around us. It wasn't like one of your towns, buildings and fences and roads forcing themselves onto the land. Our village was a part of the world around us. The air was clean, the sun burned away sickness. When we were left alone, even when we were hungry, we could live. But your people brought things that weren't a part of the air and the sun, things we couldn't fight against and win.

"We had thought we were free. We had thought we'd found a way to escape, that the only way not to be part of those things that don't understand the sun was to go deeper and deeper into the Territory, where things may happen that aren't expected, but where there's the hope of being free.

"The people who brought the sickness thought they could own the land. They wanted to force themselves on it as though it would take notice. But that's a sickness in itself. They needed to control what they thought was outside, then maybe they'd be so busy, they wouldn't have to look inside. Because they were afraid of what they might find. But they'd be lost in the Territory. Because inside the Territory, you can't even pretend you're controlling the land.

"So it's only from there, inside the Territory, you can get far enough away to see the horrors for what they are. But even we had stopped too close to the edge. My village tried, they fought bravely, and then they died sadly. That was when I learned that the village wasn't my home. Home can only be a hope that's inside your mind. You can't ever get there by trying to return."

While he was talking, Bobby Joe had been perfectly still, staring over the deserted village. Now he shifted his weight, his horse swished its tail at some flies, and it was as though Bobby Joe was speaking from a different part of his mind.

"One of the things I liked about Charley. He wasn't the kind who stopped at borders."

Bo was listening. But he wasn't paying as much attention as he might have. "You don't have to go," he'd told his mother. But she picked up the book she was going to return to Uncle Charley once she'd finished shopping. "We could all go in together," he said, "later, once we're done with the chores."

She was smiling now, but not the way Bo liked. It was tighter, as though she had to think about how to do it. "Don't forget about your Daddy's lunch," she said, as though he would, as though he wouldn't rather be with him right now instead of here, watching over Davey and saying goodbye to his mother.

"The milk's already poured." She reached out to rub her hand through his hair, and without thinking he pulled back, not much, but enough so that she noticed. Only she didn't act like it.

"A woman needs a little time to herself, away from the kitchen," she said. "You'll understand such things better when you get grown."

Bo didn't want to understand any better than he did right now. "Uncle Charley doesn't need the book," he said. "He can get along just fine by himself. There's no need for you to go." But his mother didn't hear, she'd already gone out the door.

"I figured somebody chasing Charley would be the same way," Bobby Joe said. "But it's your journey, you can end it whenever you want to."

"Head on out," Bo answered. "You can't expect me to know where you're going."

They rode quietly. Bo didn't mind, he was tired of the talking, of everybody seeming to think that what they knew of their life somehow made them in charge of his. But he'd come this far, turning back wouldn't solve anything, it couldn't make Smith any less dead.

They stopped at the mouth of what seemed like a boxed-in canyon. Bo unsaddled and staked his horse. Bobby Joe left his reins resting on his horse's neck. They built a fire and each ate a handful of beef jerky. Then Bobby Joe got back on his horse. He didn't explain, just rode into the canyon, disappearing among its shadows.

Earlier Bo might have been worried, probably not scared, but worried. Now he sat by the fire and waited. The world around him was quiet, nothing seemed to be changing. As though time moved only inside, among his thoughts, the sounds that weren't there, the shapes that hadn't happened.

He wasn't lonely. He was expecting company. But he didn't want them to just drop in, he wanted them to come invited. Not simply pop up without warning and then disappear the same way. That may have been all right earlier. Back when he hadn't known so many memories were in there waiting. But now he knew better, now he could bring them up while there was time to look closely.

Not so he could change them, he couldn't do that. The memories were already there, they had long since become facts, a part of who he was, of what he was doing. He couldn't control what they were, but he could try to understand them.

They'd been sitting in the shade, waiting for his mother to open the lunch pail and pass out the food. And her being there was part of the resting, part of the reward for the morning's work. It was almost like a holiday. Davey was trying not to, but he was beaming. Bo and his father had been clearing a ditch together, so Davey had spent the morning by himself, plowing. And he'd finished more than any of them had expected him to, even himself, and the furrows were straight as a rule and he knew that his father had noticed it.

Not that his father said anything about it. It would've been better if he had, but Davey had learned to look for the little signs that took the place of words. He sometimes missed them, they all did. And sometimes they hoped they'd only missed them when they were pretty sure they hadn't really been there. But this time Davey couldn't help seeing them. Nobody else could either, and so Davey was happy and everybody else almost was, too.

Because there were other signs, not just from his father, but from his mother as well, and Bo couldn't miss those either. He had almost forgotten them, had almost begun to believe he could keep on forgetting. But they were back. His father tried not to show them, Bo could tell he wanted to act as though nothing was wrong, as though things were still like they had finally gotten to be once Uncle Charley had gotten on his horse and left for who knew where. But even Bo's father, who never much showed how he was feeling, couldn't help giving the signs.

Bo's mother acted like she wanted to help him, to say things were still like they had gotten to be, but it was like she couldn't help it, there was something in her eyes, in the way she held her head, it reminded Bo of back then, back before Uncle Charley had taken the gun and shot Mr. Thibodeaux and the alligator.

Bo didn't want to think about it. He didn't want to see them there, pretending to be happy while all the time trying to hide the signs. He wanted to remember them being together and looking at Davey's furrows like it was a celebration. That's what families were for. When he thought of home, that's what he wanted to think about. That's what he wanted to remember.

So he quit before the chores were completely done, nobody stopped him, and he went into town where they were still talking about the tombstone and Uncle Charley. And when they started talking about who should go after him, Bo pushed his way to the front. Uncle Charley had torn things down once before. Bo wasn't going to stay around, watching it happen again. And besides, he had the right.

Then Bobby Joe rode out of the darkness and motioned toward Bo's horse. Bo saddled up and followed. Where they'd been camped outside the canyon, there'd been a moon. But the deeper they traveled inside, the overhanging ridges blocked out the possibility of light. Bo couldn't see any farther than Bobby Joe's shape riding in front of him. Even then, when Bobby Joe stopped, Bo's horse almost collided with his.

Bobby Joe got down. Bo did, too. His eyes were more accustomed now, so when Bobby Joe motioned toward a jagged outcropping of rock, Bo tied his horse to it. When he turned back around, Bobby Joe was almost out of sight, walking straight into the canyon wall.

There must have been a trail, Bo didn't know, all he was doing was following. He did know they were climbing now, and climbing steep. Then Bobby Joe was gone.

"Through here, between the rocks."

Bo went toward the voice and ran into stone. He felt along it till there was nothing pushing back against him.

"Here?"

There wasn't any answer. Bo forced himself through.

"Bobby Joe?"

"Over here."

He looked toward the voice, and only then noticed that moonlight somehow was getting through. Bobby Joe stood in the middle of a space surrounded by high walls of rock. Bo looked up and saw the sky. It was as though they were in the bottom of a deep, used-up well.

Bobby Joe was disappearing again, sinking it seemed into the ground. When Bo got closer, there was a hole with a ladder in it.

The ladder seemed old, the poles Bo held onto were gnarled but worn smooth. As he and Bobby Joe climbed lower, they began meeting light.

They were in a room, not a cave, but a room. Bo could see, even though the fire in the middle wasn't bright, the walls were too regular not to have been worked on by hands. He could see the outlines of beams.

They weren't by themselves. There were men, Bo couldn't tell how many, they merged into the darkness, sitting around the fringes of the campfire, facing toward the ladder. They seemed to be Indians.

Four men were sitting closest to the flames. They looked incredibly old, the skin on their faces not merely wrinkled, but furrowed like the ground on parched river bottoms, as though their bodies had already long ago died, but something else much deeper inside kept on giving them life.

They sat without moving. Bobby Joe said something to them in a strange language, and one of the old men nodded. Bobby Joe sat down on the fringes. Bo did, too, right beside him.

The old man nodded once more.

"These are the old ones," Bobby Joe said. "Many years ago, a long time before the white man came to our land, there were other old ones, the Anasazi, who had learned to live with the earth, to become one with it. Their houses seemed part of the rock, high up in the cracks of cliffs, on ledges it didn't look possible for birds to nest on.

"They were peaceful people. They didn't use the land, they were part of it, they shared with it. And out of what looked dry and dead, they lived well. They didn't try to conquer the land and the land didn't defeat them.

"Then the outsiders came. Not the whites, this was before that, these were merely the first of many, the outsiders who came to conquer, whose favorite tools weren't made to build or grow but to kill and destroy.

"The old ones were peaceful people. It wasn't that they didn't know how to fight. They chose not to. Many were killed. Others moved away and became part of other peoples. Some, a very few, stayed high in the cliffs, close to the rocks, hidden from those who wanted to rule over both the land and the people.

"Others, who hadn't moved too far away, would return and help those in the mountains. Because they knew that these were different, they must be kept secret, because in them was the hope of the future, of all their children, of all children yet to come.

"For the good of everyone, some mustn't become lost among foreign spirits. The outsiders would come, first one, then another, but none would ever conquer the land. They would put fences around it, they would say they owned it, but after the outsiders and their children were long dead, the land would remain, the spirit of the land would still live when the outsiders' bones were rotting in graves, submitting to the land they'd hoped to rule.

"The spirit of the land would remain, none of the old ones doubted that. But if they wanted their own spirit to survive, to be there for their children or the children of their children's children, some of them had to remain in contact with forces beyond words, forces that lived inside themselves. But that also reached outside, linking them with powers their spirits couldn't live without.

"All that the few had to do was stay loyal and wait. That was the way they would fight. They would wait, they would survive. And they would win. There was no possibility that they wouldn't.

"There is a story the old men tell about Taiowa, who created the land and the water, and he was proud of them as everyone is of the firstborn. But there wasn't anyone to share his pride. So he created Spiderwoman, who made trees and bushes and everything that grows from the ground and water. But that wasn't enough, either. So Spiderwoman made birds and animals, all the living things that don't grow from the ground but move about on and above it.

"But even these, the thirdborn, weren't enough. So Spiderwoman gathered earth that was yellow and red, white and black. She mixed them with the water out of her mouth and molded the shapes of men and women. But at first they weren't finished. There was still some soft clay on the top of their heads. But soon the warmth of the sun seemed to remove the dampness and harden the clay.

"The way the old men tell it, the story is too long. We're young, I'll tell it shorter. That first world was good, but the people drifted away from the spirit that had made not just them, but the birds and the animals and the land itself. And so Taiowa wearied and decided to get rid of the world and try again. But there were some from the first world who had remained loyal. And Taiowa told them that the soft spot on top of their heads hadn't completely hardened and it would become the door through which the spirit of Taiowa might enter. All they had to do was open it and follow the bidding from within.

"And so while the first world was destroyed by fire, the few opened their heads and were led to the mounds of the Ant People where they waited. And when Taiowa had created a second world, the people began again. But this time, too, they ignored the spirit that connected them with the earth and each other, and they wanted to control instead of being a part.

"So Taiowa destroyed the second world with ice. Except for the few, who kept the holes in their head open and waited once more in the mounds of the Ant People. But the same thing as before happened when they had a third world. The earth itself remained loyal, the things that grew from the ground, the things that moved on it and above it, everything except the people. Only this time Taiowa was wearied of fire and ice, he was tired of doing everything himself. This time he would let the people of the third world destroy themselves.

"Except for the few. Only this time they couldn't find the Ant People. So they opened the tops of their heads, and instead of staying in the mounds of the Ant People, they hid themselves in mounds of rock, where they again waited. And it's been a long time. But their ancestors had waited before, and they had been the ones who had lived. And that's the way it would be again. There would be another world. All they must do is wait."

Bobby Joe looked around the room. "So this is what's left," he said. "What you see around the campfire, these old men, they're the last of the Anasazi. Not the first ones, they have long since been dead, but high in the cliffs, far away from the outsiders, the Anasazi have survived generation after generation, until we have come to this."

"There aren't any children?"

"There are no children."

"Then who are the rest of them, the men in the shadows?"

"They are the ones who must become Anasazi. If not by birth, then by patience. They are the ones who must learn to keep alive some hope for the Fourth World."

"And you, are you one of them?"

Bobby Joe didn't answer. "It's hard," he said, "when all around, the outsiders seem to be winning. But they think winning is something you do in a straight line, that being alive is only a matter of moving through time. They think that what they're doing now will be done and then it will be over, that once they subdue the land it will be part of history.

"They don't know, or they've forgotten, what they're doing now is happening between forces inside themselves, it's only a part of their own histories. The battle they think they're winning was being fought in the time of the Anasazi, it will still be being fought a hundred years from now. If there are any of us left to fight it.

"But they don't know it. They think you do this and then you do this and then you do the next thing. But there must be some of us left who keep remembering, all straight lines end somewhere. So the outsiders must fear death, they feel that to live on, for people to remember them, they must build something on the outside before they leave it.

"The old people know that straight lines aren't the answer. There must be a going out, but then there must be a coming back in. Only circles don't have endings, only circles can go on forever. He used to understand that, too."

Bo hesitated. "Uncle Charley?"

"Until he lost patience. We were together when he did, when we got back to the village."

"The one we passed through?"

"After he found them, his son in her arms, after that he was no longer Anasazi."

"Uncle Charley was married?"
"My sister."

One of the old men got up slowly. He went to a corner and came back with a cup made from bone. He began speaking, the sounds coming from deep inside as though the path outward was strenuous. Bobby Joe spoke when the old man had finished.

"He says in the old days, back when the first stories were told, there was no need for the berries. Then the only need was to keep the top of one's head open and to know that we walk in the sky."

Bo looked confused. This time Bobby Joe didn't wait for the old man. "Today things seem separate," he said. "Even for those of us who try. But the old ones, the true old ones, somehow they knew. If you ask a white man, your father perhaps, what is the sky? He'll point upwards. There, he'll probably say, it's over your head. But the old ones knew. The sky is all around us, it's inside us. You dig a hole in the ground. It doesn't matter how deep, the sky begins at the bottom."

Another old man began to speak. Bobby Joe held the bowl in front of Bo. "Here," he said. "Eat it."

Bo hesitated.

"Do it," Bobby Joe said. "It's necessary."

So Bo did. It was dry, bitter. Bo didn't really want to swallow. It scratched as it passed through his throat.

"We don't really have any choice," Bobby Joe said. "If there isn't any connection, if the spirit within us isn't part of something outside, then we're all lost. How else would we know what we are seeing or tasting or touching, if it weren't connected with something already in us? We wouldn't even know it was there. If there were no connection we'd be lost, we wouldn't recognize where we are. Or even each other."

"And Smith?" Bo said. "Or Dute? What was the spirit inside them supposed to recognize?"

"This isn't the world that Taiowa, or whoever it was, first made," Bobby Joe said. "There are horrors out there that we've got to wait through. And some who don't deserve to will suffer. Even some of those who are waiting. But it isn't necessary for all of them to survive. Only enough to be there when the outsiders have destroyed each other."

"And Uncle Charley?"

"Forget about Charley. You've chased him far enough. You needed him to get here, if it hadn't been for Charley you'd probably never have left home.

"You'd have been trapped. Because there are too many towns back there, too many fences and people looking for borders. They think they're trying to tame the land. But it's not really the land, it's themselves. What they're really trying to tame are the parts of themselves they're afraid of, and they'll most likely fail. They'd better hope they do. Because the parts they're most afraid of may be just the ones they need the most.

"That's why we need the Territory. Because if you stay at home, you're going to let those folks convince you those parts aren't there, or at least they don't belong, they're not really you, they're things that need getting rid of. They'll try to make you push those parts they're afraid of so deep down inside, you'll think you've lost them. Or maybe never had them except sometimes in dreams.

"That's why we need the Territory. But you're already here. You can stop chasing. Journeys don't have to keep on going lengthwise, heading on out step by step. A person who's whole, who's not trying to keep parts of himself hidden, can stop and let life spread out toward him, he can let it become thicker. There's no hurry. There's no place to go, not once you're already there. You're already where you need to be. There's nowhere else to go."

"Is that what Uncle Charley would say?"

"He would have once," Bobby Joe said quietly, staring into a dark corner of the cave. Then he looked at Bo directly, more urgently than he had before. "You don't have to reach him, Bo. No matter what you think. Or hope. He's not some father you never had."

Bo was startled. He was carrying a message, not looking for a father. He already had one of those.

Bobby Joe ignored him. "Now I know," he said. "Before, when I was younger, maybe I was hoping so, too. But he's not. He's simply a man who's bitter and who insists on his own confusions. There's nothing you have to tell him, not anything he'll listen to. Stay here. Find a home.

"The spirit is still fresh inside you, all you need to do is become open to it, to be at peace with the earth and to wait. The hole in the roof, the one we came through, for you it can be like the birthing place of a woman. When we climb out, it can be a new beginning. Where everything is connected, nothing is separate, if only you have the eyes to see and the patience to open your head and wait."

New things were already beginning, there wasn't much doubt about that. He wasn't sure about connections, but something was happening inside him. He knew it was the berries, it had to be. All the time, there wasn't any question, the berries were getting ready to make things happen Bo wasn't used to.

The main thing he wasn't used to, all of a sudden there were two of him, one person those things were getting ready to happen to, and another one who was up somewhere watching. And yet it was the same person, all the time it was somehow him. He saw himself, felt himself floating, he was floating out the hole in the roof. Without effort. Floating. Nothing seemed strange about it, he wasn't dizzy or confused or half asleep, he was simply floating and when he was outside it didn't stop, not like before when he had followed Bobby Joe up the path, this time he was above it, he was moving through the air, he was walking through the sky.

Nothing felt strange. The surrounding air seemed to embrace him, the sounds of the nightbirds, the rustling of whatever was moving in the darkness seemed to be coming from somewhere inside. And now that other him, the one above, saw that the one who was floating had a direction. If there was something in the way, he seemed to go over or even around, but always he came back to the direction he'd been heading.

And then in front of him was a mountain. The floating self wasn't worried. For him, the mesas, the buttes weren't enemies. But his other self wasn't so sure. This mountain was taller than the others, and farther around.

Somewhere on the side of the mountain there was a light.

When Bo woke up, he was lying on cold sand. He could taste the grit in his mouth, and he could feel that he was alone.

On the outside.

"You don't have to go anywhere," Bobby Joe was saying on the inside. "All you have to do is wait. Reach out to what's already around you and wait."

"Only you don't have to do it here with your mouth full of sand." Miranda was getting impatient. "There's places that are green all year round, there's water always close by."

"Go on back home, Bo." Sam's voice seemed half-hearted. "While you still got a chance to do it, go on back home."

"Home," Bobby Joe said, as though it was final. "Home's not a place. It's a hope inside you. You can't get to it by going backwards. You can't fence in the wildness and pretend you've tamed it, there's too much, it's too strong, it doesn't make sense even to try."

"But you don't have to make any of it up, either," the Preacher said. "There's enough out there already, you don't have to go around eating berries."

"That's about enough," Bo said. "From all of you. There's somebody named Bo still left in here, although from the racket everybody's making, a person might doubt it."

He got up and spit and shook his head, trying to get it clearer, making sure it kept quiet. Voices were all right, so long as they stayed inside, so long as they didn't get so far outside you couldn't tell any difference.

Then he looked around to get his bearings. There was enough moonlight to see, but it hardly mattered. Everything looked the same, desert sand running between mesas and jagged boulders that seemed to be folding in on themselves, making shapes Bo couldn't separate from the shadows.

The light on the mountain was still there.

He didn't know what he was going to do. But he'd figure it out. And for the moment, he didn't mind doing it by himself. He tried shaking his head again. He could still see the light, the mountain was still there in front of him.

Or he thought it was. At the moment he wasn't terribly certain what was really out there and what had been built by the berries. Besides that, his head hurt. He wasn't in the mood for things all of a sudden to disappear once whatever it was wore off. He wasn't sure he wanted to live in a world that depended on what he ate.

But the mountain seemed as real as anything else. At least it was a direction, it wasn't just standing still.

At first he went slowly, then he started to run. Not because he was in a hurry to get there, he wasn't sure if there was any there to get to, but the night air was cold, he wanted to get warm. And it was nice to feel himself doing something while he was only one person.

The mountain was closer than he'd thought. And it wasn't a mountain, only a mesa, but taller than any others close by, and the light was about halfway up. Bo wasn't sure what to do now that he'd gotten there. But he had to do something, so he started to climb. As soon as he did, the light was suddenly gone. But it didn't matter, even without it to guide him, there still wasn't much choice. So he kept climbing, not being sure, trying to remember the direction he'd been heading.

There wasn't a moon, he had to move up by feel. There were rocks, but mostly it was clay, crumbly, dry. Each reach, each step might be up, but when things gave way he found himself sliding, at first slowly, then picking up speed until something, a ridge, a root, the jutting of a rock stopped him, and so he could begin again.

He wasn't sure why he was doing this. But right now it was a little late to ask. So he kept on climbing.

Until behind him. Beneath him. It was hard to say even what it was. Not really a sound. Or maybe it was. But something. Behind him, beneath him. Following. Bo climbed more rapidly. He tried to look down, to see what it was. Or what it wasn't. But he couldn't see, it was too dark. But now he knew what he was doing. He was getting away from whatever it was down there. It didn't matter where he was going, just as long as it was away. He only prayed against falling, not just from the side of the mesa, but closer to whatever it was down below, praying not with words but the marrow of his body, and reaching for the next foothold, the next rock.

The next rock. He listened. The noise was still there, coming closer. He pulled, the rock loosened, it was heavy, but Bo could lift it. He clawed into the dirt with his other hand, digging with his fingers, getting ready for the shock of holding on. He still couldn't see, but he could hear, it had to be just beneath him. He threw the rock with as much force as he could, too much for his other hand, the one that was holding on, and the clay gave way and he was falling, spread-eagled, kicking, grabbing, trying to find anything that would make him stop. His feet found a ledge, not even a ledge, a wrinkle on the face of the mesa. He flattened himself against the side and began edging his way along, his whole body pressed as hard as he could, he only wished he could press harder, his mouth, his nostrils, he was gasping hard now, taking in as much clay as he did air, his feet looking for places to hold to, knocking down pebbles that rattled beneath him.

Then he heard it, a stirring at first, then clearly a rattling. The smell of sour cucumbers.

"Stop."

At first he didn't know he had heard it.

"Right there," the voice said, soft, hoarse, somewhere between a hiss and a whisper.

"No farther," it said. "Stop there."

"Uncle Charley?"

"Another step," he said. "Down under you. It's where they sleep. You woke them up. Listen."

"Uncle Charley?"

"Don't talk. Stay still. Listen."

Bo did. The rattling had turned back to a stirring, but it was still there.

"Whatever you've come to tell me, boy, I'm not interested."

It had to be Uncle Charley, but Bo shook his head anyway, trying to clear it, making sure that the voice wasn't coming from inside. But it had to be Uncle Charley, Bo couldn't be making it up, because it wasn't the way he'd ever heard it before. Now it sounded strange, like it wasn't accustomed to talking.

"You didn't do it, Uncle Charley . . ."

"Whatever it is, boy, I don't need to hear it . . ."

"You didn't kill . . ."

"Because whatever it is, boy, I'm free of it. It wasn't easy, boy, but I got myself free."

"But you didn't kill him. Now you can come home!"

"Back then, back when I started running, I thought it was because I'd shot somebody, because I'd shot two men who hadn't killed an alligator."

"But that doesn't matter! Even Simon McCallister, he wants you to come on back home!"

"But I was getting things mixed up," Charley was saying, not even pretending to listen. "The reason I'd done it was because I couldn't kill an alligator or something else just as mean and old and ugly lying around in the mud down inside me. And once it came to the surface, whatever it was, I couldn't say it wasn't there, no matter how scared I was of it or how far I tried outrunning it, or how much I tried blaming it on things that were someplace else."

Even Mamma, even Mamma wouldn't mind. And Bo felt something inside him trying to push its way to the top. But there was something else trying just as hard to keep it back, like things on two sides of a door, pushing hard to force it open, just as hard keeping it shut.

"You can try telling yourself they're not down there, boy, but it's no good. Because it's no use trying to cheat, once you discover you're playing against parts of yourself. So once you know they're down there, boy, you're not going to bury them back in the mud."

But Bo didn't have time to listen. He was coming home early, too early, it was still morning. Davey and his father were back in the fields plowing. But Bo was going to the barn to get a new hame string for the plow when he heard a horse whinny. That wasn't strange. But it came from a stand of trees behind the house where horses weren't supposed to be. When he got there, he found a horse he thought he recognized, tied to a tree, grazing.

"That soft place Bobby Joe told you about," Charley was saying, "the one on top of our heads. If it ever was there, it's all hardened up now. There ain't no spirit coming in from someplace, then stretching itself out into the world. If there ever was a hole, it's long since dried shut. What Bobby Joe needs to learn, boy, if there's still a spirit, it's not in there by itself. It's trapped inside. It's trapped down there with the alligators."

He was coming up in back of the house, where the window from his mother and father's bedroom opened up toward the windbreak, facing away from the fields and the barn. He came up quietly, knowing he wanted to be secret, still not thinking about why.

"The soft spot," Charley was still saying, "if it ever was open, it's long since been closed shut. The only journeys worth taking, boy, they're gonna be over landscapes inside your mind. Those canyons and arroyos and cliffs you've been traveling through, this mountain you just climbed, they're *inside* now. And you're going to need them, boy, you're going to need places to hide behind, or maybe just get a little shade."

He was up to the window, bracing himself against the outjutting of the chimney, the bricks, cold now in the summer, scraping along his back.

They were in there. He couldn't see his Uncle Charley, he didn't want to, but he knew he was in there. He could see his shape lying on the bed, looking toward his mother.

"And the folks you've been traveling with, they're in there, too. Don't get me wrong, boy, I'm not talking about memories, I'm talking about folks that *live* in there, so what's happened, you've got your insides peopled, you're not going to have to face things just by yourself, you're not going to have to fight things all alone."

Looking toward his mother.

"Because that's what it is, boy, it's a fight, or it'd better be. Because if there's something in me that's trying to kill me, maybe I can't get rid of it, but I don't have to make it welcome, and I'm sure not going to pretend it ain't there. You better remember, boy, you intend on finding out what you are, you'd better do some looking in the dark."

Looking toward his mother. Who was looking toward him, naked, her body offering, her face glistening, with tears, with happiness, how could Bo know? He wanted to look away, to hide his face, but he couldn't. She was there, coming toward him, open, offering, her face glistening.

"But sometimes, and don't you forget this, boy, you can get fooled, there's more gators lying around than you figured on. You can get yourself trapped, like in one of them box canyons. Most of the time you've got to turn around, fight your way out. But sometimes, boy, you get lucky. You find a crack just big enough to slip through, you're out the other side. That's where I am, boy, I'm out the other side."

Toward the bed, toward Charley, who was waiting. And Bo wanted to stop looking, to stop seeing, to make himself look away. But he couldn't.

"And don't you worry about that rock, boy. There's something in everybody that wants to kill strangers. You just go back down the way you got here. Your horse's down at the bottom just waiting."

But Bo wasn't listening, because she was coming toward him, and the door inside him burst open.

"You can tell folks you caught me, boy, that's all right." It was like he just couldn't stop talking. "You just don't believe it yourself. Because any time you think you've caught me, boy, that's when the gators are going to get you."

Whatever it was inside trying to hold the door shut gave way, and Bo didn't care anymore about snakes down below or the narrowness of the ledge.

Whatever had been trapped inside Bo was breaking free. "She wants you back, too, God damn you to hell," he yelled. "She wants you back, too, but God damn it, you can't have her!"

And Bo was leaping toward the voice, not caring about the snakes or the ledge or the fact that he couldn't see. He was throwing himself toward the voice, scrambling, pulling himself across rocks, recklessly finding footholds as though they'd been intended.

He knew he'd guessed right, he was headed in the right direction. He knew he was getting closer because he could hear Charley moving, too, fast, not worrying about the noise.

"Ease off, boy," Charley was saying. "Ease off! What I'm trying to tell you is we're both free!" But the voice sounded winded, even more raspy, as though he was using words only to keep Bo away.

But he couldn't. Bo was moving with a fury, climbing, clambering, he didn't need to listen. Charley was moving too loudly, trying to find a way.

But he couldn't. They were on a ridge, a wider one now, and Bo could sense they were on it together. He lunged across the darkness and struck against something that wasn't rock, something yielding, and he held on while Charley tried to kick him away, but Bo held on to cloth, to bone, he wouldn't let go of the leg.

So Charley kicked harder, trying to force himself free, to pull himself higher to the next ledge, to whatever it was he was holding on to. But Bo wouldn't let go, giving all his weight, pulling desperately downward. And so they both fell, both grappling on the hard crumbling surface of the ledge, their bodies groping, grasping, and for the first time Bo was holding on to something real, not just a name out there he was looking for, it was Charley himself, and he was holding on, even though it was twisting under him, trying to get itself free, and Bo could feel the fury of its desperation, the rage at being so much as touched, of sharing the stench of his loneliness.

And now that he'd found him, Bo wanted only to let him go, to be out of its way. But he couldn't, they both seemed too tangled, grasping out into the darkness, trying to find something of each other to grab hold of, gouging their own bodies as much as the other's, gasping in the exhaustion of each other's breath.

Then in the middle of his confusion, not knowing for sure whether he was trying to escape or to subdue or even kill, Bo felt more alive than he'd ever remembered feeling. As though both energy and relief flowed along with his anger and his fear. And for that moment, for reasons he didn't have time to understand, Bo not only couldn't, he wouldn't let go.

Then they rolled too far. They'd forgotten the edge. Bo could feel his legs meeting not rock any more but only emptiness. He was still holding on to Charley, but not just from rage or hate or despair, he was holding on now to keep from falling. Because they both were flailing away on the edge, grabbing on to each other as though flesh, just because it was somebody else's, could give sustenance, provide some of the safety they'd lost from the rock.

Then Bo felt Charley's body lurch. He could feel a lightness as Charley's hands left him, and Bo knew that Charley had found the ledge and was pulling himself up. So Bo held on, not to pull Charley down, but to keep himself from falling, to lift himself up alongside. But Charley kicked away, breaking Bo's hold, and Bo was falling, his hands clawing furiously until they found something less yielding than Charley's body, something unmoving, and he was holding on to the ledge, hanging, but holding desperately, and he knew that Charley was standing up above him, breathing heavily, looking down into the darkness.

"Hell, boy," Charley's voice was thin and wheezy. "Hell, boy," he said. "What you got to figure out, you trying to catch me or you trying to kill me?"

Then Bo could almost hear what Charley was getting ready to do. He could almost see Charley's leg drawing back, his boot arcing through the darkness, he could hear the sound as it moved toward him, before he felt the explosion against his face and felt the release of his own falling.

Things then were quiet and strangely familiar. Bo was lying on cold sand, the taste of grit feeling at home in his mouth. Except he hurt in ways he couldn't have imagined. He felt waves of nausea flowing through him, threatening to suck him under and drown him. But Bo didn't mind. It felt good to drift slowly downward. Except now the darkness had shape, walls and shadows, like the inside of a cave.

They were there, all of them, standing there looking toward him. The Preacher, Bobby Joe, Zeke, Jeremiah, and Sam. Mrs. Butters, Smith, Mendoza, even a young man Bo didn't recognize who was wearing a blue uniform. And each one of them was motioning for Bo to follow in that direction, but he couldn't follow them all. And besides, back behind everybody, almost hidden, there was Miranda, waving slowly like she was under water and waiting. Bo tried to get to her, but he kept tripping over the others until finally he fell. And while he was trying to get up, Flake was beside him, wiping Bo's brow with his bandanna, and then Bo realized that everybody wasn't there, somebody was missing. So Bo pulled himself up, even though he felt the pain beating unbearably through him, Bo pulled himself up so he could look behind him, away from the crowd, but there wasn't anything there and then he was calling out, not in his dream now, "Uncle Charley," he was yelling, "all of that doesn't matter, God damn you to hell, it's time to come home! Uncle Charley!" he was yelling . . .

But there wasn't any answer. Bo struggled up until he was sitting. "To hell with Uncle Charley," Bo said quietly. "To hell with both him and his alligators."

Off in the distance, right at the edge of the world, some light was just starting. But closer by, Bo could see his horse was standing, not even grazing, just waiting. So Bo made himself try to get up.

It didn't work. And when he hit the ground, his mouth got even more full of sand. Bo didn't mind. Lying there was a lot more comfortable than standing.

"That's fine," the Preacher said. "There's a heap of things we need to get started making sense of. I don't reckon there's any better time, why don't we just lean back and do some sorting?"

No, Bo said. Not just yet, he'd deal with those things later. Once he was traveling through landscapes that felt more familiar. After the Territory was somewhere behind.

"That's all right, boy," the voice said, and this time it wasn't the Preacher. "You go ahead and start traveling."

Bo had liked the other voice better. He'd already heard enough of this one. And the last time it stopped talking, things began hurting and falling.

"Go ahead, boy, mount up and start leaving. Just don't think you've lost me, boy, don't you even begin to. Because you know I'm down here, down alongside the snakes and the alligators. Except you don't know just where. Because you may have chased me, boy, but you ain't caught me. You ain't caught me or killed me either and don't you forget it.

"So whichever way you plan to be going, boy, I plan to be heading there with you."

Bo shook his head and made it be quiet. He had enough to do right now without worrying about Charley.

So he tried again, and this time he stood.

He swayed a bit, then he stumbled forward. Once he got started, he said to himself, once he managed to get on his horse, the trip home was bound to be easier. He'd traveled most of the roads, he'd met a lot of the people. He'd know what to expect. The way back home was bound to be easier. At least that's what he thought at the time.

Acknowledgments

My father-in-law, Lance Wingate, an ex-rancher from Orange, Texas, knows how to tell a good story. One of his favorites is about his Uncle Bob who thought he'd killed a man. So he ran off to Indian Country and came back twenty years later with an Indian wife.

There was more to it. I'm sure I missed a lot, because even while I was listening the first time, my mind started drifting. What was it like to come back? Settling down must have been comforting, but after what he'd been through, wouldn't it have been kind of boring? On the other hand, why'd he wait so long?

Uncle Bob wouldn't leave me alone. Wouldn't somebody have tried to find him, to tell him it was all right to come home? Or maybe Uncle Bob wasn't interested in coming back. Maybe he didn't even want to know that he could.

That's when, out of nowhere, I saw the mountain. It was dark and a boy was scrambling up it, trying to reach someone who didn't want to be found. And the boy was frightened, not just by the strangeness and the night, but because he didn't know who it was he was chasing, since he knew by now that the man he was after wasn't any longer what he'd been.

It was the night on the mountain that made me want to tell the story. But I had to get there. Then I remembered another story Lance told me, this one about a butcher who dumped his refuse into Cow Bayou. This brought alligators, so the town hired a local alligator hunter to get rid of them. The alligator man got careless and wound up dead. So the civic leaders sent away for a more professional, out-of-town man who finished the job.

But Lance must have gotten the story wrong. Because now I knew what had *really* happened. It was the out-of-town man who wound up dead. Uncle Charley killed him.

I had my ending. I had my beginning. All I had to do now was get from one to the other.

I drove around Texas looking at landscapes. I didn't want to get too tied down to the way things were on maps. If I wanted the Big Thicket to be at the bottom of Palo Duro Canyon, that's where it was going to be. But I wanted to know for myself what Bo was seeing.

I started reading. I wanted overtones of history; I wanted the feeling of folklore. I wanted old tales that I could turn upside down, shove together, stir around. Among the authors, collectors, and editors I pilfered were Francis Edward Abernethy, Dee Brown, Henry Chafetz, David Dary, Robert DeArment, J. Frank Dobie, Richard Erdoes, T. R. Fehrenbach, Campbell and Lynn Loughmiller, D. W. Meinig, Americo Paredes, Ross Phares, Ross Santee, the editors of the *Time-Life* Books multivolume series on *The Old West*, Walter Prescott Webb, and Ray Williamson.

For those I've left out, and I'm sure there are some, I apologize.

Some readers may recognize in particular a gambling strategy from Robert DeArment's *Knights of the Green Cloth: The Saga of the Frontier Gambler*. I'm sure some will notice the occasional touches of Big Foot Wallace in Flake and the larger traces of J. Frank Dobie's description of Ben Lilly in Zeke Butters. The Native American myth that Bobby Joe tells comes from Dee Brown.

I also got help from the University of Delaware in the form of a sabbatical and a summer grant, both of which aided greatly in *Charley*'s completion. I have been blessed by colleagues who have read draft after draft and haven't been bashful about letting me know what they thought.

I feel a special affection and respect for the people at the Southern Methodist University Press who helped me get *Charley* ready for publication. Time and time again, Kathryn Lang, Keith Gregory, and the late Suzanne Comer demonstrated their sincere concern for literature and for writers. It seemed more than just a job, and I'm grateful.

But most of all, I'm grateful for those stories about runaway uncles and alligators. Of course, I suspect that Lance isn't much more reliable than I am. I just hope I can tell as good a story.

About the Author

Cruce Stark grew up in rural Mississippi and small-town Texas. He is a graduate of both Southern Methodist University and Harvard University and now teaches in the English department at the University of Delaware. While he is proud of his scholarly achievements and publications, his heart, he says, belongs to fiction. *Chasing Uncle Charley* is his first published novel.